D1237262

The Strange Case of Deacon Brodie

By Forbes Bramble

STONE

THE STRANGE CASE OF DEACON BRODIE

THE STRANGE CASE OF DEACON BRODIE

Forbes Bramble

COWARD, McCANN & GEOGHEGAN, INC.
NEW YORK

First American Edition 1976

SBN: 698-10723-3

Library of Congress Cataloging in Publication Data

Bramble, Forbes, 1939-
The strange case of Deacon Brodie.

1. Brodie, William, 1741-1788—Fiction. I. Title.
PZ4.B8148Su [PR6052.R2687] 823'.9'14 75-31754

Printed in the United States of America

'I, William Brodie, late Deacon of the Wrights in Edinburgh, and sometime member of the Town Council of said burgh, considering the certainty of my death and the propriety and expediency of recommending my memory by some good offices to my friends when I am no more, do hereby execute my last will and testament in manner following, that is to say—

Having a Royal Successor to my means and estates, and nothing else to dispose of but my good and bad qualifications, I dispose of these as follows:—

1mo. To the Right Honourable, (for a few days to come), John Grieve, Esq., I give and bequeath all my political knowledge in securing magistrates and packing corporations, hoping he will use the same in effecting a seat for himself at a certain board, to which he has long had an eye, on the first vacancy.

2. To James Donaldson, I freely bequeath my sobriety and good breeding, which may save him from being kicked out of company on occasion of his petulance and ill-manners, as was lately the case at Archers' Hall.

3. My charity and good deeds I humbly bequeath to the ministers of the Gospel in Scotland, with this injunction, that they do not retail them among their hearers, but put them in practice amongst themselves.

4. To the Magistrates of Edinburgh, present and to come, I leave and bequeath all my knowledge of the law, which may prevent their being under the necessity in future of borrowing from any of their Jameos [their clerks], who are as ignorant as themselves.

5. To my late landlord, William Charles Little of Liberton,

Esq., I leave my whole stock of economy, pride, and self-conceit, knowing he has very little of his own.
6. To William Creech, bookseller, who has favoured the public with an account of my trial, I give and bequeath my honour and generosity, referring the world to the note prefixed to Mr Morrison's appendix.
7. To Hamilton, the chimney-sweep, I leave and bequeath my dexterity in cards and dice, which may enable him to refund himself of the five guineas, two half-guineas, and six shillings, which he prosecuted me for, when he meets a pigeon, which I advertise him he is not likely to do either at Clark's or Michael Henderson's.
8. To my good friends and old companions, Brown and Ainslie, I freely bequeath all my bad qualities, not doubting, however, but their own will secure them a rope at last.

My neck now being about to embrace the halter, I would recommend it to all rogues, sharpers, thieves, and gamblers, whether in high or low station, to take care of theirs, by leaving-off their wicked practices, and becoming good members of Society in future.

Written with my own hand, and dated Sept. 26, 1788.

WILLM BRODIE'

(The Will of William Brodie, written in Edinburgh Tolbooth)

CHAPTER ONE

Edinburgh and London

The room smelled of age, death and broth. Francis Brodie lay propped up in the bed alcove of the main room, with the curtains pulled back, and watched the light slowly increase until dim shapes became visible in the overall blackness. The fire had died during the night. The lack of light worried him and he strained his eyes for the dawn. He had asked for the fire even though it was June and the nights warm. Jean and Jacobina, his daughters, had taken turns to sit by him. He wondered if anyone was with him now. Unable to move his head, he could only strain into the black window of his field of vision.

He had not slept. His brain was alive and active but with lapses of concentration when he was not aware of events external to himself. He had his speech, although painfully low, harsh and stuttering, and he had his hearing. Listening for perhaps a minute with great concentration he decided he could hear the sound of breathing. Jean or Jacobina by the fire. Probably Jean, as Jacobina would have gone home to her husband. The involuntary juddering and rattling of his limbs continued, twitched by uncontrollable muscles. He stared into the dark at the end of the bed, feeling it shake and tremble as though unrelated to his being except for the pain of the muscular cramps. The disease that took away all motion had no right to leave him pain. The doctor had told him that for seventy-four he was remarkably fit for his age. He doubted if Death cared about the doctor's diagnosis, preferring to make his own judgements. He wondered, as he had wondered often, what dying men thought about. That was the secret, so that you should know when the time was really coming.

In a few minutes the light had increased sufficiently that he could make out a shape that must be a figure asleep in a chair by the fireplace. Impossible to tell who, but by the disposition of bulk, a female shape. No legs sticking out. Men stick their legs out, women draw them in, he thought. On my chair. I made it. By my mantel. I made it. Francis Brodie, Deacon of the Incorporation of Wrights, master-craftsman, cabinet-maker, Mason of Lodge Kilwinning, Canongate. As I have made my own bed, so shall I die in it. As Cecil died on it. Was it only five years ago? He tried as he had tried before to move his left hand towards the side where Cecil had slept, almost expecting in his state of suspended animation to find her there. As if what would happen in the end, would literally come true—that she should be by his side. He felt some minute response in his hand, some tingle as if the messenger of will had arrived at the right muscles and delivered his piece. But the muscles were not even resisting or stubborn; they were deaf, or dead.

When, at the end of each clear day of his dying, the sun set, the big west window would glow, as though he were outside watching a house, consumed within by flame. Now as he waited for the light, he wondered if he should ever see that today. A second is an hour, an hour is an ecstasy, a day is forever. He urged and implored the light to come, the sun to rise, the day to begin, this his last. As he had done yesterday, and the day before yesterday and the day before that in the four eternities of his illness. He had asked himself what the point was of being a fit and strong man if it only meant taking the longer dying. A weaker man, the surgeon said, would have died the first night. He had found the answer. The dying man is a miser of seconds and he had accumulated them beyond all human right. The pain had been bearable. If the illness ran its usual course he would have one almighty spasm and lose consciousness forever. I am at peace with God, he thought, I have only that to fear.

His mind ran blank. For a few seconds he lay there, then in panic, as though a vacant mind would produce a vacant body, his thoughts ran on, tumbling over themselves, shapeless and formless. Flashes of things he could not retain. Then he remembered William. Where had he been all that long night. He could not remember that he had visited him the previous evening, or in the night at all. He could remember friends, faces. Neighbours and guild-brothers. He had been tired, they had been turned away. But Will had not been there. He would come in the morning. Was he afraid of death? Did Will think it was a night thing, to be avoided, and keep away? The dark angel was too familiar with his house already and had shown scant respect for any hour. Little Helen, and Cecil. Little Ludovick. Both the little Ludovicks. Little John. The second one we never named through grief. That was the first child that died. We were unaccustomed to it then.

The light of dawn slid in through the south windows. It seemed to Francis to pulsate like the northern lights, taking on an intensity that was immediately followed by darkness. A green after-image floated like the Aurora behind his eyes. It must be nearly five o'clock. The Town would be waking. The noises would start, that meant that life was in order again, today. He yearned for the noises. The doors being flung back, domestic shouts, early caddies and sedan chairs, the carriers calling to each other, slithering and cursing their way up the Lawnmarket to meet the Glasgow or London coach or the carriers from Inverness or the borders in the Grassmarket. Or to take anonymous Burgesses and Lords of Session discreetly home, heaving and hawking with the motion of the chair and swearing never to touch the stoup again. Or they carried desperate profligates who had been lent the price of their fare, who were already promising they would go back tonight and straighten out their losses. Where, for that matter, was Will? A little gaming was in the nature of a man, but he was showing a certain streak of recklessness, loose talk and wild ideas. A young man should have his length of tether, but it should be staked out. Who would do it now?

The workmen would arrive soon and he would hear them tramping down the Close, whistling. Brodie's Close. The sign of Palladio's Head. Business would go on as usual; life as usual. The sound of saws in the timber-yard at the end of the Close. Saws on steel and brass. The breathy sigh, sigh, sigh, of a sharp plane on sweet wood. He longed for the smell of it, instead of the stale stink of the room. The clean acrid vapours of shellac, even the meaty, fish-head stench of boiling glue had better savours than the thin sweet smell of his own bed. The scavengers must come soon with their barrows, with their shovels grating against the cobble-stones. The upper part of the Lawnmarket was kept respectably clean. Windows could be opened, letting in the delicious sounds. Trade was good. The New Town would provide work for hundreds. He had told Will and told him. It was theirs for the taking. So much work and we must have a part in it ...

He could see the interior of the room more clearly now. The figure on the chair looked like Jean. She stirred because of the light, but did not wake. Francis could not call her if he tried. His voice would not have awakened Cecil, if she had been by his side. Aye Jean, aye Jacobina. He would think about Will later when the light arrived. When life was firmly back from another night of hesitating. Then he could sort out the confusion of light and dark that disturbed him and that he could not determine. He had spoiled the boy. Given him everything, set him up, never been too critical. But Will did not come, in the night when he was needed. I deserve it as a father, he thought. William could be the angel or the devil. If only he would concentrate on his work. But he did, so where was it? His comings and goings and incivility to questions. Something secret in him. His fine clothes and clever ways. His fine work was a damnation because even that gave you doubts. Beautiful work, and yet he seemed to think no more of it than a sawyer does of a log. Put your mind into it, Will! Study it, study the catalogues of Chippendale, the discipline of Palladio. Fine work in this very room. A grand oval mahogany table and six chairs, upholstered over the seat and down the side in their own manner. A china cabinet, mahogany faced, the wood perfectly matched and elegantly glazed, the fret-work thin as two straws. If only he would study design he could take it all forwards. Palladian form.

He could see the coffered plaster ceiling now, with heavy pendant plaster-work that appeared to defy gravity. Lord Cullen had had it put there—a man of taste. Unprompted words jettisoned themselves into his mind . . . palmettes, triglyphs, acroterion, modillion, dentils and fascia, pediments triangular, pediments segmental, pediments broken and open. Ogee, ovolo, cyma recta, torus, cavetto and scotia. Egg-and-dart, bead-and-reel . . .

'Faither! Faither!' He was aware that Jean was bending over him, her face white and anxious. To his surprise it was quite light now. Quite suddenly. Where had he been?

'It's a'right lassie,' he breathed, rather than spoke. 'I'm no' deid . . . I'm here. Aye, still . . .'

He saw by her face that she had thought him dead. Maybe death came just like that, a jumble of the mind wandering on endlessly, and she had only just retrieved him. He must be wary.

'Tell Young and Trotter that Francis Brodie is still alive and in business in a manner of speaking. No doubt you will receive their regrets!'

Jean Brodie had to bend low to his dry lips to catch the breathy rasp of his voice. His breath smelled like an old dog's.

'Where's Will?' he exhaled.

Jean tried not to recoil.

'He'll be here soon enough.'

'Aye, so ye say. But where is he? He's not in the house?'

'Is there anything you want? Can you manage a bite or a

drink? The surgeon said you was to try broth ...'

'No, Jean. I was lying watchin' the light. That's all a sick man like masel' wants tae see. Another day. And my son. Have I not done well for him, Jean?'

His voice was taking on the querulous tone she recognised in everything he said of Will.

'Of course you have.'

'And has he not been a sore failure to me? Has he not?'

'No he has not. He's a credit to you. He's a fine craftsman. You said it often—he does grand work.'

'He does what I do.'

'And that's grand work!' She was trying hard to ease his mind.

'Ye don't understand.'

His body was raked by a progressive shaking that started at his legs and seemed to run up him like a shock, rattling his limbs and teeth. Jean, powerless and fearful, watched the spasms and shakings until they ceased. The surgeon had given her no hope. Any one of these seizures could be his last. The surgeon had said that he was seventy-four and it was only a matter of time—then charged good money for this wisdom. The old man looked frail as a moth in his night-gown, yet when she undressed him to bathe him, his muscles were hard as hawser under the loose flap that had become his skin. She straightened his night-cap, which had, with nasty mockery, slipped rakishly over his left ear. It was a tough, hard body, to which death came equally hard. By any ordinary standards he had exceeded his span by weeks.

'He'll have been at his damned Cape Club, or Clark's or Johnnie Dowie's, playing the rakehell. That's where he'll be. Gaming and drinking with his fine friends. Fine for the Tolbooth. I don't like the way o' it. Who will keep a check on him when I'm gone? A canny unbroken devil like that, and my fault, for I indulged him and never had the bridle on him to keep his spirit quiet! There will be no greetin' when they put me doon and under. Jean, the man hasna' come ... ! I have heard the talk they spread ... these literati ... their "new orders" and their "humanism" and their "revolution" ... verra clever talk, no doubt, and all founded on a pair o' dice, a pack o' cards and a bottle. That's the French way! Is that no' so wonderful easy ...'

'Don't talk. Ye get excited. He'll be here.'

'Aye, no doubt. There's yet the will! I would alter it but I havena' the body. Now what sort of a state is that to be in?'

'You would not, father. If you wanted to, you could. You know fine!'

Jean tucked the blanket around his shoulders in a firm and final way.

'I'm tuckit in lass!' he declared irritably. 'I canna move, I was never untuckit. And that will not keep me quiet, your woman's ways!'

'Please?'

Jean let the one word hang on the silence and held the old man's glazed eyes, until he looked away like a dog.

'I want to see Will.'

'I know, father, he'll be here soon!' she sounded irritated now.

'Aye, well he'd best be soon, or he'll miss me!'

William Brodie was still fast asleep beside Ann Grant. The main apartment in Ann Grant's 'land' in Cant's Close had none of the elegant features of the Brodie house. It was small by comparison, with little windows and bottle-glass lights. Cant's Close itself was long and narrow, no more than three feet wide and overrun with building so that it felt like a miner's tunnel and smelled too much like a sewer. It eventually opened out towards the Cowgate to let in some air and light, but it was scarce and fickle, and filtered through gaps and shafts in the grey stone walls on all sides. It became tired and wan at having travelled so far to get there, and was stale on arrival.

Despite its small proportions, the room was well furnished. What Will had not made he had selected himself. He was not mean with Ann Grant. The bed alcove still had its curtains drawn close. Few of the busy sounds from either the Cowgate or the High Street penetrated into this stone abyss. Noises were local. Children crying, men leaving for work, shouting, forgetting things, coming back, more shouting. Ann smiled and lay half awake. A woman's voice cut in decisively. The man's feet clopped away again. Ann lay with closed eyes and began to remember that there was some reason why she should be awake and not in this warm half-way pleasure.

She was thinking of Francis Brodie. Insidiously it grew upon her from a suspicion to a fact, and then she was awake. Eyes still closed, she could hear Will's deep breathing. No surprise. She wondered if Francis Brodie was awake this morning, or while she lay warm, was he stiff and formally dead? Pennies on his eyes, and Will not there. Will with his woman, his mistress, the night that his father died. She considered. As for being his mistress, it had been so long she was more like a wife, and she was proud of it. There was many a fine lady in the 'lands' who would have exchanged their old bags of wind for Will Brodie.

But it was not decent he should be there when his father died. The wrong bed at the wrong time.

She had tried to get him to go home last night. He had come in at two, reeking and reeling, so elated he could hardly speak. He had pulled out the silk pockets of his trousers and slammed guineas on to the table, showering gold. All won at cards. Twenty-two guineas, no less, and a cock, the best cock in the world, fighting tomorrow in the main at Henderson's stables. The world held high joys, he had roared, for men who were willing to take them. But take her he had failed to do and collapsed into bed fully clothed and snoring.

She was glad. What the world thought of morals she could not care, but she felt it was not right to be embraced in fornication while the old man was dying. The two things were somehow too much alike. Will moved beside her and suddenly spoke in his slow careful fashion, as though he was moulding each word with his tongue.

'Are you awake?'

'Aye.'

His left arm burrowed beneath her, hand over her left breast, held it cupped and full.

'I was little use last nicht!'

'I'm glad o' it ...'

His hand stroked her. She pulled away, holding his hand firm.

'No, Will, not now—it's not proper.'

There was a pause as he tried to comprehend her meaning. She waited, knowing the ways of men.

'How do ye mean? It's the most proper thing I can think of, considerin' as we were made one in, one out to dae it! Ann, lass ...' He forsook words, as she knew he would, and rolled half over on her, burying his face in her breasts, hands stroking her belly, caressing its roundness lightly and riffling with thief's fingers over thighs and fine hair.

'No, Will! Get off! The old man is dying! I'll no' be pleasurin' you while your own faither ... it's no decent.'

He lay back and stared at the ceiling, thinking. She said nothing, knowing it. They knew each other well after these twelve or thirteen years. She had even thought they might marry, but knew they could not, even if Will would. He was good to her. A lusty man, an irregular man, fussy of his appearance, intemperate but generous. When he needed her, he needed her with immoderate passion, and she had known enough men before to make comparisons. Then for days after his visits, perhaps weeks afterwards—nothing. He would call for an hour, passing through on business, talk, leave money, gifts for the children—often something for the children. He would play with them and sing songs and move on, leaving as little trace of his passing as a moonbeam. She had no other men. It was agreed upon, not by finance, but by her nature. All their children would be his. Cecil, Willie and the one on the way. She felt secure. They spent long relaxed and domestic hours. She felt free to argue and even reject him. It was normal, as between man and woman should be. Then he would be gone and there would be always that slight secret thing. She thought it might be other women and had tried to discover him in a hundred small ways that never got anywhere. 'Women,' he would say, 'do ye think a peel-wersh wee person like me would have the puff for it?'

But still there was something undiscovered and withdrawn. The irregularities of his comings and goings were in themselves a contrived discipline, as though he were afraid he should ever establish a pattern. Yet, she thought, looking at him, there was nothing peel-wersh or weakly about his shoulders and arms. They were broad and muscled with his work. Strong with planing, sawing and shaving. She worried about his gaming and gambling and cock-fighting. She realised she knew nothing about the hours and recreations of gentlemen, where these things were considered not only right and proper, but were the rage of the 'fancy'. Her own father had been a God-fearing, breast-beating bible man, keeping timely hours. But they had been poor and times had changed. Great men like the Lord Advocate, Burns or Boswell mixed freely in taverns with the Edinburgh trashery. In her father's house, no candles had burned after the hour of ten, except to read the Bible.

'As wax melteth before the fire, so let the wicked perish at the presence of God.'

William was very disturbed and elated. He had waited for this moment for a long time. It had seemed that the old man would never go. Yet he had no reason to hurry him on. Almost everything about him could be bearable, except the everlasting burden of being his son. William was stricken with guilt at the colossal ingratitude of his position towards his father's generosity.

And yet, he thought, none of that generosity was towards William Brodie, but rather to the son and heir of Francis Brodie, that the name Brodie might thrive and be illustrious, if anything could shine in the verdigris that tainted Edinburgh. They argued continually, his father seeking for some obscure purity that he could not understand and in the search for which William was not prepared to join. William Brodie, son of Francis Brodie, because of Francis Brodie. Guild Brother, Burgess and Deacon out of Francis Brodie, by right of marriage to Cecil née Grant, daughter of William Grant, Burgess and Guild Brother, wife of Francis Brodie. His mother, deceased. And out of me, he thought, there will be nothing but bastards. To them I will leave everything, for Edinburgh to talk about. Two here, a third on the way, and one by that whore Jean Watt, the which is no more my son than Moses except she claims it and I cannot prove otherwise.

Poor Francis, if you knew what your good coin has brought. No lukewarm wives with their four o'clock refection, sipping tea and gossip. No fussing over sedans and gowns and servants. No dullard dinners. Spurs and feathers, coin cards and dice. That was the style of it. Times had changed. The world was changing. Death reaps and misses one stalk in his stroke. I, William Brodie—a mere chance. All men are equal from birth yet spend their whole lives trying to disprove it.

He looked slyly sideways at Ann Grant, who saw the look but lay still and said nothing. He thought that she would have made a good wife had he ever the intention to marry. It was a sore temptation. How it would have scandalised the Town! But William Brodie, gamester, cabinet-maker, Guild Brother, Burgess, Mason and card-sharp would be revealed. Let it lie, let them all be. The self-perpetuating Deacons and Councillors of the Town of Edinburgh would come in and out like the tide, with no difference but the height of the rubbish they left behind. Yet through them and within them there was undreamed of freedom for a man who was willing to take the chance.

He would go to the old man, he would play the game. Thought of that way, he warmed to the idea. The stakes were high. He must secure his legacy. 'How are ye, father? Are ye feeling well the day? Is there onything I can dae?' He would fawn on him without overplaying his part, and spoon broth into his open gullet, watching the old man trying to grapple with the truth. There was a challenge in that. To watch the belief in the old eyes, become relief, willing to believe, like everyone else, nothing but good of a Brodie. Yes, he would tell him, yes, I will marry. Who? A Bailie's daughter, what else? Or a Writer's. From nowhere to the edge of real power in two generations. Where might they not go?

To Parliament, he thought, Lord Provost, the moon. Tytler was building a balloon that would take him to the moon, so he said. They had talked of it in Canongate Kilwinning Lodge. The moon—with a trail of angry black smoke over the top of Edinburgh town, looking down to see them as they really were. Wee, wee men in three-cornered hats covering their wee, wee minds. All Edinburgh in a hand's span.

'Ann, I'll go and see him.'

She sat up.

'It's right you should, Will. Death is an awfu' state of bein' alone.'

Will laughed.

'Aye, but you're mair alone after!'

'It's no' a thing tae laugh at!'

'No, maybe not, but I've seen it often enough. Sometimes it comes as a blessing, sometimes as an agony, others as just a flicker. Ye're a Christian woman, Ann. It should be a fulfilment. There is one thing in this life that is uniquely your own, and that only you can do, and that is die! There's no one else can dae it for ye!'

He got out of bed, naked. His broad shoulders emphasised his skinny shanks and hollow thighs. He started to dress from where his clothes lay neatly folded on a chair. Ann had lain them there the night before.

'You're good to a man who is not entirely himself. Ye keep me well turned oot and fittin' for a Councillor! God, I'm dry!'

'You get there sober, Will Brodie! The old man's not fit for a face full of convivial breath.'

'His breath is no' as sweet as a new sliced apple neither. But I'll not drink. I have a good cock at a main at the Grassmarket this afternoon. He'll need nae charms nor hocus-pocus. You shall have his take, my love, for being a mistress sans pareil. And give a kiss to the children, and here's a shilling each for them.'

He pulled money from his purse.

'And here's five guineas to ye, Ann, for what I intended.'

'Away, you'll mak' me blush.'

'Have ye thocht, Ann, that I will be a rich man?'

'Aye. But what will ye do wi' it?'

He had resumed his coat now and was adjusting his shirt ruffles in a looking glass. His waistcoat was of white silk with pearl buttons, his coat and trousers of light grey, the coat lined with white silk again. His cuffs and ruffles were of cream-coloured lace.

'I expect I shall put it tae guid use!'

He came over to the bed and kissed her.

'Don't forget the barber, Will. And come earlier next time and kiss the weans for yoursel'.'

He walked to the door and collected his black three-cornered hat and cane.

'Just pray for the cock,' he said, and as an afterthought, 'and the old man.' He tipped his hat to her formally, and left, closing the door quietly.

The crowd in the Grassmarket seemed to be detaching itself from the White Hart Inn. As was usual at this hour, sober men were exceptions. Having lunched on a 'cauld cock and a feather'—the braggart name for a large brandy and a handful of raisins—there was an excited and general drift to Michael Henderson's stables. The place was alive with carriers and their carts, a number of which added to the confusion by being allowed to drift untethered about the market while their drivers united the bonds of friendship, severed as long ago as last week. Sober carriers swore and lashed out at the straying ponies, which immediately kicked up their heels and careered around with their loads swaying and clattering. Highlanders swore at Lowlanders in the Gaelic, and Lowlanders gave as good as they got. As neither understood the other, they all seemed satisfied.

The interior of Michael Henderson's old feed barn was impenetrably gloomy at first sight. Brodie, the warm glow of three unstinted brandies burning inside him, picked his way carefully through the human mêlée. He had been shaved, and in doing his duty to his father, had not forgotten to change both his shirt and waistcoat. He brandished his silver-topped and silk-tasselled cane with a flourish as he walked, acknowledging the greetings of friends with a lift of his hat. Even in the gloom his light-clad figure was easily seen, and people moved aside for him. Close to the pit, where all backs were turned, he had to push his way through the tightly packed, hoarse-tongued spectators. His shoving progress met with curses and shouts, but seeing who he was, he was allowed through. Brodie's cock was fighting today. He was slapped on the back and wished good luck.

'Will he win, Mr Brodie?'

'Whit was his last main? Does he kill? Tell us, Mr Brodie?'

'Gie us a tip, Mr Brodie!'

Brodie waited until he reached the edge of the pit, then called back to them: 'I never advise a man how tae lose money. I have found through experience that most men are good at it without any previous training!' There was a roar of jibes and laughter. Brodie turned and, looking, saw a tall lean man, standing on the edge of the pit. He was dressed with little grace in well-worn heavy cloth, but commanded his crowd like a ring-master.

'Michael!' shouted Brodie.

The tall man crossed the sacred boards of the pit. Any other man stepping on them would have instantly been hurled off. The tall man held out his hand.

'Good-day to ye, Will! Full house again. Sit down. How's your red cock?'

'Better than Macfarlane's, I've little doubt.'

'Aye. And how's your faither? I heard he was near the end.'

'He is. But not gone yet.'

'You devil. And you here!'

'Ye ken me, Michael. I have paid him a visit and made my peace. It would be indecent o' me, do you not think, tae sit there wi' a glass ower his mooth, sayin' just blaw a wee bit, faither, so's I ken ye're still alive!'

'Come on now, Will, that's nae way tae talk! The old devil's been guid tae ye!'

'He has that. I have been near smoored wi' guidness!'

'And I'm thinking you will be a wealthy man.'

'I have been assured o' it.'

'Ye devil, Will. This morn?'

'Aye. But he's still ower fond I should marry!'

Henderson roared with laughter.

'Old men are gey like the lassies!'

A small man, dressed in a rough grey waistcoat and breeches with canvas leggings, stood in the middle of the pit. He was shouting at the top of his rather squeaky voice and flapping his arms up and down, for all the world like a cock himself:

'Shentlemen!' he was roaring with a Highland brogue. 'Shentlemen! Will ye clear the pit please of bottles and arms and hats an' sich things!' No one paid him the least attention, which made his arms pump up and down even faster with rage.

'Ach, it's wee Jamie,' said Henderson, 'leave him at it the

whiles, he's quite happy. He's a good man, he wears them doon in the end.'

The lower windows of the barn had been boarded up for most of their height to prevent disorderly crowds from forming outside. Light only fell from the upper windows and this was scant enough. The press of bodies already produced a sticky heat. The din of shouting, bragging and cursing made it impossible to speak without shouting oneself. Somewhere a high refined voice was wailing that he had lost a purse and five guineas to some damned thief. He kept shouting monotonously, 'There is a thief in here! There is a thief in here!' As there were most certainly many thieves in there, no one was in the least interested, the men next to him hardly giving him a glance. Henderson motioned with his hand and a bench was set up at the side of the pit for the cockers, and they were cleared some space, which they occupied like six kings in a row, among them William Brodie. The pit, in accordance with the rules, was twelve feet in diameter and eighteen inches off the ground, made of timber boards. Unlike the degenerate English cocking of which they had all heard, there was no carpet on the boards, but a canvas cloth covering, rolled up at the edges to stretch it tight. The pens stood behind their cockers, each covered with a cloth so that the birds should not see each other until upon the pit. The two setters-on for the first fight now climbed on to the pit, exchanging good-natured cracks and violent insults with friends and foes in the crowd.

'There is a thief in here! There is a thief in here!' The monotonous sing-song voice continued, from another part of the barn.

'There is a thief in here! There is a thief in here!' voices mimicked him with roars of laughter. The hopeless calling ceased. Alongside Brodie sat the other five pitters—a Writer, a big-faced flesher, a glover, an unknown farmer, bulky and overclad for the heat, and another man unknown to Brodie but well dressed in sporting fashion. Jamie waved his arms up and down and the crowd, sensing that the fighting was about to start, grew noticeably quieter. Few men appeared to be sober. Thieves, advocates and inn-keepers pressed tight with soldiers, traders and caddies. Scavengers, Town Councillors and a Bailie pushed and heaved for the front. The cocks could be heard crowing and beating their wings.

'Shentlemen, shentlemen!'

By sheer persistence Jamie was making himself heard. A drunk, clutching a bottle of claret, tripped over a leg and spilt a gob of wine on to a soldier's coat. The soldier promptly and dispassionately punched him in the mouth so that he flew backwards unconscious on to the hay bales provided. Henderson's men took the figure out, where it would be propped up in the street. The shouting became a murmuring, low, excited and intense. Brodie felt his heart beating. This was the feeling he came for. The tension that made men sweat, that made drunk men sober and sober men drunk. The chink of coin could be clearly heard like primitive impatient music.

'Shentlemen, may we please have yout attention. All the birds have been weighed before Mr Henderson who is satisfied hisself that they is all within the weights as permitted in the rules and is evenly matched. There will be three fights, each to the death.'

The crowd roared and cheered.

'I repeat, there will be three fights to the death or until a bird is disabled and, put beak to beak, refuses to fight. The other bird then shall be the winner. No shentleman who is a cocker shall in any circumstances enter the pit, nor clean the beak or eyes of his bird, nor adjust his spurs! Nor prod, nor poke, nor in any other way provoke or spike or prick the bird to carry on! No fight may be abandoned by any cocker nor his bird withdrawn for any reason unless he accept he loses! And, shentlemen, it is a rule of the house as most of ye know that all bets shall be paid immediate. Brawling and fighting in the house and disturbances are forbidden and those taking part will be removed immediately!'

There was a great cheer and a wave of laughter and applause. Jamie, very red-faced and sweating, stepped out of the pit, followed by the two setters-on who went to their respective pens and brought out the two first cocks, both greys, belonging to the farmer and the flesher. The din that broke out at the sight of the birds was like a mob at an execution. Bets were freely shouted and taken between owners and onlookers. Brodie too, all decorum gone, had leapt to his feet, eyes flashing.

'Ten guineas on Galloway's grey!' bellowed a puce-faced baker, the flour still in his hair.

'Taken!' shouted a hard-faced man who might have been an advocate or an undertaker.

'Twenty on the other yin!'

'Taken,' roared Galloway the flesher.

The bedlam steadily increased as the setters-on strapped on the spurs, under the cockers' watchful eyes, and held them up to be checked. Brodie, having placed three bets of ten guineas on the farmer's grey, sat back, his face glowing. His normal pallor had disappeared. His heart beat fast. He watched the cocks eagerly for any sign, any give-away trace of ill-health or cowardice. The beautiful birds flapped and their feathers and beaks gleamed and shone even in the dull interior. They glared furiously, darting their heads, while spurs were bound. These were of needle-pointed horn, set in a steel mounting and pinned and whipped into the leather leg-piece that was wrapped firmly round before binding the whole in place with leather thongs. The spikes stuck out over an inch, vicious as huge thorns. On seeing each other the cocks immediately tried to attack. The crowd cheered, the setters-on held them expertly tight. Frustrated, the cocks puffed out their feathers and Galloway's cock let out a blood-curdling scream. The farmer's cock eyed it with glittering contempt and hung its head, with its beak open and tongue partly exposed, making a low moaning noise. Its eyes were full of malice. Brodie felt a sense of the wild animal madness in the beasts' hearts. A fury without fear. On the contrary, they relished it. He thought they were magnificent when you compared them with men.

With a yell from the crowd, the two birds were released. They hurled themselves straight at each other, half running, half flying. What happened on impact was so rapid it was difficult to follow—beaks, claws, spurs ripped, pecked and lunged. The cocks had no concept of retreat. Blood spattered on to the canvas and the crowd screamed, as though it was theirs. Feathers, flesh-ended and torn out by the stump, flew all over the canvas. Galloway's cock struck an eye from the farmer's cock, gashing open its head. The crowd yelled or booed. The bird, unable to see or understand why, shook its head vigorously, as though this would restore its sight. It showered blood on the floor. Galloway's cock leaped in the air, and with a terrible downward thrust, pinned the unfortunate bird's head to the canvas in both claws. In one deft move it picked out the other eye, and crowed. The helpless bird got to its feet while the grey was momentarily off balance and staggered round in circles, the crowd screaming or groaning, or punching their hands with their fists shouting, 'A kill! A kill!' Galloway's grey stood watching his victim with every appearance of satisfaction. He gathered himself up and launched himself at the farmer's grey, and cut it open with his spurs. The wing tendon was severed and the sightless bird flapped desperately, one-winged.

'I win!' bawled Galloway. 'It's finished. I win!'

His cock, still not satisfied with its ruin, flew at the bleeding grey with its spurs again, kicking and clawing at the mangled head and throat. The farmer's grey just bubbled blood now, and thrashed feebly round in a circle. Galloway's grey stepped off and eyed it. It beat its wings and crowed, inciting the dying animal to fight. It seemed disappointed and puzzled with the brevity of the affair. Jamie and the two setters-on, wearing thick leathern gloves, stepped up on to the pit. The surviving cock's pen was dumped on the side of the pit and the setters-on tried to drive it towards the pen. It seemed reluctant to leave, crowing and flapping its wings, its head on one side, glancing all the time at its twitching enemy. Galloway was making a great fuss by the pen, rattling a bowl of barley.

'Come home, ma beauty, come home—you owe me ten guineas, man—I'll thank you—come home, ma beauty, come home—away here!'

Rattle rattle.

'Can you no' bring him in!'

The setters-on managed with their leggings to push the cock in the direction of the pen, advancing carefully as it still seemed inclined to violence. Galloway was calling in his bets.

'Currie, and I'll have your five in too. Mind that. Let me get ma' bird in!'

Jamie picked up the dying grey in his gloved hands. The spurred feet still kicked. He flung the bleeding wreckage towards the farmer, who shrugged and said with bitter humour, 'Throw it oot the back. I'll no be needin that yin again!'

Will Brodie, heart racing, was paying out money. Thirty guineas. He hardly knew or cared who he paid it to. That was just the preliminary, his own bird was next. His red, against Macfarlane's black.

'Tak yer money. Here, awa!'

His hands shook as he counted guineas in hands that seemed unconnected with drunken, red, floating faces. Jamie was back in the pit. Brodie's red and Macfarlane's black. That would be a fight! None of these thirty-second whangs!

'Shentlemen, shentlemen! That was quick work, was it not now. Shentlemen, I beg of you to settle your affairs, for we canna restart wi a' this din!' His arms were pumping up and down again. His feet were scuffling in a pool of purple that the canvas had soaked up, and which squelched beneath his brogues. The canvas was covered with such dark stains.

'Next we have Mr Macfarlane's black, and Mr Brodie's red. Oh aye, the weight, I mon give it to ye. Mr Macfarlane's four poonds and three ounces, Mr Brodie's four poonds and four ounces!'

He climbed down from the pit. The setter-on took Will's bird from its pen. Brodie gave him from his coat pocket the vicious prongs which he had made himself. He prided himself on them. No pair of Brodie spurs ever tore or broke. His foreman cabinet-maker had pinned and bound the steel setting and whipped it into the leather. The setter-on had deftly wrapped the leather bands round the bird's legs and, holding it prone, had bound them on with thongs. He now offered the bird, legs foremost to Brodie, who in a fluster of excitement felt the bindings and, considering one too loose, undid it with trembling and clumsy hands, to pull it tighter.

'Let me do it, Mr Brodie,' said the setter-on, 'it's ower exciting for the cocker an' we dinna want it fleein' loose!' The man re-strapped the leg, while the cock contrived to wind its head round the man's legs, upside-down, and glare indignantly at Brodie. Brodie murmured endearments to it, calling it his red beauty, king of birds, a very paragon of cocks, a brave soldier, a veritable tiger. The bird blinked and continued to glare.

Macfarlane was beside his bird, whispering exhortations into its uncomprehending ears, crossing himself every few seconds as though immersed in prayer. His bird made attempts to peck at him which caused Macfarlane to sit back heavily on the floor to roars of derision and laughter. Macfarlane regained his crouching position with as much poise as possible and continued his incantation, which culminated in his producing a bundle of heather tied round a rabbit's foot, which he waved over the bird like a priest making the sign.

'Twenty pounds on Brodie's red!' shouted Henderson. He knew, for he had trained it.

'I take that!'

'Thirty on my ain!' yelled Brodie, now satisfied with the bird's legs.

'Mak' it forty!' bellowed Galloway, glaring at him. Brodie had bet against Galloway's bird.

'Fifty!' replied Brodie, a strange and triumphant glow spreading over him.

'Sixty, if ye can afford *that*!' yelled Galloway, but looking less pleased. All other betting seemed to have fallen into a hush. This was the battle of giants.

'Seventy, if *ye* can afford that!' Brodie spoke quietly now, there was no need to shout. He felt quite calm and curiously elevated. They were all in the palm of his hand. They worshipped money, they were awe-struck by the show. Brodie was bound to win, for the money meant nothing to him, he did not even consider it. But Galloway cared. The crowd broke into spontaneous applause, cheers and hurroos.

'Seventy then,' Galloway replied truculently, and immediately turned his back and sat down. Brodie smiled slightly to himself, bowed neatly to the crowd and doffed his hat to them. He then too sat down. Pandemonium followed. Bets flew. Compared with the first fight, stakes were high. Brodie always got the middle fight in a three-fight main. In the first fight, inferior birds were put on, and the money was warming up in the pockets. By the time for the second match, the crowd was red-hot with triumph or defeat, and determined to go on. By the third match there was usually a noticeable chill. Losers had lost too much, and winners could find no one to take their bets. The middle match was the best.

Macfarlane's black was an evil-looking bird, glossy and crow-beaked, but Brodie's bird had the big thick legs of a real fighter, with a long wiry neck and exceptional speed. It had plenty of experience in training, but so had Macfarlane's. These were no farmyard roosters.

Macfarlane called across good-naturedly.

'Worried, Will, about yon wee red skitter o' yours!'

'Celebrate my victory, Peter.' He took a flask from his pocket, poured himself a brandy and tossed it back. 'Join me. It will be a dolorous occasion for you and yon black craw in just a wee while. Enjoy it while ye may!'

Macfarlane smiled grimly and shook his head.

'I've no need for Frenchman's courage, Will Brodie!'

'Maybe no'. But maybe as a restorative!'

The crowd followed every exchange eagerly, but their expectation of a long verbal duel was spoiled by Jamie hopping out of the pit, with a yell of 'They're away!' The setters-on released the birds, which flew at each other so that they seemed to meet in the centre in an explosion of feathers, some of which rose feet in the air, to idle down like snow. The birds raked each other with their spurs. Hooked beaks appeared from most unusual angles and positions, spitting feathers. Wings beat and flapped and covered everything like a violent mating. Will swore to himself. Suddenly blood jetted on to the floor. There was an unbearable silence while they strained to see which bird was cut. It was not clear as both were marked with blood. The furious rustling and scuffling continued. Each bird had hold of the flesh of the other and would not let go. Like wrestlers locked in a hold, they circled round and round, kicking out with their spurs. The crowd began to chant, according to their fancy. Macfarlane was straining forward on the edge of the bench. Brodie affected to lean back and fold his arms with a smile, brushing idly at his immaculate clothes. The money was going on Brodie's red now. It seemed as though hours passed. The sweat ran down inside his shirt, but still he smiled and crossed his legs. After nearly five minutes, the two birds, as though by mutual consent, backed off and surveyed each other. The black cock looked the more dishevelled. It did not seem to have the strength. Brodie's strutted, flapped its wings and screeched. The crowd cheered. There would be a few moments' pause then the second round would start. Brodie, his heart pounding knew his bird would win. The two cocks flew at each other with renewed savagery.

* * *

About this time Francis Brodie died. He knew, no more than Macfarlane's black cock, that the life was seeping out of him. As he had been expecting it for days, it took him unawares, in one violent shudder, then nothing. Jean, by his side, felt that death made a mockery of the Palladian ennoblement of man.

Picking his way between carts, animals and men in the Grassmarket, William Brodie was light-hearted and a little drunk. His winnings felt heavy in his pocket. He could still faintly hear the bestial roars of the crowd in Henderson's as the third and last pair of cocks were unleashed. It was beginning to get chill and the sun was low. The castle high above had taken on its customary night-black silhouette. Long dark shadows from the 'lands' occupied the streets, so that the falling sun was allowed meagre space of narrow golden rails across the cobbles.

He made his way by the West Bow to the High Street, his mind guiltily pre-occupied with this light-heartedness. He knew he should be worrying about his father, whereas in fact, about the matter, he felt absolute indifference. Perhaps it was the dark gloom of the West Bow that affected him. Despite himself, there was a nagging guilt he could not suppress. At the same time he would not admit it to himself. Yet he knew he was going home involuntarily. He had to know. There was, after all, money in it, he told himself. But at the same time he knew that was not the real reason. He was assured of the money anyway. He wanted to see the old man dead. He was still trying to convince himself that this was not a pleasure, when, at the junction with the High Street, he was hailed loudly. He felt a surge of annoyance, recognising the voice, and realising he did not want to be delayed. The large and puff-bellied figure of Bailie Dickson was moving down the High Street just behind him, with that care that people use, walking on ice. He stopped and waited until Dickson caught up with him.

'Good day to you, Mr Brodie! Aye, and how's your poor father?'

Brodie lifted his hat, with the formalities of the day, and rested his hands on his cane.

'Good day, Mr Dickson. He is not improved in any way. In fact I fear the worst at any time. I am just on my way back tae sit wi' him.'

'Aye aye. It's a trying time. I had it myself, mind. Sore grievin'. I'll walk with you if I may. That is if you can abide ma slow pace. I'm not that steady on the cobbles ... I suppose he wants nae visitors?'

'He's beyond that now.'

'Aye, he would be, he would be. Peace at the end of the road. It's a sore loss. It is indeed.'

There was a pause as they edged their way down the High Street at Dickson's pace.

'And you'll be managing the firm on your own now ...'

It was not a question.

'You'll be a substantial man.'

'I suppose I will,' said Brodie, determined to lead the conversation by the nose, 'but my faither has not been that active these ten years, God rest his soul. He was a good man and a good worker. Everyone said that of him.'

'A good man he was. A good man. Aye, and his work the best. Craftsmanship,' said Dickson as though he had invented the word, 'that's what you call it, craftsmanship. Mind you, some of it was ower deep for me. This Renaissance and his proportions. Aye well. But inventive, with always the latest things.'

What is he after? thought Brodie. It was soon out.

'You have a lot of work on. There will be no difficulty, I suppose, in completing it? I ask, you understand, not for ma'self, but the Council is bound tae ask, and the best way o' allaying fears is no' tae let them arise. Ye ken Shaw and his ways. And Simpson is keen on havin' things well ordered. It will be my duty, you see, to clear your accounts, and I would not like to see anything not done and you held to any loss for it on account of a bereavement ...'

Brodie controlled his rage, and his face remained bland and smiling. The carrion crows were gathering. But carrion crows are cowards.

'Mr Dickson, I thank ye for your courtesy. As a gesture of intention, I think it would be only proper, do you no', if I finished the work a wee bit earlier than expectit? Tae remove these doubts that folk may be harbourin'. And at a very reasonable price.'

'Mr Brodie, we have complete faith in you as a man and brother, ye ken that!' He paused. 'But I think that would be a politic sort of move for cementing things for the future. The Provost, I ken, would be appreciative of it.'

'The Brodie business will serve Edinburgh well, Mr Dickson, ye can depend on it. For yourself, ye ken well that you have only to call on me. It was my faither's axiom as it is mine, to turn out handsome work, and not exact a usurious price.'

'I ken it well, Mr Brodie. Ye have what tae start this next few months. Much work, is it not?'

'For the Council, Mr Dickson, I have a good degree of Wright work. And there is the cabinet-making too.'

'Fine cabinets Francis made.'

'And all the Council's work is ordered up and timber to hand.' He was furious with Dickson and all his sort. Furious with their interference and inferences and their penny-pinching nosing and poking about in affairs. Their pompous assumption of public rectitude.

'I have as you know, quotations before the Council for bits and pieces listed at the Tolbooth and the Exchequer building. You will no doubt have noticed on Sundays that the work is coming on fine on the windows to St Andrew's Kirk, which will cost a hundred pounds or more, doors and stalls to the Fleshmarket, which is a big contract, with all framing and locking and the like. The Public Market work and the Leith

Pier have to be started and cannot be under fifty pounds apiece. Work on churches—there is always work on churches. And you yourself were moving the work to our fire engines and the fire cocks. I think I can do all that. Is there any doubt tae it?'

'It's in capable hands, Mr Brodie, very capable. I like tae see hands well occupied. I dinna hold wi' all this drinkin' and cock fighting as ye ken. Did you hear the noise down at Henderson's stables in the Grassmarket? Terrible!'

'Were you at the Grassmarket yourself?'

Dickson stopped dead and stared at Brodie, his face colouring.

'Not at the cock-fighting, Mr Brodie, God forbid, but in the Market at the carriers.'

'So I took it, Mr Dickson.'

'Aye. They can never get things right. It's a terrible age we live in, Mr Brodie. Drunkenness and confusion everywhere. Respectable folks must aye cling together in these times, is it not so, Mr Brodie.'

'It is so, Mr Dickson.'

'Well, we're at your Close, Mr Brodie. Give my regards to your faither, if ye can. From me and his friends at the Lodge. You'll be a busy man, Mr Brodie, so it seems, for the work you have tae do. Good day tae ye!' He lifted his cocked hat and waddled off down the High Street. The same portly figure had stood at the back at Henderson's and made thirty guineas on Will Brodie's red.

'Good day,' called Brodie, 'and thank ye!'

He smiled his down-turned smile and went down the black alley of the Close.

Francis was laid out with guineas on his eyes. It seemed so appropriate to William he nearly burst out laughing. Jean, Jacobina and her husband Matthew Sheriff were all there. They sat by the fire, sipping wine. Will came carefully into the centre of the room and stopped dramatically in his tracks. He knew he must play his part skilfully.

'Oh God!' he cried, 'He's not dead!'

This did not sound very convincing to him, but some irony persuaded him to try it. It apparently convinced the others. Matthew got up.

'Aye he is, gone this last hour. I'm sorry, Will, you missed him.'

He made it sound like a business appointment. Matthew was a realistic man.

'I saw him just this morning,' said Will.

Jean was more forthcoming.

'If you had stopped in this morning,' she said acidly, 'and not gone out drinking or whatever you've been up to, you could have been with him. We sent Robert Smith out looking for you round the taverns. You werna' even there!'

Brodie ignored the accusation.

'I never thought he was that bad. Let me look at him ...' Matthew came over to Will's side. 'Alone please, Matthew, just for a minute.' He contrived such humility, that Matthew, looking surprised, stepped back, then resumed his seat by the fire. The sweet apple smell hung about the bed. Conscious of the hostility of his sisters, he bent over and stared down at the dead man. He found he enjoyed it enormously. It was a thorough, pure pleasure, that made him want to giggle like a child. The grotesqueness of the golden eyes quite delighted him. He was delighted by the caprice that both guineas had not been placed the same way up. Heads I win, tails you lose, he thought. How are things behind your gold-stopped eyes, you old bastard? He had an overpowering sense of being free at last from the loving octopus embrace that the old man had exerted. Love like that was like the clutch of a drowning man, that takes you down with it. His face was slack and meaningless now. That, thought Will, is all you get out of a good solid life of Wright's work—two golden guineas. But not for Will Brodie.

* * *

Entering John Clark's tavern was like stumbling through the subterranean smoking passages that feed a volcano. It was hot, dark and sulphurous. To those entering from the street, the air was at first unbreathable, and Will Brodie broke into a fit of coughing—a habit so common they called it 'taking the air'. Small glimmers of orange fire that came and went, and moved their position in the darkness, indicated a group of pipe-smokers, lost in a toxic cloud. Towards the far end of the series of drinking recesses, that afforded privacy for every kind of business and pleasure a gentleman might desire to conduct, an open fire gave light and heat. Candles on every table augmented this. Some were stuck to the bare boards in their own wax, some in wine bottles. As the cellar almost entirely lacked natural ventilation, the thick smoke was only disturbed by the entrance of customers, when it would rush and eddy towards the door.

Brodie, pausing for a few seconds until his eyes were accustomed to the gloom, saw his companions and made his way towards three men round a table, whom he could dimly see playing with dice. Voices called greetings to him from tables on either side. He doffed his hat and replied in kind. Some voices he recognised. Some seemed quite unknown. Some were famous voices, heard in public places and thundering from the Bench. Some were voices he recognised from the cock-pits. At first he was annoyed that he had been noticed. But on consideration it was rather the opposite. If he was noticed coming in, he would be just as noticeable leaving, especially if it seemed at an untimely hour amongst such late birds.

One of the three men was Michael Henderson of the Grassmarket. Of the two others, Will Robertson was a fellow Cape Club member, and Thomas Wilson was a respectable enough tanner, not given to gaming, but over-fond of spectating through the bottom of a glass.

They had already been drinking for some time and were gesticulating and shouting with some abandon. This last was more out of expediency because the din in the cellars was so deafening that only a moderate bellow could be heard. Somewhere in the darkness of the booths, women giggled and squealed. Henderson, who was facing him, saw Brodie first. He removed the dice and box from the table with skilled legerdemain, but not so fast that Brodie did not notice. Henderson made great sweeping gestures to Brodie that he was to join them. Beside these indifferently clad companions, Brodie looked immaculately dressed—almost of a religious purity in the whiteness of his silks and brocades. He sat carefully on the bench by the table, looking like an angel who had descended into infernum. They exchanged formal greetings.

'What happened at the last fight at the main, Michael?' Brodie cupped a hand to his mouth and shouted. Henderson leaned forward.

'A black and a red. The red lost. No good!' He bellowed suddenly over his shoulder. Everything about Henderson had a power and vigour that Brodie admired. 'Johnnie!' he shouted, 'Mr Brodie would like a drop o' vinous refreshment!'

This was addressed to Clark, the inn-keeper, a short thickset man who stood over the fire, drawing on a long-stemmed clay pipe. Clark removed the stem from his lips, and with a deft movement of it, indicated the waiter, then Brodie, replaced the stem and continued his conversation with his companion. The waiter, a lad of fourteen with auctioneer's eyes, noted the minute gesture and shortly arrived with a pewter pot of claret which he set on the table before Brodie, wiping the boards with a cloth. Brodie's clothes encouraged such little considerations around him that others did not receive. Another gesture of Clark's pipe stem sent the harassed lad off immediately on another errand of mercy. Clark never wrote the tally down, but kept it in his head. No one had ever argued that he was wrong.

'Did you win today then?' Robertson was trying to shout at Brodie. Brodie laughed and took a drink.

'What's that to you then?'

'Now now, Will,' said Henderson, 'we have always been most solicitous for your welfare!'

'I saw the ivories, Michael! You can put them back on the table!'

Grinning, Henderson replaced the dice and box.

'Your eyes were always too sharp, Will Brodie!'

Brodie wondered if he should break it to them now, as though it were a burden, or seem to enter into the spirit of things, but woefully, so that they would be bound to ask. The latter seemed better, because if they started gaming, they would feel more ashamed and would spread the sense of their ashamedness when they spread the news. This suited him very well. He felt in his pocket and took out five guineas, which he laid in two piles, two and three, to remind him of Francis's eyes.

'Maybe,' he said, 'but you gentlemen talk too much for me. If ye are determined tae twist ma arm, then I maun put ma money on the boards. But only the five, and not long.'

'Away with you, Will!' Henderson grinned hugely and began to stack up coins. 'Whit new little trick is this?' Robertson was following suit. 'Are you not in, Thomas?' Henderson demanded of Wilson.

'No,' Wilson replied, his voice already taking on a certain full tone, 'I'm only a mootie poor tanner—I canna afford these expensive pastimes!'

'Away!' said Robertson. 'Ye're rich as an auld widda!'

'Aye, but mean too!' Wilson replied to their laughter. 'Ye ken I'm no gambler, but nor am I one of your gulls nor a wee fat pigeon, nor ony other little birdie ready for pluckin'! So play on, an' I'll keep a watch on the state o' things ower a bottle.'

By the yellow light of the candles and the orange-and-red flicker of the fire, the dice were rattled and kissed and coddled and cursed. Henderson was pulling in guineas. Brodie waited for the right moment, when Henderson raised himself.

'How's the old man then, Will? Still hangin' on, as they said o' the man in the gibbet!'

'He's deid.' Brodie contrived to put into the two words a flat melancholy. He shuffled two guineas about on the table with the tips of his fingers. The others froze, then looked embarrassed, as he had known they would.

'That's awfu'!' said Henderson. 'I didna' ken, Will. Tak' your money back. I'm grieved I brought ye intae it. It's no civil tae tak the money aff a man who is bereavèd.' He pushed three guineas back at Brodie, who let them lie.

'No. They were fairly won.'

'Ye canna be expectit tae concentrate. Tak' it back!'

'No, Michael. We have a gowden rule, do we no', that a bet is a bet, and once ta'en canna be refused. I cam' here the nicht for a moment or twa's distraction frae the affais at hame. I didna' want tae spoil your pleasure and thus me ain by tellin' ye. I've lost the money. It's nothin'. But I think ye will onnerstan' me, gentlemen, if I tak' ma leave early. It has been a distress—no' just for me, but for the girls.'

'Of course,' said Henderson, standing when Brodie stood up, as though at some reverential occasion. The other two were muttering inadequate but polite condolences, and running out of these, sat shaking their heads in an absurd owlish fashion. It was all Brodie could do to restrain himself from howling with laughter. So much pious sympathy was really too much. He managed to bow to them with a crisp courtesy and made straight-faced for the door. He walked slowly, to be seen going. He knew Henderson would spread the word. Voices called to him from dark booths.

'Off already, Deacon!'

'Goodnicht to ye, Brodie!'

'There's Will! What's the matter, Will?'

He raised his hat in the correct directions, and walked up the steps to the street door. Stepping out into the street, his mouth curled down in an open grin, and he took three swaggering strides, twirling his cane in a theatrical manner, before resuming his sober gait. His face was now blank again. The whole of Edinburgh would believe nothing ill of Will Brodie tonight. It was against human nature, with the old man laid out and the candles burning. The perfect night for a little excursion.

He had made the key a good three months before when Thomson had come to the Close asking for new shelves and drawers, with brass handles, air-tight, for his 'nicotiana tabacum'—twist, flake, rubbed, navy cut, snuff and black cheroots. In common with all Edinburgh shopkeepers, Thomson was accustomed to open the shop in the morning and hang the key on a nail behind the door. While surveying the excellence of his carpenter's workmanship, it was a matter of a moment to make a quick impression on the putty which he carried in a japan-black tin.

The idea of taking his father's wig with him had only occurred as an afterthought, but now he savoured the full relish of it. In one pocket with the key he had a pistol, ready loaded with ball. In the other hand he had stuffed a jemmy and the wig. In addition he carried a dark-lantern, concealed beneath the cloak. He pulled the crushed wig out, straightening the crumpled curls. He felt a hysterical desire to laugh at the sight of it. Pulling it on over his hair was like committing sweet sacrilege. A real wolf in sheep's clothing.

Besides the cloak, his whole appearance had been transformed from the angel of day to the dark angel of night. He wore black trousers and stockings, waistcoat and gloves. He hardly seemed to exist in the narrow darkness of Edinburgh streets. It gave him a dangerous delight to know that, by stepping back into the shadows, he dissolved. He had practised it a dozen times, huddled in some doorway while the town guard tramped by unnoticing.

Lastly he had a cloth mask of the type worn at masked balls. With this on, he was dark as old Sootie himself. He moved carefully along the Cowgate towards Assembly Close and Fishmarket Close. Thomson's tobacco shop, emporium of nicotiana, lay just beyond, tucked in the dark beneath a brooding pinnacle of a tenement.

He listened. From taverns nearby came the sound of shouting and singing. A fiddle played frantically. Feet thumped on boards. Children cried. Above, people coughed, doors slammed. The street was however deserted, just for this moment. He must be quick. With his heart thumping he put on the crêpe mask. This was the decisive move. Until that motion, he was a sober citizen, decently if sombrely clothed in black. With the mask he was outside the law. Taking the key from his pocket, he carefully eased it into the lock of the big iron-strapped door that Thomson fondly believed would give him protection from the common felon. He turned the key carefully, restraining the bolt from shooting back noisily. He listened carefully for any noises of alarm, and looked up to see if any candle was being lit. All he could hear was the domestic throbbing of the town and the steady trickle of the gutter. The key worked smoothly. He had had time to take a clear impression and he had left the lock well oiled. He removed the key from the outside, and turned the handle that lifted the latch. He stepped quickly inside. His heart pumped so that the blood sang in his ears. The excitement was potent.

The room he had entered was vacant. Brodie stood for nearly a minute, absolutely still, until his eyes had become accustomed to the moonless black; he had fallen over a chair once by moving too soon and brought the whole household streaming after him. Certain he had now adjusted to the lack of light, he carefully lifted and replaced the latch so that the door would appear closed. He did not lock it. Everything inside was very familiar. Every shelf, counter, rack, tobacco-box, cabinet and chest had been made in Brodie's Close under his personal supervision and installed less than three months ago. Mr Brodie was a conscientious man who visited his sites often. The work was fine and the wood was good. Above all the price was reasonable, a matter that Will Brodie now hoped to resolve to his greater profit. Thomson was a religious, pernickety man who had been broken in and haltered by an even more religiously imperious wife. His saving grace was an altogether human passion for the water of Speyside and the Loire.

'I'll no' be standing about in your way,' Thomson had announced obligingly. 'Ye'll work better if I clear out for the day.' And the next day, and the next, leaving the premises in the hands of Brodie's workmen for ten days. Brodie merely had to wait until the men had gone for their ale, to slip in and take a putty impression in his japan-black box. Thomson was not only a fool, Brodie considered, but a bigot. He had tired of listening to the man's analysis of Scotland's ills. His lamenting of the passing of the old days, the decay of patrimony and the threat of revolution and anarchy. Brodie had decided then to relieve Mr Thomson of some of his undoubted wealth. Since the American War was slowing down trade, it seemed none too soon.

Brodie moved cautiously over to the small counter, little more than a desk, where Thomson kept his money in a locked drawer. That could be forced with a knife blade. Brodie took the dark-lantern from under his cloak and, setting it down on the desk, took out his tinderbox and touch-paper. He struck it and, on the third spark, it lit. He quickly lit the candle and closed the lantern shutter. In the slit of light the gilt lettering on the tobacco drawers lining the walls glittered and sparkled. The names were magical to Brodie. Ships sailed and crashed through the seas of the world for them, so that Glasgow tobacco-lords could strut and hold court in their scarlet cloaks and gold braid. Virginia, Latakia, Vuelta Abajo Cuba, Bahia Brazil. Packets of cheroots. Burmese, Dindigul, Lunka, Kentucky and Kanaster Varinas, Margarita Venezuela. Not for the first time he considered Edinburgh's small pretensions. Cut, cake, plug, roll, bird's-eye twist, black twist, pigtail and liquorice. Honeydew sweet Cavendish for chewing. Aromatic wooden drawers of snuff. Romantic, free-booting, free-trading smells from places far removed from the smell of sawdust in Brodie's Close. He wished he had run away to sea as he had once intended. He closed the lantern further, lest the glittering gold should catch someone's eye. Taking the pistol from his pocket, he laid it on the desk, uncocked.

He methodically pulled out the drawers of the desk, leaving the locked one to last. With Thomson away, his servant would be with him. He had only to shield his light from the street. The 'Town Rats' had just enough intelligence and curiosity to investigate a flittering light in a shop at night. The drawers of the desk contained nothing but receipts and bills. He replaced all these carefully. His plan was to lock up on his departure, leaving no trace of theft. Thomson would not return for days and would have no idea when the crime had been committed. The locks would be examined and found secure. The servant could not be blamed for he would be away. Who then could be blamed? Brodie? That was unthinkable. Some magician with pick-locks? The press would make a column of that. He moved to the locked drawer, smiling. Thomson would ask him to change the door lock again. Taking the jemmy from his pocket, he stopped. He could not bear to wedge it into the mahogany. It was a beautiful desk on which he had spent many hours. The drawer would have to be broken unless he could find a knife, and why should Brodie break Brodie's work? The joints were beautifully dovetailed, the lock fully inset.

While he considered this, he opened the drawer of cheroots behind him. There were bundles of them tied with raffia, like earthy roots. He thrust these into his cloak pocket. He would have much pleasure in offering them round after a decent interval. On the side was a cheap paper knife of poor steel. He inserted this between the lock and the keep, but it began to bend. Brodie was furious with himself. He should have thought of it beforehand. He took the knife out and straightened it with his fingers, wiping the sweat from his hands, and tried again. While so involved, he did not see the pale light that wavered down the stone stairway into the shop. Thomson had reached the foot of it before Brodie heard the night-gown rustle.

'Who's that in there!' shouted Thomson, sounding terrified. Brodie dropped the paper knife and jumped for his pistol. He pointed it at Thomson, who was carrying a candle in a holder, and trying to see into the gloom. He raised it higher and, seeing the man and the pistol, let out a strangled yelp and froze. Brodie, equally startled, had just managed to comprehend who it was and that Thomson had not in fact gone away. His immediate thought was that it must be a trap. He cocked the pistol and glanced at the door. The sound of the pistol hammer locking back made Thomson speak.

'Don't shoot! I haven't seen you! Take what you want. Leave me alone!'

Brodie backed cautiously to the door, opened the latch and peered through the crack. There was no one in sight, nor any sound of feet. Thomson was shaking, so that the candle he was holding produced fluttering shadows. Brodie realised he must get out quickly before the man recovered his wits enough to dash back up the stairs and start shouting. He smelled his own sweat and it smelled of fear. Thomson, seeing him opening the door, suddenly gained courage and screamed, 'Thief!' Brodie turned to him and, unable to resist the gesture, doffed his hat.

'Guid nicht to ye, Mr Thomson!'

'Thief! Thief!'

Brodie found it irresistible. He doffed his hat again.

'I'm truly sorry, Mr Thomson, that this visit did not prove more profitable to me, but in the circumstances of your womanish screechin', I maun wish ye guid nicht!'

With a bow he was gone, thrusting the pistol, uncocked, into his pocket. He walked quickly, not running, into the darkness, doubling down the first wynd on his left towards the High Street. He could still faintly hear Thomson's shouting. The man was on the street now, more confident. He passed through the blackness of Bell's Wynd. The mask and wig were slipped back into his pockets. He then turned north again towards Libberton's Wynd, walking beneath the buildings that overhung the road. black in blackness, the bundles of cheroots thumping his side. He felt wild and exhilarated, and began to sing quietly to himself as he walked.

'Youth's the season made for joys,
Love is then our duty.'

Thomson had at last managed to attract the attention of the Town Guard, who came puffing up, red-faced and exhausted, their heavy pikes all askew. The sergeant demanded to know if he had seen the man or could recognise him again.

'How could I?' said Thomson. 'He was dressed all in black and wearing a black mask! No one is safe in their beds, Sergeant. He would have shot me!'

Thomson forbore to mention that he thought the man had looked and sounded very like a respected Deacon and Town Councillor. He had heard a thing or two before, but there were always malicious rumours.

Jean Watt was lying in that state of comfortable suspension that immediately precedes sleep when he opened her door. She heard the key in the lock and, not being entirely sure whose key it might be, called out, 'Who is it?' and immediately regretted doing so.

'Who were ye expectin', my chicken?' came Will's voice. He entered the room in a dramatic swirl of black cloak which she thought looked purposely dramatic. She giggled to hide her mistake.

'Ye could have been a burglar!'

'With a key?'

He sounded suspicious and despite his smile was casually examining the room. She knew that was how it was with Will.

'Ach, I knew fine it was you! Who else? Be quiet, you'll wake Peg and the bairns.'

'Peggy hears everything, but she says very little.'

'Are ye sober?'

'Of course I'm sober!'

'Well, will ye tak' off your clothes and cam tae bed, or am I tae wait a' nicht! And me needin' ma sleep!'

She turned back the bed clothes invitingly. Jean Watt was dark-haired, dark-eyed and attractive. She wordlessly gathered her linen nightdress by the hem and pulled it up to her chin. Will, swearing to himself, tore off his cloak and shoes and scrambled down over her.

'Tak your time, Will Brodie! Dinna wouf a guid thing! Ye smell terrible o' tabacca!'

'You're a devil, Jean, you're a devil!'

Jean smiled contentedly and knowingly over his shoulder. Men were such excellent plain fools.

* * *

James Street was dirty and narrow. It ran directly into the market from the Long Acre, parallel to Bow Street. The whole place was strident with the smell of vegetables, fruit and horses. Rotten produce littered the gutter, where it was picked over by destitutes of every age, who dodged the cart and carriage wheels. The stalls that littered the street and formed the market area were no more than timber shacks, their construction clearly showing their origin from ships' ribs and planks. Many of the Seedsmen and Growers had their market gardens near the ports of Gravesend, Rochester, Tilbury and the Hackney Marshes. Business, even on a cold February day, was vigorous and noisy. Hundreds of horses milled about in the narrow streets, trampling on unwary porters who swore and punched them in the belly or on the nose, causing the animals to rear and plunge, adding to the confusion. The street smoked with their droppings in the crisp air.

If the traders were wealthy, they took good care to conceal it. The houses had once been fine dwellings, built for the gentry, but these last twenty years had seen them move west to the new Mayfair. Their fine ground-floor rooms were now deep stock-rooms for winter store and seed. The formerly clean streets were a disgrace. Even at this time of the year, with the breath white on everyone's lips, John Field found himself nauseated by the pungent stew of smells.

He was walking briskly, because of the cold, and in doing so ran the risk of collision in the organised affray of the market work. He reacted too slowly to a dray horse, which shook its head, wet with slobber, knocking his hat half off and spraying him. Then he collided with a drunken porter who would have hit him had he been able to stand, and with a large man carrying a basket of apples. Disabled by his burden, the large man cursed him venomously with the even tone of a man well accustomed to it. John Field's mind was on potatoes, and seed. These he would be buying for sale to the Islington farmers, and he was late. Other seedsmen had been travelling lately and undercutting his business. His fourth collision with an over-dressed and rather vulgar-looking man hardly surprised him. They all seemed to be human ninepins. The rather over-dressed man detained him with a shout.

'Hey, sir!' he shouted. 'You've dropped something! You want to watch what you're doing!'

John Field would have passed on but, following the man's pointing arm, stopped. Nestling in the ooze of the gutter was a white leather purse, quite new by its look, drawn tight with a leather string. He looked back to the man.

'It's not mine.'

'Well, it's not mine either. Let me have a look.'

The man bent quickly down, and seized the purse, gesturing to Field to accompany him. Field, curious, followed to a quieter corner of an alley.

'We should hand it over to the Justice,' said Field.

'What? And let that scoundrel have it?' the man replied.

'Then we should advertise for the reward.'

'Who will pay for the advertisement? Let us have a look, at least.' Field hesitated. He wanted to be about his business, but the man was feeling the purse cautiously. 'It's a ring,' he said, leaning over to whisper to Field. 'I know a spot where we can have a look at it in peace.' He motioned with his head to an ale house further up the street.

'Very well,' said Field. He was not so prosperous as to turn down a chance like this. The man was right. The Justices had a way with things like rings, and to advertise would only involve trouble, and who was to see the prospective claimants and deal with them and who was to know who would be genuine or not?

'But why should you share it?' he asked, nagged by a last doubt.

'I wouldn't have,' the man replied, 'only I thought you dropped it. I sort of said it out loud without thinking.' He shrugged. 'Next time I'll mind my mouth.'

Field nodded, satisfied. They walked to the ale house, and, entering, the man led him to a small bar at the rear, which was deserted. The man appeared to know the place.

'Do you work at the market?' Field asked.

'No,' said the man, 'I've been coming here for years though. Trader, you see. Now, let's have a look at it.' With blunt fingers, the man unpicked the leather thong which had been tied in a true knot. Field was becoming quite excited. The man tipped up the purse, and a brilliant cluster-ring fell on to the table. The man let out a gasp and clamped a hand on it.

'God look at that! Here, keep it hid in your hand. There's paper in here. Money!' The man fished about, and produced a slip of folded paper which he flattened out. 'No luck! It's a receipt of some sort. Only the ring. Let me see it!' Field handed him back the ring, and curiously picked up the piece of paper. He read upon it the date, Feb. 2, 1784, and in a sloping but unrefined copper-plate the wording, 'Bought of William Smith, one brilliant diamond-cluster ring, value £210, and received at the same time the contents, in full of all demands, by me, William Smith.' Field was speechless. He jabbed a finger at the paper, and tapped the man on the shoulder.

'What?' said the man.

'Look!' squeaked Field. 'Just look! It's worth a fortune! Two hundred and ten pounds!' The man seized the paper and read it. He seemed equally impressed, but this seemed only to spur on his practicality.

'Fifty-fifty,' he said.

'Right,' said Field.

'But how? Can you buy your half?'

'You're joking. Can you buy yours?'

'What do you think? I'll get us a drink. Ale?' Field nodded. This was going to be a problem. The ring lay on the table and glittered at him. He was conscious that they must get rid of it fast, but how? He was suddenly aware that the man was in conversation with another well-dressed-looking fellow who had quietly entered their part of the bar. The newcomer was looking at the ring. Belatedly, Field covered it with his fist. Both men came over to the table, the trader carrying two quarts of ale. Field felt panic. 'Oh, God,' he thought, 'we've been discovered. It's the owner!'

But instead of hurtling accusations, the trader introduced the newcomer.

'Here's someone who can help. A friend of mine, going by like a gift from the Gods.'

'What does he want?' asked Field suspiciously. 'I don't want any part of this. Why are you bringing him in?'

'Don't get excited, friend. May I introduce Mr Humphry Moore, who will enable me to dispose of my half of our assets, which he cannot do without you disposing of your half—at no loss to yourself, I assure you. Mr Moore will be content with a small offer I have made him of percentage from my share. Otherwise, as I see it, we are stuck.' Moore held out a hand.

'How do you do, Mr . . .?'

'Field.'

'Mr Field.' They shook hands. Field noted the warmth of Moore's handshake. Evidently he did not mind being a party to this business.

'Unfortunately like yourselves I do not have the ready money to relieve you of the ring and dispose of it myself. It is this damned indivisibility that is the problem. If only we had some cash!'

'How much cash?' said Field impetuously.

The two others exchanged glances.

'How much have you got?' said Moore.

'None on me. But I have some money at my lodgings.' The other two sat down. The trader spoke.

'How much at your lodgings?' As Field hesitated, he continued, 'Look, as I see it, friend, without money we have no security and have no chance. Mr Moore here knows a man who will give us good value for that ring. Not its full value naturally, but I do not expect you are green, Mr Field, if you will pardon my little joke. We must get what we can.'

Moore spoke: 'Hold hard. I understand how Mr Field feels. I tell you what. Mr Field has no way of knowing he can trust us. That is right isn't it, Mr Field?'

Field nodded.

'I propose Mr Field retains the ring, and gives us money in security until tomorrow when I can readily dispose of it. How much money have you, Mr Field, and do you not think that solves the problem. You have the ring, and it is we that take the risk. I think that's fair.'

Field considered, and felt the ring in the palm of his hand. He made up his mind.

'About forty to fifty pounds. My lodgings are at Chelsea.'

The trader looked at Moore. There was a silence. Moore shrugged.

'It is not really your half of the value, but I suppose it will just about do. You look an honest man, Mr Field, and I'm sure you are.'

Within an hour they had arrived at Field's lodgings by cab. The trader entered at Field's request, Moore saying he would remain in the Five Fields tavern and wait for them later in the day at the Cheshire Cheese, not wishing to inhibit the celebrations of Field and the trader, but having other business to see to concerning the disposal of the ring. Field proved more difficult to persuade than anticipated, when the trader got him alone. After several more convivial ales they returned to the Cheshire Cheese with only twenty guineas and four doubloons, Field stoutly maintaining that the sum of forty to fifty pounds represented his total capital and that he must have something to buy seed and potatoes. Moore was already there, waiting for them. The trader made what Field thought was quite a good job of presenting his case to Moore. Moore was at first disposed to be truculent and disappointed, but finally settled for the sum offered, handing Field the ring.

'We will see you tomorrow, friend,' said Moore, 'when we should get a more realistic return on its value. Meet us in Hatton Garden at the corner of Saint Cross Street at ten in the morning. You leave us little security considering its value!'

'You can trust me,' said Field, feeling somewhat nervous at his responsibility. 'I will be there exactly as planned.'

'Well, you will get your money back then, and the hundred that we hope will be your share. I hope you are aware of the risk we take. We have never met you before in our lives.'

'Yes,' said Field, 'yes. You can trust me.'

'I hope so, friend, for we shall certainly report on you if you don't.'

This sour note jolted Field into a degree of sobriety.

'I am no cheat. I shall be there,' he replied stiffly.

It was after he had patiently waited for nearly two hours that

John Field had the courage to enter a jeweller's shop, much further down the street. The man put his glass to his eye and grunted. He put the ring back on the counter and scratched his cheek.

'Are you being serious, sir?'

'Well, what is it worth? It was left to me by my mother.'

'Was it, sir? Well, I hope she didn't pay much for it, sir. It's trash!'

'It can't be!'

'Glass diamonds.'

Field stormed out of the shop, white with fury. He vowed revenge and made for the Justices' Office, gripping the ring.

CHAPTER TWO

The Council

The long mahogany table was strewn with papers, quills, ink-stands and ledgers. The room was heavily oak-panelled, reducing the light, and had become warm. Councillors rustled and shifted, pulling at collars and waistcoats. Some lay back in their chairs and thought of cool ale. David Stuart, former Provost, was on his feet speaking. An elderly man, dry-skinned and grey, he commanded great respect.

'We have always had a good reputation for the civilised manner of the despatch of our criminals,' he was saying, 'and I think we may say that we have always kept before England in this matter. It is a matter of disgust to all Scotsmen that the English, who are generally held throughout Europe to be a race of tender sympathies, did not abolish pressing to death until only thirteen years ago! Thirty years ago, that humane race still suffered women to be burned alive for murdering their husbands, a crime they quaintly called by the name of "petit treason". Being a tender race, they retain as capital offences such notable crimes as the destruction of ornamental trees!'

There was laughter from the Councillors.

'The French, who have more enthusiasm even than the English in these matters, do of course, execute by means of hanging. They also practise such disgusting and barbarous customs as burning alive and breaking on the wheel, which I believe they greatly enjoy. It is not my wish that we should be seen to be in the forefront of zealous despatch. I even understand the French clad the man to be burned in a shirt soaked in sulphur to ensure a good blaze! They also use torture by water to extract confessions, which we might expect in a Catholic realm, and they suspend their unfortunate criminals from the ceiling in Besançon, I am told, and attach weights to his legs until he is near rent apart. However, this idea from Newgate does seem to have about it a humane design. It may be admitted that it is the English wish to speed the process up—they having more criminals to despatch, as I believe, than they can readily cope with. To this end they execute them six at a time. I do not believe we shall ever have to come to that!'

He sat down in his leather seat with a dry little cough. Bailie Dickson rose.

'It is merely my contention that what Mr Brodie has said about the use o' a trap tae produce a drop, is more humane. The folding awa' o' a ladder does nae mair than strangle the man.'

Brodie got to his feet, and Dickson sat down.

'It is, ye see, founded on sound anatomical principles,' said Brodie.

'Aye, and no doubt it will cost money!' said Bailie Galloway, a diminutive figure in a coat green with wear. 'Principles are aye things that cost someone or other!'

'The principles,' said Brodie, ignoring Galloway, 'are that the fall dislocates the vertebrae o' the spine at the base o' the skull, rendering the man immediately insensible.'

'What for,' said Councillor Simpson. 'Should we go out of our way to prevent a criminal from suffering? I put it to ye, that suffering is inherent in the punishment, and wi' oot it, where's the punishment?'

There were some murmurs of assent. Lord Provost Grieve spoke from the head of the table. Behind his head on the high-backed leather chair, the arms of Edinburgh glittered in gold.

'I would have thought, Councillor Simpson, that the punishment consisted of being deprived of life, and no' in suffering. In this I believe I correctly interpret the law of Scotland. We have little sympathy, I hope, with the idea held by other people, and I am sure ye all ken what I mean, that sufferin' is good for the soul. Sufferin' affects only the body. The soul maun tak' its chance after death, and that seems tae me tae be the punishment our law sees fit.'

There was a strong murmur of agreement at this. Councillor Jameson rose to his feet. He was a big man, prosperously dressed, and perspiring amid a confection of lace ruffles that forced his cravat tight up to his chin. He had a business interest in it, as had Will Brodie.

'I agree with Mr Brodie's proposition. We dinna want the embarrassment attendin' upon sic cases as "hauf-hengit" Maggie Dickson. I ken it may be sixty year ago, but we have had some long struggles syne!'

'What a sin,' said Galloway, 'to delay the refection of the Councillors by presuming tae tak' so long tae die! This invention seems tae me to be inventit' tae stop the broth getting cauld!'

There were shouts and protests from several of the Councillors at this. Provost Grieve banged with his gavel.

'Mr Brodie, you have I believe prepared some drawings of this device. I am of the opinion that we should see them.' Brodie unfurled a drawing on the table, and rolled it backwards so that it would lie flat.

'Would ye be so good as to explain briefly what must be done.'

Brodie got to his feet.

'It is a simple matter, Lord Provost. At the moment the arrangements are clumsy. We use the same beam in the Tolbooth wall, thus incurring no extra expense, but it will be necessary to have a new door straight to it, thus avoiding having to construct steps each time. Then, instead of collapsible steps which must be removed with some vigour, and have on occasion known to us been kicked awa' too previously, we construct a platform as shown which has a trap door on a hinge. This as ye can see is held in place by a catch operated by a lever —the drawing is to my design but is similar I believe to that in use at Newgate. By a simple pull of the lever, the trap drops sharply awa' with the weight o' the prisoner, precipitating him some feet. The force of this drop, being so abrupt, is sufficient tae dislocate the vertebrae as already mentioned.'

'How much will a' this cost?' demanded Galloway, his mean little eyes sceptical.

'About twenty-five pounds for the Wright work and the same for the Mason,' said Brodie.

'A' that for a door in the floor!' exclaimed Galloway. 'It's ower dear for a criminal, ower dear!'

'It will also be necessary to rebuild the shops and the parapet end of the Tolbooth tae tak' the weight o' it, and tae provide a decent deep drop.'

'Lord Provost, this is a waste of citizens' money!' Galloway exploded. 'Whatever next! And how much will the rebuilding o' the shops cost?'

'I can't say until they have been examined.'

'Oh, aye, so that's the way o' it. Ye must have some idea!'

'Perhaps another fifty pounds.'

'Fifty poonds! Fifty poonds!' Galloway was shaking and pounding the table with his small white fists. 'It's ridiculous for a hengin'. An' what's the rope to be o'. Crimson silk?'

The Lord Provost banged with his gavel. Galloway continued, to the table at large.

'I ask ye all, is this no' a ridiculous extravagance? We should have a tax on the theatres tae pay for it onyways. If it wasnae for them, we might have less use for it. Aye, an' use their curtain cords!'

Bailie Shaw joined in the commotion, his bellowing voice eventually achieving the silence of others.

'We live in a time of depravity!' he declaimed in the voice of a preacher. 'And the depravity costs us money! Now we are to pay twice over—once when they steal our money and twice when we hang them! If the Lord Provost will pardon my saying so, when his Grace the Duke of Queensberry introduced Mr Gay and his deplorable plays to our town and lodged him with Allan

Ramsay, he did us the disservice of doubling our crime overnight!'

The Lord Provost rapped repeatedly with his gavel until there was silence amid the uproar that followed.

'Bailie Shaw, I do not know there is any substance to your assumptions. They are out of order in the matter under discussion.'

Bailie Galloway was not to be diverted: 'With respect, they canna be out of order when we are considering the spendin' o' at least a hunnert poonds for the hengin' o' people enticed frae the paths o' righteousness by such-like public performances which are a disgrace to our city, which corrupt the young, which mak' oot that to rob an' murder and steal folks' possessions is somehow an act o' heroism and even humour ...'

He paused to draw breath. Shaw continued, for him: 'It is written in the Book, my Lord Provost, "Pleasant words are as an honeycomb, sweet to the soul, and health to the bones. An ungodly man diggeth up evil: and in his lips there is as a burning fire." Proverbs, Chapter sixteen!'

Lord Provost Grieve looked at Galloway with a gleam of distaste. 'As we are quoting the good book, Bailie Shaw, is it not written in Proverbs, sixteen, that "the Lord hath made all things for himself; yea even the wicked for the day of evil"?'

Shaw was offended. His thin sallow face took on a fanatical look.

'The heart of the righteous studieth to answer: but the mouth of the wicked poureth out evil things!'

'Yes, I know, Bailie Shaw. I know also that "a wholesome tongue is a tree of life: but perverseness therein is a breach in the spirit". Is that not so? But I am sure we are here for a meeting of the Council and not a catechism.'

Bailie Galloway was still determined to speak. Brodie continued to stand with the plan in front of him, a broad smile across his face.

Galloway, his voice shaking, said, 'With the Lord Provost's

permission I should still like tae point oot that when yon Mrs Siddons appeared at the Theatre Royal, durin' the General Assembly o' the Kirk itself, all important business was transferred tae the days she wasnae actin', as all the young members o' the Kirk were in the theatre at three in the afternoon. Crime and the Theatre are not unconnected!'

Shaw shouted his assent, while many others roared with laughter.

'I hope,' said Grieve, 'that you are not suggesting that our recent outbreaks of robberies is being conducted by a member of the Kirk?'

Shaw went red with rage, but fortunately was speechless. There was a good deal of undignified clapping and laughter. Grieve continued:

'As we are to vote whether or not to construct a new trap, as Mr Brodie calls it, for the more humane despatch of convicted felons, I feel we should do so now. The study of the good book may, I feel, quite properly be conducted at home by the fire, but we can hardly dae our Council business there, by your leave. Those in favour of the new machine please show. Thank you gentlemen. You have a majority, Mr Brodie. We must ask you to make a survey of the Tolbooth, with Convener Jameson. Mr Hill has experience in these matters too and if it is agreeable perhaps the three gentlemen might prepare a report. Thank you, Mr Brodie, for the pains you have taken in showing your plan.'

Will Brodie took the drawing off the table.

Galloway and Shaw had both half-turned from the table, furious.

'I have in my workshop a small model I have constructed,' said Brodie. 'Perhaps the Council might be pleased to look at it when next it sits and examine its principle?'

The Lord Provost nodded his assent.

Will Brodie sat down with his secret smile.

CHAPTER THREE

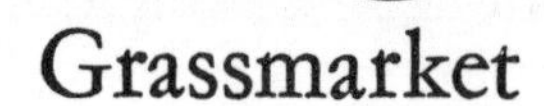

Grassmarket

George Smith was eating at a large scrubbed table; in front of him on a distorted pewter plate he had a cold beef bone. On this there was only a meagre scraping of meat, encased in a ring of marbled fat. He picked nuggets of bread from a lump on the table and compressed them between thumb and fore-finger before eating them. From time to time he pared a frag-ment of meat from the bone with his clasp knife, washing the dry mixture down from a lidded quart pot of ale. He ate with little enthusiasm and in silence, watched by his wife.

Smith was a heavy-browed man with a distinctly large head and protruding jaw. He had the appearance of a man who had once been robust but had recently been ill—rings beneath his eyes had not filled out, he had hollows in his cheeks and loose flesh drooped in dewlaps about the base of his neck. His clothes were in bad condition and hung about him loosely. His wife Mary who sat patiently across from him, watching, was anxious and over-aged for her years. Her clothes had washed thin across her shoulders and elbows so that the cotton was discoloured with the flesh-colour beneath, and the wool had become loose-woven and fibrous like hessian. Her face was pinched and pointed, and her eyes seemed dull and lethargic. Her anxiety was that of a working-dog regarding its master. She was not a clever woman, nor particularly attractive, but she was faithful. In their relation-ship Smith was the master. She might have been waiting for the bone.

The third person in the upper room in which they were sitting was Michael Henderson. Lean-faced and relaxed, he reclined with his clay pipe on a wooden bench set in the window bay, where he could look out over the activity in the Grassmarket. From the White Hart tavern a steady stream of travellers and carriers emerged, to continue their journeys or commence the day's business, having refreshed themselves. Highland drovers would still be asleep in the straw of the stables, oblivious to the bellowing of their beasts. Golden-yellow light, as yet lacking any warmth, gilded the wet cobbles, damp from dispersing mist. Henderson puffed smoke and enjoyed the scene. He had eaten early and well, and his lodgers ate what they could afford. He was however a fair man, and tried to give value, as the presence of beef instead of mutton indicated. He idly watched the cobbles drying, each from the centre becoming grey, rimmed about the joints with black mire. He would finish his pipe and go back to the stables again. This total silence between the Smiths was strange. Usually they exchanged a few words, and Smith talked of the day before or the day ahead. There was something in the air between them.

Puffing smoke, he said, 'I can't sit here forever. Time I was out and about. I will wish you good-day.'

He swung his legs off the bench and regarded the dying glow in the bowl of his pipe. Smith stopped the movement of his jaws and swallowed. His wife nodded to him, urgently, meaningfully. He ignored her.

'Mr Henderson . . .' he said. Henderson stopped on the bench, aware that he had precipitated the matter whatever it was. '. . . I know it is an imposition on you, and that I have no call on you to ask.' His voice had a strong Birmingham accent, nasal and difficult for Henderson to understand at times.

Henderson said equably, 'What is the matter, Mr Smith. You have paid your bill until the end of the month. You have discharged all your obligations to me. Can I be of some service to you?' Smith paused and said his piece slowly.

'When I arrived here, as you know, I had only my goods and the horse and cart and a few bits and pieces about me. I know you have been most generous and introduced me to ... parties of your acquaintance. You know where a man might have a guinea or two on the cards and other gentlemanly pursuits.'

'Aye,' said Henderson, 'that's so. And have made a guinea or two as well. And, as I have said, I cannot complain that you have not always paid your rent and score. Have you noticed,' Henderson continued, with practised circumlocution, indicating the scene outside the window with his pipe, 'that we have more oil-lamps around the Grassmarket than formerly. It is either some extravagance of the Town Council, or we have become prosperous through the Act of Union at last! Our English cousins, Mr Smith, knew well what they were doing with us Scottish simpletons!'

Smith, with a touch of impatience, said, 'Mr Henderson, I know your views on the English ...'

'I have no views on the English, Mr Smith, only on England!'

'What I need, Mr Henderson, is a steady job. Regular employment. This is a chancy sort of business living by cards, and a man is as soon down as he is up. With my wife here with me, we could do something steady. I was trained as a locksmith in Birmingham before I became a traveller, did you know?'

The oblique Henderson was not going to be drawn into a straight reply to that.

'Aye, I daresay it was a rash move ye made, this moving from England, where ye might have been a better-off kind of a man. Have ye never thought that ye might be better returning there?'

Henderson glanced at him quickly as he said this. Smith took the bone of beef and carved a knuckle of meat out of it. His face remained impassive. Henderson thought it remained too much so.

'We never know how these things will turn out,' Smith replied. 'Are you telling me that, in a city that can afford more oil-lamps, you are so well-endowed with locksmiths as well that you have no use for my trade?'

'I cannot speak for Edinburgh, Mr Smith!'

'Well, is it so?'

'There is use for locksmiths in the town.'

'Then I only ask you the favour of putting it about that there is one here in need of employment.'

'You have decided to settle this side o' the border then?'

'We have.'

'Aye, well. But I have no guarantee, if you pardon me for being so blunt, that your work is of the best. I believe everything ye say but other folk are inclined to be disbelievin'! Folks are not trusting, ye know!'

'Mr Henderson, when you believed me, you had my horse and cart as security!'

Henderson suddenly smiled. There was genuine amusement in the dark eyes.

'That is true, Mr Smith, and I like you for it! I will put in a word for ye.'

'With Brodie?'

'So ye know your man? That's a high ambition. He has the biggest business in Edinburgh.'

'Please ask him,' said Mary Smith. Her face was not unattractive but had a soft simplicity that detracted from it. Almost stupidity.

'You have met Mr Brodie over cards I believe?'

'I have. A substantial man and a gentleman. I like his style.'

'Can you make locks and mend keys?'

'I can. There is not a lock in this city I could not master, given a little time.'

'You can tell Mr Brodie that yourself. I will arrange an introduction for you this evening. There is a game for the fancy at Johnnie Clark's. Mr Brodie will naturally be there. He may well have a use for you.'

'That's very kind of you, Mr Henderson ...' Smith began.

'Not at all. You could be useful to him.' Mary Smith was mumbling grateful thanks, to which Henderson inclined his head. 'Be honest with Mr Brodie. He will want to know all about you.'

'What else!' said Smith, throwing out his hands palms upwards in a gesture of frankness.

'But take my meaning. He will want to know *all* about you. It is not for Michael Henderson to ask why a traveller cannot return the way he has come.'

Smith looked hard at Henderson, and nodded.

'I take your drift.'

Henderson smiled, stood his pipe on the stone mantelshelf of the room, and left. Mary Smith took George Smith's arm and smiled.

The Royal Exchange was always discreetly busy in the subdued way favoured by banking houses. In the same discreet way, Brodie knew all comings and goings were noted. It was after all a matter of business importance to know just who was dealing with whom.

Dressed for the daylight hours in customary style, he wore white stockings, grey trousers and waistcoat and a dark grey coat lined with pearl-grey silk. He strolled with his slightly bent-legged gait across the inner courtyard, planting the tip of his cane on the cobbles like a man spiking leaves. The silver buckles of his shoes sparkled in the sunlight. Bankers, dressed almost exclusively in black with severely minimal ruffles, raised their hats and wished him 'Good-day'. The younger men envied his flair, while the older curmudgeons muttered after he had passed, that Brodie went too far. Brodie knew it and it amused him. It was good to be known so well and so very little at the same time. Lawyers particularly, he thought, will always seize on the visible man. He enjoyed their respect.

Even within the courtyard he could hear the muffled banging of his men at work. He entered the building and walked to Johnston and Smith's. The outer door of the counting-house gave directly on to an open common stair that raised the floor up about four feet. The door was shut, and he knocked. An elderly clerk opened it just sufficiently to recognise the visitor, then threw it open to allow him in.

'Good morning, Mr Brodie. Have you come to see the works?'

'I have.'

'I hope they will finish soon. We are near deaf with it!'

Johnston himself was sitting at a huge severe mahogany desk, elevated above the floor so that he overlooked the counting floor as a judge overlooks the court. The counting-house was divided by hip-high rails and miniature partitions into territorial domains over which each clerk had deputed authority. Some clerks were alone with their morocco-bound ledgers, scraping away with quills. Others were huddled discreetly forward, in close conversation with their clients. Off the main counting-house there were a series of panelled private rooms, where, when the business became substantial, they would retire for privacy and port. Brodie noted the considerable quantities of banknotes that lay in open cash drawers, and marvelled, as he had done a hundred times at the unimaginative nature of his fellow men. For less than lay in one room, men were prepared to sail to India or America. Were prepared to spend years and take great risks for something that could so easily be had within a mile of the Cross.

Johnston, looking up from his accounts with the lofty air of a schoolmaster overlooking his essay class, caught sight of Brodie and, raising his hand in recognition, came lumbering down from his dais. He joined Brodie in the common area, separated from the remainder by a partition, that served as a reception hall. Beside and behind the door on a gleaming brass hook, as though to draw attention to it, hung the key of the main door.

Johnston was a big man growing fat. He held out his hand and energetically grasped Brodie's, thrashing his arm up and down. 'Good morning to you! Your men will finish in time, I hope? But of course they will! No offence, for they are doing a fine job, but my, what a pease-bruizle! And this banging is driving us all mad!' He shook his head good-humouredly enough, however, and a small cloud of powder shook out of his wig and settled on his shoulders, which already looked lightly frosted. Brodie smiled sympathetically. 'I'm afraid Mr Johnston, that, despite the wonderful age we live in, it is still impossible to do work without dirt or noise. Maybe one day we shall come to it—silent workmen. But how shall I know they are working?'

Johnston laughed good-naturedly, but nonetheless persisted: 'They will be gone tomorrow? That was what you told me last Thursday, do you mind?'

'They will be gone tomorrow. I have come round now to be sure of it. Can I go through to them?'

'Certainly. Let yourself through. You know the way. Do anything that will speed up the end of this banging!'

He opened a small wooden gate and Brodie passed through the counting floor to the private rooms. There his carpenters under his foreman Robert Smith were finishing off the mahogany mouldings to two new panelled rooms. It smelled of sawdust like snuff and fish glue. A small fire burned in the hearth on which the glue-pot simmered. Rab Smith came over. He was the same height as Brodie, but stocky and solid. The men looked up, greeting Brodie respectfully, then continued with their work, mitreing, glueing and wedging, and hammering.

'How goes it, Rab?'

'It'll be done in time.' Smith wiped his hands on his apron. 'The old fellow out there is aye complainin' about the noise, but what can I do?'

'I've spoken to him about it. Don't worry. Let me look over the work.'

'Aye. Take a look.'

For ten minutes Brodie engaged himself in careful inspection of his men's work. He examined junctions and joints, external and internal returns. He looked at the stopping and filling and staining. With Robert Smith he discussed quantities of nails and glass and the amounts of off-cut timber and waste. They discussed polish and shellac and veneers. Brodie loved the spicy, aromatic smell of sawn hardwoods. The minutes amongst his men's work gave him real pleasure, as when he made a piece himself. At these times he became totally absorbed in the perfection of it. In the design of it he was interested but cared little for invention. In the construction and detail he put his heart. This, Francis had never been able to comprehend.

William, in his imagination, had always been able to see the slow miracle of transformation from the standing wood in Honduras, Cuba or Haiti. Huge hundred-foot giants toppled in ocean-green forests that rang with the echo of axes; logging camps by steaming tropical rivers, resounding with birds by day and droning with malevolence by night; logs hoisted by sweating negroes on timber gantries with only rope tackle and quivering muscles. Guttural shouts. Whips and gang-masters. Shipped across the Atlantic, to be sawn, with such difficulty, into plank and matured. Finally the verdure of these forests, passing through his hands, became the polished partitions of Johnston and Smith or the mahogany chest of Mrs Ross of Pitcalnie. The transformation was absolute, and delighted him.

When he had finished, he returned by the same route he had entered. Johnston called to him good-naturedly: 'On time then, Mr Brodie?'

'Finished tomorrow,' said Brodie.

'Good day, and thank you. Will you see yourself out?'

'I will.' He always did. Putting on his hat he walked in a leisured fashion to the reception area. Here the partition, built to lend discreetness to the transactions of the counting-hall, equally concealed the main door from that room. Behind the partition, Brodie moved with speed. Looking quickly round first, he took down the original key from its brass hook. From his pocket he produced an identical key of bright iron, which he compared with the original by quickly laying one on top of the other and checking their alignment. Nodding to himself with satisfaction, he re-hung the original and in a moment was closing the door behind him. The whole thing had taken under ten seconds. No one could have known other than that the Deacon was walking slowly.

Outside he strolled back across the court, the lifted sun shining full in his eyes until he passed out through the narrow way and into the High Street. Here the height of the buildings still obscured the sun except for brief slots between gables and chimneys. The High Street appeared a sinuous wet snake, splashed with patches of yolk yellow. He had a peculiar notion to walk north and examine the new works to the Tolbooth.

The works were a burning source of rancour with him. Although the idea had been his own, by virtue of his statutory two years out of office as Deacon of Wrights, and the tardiness of the Town Council in promoting his plans, the work had been passed to the new Deacon, Thomas Hill, and Councillor Jameson. With a show of good-will that was entirely false, but which at least gave him some satisfaction, he had handed over his plans. Deacon Hill now claimed of course to have improved them so that they no longer bore any relationship to the original. Not only that, but last year the pair of them had obtained a vote by virtue of Lord Provost Grieve to rebuild the shops and parapet to the west end of the Tolbooth, beneath the trap and beam—at the handsome price of seventy pounds, *exclusive* of Wright's work, and trap machinery. Brodie had forecast to all and sundry that Hill's trap would never work, and that the prisoner was more likely to die of exposure than of hanging. In truth, the design was very close to his own and he was perfectly satisfied, to his disgust, that Hill had followed the plans well, and done a good job. To lose work like that, with all the prestige it carried, was not good. Besides, it gave Brodie a thrill of exhilarating terror to stand upon the very trap and look out over the Lawnmarket, picturing the mob of tens of thousands, yelling, fainting and hanging out of every window to get a view. He loved the theatre. He thought of the platform as a stage on which the last act would be performed to an audience never equalled in size except in the Colosseum in Rome. It was a sacred spot, which he had set his heart on creating. Already he was thinking of future improvements so that, when Hill lost office, he might return to the work. If cathedrals should be mighty buildings, although so thinly filled, why should a temple of death with its universal popularity be so badly appointed? Was not this platform a more immediate method for the disposal of immortal souls than any fine, polished altar?

There had been a good deal of outcry from pious Edinburgh gentles about the purpose of it all. But the construction of the new place of execution had excited the imagination of the ordinary folk, long accustomed to the Grassmarket as the scene, and the use of the folding steps.

Brodie thought of Wilson the smuggler, so endeared to the mob. Of Maclean the highwayman, hero of Gay's opera. They had been wild men, but gentle and courteous in their way, solicitous of the safety of their friends, darlings of the crowd. How few of Edinburgh's worthies would go like that, bemoaned by tens of thousands, cheered on by adoring crowds! Surely it could not be a bad way to die.

As he walked up the High Street towards the Tolbooth, he sang to himself, just audibly, Macheath's song from *The Beggar's Opera,* his favourite work.

> 'Let us take the road!
> Hark! I hear the sound of coaches.
> The hour of attack approaches,
> To your arms brave boys and load!
>
> See the ball I hold
> Let the Chymists toil like asses
> Our fire their fire surpasses
> And turns all our lead to gold!'

* * *

Gilmore the Hairdresser's shop was directly below the projecting two-storey portion of the Tolbooth. Out of the gable end from which it projected, sprouted the substantial oak beam. It appeared to have a menace of its own, and it made Brodie's hair prickle just to look at it. He entered Gilmore's. The shop smelled of pomade and powder. Around the walls on pegs like so many scalps from victims of the beam above, hung every example of false hair. The conjunction of the shop and scaffold amused Brodie who never omitted to remark that he assumed Mr Gilmore could rely on a cheap supply of new hair from now on. Mr Gilmore, a man of easy ways and little concern for the boot-soles suspended above his head, would laugh and wink, and heat his tongs over the spirit lamp that burnt blue.

'I'll dae more business by making them look pretty first!' Mr Gilmore prattled on happily about perukes and full bobs, naturals, half naturals, curley roys and airey levants until Brodie was forced to interrupt.

'How is Mr Hill's work proceeding?'

'Well enough, I hear. I doubt he'll finish it in his term.'

'I must go up and see.'

'You can make your way up round the back. They have a ladder leading up.'

'Is Tom Hill up there?'

'No, Deacon. He'll be at his ale.'

Brodie passed through the back of the shop to a passage, where he found a ladder leading to the platform. He mounted the ladder and inspected the work, making a grimace to himself. Hill was a good carpenter, but would never make a cabinet. He walked over to the trap, not yet complete, and inspected it in thorough detail, pulling the lever which was not yet operational, and examining the release and drop. It was exactly like his own designs. Straightening up, he realised that he now had exactly the last view that a condemned man would have of the world. Without the shouts and cheering of the mob, without the red coats of the Town Guard, the glint of their pikes and Lochaber axes, without the bows, frills and bouquets of the ladies of pleasure, without the smell of new jute rope, it was commonplace enough. Indeed, viewing it with complete dispassion, it was depressing and drear, even on a fine warm summer's day. The tenements on each side of the Grassmarket were soot-clad and ill-tarred. Their bow windows sagged and the sashes were cracked. Napier's laboratory, the new spectator's gallery, had a mortar and pestle hanging over the door. The pestle was painted a disquieting blood-red. Brodie could not keep himself from glancing up at the beam. Two stout iron hooks were embedded in its underside. The wall of the Tolbooth, into which the beam was let, was in terrible condition. Rubble stonework was exposed where the harl or render had fallen away. Being a gable end, it was streaked with rainmarking. Small plants struggled to survive in cracks high up. Brodie walked quickly away, feeling suddenly that it was a dreadful spot. As a backdrop it needed vast improvements. In his mind's eye it would be painted with glorious scenes. Men with their eyes turned heavenwards like Christian martyrs. Gilded mahogany should surround them, and fine funereal music should be played by a chamber orchestra. Something solemn like Vivaldi and Purcell which he had heard at a concert. Men lacked so much imagination. The shadow of the beam swept across the platform like a huge sun-dial, emphasising that life passes whether we use it or not.

Brodie was worried. The exhilarations of the morning had lifted his spirits to a dangerous degree and he had been taking risks, which was never good at John Clark's tavern. There were too many fast hands and sly eyes beside his own and he had already lost fifteen guineas. His mind was on the counting-house, and the key in his coat pocket. Four of them were playing faro—Brodie, Robertson, a big rich farmer up from Ettrickdale, called Milne, and Henderson. Milne was refusing to be fleeced. The gull had become a kite and was well up on all of them.

Robertson was the first to complain.

'There's no winning for me! What's wrong with these cards?'

Milne, who was half drunk, grinned broadly.

'Nothing!'

Henderson, knowing the way of things, turned to the farmer. 'Look, we none of us have a chance. You're handsomely up on all of us. I can see you're a man for a gamble. Change to dice for a bit!'

The farmer hesitated. Brodie said quietly, 'If a man's in luck, the instrument of it rarely makes any difference. It's no use, Michael. You merely change the means o' our misfortune.'

'Have you a pair of dice, Will?' said Henderson.

'I have, but I doubt if they'll do much good.'

'Mr Milne,' continued Henderson, 'you have been winning well and we have paid like gentlemen without complaint. Would it not be a gentlemanly thing just to give us the choice of the weapons before the execution!'

The big farmer roared hugely.

'Aye, ye put it grand! All right, gentlemen, show me the weapons!'

Brodie produced his loaded dice from his coat pocket. He handed them to the farmer. No inexpert hand would be able to make proper use of them. Brodie caught Clark's eye. The pipe was withdrawn from the lips, the stem was pointed, and pots of claret appeared at their sides.

'Your health, Mr Milne!' declared Brodie.

'And yours, sir!' roared the farmer. 'I came here to sell beef, but it is a wonderful thing that I have doubled my money!' He rolled the dice experimentally, and drank deep from his pot. Brodie, turning slightly aside in the igneous hell of the cellar, winked at Henderson. Now the fun could begin. What with the two regular women and others, and keeping the house, and paying for the feeding and training of the cocks, and the price of claret and cards and dice games, life was becoming expensive.

In an adjacent booth three men sat in the shadow, where no

light could catch them. They too played cards, but for low stakes, and their drink was Edinburgh Ale. They talked together sporadically throughout their game and remained watchful of the four men opposite. Their game was only a diversion.

One of the three was George Smith, awaiting his introduction. The other two had become his frequent companions through common poverty. Smith had been two months at Henderson's convalescing from pneumatic fever, and in that time everything he possessed had gone to pay the rent. He was becoming an impatient man now as he had waited nearly two hours and it was approaching ten o'clock.

'Damn it, will he never stop! They are just settling in!'

Smith's two companions were very different men. The first, Ainslie, who had at one time been an Edinburgh shoemaker, but now lived by his wits, was small and wretched-looking. His hair was sandy and straggling and his face pinched. He looked as though he had attached himself to the other two for support. To them he was useful for his local knowledge. Ainslie had the kind of appearance that enabled him to become lost in any crowd in an instant—an advantage he put to common use.

The other man was the well-dressed John Brown, calling himself Humphry Moore, seeking refuge from his English conviction on account of a charge proved by Mr John Field regarding twenty pounds and four doubloons. Mr Field had, with remarkable persistence, found his man and had him tried, and convicted and sentenced to seven years' transportation. The ingenious Mr Brown had, however, managed to escape and had now taken refuge over the border.

He listened to all that was said and took mental notes. He particularly took note of Mr Brodie and how he played the dice. Mr Brown was not unskilled in such agile arts and recognised them for what they were. Mr Brodie interested Mr Brown but so did many other things and he would await his time. He spoke to Smith.

'He will win it back, and clean out our bluff friend into the bargain.'

'How's that?' asked Ainslie.

'You'll see.'

'And how long will that take, do you think?' demanded Smith.

'Not very long.'

Brodie was beginning to empty Milne's purse with reckless haste. It was how he felt. His elation transcended discretion. Had the farmer had more shrewdness about him, or less claret in him, he must have been suspicious of such constant luck. The enigmatic Clark watched admiringly from his elbow-rest by the fire. He enjoyed seeing the work of a professional. However, he had reservations about such speed. He had never seen Brodie quite so blatant. One day, if he kept it up, it would lead to trouble.

Milne had begun to sweat heavily, the drops running down his side-whiskers and staining his collar. Clark, wise in these matters, despatched the harassed lad with more claret without waiting for Brodie's orders. Brodie was too involved to take account of such things and Clark wanted no trouble when the 'kill' came. Milne had already taken to roaring insults at the dice, having tried and discarded kissing, then coaxing, then pleading.

'Come on! Damn your black-hearted spots! If the leopard canna do it, you canna do it! Come on now! ... God damn!'

Brodie, to keep up appearances, coddled his agents.

'Now, my beauties, see what you can do for Will!'

He gave them the token violent shake, followed by gentle, settling taps and a subtle tip of the box that sent them out at the right angle and speed. Brodie had not only taken back his fifteen guineas from Milne, but had gone on to take a further twelve. As they turned up a six and a five, Milne suddenly burst out,

'No, no more! I will play no more! The devil's in those

things!' Heads turned throughout the cellars, people leaned forward and stared around the ends of booths.

'I have lost enough to you pretty gentlemen, thank you! But that is my cattle money. That is my stock! You have made a fool of me. What sort of chance am I supposed to have agin things like that?'

He pointed at them as Macbeth must have pointed at Banquo's ghost.

'They are possessed! Or they're wrong!'

He snatched them up and looked at them as closely as his fuddled brain and sight permitted. Clark unhooked his elbow off the mantel and wandered over, the pipe stem still in his mouth, emitting a thin stream of smoke from his lips.

'Excuse me, sir, but you are makin' a great cleck which could be taken amiss by my customers. A great deal o' cleck.'

'I've lost twelve guineas!' cried the farmer tragically. There were roars of laughter from the people all around. Remarks.

'Pour soul!'

'So much!'

'My, that's heavy gambling!'

Clark addressed Milne impassively.

'And were you not fifteen the better off, but a few minutes syne? You shouldna play games. Life is full o' both tragedy and triumph, and you have had both.'

With this mock-solemn utterance, Clark stood arms akimbo over Milne. The smoke still trickled from his lips. Milne looked desperately around the room for some support—a sympathetic face—but, seeing them all staring at him with wicked merriment, staggered to his feet and made for the door.

'I have lost twelve guineas!' he wailed. 'It was my cattle money!' He stumbled unsteadily out into the street.

'Poor man, and it just ten o'clock too!' said a voice from the dark, amid roars of laughter.

Clark bent down and whispered to Will.

'You pushed him too hard, Will. You shouldna'. I've tell'd

you!' Will, who had sat silent throughout, smiled at Clark.

'I'm on my way, Johnnie.' To the other two he said, 'I have to visit my respectable friends!'

Henderson laughed with apparent good-humour, but secretly like Clark he had been worried by Brodie's recklessness.

'And they don't gamble. Will, afore ye go, there is someone I have been meaning to tell you about. Can you use a locksmith?'

Brodie looked at him sharply.

'Why?'

'The man I have had at the stables these two months. That was taken ill with fever. The Englishman. He is recovered and looking for a job. I promised him I would ask you on his behalf.'

'Is he good? Has he references?'

'I don't know, and he has no references, but he is lately from Birmingham, where I believe they know their craft. If you should want one reference, however, I can tell you he has no intention of going back!'

'I see. Well, maybe I can, Michael.'

'He's over there, waiting to be seen.'

Brodie glanced in the direction indicated.

'All right. I'll have a quick word.'

Strange notions were flickering through his mind. He was on a heightened plane where his thoughts raced and mortals seemed unable to reach him. A heady recklessness in which fate seemed to be dealing him nothing but royals. Robertson tactfully got up with Henderson and the two of them moved to a further part of the room. Henderson motioned Smith over. Smith had been intrigued by the previous scene. This showy little man was no fool.

Brodie looked up at Smith, almost challengingly. He, Will Brodie, was no fool about locks. Smith returned the look, unabashed. He had an Englishman's jaded view of these Scots gentry.

'You are a locksmith, Mr Henderson tells me.'
'I am.'
'You have left England?'
'Yes.'
Brodie motioned him to sit down.
'By that, I mean you have left for good.'
'By that, I mean what you mean.'
'You can handle any wards? Any lock?'
'Yes. A blank coated with wax ... make an impression. The easiest business in the world if the public only knew it. I can make a Barron's lock, and I can make a key for it—before or after fitting.' Brodie was impressed. The Barron's lock was the newest and best.
'What is your name?'
'George Smith.'
'Well, Mr Smith, you are the only man in Edinburgh, I think, beside myself who can manage a Barron's lock. Too many of them would make life difficult. Luckily Edinburgh is behind England in these things. They are too difficult.'
'To make or to open?'
'You are alert, Mr Smith. There may be work for a man like you in Edinburgh, if you have a still tongue and a good business head. I have a large business as Wright and cabinet-maker. You knew that?'
Smith nodded.
'I will let you know directly. I have to go now to Johnnie Dowie's. You know it?'
'The gentleman's tavern—the one they call "The Coffin".'
'Indeed. Call round to my timber yards tomorrow and we will see what you can do.' Brodie got to his feet.
'Can I consider myself hired, Mr Brodie?'
'I know nothing about your background—or your discretion.'
'I am discreet enough, Mr Brodie, to hold my tongue when I see loaded dice.'
Brodie stared at him in silence. A slow smile crept into his

eyes, and the corners of his mouth drooped.

'I think you can, Mr Smith. I look forward to tomorrow.'

He left, bidding his friends good-night but scarcely noticing them. His mind was in a turmoil, considering the possibilities that presented themselves. He felt that he was seeing more clearly than he had been for a long time. There was nothing in Edinburgh that two or more men could not achieve, working together. One man always took a risk. He had no look-out, no protection at his rear. Two or more men could select the most difficult, most exciting, most outrageous targets. The University. The Excise Office. The Council Chamber itself! Anything. He sang quietly as he walked.

'I sipt each flower,
I chang'd ev'ry hour,
And here ev'ry flower is united ...'

In his mind's eye, they swept through Edinburgh like a black plague from hell. Worthy Councillors and Clerics would tremble with fear behind their curtains. The citizens would line their windows and cheer Brodie! Brodie! Brodie! as they had cheered Wilson, or Maclean. And who would catch a Deacon!

A yell from above interrupted his dreaming and sent him diving for a doorway. He just avoided a gout of filth that splattered on the gutter. He had forgotten the hour.

At Johnnie Dowie's tavern, the words were as intoxicating as the fine ale, and were dispensed with the liberality of blown snow. The tavern was entirely without light and consisted throughout its length of a series of windowless rooms, ending in a single black, oblong-panelled room appropriately called 'the Coffin'. This was lit by numerous candles, so that the throng of men's faces, packed in that small area, waved and moved like corn in the wind, their features becoming distorted this way and that by the whim of a draught or an emphatic gesture. Brodie listened, fascinated, at the edge of the group of men, it being impossible to burrow any closer. The centre of this verbal hurricane was Robert Burns, in Edinburgh these last few days to see Creech the publisher. Burns was in a wild state. With him were his friends Nicol and Masterton, while packed nearby were those others who could cram in: Creech, David Herd, Naysmith, Raeburn and John Beugo; Home and Cruickshank; Lawyer Dunbar and Dean-of-Faculty Erskine, amongst many others. They drank Younger's Edinburgh Ale, sticky as black molasses, and listened, occasionally joining in. Burns, in consequence of his belief that he would daily have to flee the country for Antigua, or do penance on account of Jean Armour, had been living each day in Edinburgh as though it was his parting. Reckless words poured from him and those around him. Restless words that thrilled Brodie as much as easing open a door, pistol in hand. Burns was declaiming against the State, the Government and women, and the oppression of men by all three with equal vigour and fluency.

'I am, as I have said, one of nature's rueful-looking, long-visaged sons of disappointment! That men have made a Pernassian Pegasus of what I have called this spur-galled hack, has only served to give me the appetite of the former with the vindictiveness of the latter! This flying steed of man's injustice can be in many places. It is not earthbound. I have the holy beagles on my heels! With my steel hoofs I should crack open the pate of so-called democracy like boys crack thin ice on a swamp, to let the stinking gases out! What have we in this stone-built ant-heap, but a parasite queen? This is no democracy when the Council perpetuates itself like the Aztec snake that engorges its own mouth, as the night follows day. And don't blame that on England, for we have made it ourselves. Nowhere are men free. Not even in bed!'

Willie Nicol clapped him on the back.

'What are we to have then, Rab? A revolution? What say you to it?'

'I say nothing for it. At least not in front of lawyers! Revolution is a wheel driven by blood for the purpose of crushing bones. Why should there be taxation without representation? Walpole refused to do it. Burke spoke out against it. Locke said that every man had a property in his own person, and that no man had a right to it but that man himself. That essential right is denied to us by the female sex, devil take all Governments!'

'Would you not then fight for liberty?' asked Allan Masterton, teasing.

'Ah, Allan, liberty is too important for that. It is better thought about than fought about. Each excludes the other. But the use of thought does not exclude the use of darts, barbs, pikes and arrows of the pen and pamphlet. A thinking man may choose his target, while a man caught up in the thick of the action may only lay about him under terror of death.'

The evening passed on. Words and ale, words and ale. Brodie slipped away with a confusion of notions tumbling in his head. Part of the system, within the system, against the system. A thinking man's position. He felt for the key in his pocket. I am the worm within the good apple which is the face that Edinburgh puts on, he thought. I will eat, eat, eat, until only the skin is left and I have become fat. The skin will shrivel and collapse. The apple must be cleaned out before the worm dies.

Reaching the entrance to the Royal Exchange, Brodie slowed his pace. He had changed at Jean Watt's house and wore his black cloak and clothes. He moved over the cobbles carefully. His shoes made no noise. At the foot of the outside stair, he put on his mask. His eyes glittered in the moon that occasionally burst through turbulent clouds. The clouds excited him like the words. It was an exciting night. He pulled the key out of his pocket, and pressing himself close to the door so that his form blended into the darkness of the doorway, he inserted the iron key in the lock. The lock turned with scarcely a noise. Brodie's men had left it well greased. Inside, he immediately locked the door again. From his pocket he took the dark-lantern and tinder-box. He stood the lantern on a desk while he struck the box on to the touch-paper. At the second strike, the paper lit, and he then lit the lantern and slid the shutter to, so that a thin rectangle of yellow light seemed to shoot out across the room, glancing off polished mahogany. Picking his way between chairs and the low rails, he methodically searched the clerks' desks, deliberately leaving Johnston's mahogany dais until last. It was there he expected to find the money, but he was in no hurry to spoil a good thing. Everything that he extracted, he put back with great care. It took him nearly fifteen minutes to go through every drawer in each of the clerk's desks. In them there was not so much as a single guinea or note. He had expected as much and knew he was deliberately prolonging this routine search to heighten his anticipation of what he would find in Johnston's mahogany throne. Closing the last desk drawer, he turned the lantern so that the yellow rectangle isolated the elevated dais. He went up the four steps that led off the counting-floor and regarded the arrangement of drawers. The desk was a beautiful piece of work, at least thirty years old and before Brodie's time. The Deacon wondered if it could have been made by his father. It had all the appearance of his workmanship. He hoped so, smiling to himself at the delicious irony. He mentally sent up a small prayer to the God in whom he had no belief.

'If there is a god anywhere, then please, god, make this my father's work.'

He was struck by a second thought, the magnitude of which made him snigger.

'If my father has escaped hell-fire and there is a heaven, please god, let him be watching, and see what I am doing!'

He began to hum to himself softly, taking from his cloak a set of pick-locks and a thin sheet of flexible steel. The desk had a fold-down top, and was lined inside with pigeon-holes and drawers like a secretaire. From the fretwork around the gallery of the desk, Brodie was more than ever convinced that

Francis might have made it. He picked the lock that held the top shut, with a few deft twists and jerks of a small skeleton. He knew the type of lock backwards. Simple double wards. Inside, the drawers were not even locked. In the second drawer down on the right, ludicrously concealed beneath a draft agreement, was a tape-bound block of bank-notes that made Brodie gasp. The bundle was an inch thick. He riffled through it. There were notes of several banks, separated by slips of paper—Royal Bank, British Linen, Glasgow, Dumfries and Perth General. Some Dundee notes from Jobson's and a small number of notes from small bankers. In the bottom of the drawer there was even some silver. Brodie quickly pocketed the notes and silver and shut the drawer, after re-arranging the draft agreement as it had been before. He folded up the last page of it so that, at a casual glance, the contents of the drawer would appear at the same height as before. Folding down the lid, it took a short time to re-lock the desk, because Brodie's hands shook so much that he was awkward with the key. That done, he picked his way back to the main entrance door and, standing the lantern on a desk, he could not resist counting quickly through the money. There was over seven hundred pounds at least. A fortune undefended. He found himself quaking, not with fear, but with hysterical excitement, which he fought down. He must remain careful. Using his false key, he very gently unlocked the outer door, lifted the latch and opened it a fraction. There was not a sound outside. His eyes still could not see into the darkness properly and he extinguished the dark-lantern, re-latching the door while he waited for it to cool. When he opened the door for the second time, the moon was partly out of the cloud and he could see the courtyard was empty. He put the lantern away in his cloak pocket, stepped outside and quickly inserted the false key and locked the door without trouble. He remained in the doorway shadow, listening. Nothing. Keeping within the black crenellations cast on the cobbles by the moonlight, he walked softly to the court entrance, and here took off his mask. Stepping boldly into the High Street, he instantly became Deacon Brodie, respected citizen of Edinburgh. The worm, he thought, has taken a substantial bite out of the apple. He could not wait to hear the screaming.

He made his way at a leisurely pace to Jean Watt's. Opening the door carefully, he listened. She did not call out and he could hear her breathing. It would be better to awake in his own bed in the morning. He crossed carefully over to a chair on which he had hung his coat and silk stockings. Retreating to the door, he sat down near it and quietly changed his stockings and took off the cloak, changing back to his former clothes. From the cloak pockets he took all his implements and the thick block of money. He carried the chair with his cloak and stockings slightly back into the room. Stripping a pound note from the bundle, he tucked it under the cloak. The avaricious witch would forgive him. He could smell her warm sleepy body. He could imagine it well. He decided he had better leave.

The captain of the Town Guard, marching with pensioned-off patrol, saluted him, as he walked up the Lawnmarket. Brodie wished him good-night. It gave him no concern, as the captain saluted everyone, without any recollection whatsoever. It amused Brodie, however, to feel the bundle in his pocket as they tramped past.

CHAPTER FOUR

Horses for courses

Brodie was fast asleep when he was awakened by the vigorous shaking of Jean.

'What time you came in I don't know, and where you spent the night before I will not ask! But now you're here, you had better attend to your business. It's late, and past eight o'clock! If it wasn't for Robert Smith, I don't know where the business would be. We had two orders in yesterday, and you not even here to see the lady and gentleman! I don't know what you think father would have said!'

I know, thought Will with satisfaction, exactly what father would have said. He let her continue without interruption. A good sailor lowers his sails and drops anchor until the force of the storm is spent through hurtling itself at nothing.

'And have you heard,' she was ending, 'the whole Town knows about it except you, I daresay. Johnston and Smith the bankers were robbed last night of a very fortune! There is nothing safe in this town, and me without a man in the house to guard me!'

Brodie sat up as though shocked.

'Johnston and Smith! That's terrible news. Terrible! I was doing work for him too. What happened?'

'I don't know the details. But what I am told is that it was not broke, but opened with false keys or pick-locks. There is over eight hunnert pounds gone! Imagine. All that in cash. They think they will never get it back. Poor Mr Johnston is in a terrible state.'

'Aye, I imagine he will be. I must go and see him immediately!'

'You do that. I'm glad to see you take some interest in the social graces instead o' all your known vices!'

'Jeannie, Jeannie, I will see the good man. I will offer our condolences, yours and mine. And I will find out whatwith he intends to pay my bill.'

'Will!'

'Now, Jeannie, you said that you are concerned that I am not paying the business enough attention. It is a simple enough affair. How do I know the good man can pay? I have done over a hundred pounds of work there, and all human feeling aside, it is not my money that is gone!'

'I sometimes wonder about you, Will! Have you no sense. Give the man time and don't be pestering him today.'

'I won't pester him, I promise you, but it is as well to mention these things in passing! Now out of the room while I dress!'

He was bursting with impatience. The scene was set for the most elegant piece of dramatic irony, and he must get his words right. He should dress sombrely today, almost in mourning. And he must proceed fast, for now their minds, however atrophied, would be moving along the line of false keys. They must already be wanting to speak to Brodie, and he would get in first. It presented him, he thought, with the greatest, the most noble challenge so far, in his career as an amateur actor and cynic.

The whole courtyard of the Exchange was full of both the concerned and the idly curious. The Town Guard, looking particularly baggy-trousered in the broad light of day, were making a brave show of maintaining order. Ten men were posted about Johnston and Smith's door, to admit only those with legitimate business interests. Their appearance of discipline was marred by their obvious delight in exchanging heavy witticisms with the crowd.

Brodie pushed his way through to the Guard. He was immediately recognised, and they stopped talking and sheepishly attempted to adopt a military stance. Those who had laid their pikes aside on the Exchange wall made as though to collect them, then stood to attention without them, ill at ease without their supports.

'Good day to you, Deacon,' said the sergeant, in careful Highland tone, 'do you want to enter?'

'I do, Sergeant.'

'Come this way,' and he went to the outer door and opened it for Brodie with some ceremony.

Immediately inside the door was a huddle of men, talking hard and earnestly. The word had spread fast. There were other bankers, Councillors, Bailies and of course Johnston. Johnston looked up and, seeing Brodie, said, 'Excuse me, gentlemen, here is Mr Brodie!'

Silence fell. Brodie advanced and took off his hat.

'Mr Johnston, this is a terrible thing to befall you. I have come to offer my heart-felt condolences, and if I can be of any assistance to you, I would like to look at the locks. I understand from my sister that these have not been forced?'

'Mr Brodie, it is good of you to come. This is a terrible, terrible thing. This is the worst robbery I have ever heard of. This is a monstrous and inhuman crime. This is a barbarous crime. The like of this I had never thought to see in our own city, is that not true, gentlemen?' There was a general murmuring of assent. 'I am ruined! So much money! This is unbelievable!' The big man was white and visibly trembling. 'I still cannot believe it. It shakes my faith in God and mankind. Why should I be singled out for such a depredation? They must be made an example of, they must be hung! Hanging is too good for them. We treat criminals like pet lambs. They are coddled and nursed to the gallows as though they had human sensibilities. This is a monstrous and inhuman crime. Who would do this? How was it done? We must all find out, or God knows, none of us will be safe. This is some monster!'

'Mr Johnston,' said Brodie, 'this is no amateur criminal. This is a skilled and determined piece of work. You have one of the finest locks in Edinburgh on your door. How was it done?'

'Look, Mr Brodie! You tell us! There are no marks, no scratches, the door has not been forced.'

'Was it locked up?'

'By myself! I lock it every night, and take the key home with me. The lock has been opened by a key, there is no other way.'

Brodie affected to give the lock a minute examination, squinting through the key hole, lifting the latch and examining the door jamb.

'May I see the key, Mr Johnston.'

'I would welcome your opinion, Mr Brodie.'

There was further silence as Brodie looked at the key, held it up to the light, and finally inserted it in the lock, opening and closing it.

'There is no doubt,' he said, 'that this lock has been opened by means of a false key.'

'Could that be done, Mr Brodie?'

'Yes, by certain skilled members of the criminal class. Or perhaps a duplicate key was made when the lock was installed?'

'The lock has been on that door for ten years.'

'Perhaps some locksmith kept a copy. These things can happen. Perhaps that copy has fallen into criminal hands.'

'Is that possible. After all this time?'

'I do not do it myself, Mr Johnston, but it is sometimes the practice of locksmiths to make a duplicate key in case the original should be lost. A locksmith must somewhere keep a record of where these keys belong. If both these items of information should fall into unscrupulous hands, then a crime like this is possible.'

'Aye, Mr Brodie, that is so. I had not thought of that. Some locksmith might have the answer.'

'Quite innocently. It may have been stolen from his shop. Have you no idea who made the lock?'

'None. It was here when we removed to these premises. The last owner is dead.'

Bailie Galloway, a vulture who never missed a corpse, burst into a jeremiad with customary relish. Brodie was reminded again of the rodent look of his eyes.

'It's an age o' moral depravity, with madmen freely encouraged! There is ower much reforming zeal and not enough punishment. And as if we do not have enough madmen o' our own, we import them and their ideas from England and France. What with Wilkes and such like, and the theatres and the dancing and the lack of attention to the Sabbath, we must expect it! I have said it often enough! No lock is safe! The sanctity o' property is the basis o' democracy! And we have folk worrying about improving how we hang them!'

He gave Brodie a spiteful look. Johnston, on whom the point was lost, dismissed the Bailie.

'Aye, we know. We've all heard you. Often. But what about my money? I must away to the Fiscal again.'

'Of course,' said Brodie, 'if someone could have removed the key and taken it to a smith, then the smith could have made an impression of it and then made a key for whoever removed it. The smith may be an innocent man who thought he was doing an innocent trade. It might happen that way.'

'But no one could remove the key! I can see everyone that comes and goes,' replied Johnston.

'Well then, it's a mystery to me,' said Brodie. 'There's no insinuation intended, you understand, but what about your staff?'

'Mr Brodie!'

'For their sakes, Mr Johnston, it would clear them.'

'There's sense in that. I shall offer a reward.'

Galloway nearly exploded. His spittle sprayed over Brodie's cheek. The Deacon elaborately wiped it away.

'What for! Pay money to get back your own! Devil take it, man!'

'Bailie Galloway, you are too free with my money!'

'Sir!'

'When you have eight hundred and thirty pounds, cash, to lose, I'll take note of your advice and any adversions on the subject!' said Johnston, whiter than before. 'Come, Brodie, you are a business man,' he took Will by the arm and walked a little away from the others into the counting-hall. 'Do you think I will ever see it again?'

'I think it very unlikely.'

'What should I offer? Twenty guineas? Thirty guineas?'

'You may only recover part of it. What of a reward for informing on the thief?'

'Oh damn it, Brodie. All this hanging stuff I was shouting. What use to me is hanging? Aye, it may be a sad reflection but the first thing a man feels the need for is revenge, then after that comes sense. Here I am—one moment I'm shouting hanging like the mob. In a state of sense, and reason, all I want is my money back! What use to me is a dead felon? So much meat on a string. It's a tempting place, the knacker's-yard of the righteous! The devil and the Fiscal can have their bloody dining. It's the money I want.'

Brodie looked at him thoughtfully.

'You're a good man, Johnston.'

'Aye, maybe. But I'm a practical man and a mean man. It is my business to be so. And I want my money back. How much should I offer?'

'I think you should offer so much for, say each hundred returned. Ten guineas.'

'Aye, it's right in principle, but over generous in matter. I'll offer five. That's one twentieth o' the sum, and quite enough.'

'You must be the judge of that.'

'Aye, well that will do. I'll away to the Fiscal and tell him.'

'My sister sends her condolences.'

'That's very kind of her, I'm sure. Please return my compliments. Now if you'll just excuse me ...'

'But there is just one question.'

'Aye?' Johnston paused, annoyed at being detained.

'Do you want my men to finish.'

'Oh aye. Aye! Today it was.'

'I'll see to it.'

As he spoke, he dismissed his earlier idea of demanding his money and was already vowing to return some part of what he had taken. He had cleaned the man out, and Johnston after all was really a good man. His cynicism he found was hollow and the delight had gone out of it. He cursed himself for getting to know the man. It brought out a side in him that he felt uneasy with. A side that could be destructive to the enjoyment of life. Johnston hurried away and, after some social talk with the others, Brodie left as well. The Town Guard, stiffening to their form of attention, looked tired and arthritic. Brodie felt badly in need of the sweet music of the gill bell and a stoup of restorative claret. He wondered what Macheath would have done.

Brodie's workshops and timber-yard were down the far end of Brodie's Close. Here the Close opened out to provide a considerable courtyard lined with two-storey buildings. Many of these were workshops, with sleeping quarters above. The timber-shed itself was wooden-slatted but otherwise open to the air. This was the largest of the buildings, and stood in the centre of the court. The place was full of the smells that Brodie loved. Lacquer, resin, wood.

Robert Smith and Brodie were seated in Brodie's office, which looked on to the court at ground level. They had been reviewing business for the last hour. Smith had been complaining about the volume of work that Thomas Hill had taken from the Council during his two years as Deacon of Wrights.

'Never mind, Rab,' said Brodie, 'I'll be back come September. There's no one else. I can tell you now, we will have our work cut out on doors. The Council is to pass a resolution to lower several streets, to stop the rain and filth ower-lippin the sills. And not before time! And we have enough cabinet work. However, I do not want us to lose our place as wrights. I know fine that your heart is more fixed in the joinery trade. But the two are hand in hand. The wright work brings in joinery, and so the other way too. You know the eeries and orries o' all this as well as me. With Hill it's all cuittle and no skill. I went ower his work at the Tolbooth. It is indifferent ordinary sort of stuff, but the devil has had the contract extended to two traps! That's his cuittling—up! And then we have Young and Trotter. They hover like vultures round my trade, Rab! But they have no wright work and are the worse for it. We have the right balance and must preserve it.'

Smith seemed mollified by this, if not entirely satisfied.

'Aye, I know you're right, Mr Brodie, and it may not seem good business. It's a thing of the heart, ye see. I am happy at the cabinet-work. There is a challenge in that. But too much of my time is taken with ower-lookin' the joinery.'

'I understand that, Rab. If I could get another foreman as good as you, I would have him for that work. But where do I get him?'

Thus flattered, Smith smiled.

'You could always get round me, Mr Brodie. I have no defence for it.'

'It's the plain truth.'

Smith looked almost bashful but said nothing. Brodie continued. 'Can we use another locksmith? I have found one from England.'

'To work here?' Smith's eyes took on a cautious look.

'He would work on a contracting basis. We have no need for him to have more than the use of the workshop.'

Smith nodded.

'Then I don't see why not.'

'Especially as we shall have the doors of Bridge Street to do almost immediately. There will be lock-work on that.'

George Smith had been nervous all morning. Edinburgh was talking of nothing else but the bank robbery. It was being said that a locksmith was involved. In the irrational manner of a man with a guilty past, he expected at every corner to be stopped by the Town Guard, or be leapt upon by some hallooing citizen. Reason told him that only Henderson and Brodie knew his trade, and Henderson never said anything. Smith had told his wife that he had a feeling about Brodie.

'He is not what he seems,' he had said. 'He's a deep and crafty fellow, I'm telling you, Deacon or no Deacon.'

Mary Smith had looked at him with a hint of anxiety in her dull and withdrawn eyes.

'Be careful, George. We've done running. Where would we go?'

'I'll be careful. He is a rich and respected man. Too respected to be suspected. These worthies are a parcel of fine thieves. With care it can do me a lot of good.'

'No more trouble, George, please!'

'Beggars can't be choosers.'

'We are not beggars!'

'No? Then we have about two days to go. In our position we should be glad for work. This Brodie has a fine opinion of himself. They think themselves fine fish. We'll see if he's as good as he thinks he is!'

Despite his brave words, he was afraid. He had an instinct that it was closer than an outside chance that Brodie had had some part in the bank's misfortunes.

When he entered the yard, Brodie was standing in a workshop doorway, chatting to a man within. Smith was impressed by the scale of what he saw. He had underestimated the size of this business. It was as big as anything he had seen in

Birmingham. His apprehension increased. Brodie saw him immediately, and came over to shake his hand. 'Good morning to you Mr Smith. I have been waiting for you. I'm glad that you turned up.'

'You employed me last night, Mr Brodie!'

'Yes indeed, but we agreed that I should see what you can do with a lock. Come this way.'

Brodie led him over to one of the workshop doors. This he unlocked with a key from a ring. Inside, the room was fitted out as a locksmith's workshop, with a bench, vice, small forge, hammers, saws, files, and racks of keys, locks and picklocks. The forge was dead but Smith noticed by the ash that it had been recently used. Everything seemed to be in good shape. Brodie obviously worked in both brass and steel. Discarded locks of all sizes and ages were piled in a corner, for parts. Brodie propped himself elegantly on his cane.

'Shut the door, Mr Smith. This is the shop that you will use, if we are agreed. Look around.'

Smith needed no bidding, but was casting an expert eye over everything. Brodie spoke again.

'You never told me, Mr Smith, why it was that you cannot return to England. Mr Henderson tells me, if you will forgive me, that you will shortly be in need of money to an extent that it will be impossible to return.'

Smith stared at him, quite calmly.

'I think you know, Mr Brodie, why I cannot return. The way you ask, proves it. Be direct with me, Mr Brodie, and I'll be direct with you.'

'I think, Mr Smith, that the law may not be your friend.'

Smith merely stared.

'Man, that is nothing to me! I like a man with some nouse about him. I'm not one of your kirk-dreerie, sable-bearing Bailies. It is my opinion that any man who is a man, has something he would keep from others!' He beckoned to Smith. 'Take these locks here. They are all shot. Can you open them?'

Smith silently helped himself to a selection of pick-locks. Examining each lock in turn, he selected one pick-lock, and feeling inside the first lock with it, turned it back at the first attempt. Brodie said nothing. Within five minutes and without attempting any of the locks more than three times, all the locks had been shot back again. Smith returned the pick-locks to their hooks. Brodie looked at him eagerly. Smith noted the animation in his eyes.

'You are experienced, Mr Smith. There is work for a man of your abilities in this town, if you will join me. We have awful careless merchants. They have a deplorable habit of leaving their keys ahint the door. Now look what happened to the bankers last night. Very careless! And there are many others for men with some courage and a certain turn o' mind. Are you o' that turn of mind, Mr Smith?'

'I had considered if you might ask me that, Mr Brodie, from what you said last night. It seems to me that the money is quite good for this sort of thing?'

'What manner of thing is that, Mr Smith?'

Smith looked at him carefully.

'I am, as you said last night, alert, Mr Brodie. You have a fine way with tickling the ivories. I have heard there was a terrible depredation at the bank last night. The very one you was working in!'

'What are you, Mr Smith. I'll take no skoddy fellow who'll bear a mind to rat!'

Smith was offended.

'Mr Brodie. Had I the mind I could have stagged you there and then!'

'You were not always a locksmith, my clever man. Henderson tells me you were last a flying stationer.'

'Mr Brodie, I think you are a sport and cracksman.'

'Be honest with me, Mr Smith. Have you never cracked a crib?'

Smith laughed.

'Who can overhear us here?' Brodie nodded. 'Then I am a very pyking rogue! And, Mr Brodie, you have got yourself in an elegant position for such work!'

'Mr Smith, I have decided that we could do business together if you are able to stand mum. Henderson has given me good reports of you.'

'My wants are pressing at the moment, Mr Brodie, and I would like to clean the slate with him.'

'I have expenses, Mr Smith, such as a gentleman incurs, if you take my drift. We must pay for these small indelicacies that life has to offer. I will come clean with you. I find it necessary from time to time, and indeed a great pleasure, to avail myself of some items of ready value that are about. Unfortunately, and you will agree it is a small vice, there is not always time to consult the owners first!'

Smith laughed.

'Mr Brodie, I had that small vice myself.'

'I have a fondness for the chances of life. From the accuracy of your sight, I take it that you are a pigeon-fancier?'

'A veritable kite!'

'How much do you owe Henderson?'

'Ten guineas.'

'Then take twenty on account. It is essential that you have some respectable occupation. I cannot employ a locksmith full time. Let them suspect the others. You have a wife, I believe. We will take a shop as a front. The accommodation will come in useful. A place with a handy cellar. Smith my foreman has his suspicions, but he knows nothing and will say nothing as long as he is not told. Give him no cause for suspicion, he is a good workman. Can your wife be trusted?'

'She knows I am no better than I am.'

'I am taking a chance with you, Mr Smith. If you breach it, there's no one will believe it.'

'Then I take a bigger chance with you!'

Brodie smiled, for the first time.

'Then we will take the air together. You must have some better clothes, or you will draw attention to yourself. I am accustomed to stroll each day, so that no one remarks upon it. It is surprising how much a man can learn from idle gazing and curiosity. There is a prospect in every street. But I am hindered by getting rid of it. Have you connections?'

'I had.'

'In England?'

'A Scotchman called Tasker in Chesterfield. Not inconvenient from Birmingham. He had the hounds at his heels.'

'Excellent,' said Brodie. 'Let us have a gill to clear our throats and heads and sharpen the power o' the eyes.' He was clearly delighted, and walked fast, rolling with his springy gait. Smith had to hurry to keep up with him, which he still found difficult after his illness. Before long they had strolled the Lawnmarket and High Street and had compiled a list for further examination. They agreed to meet regularly in Clark's.

'You see, Mr Smith, even the veriest white pigeon or sucking dove is better played by combination!'

* * *

Edinburgh Evening Courant, 1786.

On Friday evening last (the 12th August) the lock of the outer door of the compting-house of Johnston and Smith, bankers in the Exchange, was opened by some wicked persons, as supposed by a counterfeit key, and eight hundred pounds Sterling stolen out of their drawers, in the following bank notes, viz:—

	£	s	d
Of the Royal Bank of Scotland	£194	9	0
British Linen Company	362	2	0
Dumfries Notes	126	0	0
Glasgow Notes	64	10	0
General Bank of Perth	32	0	0
Dundee Notes (Jobson's)	40	0	0
Several small Notes and Silver	11	1	0
	£830	2	0

It is entreated that every honest person will give the Magistrates of Edinburgh, or Johnston and Smith, notice of any circumstances that may fall under their observation for discovering the offenders; and farther, the said Johnston and Smith will give the informer a reward of Five Pounds Sterling for every hundred pounds sterling that shall be recovered in consequence of such information. As some smith may very innocently have made a key from an impression of clay or wax, such smith giving information, as above, so as the person who got the key may be discovered, shall be handsomely rewarded.

* * *

The weather had turned surly and a squally rainstorm buffeted the town, puffing out of the blow-holes formed by the wynds and closes. The runnels showed white water like Highland streams. It was a night for convivial company and people kept indoors.

In the 'Isle of Man's Arms' in Craig's Close, the Cape Club were meeting in a large upper room, behind a solid pine door. The door was firmly locked for an initiation.

Two long trestle tables had been butted together to accommodate the thirty or so members, who at the moment were engaged in jokes and chatter. The table was well laden with bottles of both claret and ale. A full-bellied whisky-jar passed to and fro.

The Sovereign, Sir Stick, sat at the head of the table. Before him on a crimson velvet cushion, befitting the royal regalia, lay the two ceremonial steel pokers of the club. These were of even length of about three and a half feet, but one was of much smaller girth than the other. The larger poker was the size of a small mace. They both shone like polished pewter in the light of dozens of candles. The Sovereign wore his cap of crimson silk velvet, embroidered on the front with the emblem of a pair of clasped hands in blue. The creation was topped with a circlet of white beads and some grey fur that looked like rabbit.

The Sovereign looked down the entire length of the tables to the applicant, who sat at the far end, flanked by his sponsors. He solemnly stood up, and all conversation soon ceased.

'Sir Knights, we have tonight an applicant who is desirous of admission to our most capital knighthood of the Cape. This applicant having been balloted for, has been found to be a worthy candidate, and we are satisfied with the abilities and qualifications of him to join our most noble order, in accordance with our rules. Then, Sir Knights, I ask you to stand! A thing you must ever be ready to do!'

There were some roars of laughter and aside jokes, as the members got to their feet. Brodie, who was among them, looked forward as they all did to the obligatory tale that the man would have to tell. They had imbibed well and the company was disposed to treat any witticism kindly. The members were mainly merchants and manufacturers, although David Herd the writer and John Bonnar the painter gave the Club some pretension to the Arts. There were glovers, opticians, skinners and grocers. An insurance broker, engineers, printers, surgeons, a tanner and druggists. Bakers, lawyers, officers of the City Guard and the Excise. Tailors and a fish-hook maker. The Sovereign, James Hewitt alias Sir Stick, continued.

'Stand forward, sir, and be presented!'

There was further laughter as the applicant, a young man of about twenty five, walked the length of the table with his escort of two Knights. He was plainly embarrassed and delighted at the same time. He dropped on one knee as he reached the Sovereign, in a gesture of submission. The Sovereign motioned him to get to his feet and, picking up the large poker, held it aloft. There were sniggers of laughter, at which the Sovereign frowned.

'Silence for our solemn ceremony!'

He turned towards the young man.

'Put your right hand on your left breast.'

The young man did so.

'Now take this poker in your left hand, and hold it!'

The young man, taking it by the handle, and having to grasp it with his left hand, found it impossible to keep it anything like level. His arm dropped so that the handle of the poker almost rested in his crotch, the steel instrument sticking up indecently at an angle. The Knights contained their mirth with difficulty.

'Now swear the words!'

The young man, now perspiring and desperately trying to keep an air of calm, solemnly and firmly spoke the oath.

'I swear devoutly by this light
To be a true and faithful Knight,
With all my might, both day and night,
So help me Poker!'

The company broke into roars of mirth. The perspiring young man, his ordeal far from over, was relieved of the wavering steel emblem by the Sovereign, which he then reverently kissed. The Sovereign then picked up the smaller poker and, aiming blows perilously close to the young man's head, shouted one after the other the three words of the club's motto.

'Concordia!—Fratum!—Decus!'

He replaced the poker. The young man's escort returned to their seats and the whole assembly sat down. There was a hushed air of expectancy. The Sovereign said,

'Sir Knight, in order that we can judge of your valour in the field of combat and can dub you by good and honest name, we must ask you to recount a deed that befits a man, so that we may judge!'

There was great cheering, and pots were thumped on the table. The young man gulped with nervousness.

'Sovereign, Depute Sovereign and Knights, my story is of a man more sinned against than sinning, for as you will see, I was caught in a position where I was unable to withdraw from the situation!'

This produced laughter, and, encouraged, he stammered on.

'In the course of my trade, in which I am employed by a merchant whose name I cannot of course reveal, but who is of a considerably greater age than his wife ...'

Cheers.

'... I have naturally come in contact with her ... metaphorically of course!'

There was laughter, and thumps of approval. The young man warmed to his theme. Some men lit pipes and settled. The bottles passed from hand to pot to hand.

'The lady, after I had only been engaged in my work for a few weeks, made certain blandishments which no gentleman could ignore ...' The young man's narrative went on. Furtive meetings in the shop, indelicate explorations behind the counter, the animalism of unsatisfied lust. Brodie listened delighted, and tried to imagine who the merchant might be. The goatish pleasure he got from this grossness was twofold. He delighted in the downfall of the worthy and the old, and again he delighted in befouling himself. Dressed in his usual unsullied manner, he considered it an intrinsic part of his artistry. Brodie, Mrs Siddons, Mr Woods. His however was the real 'tour de force' for it continued after the curtain was pulled. These knights so frequently invented the episodes they so honestly declared, whereas he had not told one quarter of the truth. Nor could he without cuckolding a proportion of the members. His double enjoyment was to watch them enjoying the story, knowing as he did the more intimate details of certain of their wives.

'Finally, I agreed to go to her house, because the lady was impatient! She told me we had two hours because he was away drinking. Naturally I was cautious. However, when I got there, we had the land to ourselves. Very soon she had shown the willingness of her disposition, and it would have been cruelty not to have shown the willingness of my own!'

There were more cheers and guffaws. The young man was perceptibly more crimson now, as the story had advanced, but he had gained in confidence. It was like watching a chick emerge from its shell and very shortly take steps, then eat, then flap its wings and become a bird.

'In the middle of our encounter, when our position, due to the lady's ardour, had no longer become defensible, what did we hear but a key in the lock. "It's him!" she shouts. "The bugger's back early!" Gentlemen, you will appreciate I was distressed at such news and the manner of its expression. Naturally I intended to leave with all possible decorum, as they put it, by the rear window. But she would have nothing of that. Before I can move, she has stuffed me into the press. The master of the house arrives. "Hello!" he shouts. "Come here, hinny!" and collapses on the bed groanin' and snorin'. She comes over to the press as though to look at clothes, but pulling up her kirtle like a fisher-wife pursues the issue. Now, sirs, I could not retreat for the press and she was most pressing. So I am locked upon it. In the furiousness of her attack, she murmurs and hisses in the way they do, and undoing her bodice, bares herself. By God if the master does not sit up and say, "Jean, whit are ye up tae there!" "I'm lookin' through my goons," says she, pressing close. "Sleep till you're sober, man." And thus I was, sirs, unwillingly!'

There were cries of disbelief and laughter.

'A second time he sits up. "Jean," he says, "whit the divil is a' the rustlin' aboot!" "Wheesht!" she says, "I have a tear in a bodice." And by God she nearly had. I could neither advance nor retreat, but held my ground until she was done. She whispers in my ear, "Leave when he is asleep," and in a moment is gone, closing the door to behind her. Sirs, I wait a long time, as you may understand, being somewhat wearied by all this enthusiasm. She flings off her clothes, with me watching through the opening of the door, and climbs in on top of him. But by this time he is snoring like a bear. "Damn me," she shouts at me, "this man was never any good!" At that I beat the retreat, feeling that I had stood my ground and done good service as any fusilier and duly earned my furlough!'

He bowed to the Sovereign.

'That sire, is the end of my tale.'

There was prolonged laughter and applause, in which Brodie joined. He thought the lad had made the most of it up, but there was a curious sincerity nonetheless. The Sovereign made his formal address.

'Sir Knight, we have listened to your trials with interest and compassion. We understand the importunity of the female sex! We shall call you Sir Soldier, because you faced the front, did not retreat from the assault, but stood your ground, keeping your weapon at the ready throughout, and doing your duty like a man!' Amid roars of laughter, the Sovereign clapped the perspiring young man on the back, and he gratefully walked back to his place at the end of the table, to the toasts of his friends. Brodie listened and smiled to the braggart tales that flew around. The Sovereign had got to his feet again and was saying, 'Stand forward, sir, and be presented!'

A middle-aged candle-maker strutted forward to confess his secret and indelicate vices. Brodie enjoyed it all.

At Clark's tavern, Smith, Brown and Ainslie crouched over a table like conspirators. Brown was reading from the *Edinburgh Evening Courant.*

'It says "On Friday evening last (the 12th August) the lock of the outer door of the compting-house of Johnston and Smith, bankers in the Exchange, was opened by some wicked persons, as supposed by a counterfeit key, and eight hundred pounds Sterling stolen out of their drawers ..."'

Smith whistled.

'No kick-shaws!'

'Then there's a list of notes. Scotch, and some silver, the total eight hundred and thirty pounds two shillings! Then it goes on, "It is entreated that every honest person will give the Magistrates of Edinburgh, or Johnston and Smith, notice of any circumstances that may fall under their observation for discovering the offenders ..."'

Smith chuckled and Ainslie laughed drily, ending up coughing and wheezing asthmatically.

'Oh aye,' he said, 'we'll dae that! The magistrates are sore pressed tae make an honest living and have decided now tae advertise for money! Will we not put in an advertisement ourself!'

Brown continued: '"And farther, the said Johnston and Smith will give the informer a reward of Five Pounds Sterling for every hundred pounds sterling that shall be recovered in consequence of such information. As some smith may very innocently have made a key from an impression of clay or wax ..."'

He was again interrupted by whoops of laughter, and broke into a broad grin himself, shaking his head. Again he continued: '"Such smith giving information, as above, so as the person who got the key may be discovered, shall be handsomely rewarded."' Brown laid down the newspaper, and paused very thoughtfully.

'And does Smith have such information?'

Smith was immediately alert, but in no way over-reacted. 'If I had, would I squeak?'

'But Smith's a smith. And has come into the employ of a very fancy gentleman, handy with the despatchers!' he said, alluding to the loaded dice. 'A man who, I am told, has a fancy for expensive sports and must be able with the dubs. He must be one of the family!'

Smith shrugged.

'You saw him fleece Milne, he's a broadsman and knowing.' Smith would tell no more for now.

'But not too far north?' Brown pursued.

'You know these Scotch!'

Ainslie grunted, because he felt some comment was called for, and did not understand a word.

'He appears to be a man in full feather,' Brown continued thoughtfully, 'but would he ease a bank . . . ?'

The question was not rhetorical and he continued to watch Smith with ill-concealed alertness.

'He's well breeched. I saw his works and shop this afternoon. It's as big as anything in Birmingham.'

'Is it now? And you think he might have employment for more than one . . . tradesman.'

'Let me in, Smith. Cheese your patter!'

Smith made a sudden decision to reveal enough to get Brown interested just as Brodie had said.

'Well, we were out on the pickaroon this afternoon, and staked out four or five. He has a job on them in Bridge Street where they are lowering the road. He comes back with new doors.'

'Damn me!'

'Aye, it's real enough.'

'But the bank?'

'Believe me, I don't know! We only met this morning!'

Smith looked thoughtfully at the newspaper.

'But there's something about him that is more fancy than real family, if you take my meaning. It's a sport with him and he's a sporting man. These jobs we saw. Half of them he wouldn't touch. But he's a known man here, he's treated with great respect. Welcomed to every shop.'

'Stab yourself and pass the dagger!'

In response to this dramatic cant, Smith poured himself a drink and passed the bottle. Ainslie's uncomprehending eyes went from one to the other. There was something afoot and he hoped to be in on it.

Brodie, returning from the 'The Isle of Man's Arms' with some fellow members, was in high spirits. The drink had been good, and his fortune was now vastly improved. He determined to push the less usual notes through the Council Chamber doors.

They would be safe enough there, and he could not go back to Johnston and Smith's for that was under guard. The good sense and generosity of the gesture appealed to him. He wondered if they would have enough sense to realise it was not as selfless as it seemed. He would get rid of the Dumfries notes, the Perth and the Dundee. There would be a watch out for these. The work in Bridge Street had, by the aid of his japanned box, provided him with an entry to selected shops. These he would keep for their appointed time. He had not yet made up his mind where to spend the night, and this pleased him too. He had after all done his duty by going home last night. Tonight he would choose. There was the heady witch Jean Watt, with the aphrodisiac of her untrustworthy scheming dark mind and gleaming white body. Or there was Ann Grant. Loving Ann. A place for leisure, to be nurtured as though she suckled her young. Life seemed to him to be good and full. He began to sing:

'Fill ev'ry glass for wine inspires us,
And fires us
With courage, love and joy.
Women and wine should life employ.
Is there ought on earth desirous?'

As they roared through the narrow streets, windows were opened, and all manner of things were flung at them, as they took to their heels like school-boys bellowing their good-nights and sniggering under cover. He determined to go to Ann Grant, for he was in just the mood to tame Jean Watt, and he decided he would enjoy the pleasure of spiting her. Let the whore roll and turn! Good night, sweet Francis, he thought, watching the moon break through the clouds. How do you like your son? And he has only just begun!

CHAPTER FIVE

Autumn fruits

Weeks had passed, and September had been a bitter month that hit like a fist. The first week of October was cold and sunny. Brodie was already regretting his generosity with money. His cocks had been doing badly, and there had been no money in cards since the cattle sales ended. In a burst of exuberance he had spent most of the bank money in a very short space of time. First there were presents to Ann and Jean and the five children—jewellery, trinkets, cakes and oranges. Then there was the repayment of some gambling debts to honourable company. He had set up Smith and his wife in a small grocer's shop which had a cellar that could be used as a workshop. It had all meant outgoings. Jean was continually pestering him to spend more money round the house. He bought her clothes, fabrics, silver and napery. Now she wanted him to settle a sum on her. Where was all the money that father had left, and why should she not have her portion. She kept the house, didn't she? What did he do? All right, he ran the business, but from what she could see, in an indifferent fashion. She knew he made his pieces still. His work was good, she wasn't criticising it. It was just that he was hardly expanding!—and on and on.

She was right. He should have settled some on her right away. For now it was all gone, the six hundred pounds as well. It was a dangerous state of affairs. Before the end of next week he would have to pay the men's wages, and he did not have the cash. He could sell one of his properties of course, but that would blow the whole carefully constructed fabric of his life apart. He would immediately be exposed as a spendthrift and a gambler, and his business would fall. Once a dog was on his way down in Edinburgh, he never lacked detractors.

Smith and he had become friends, meeting often to play cards and dice, frequently with Ainslie and often with Brown as well. But this passed the time rather than filled the coffers, as each man proved to be as great a cheat as the next. Even Ainslie, it had turned out, was a thorough professional at plucking a dove. This combined with his insignificant appearance, made him a valuable ally. Smith and he talked often about ways and means. They took their constitutional strolls in the afternoon, Smith accompanied by his black mongrel Rodney that he had adopted to guard the shop, which he said was a tribute to the admiral.

'Why don't we crack one of those shops on Bridge Street?' Smith often asked.

'Because, man, it's too soon after the work on them,' Brodie replied. 'There's mair fools than is natural in this town, but even a fool may trip ower the truth by mistake. We must crack a different sort o' crib first, so that it appears an epidemic o' the thing, and not particular to my work!'

They remained watchful—'on the pickaroon' as Smith called it—and during the course of several daily constitutional turns around the Council Chamber, where the goldsmiths had their shops, had come to the conclusion that, of the goldsmiths, Wemyss carried more stock than was prudent with two such felons about. Brodie now returned to get at the key. In his breeches pocket he had the flat japanned box of putty and about ten pounds, which was all that he could afford.

The shops around the Council Chamber were more in the nature of small booths in a row, tucked under the overhang of the lands above. The tiny interior was almost entirely occupied in each case by a small counter, behind which the assistant worked and served, and a recess to the side of the window where the goldsmith sat. The stock was either kept in the house at the rear or, for security's sake, in the cellar. Brodie and

Smith had noted, over a number of days, that the assistant in Wemyss' shop was sent out at twelve for ale. Being a young and cheerful fellow, he met his friends in the tavern and did not hurry back. This delay, which the assistant blamed on slow service, meant that Wemyss was alone in the shop for nearly half an hour. All that time, he would have to serve a customer himself. Smith was in the tavern, in case the assistant should for any reason leave early. In which case he was to leave after the lad and accidentally trip him up, spilling the ale. He would immediately apologise and offer to buy some more, thus gaining the necessary time. Brodie strolled down the cobbles of the arcade, his eyes on the shop door. It opened suddenly to let the lad out. Without a glance in any direction and obviously intent on his ale, he set off up the street. Brodie sauntered up to the window, and stopped. He looked thoughtfully through the bottle-glass panes. He could distinguish very little except the exciting glint of gold and the movement of a single figure beside a flame, which the figure was using, Brodie imagined, for soldering. To stand too long might appear suspicious, so he opened the door firmly, noting the massive but crude lock, and the simple bar used for a latch. Wemyss was studying a brooch through a jeweller's glass. His florid, grog-blossomed face broke into a smile, as he looked up. He kept the jeweller's glass in, so that one huge eye stood out from his forehead like a sea-anemone. The spirit lamp that Brodie had seen him using lit up his face from below in the comparative dimness of the interior, so that his features were wavering ruby smudges. His smile appeared demoniac rather than welcoming.

'Well well, come in, Mr Brodie! Honoured I'm sure and nice to see you looking so well and in good shape I see! "Embonpoint" as they say.'

Clearly Wemyss had no idea what he meant. Brodie was his usual sallow and rather slender self.

'And you, Mr Wemyss,' he replied, 'you are looking more than ever your usual self!' Wemyss was oblivious to the insulting nature of the remark, and glowed with satisfaction. He radiated it, Brodie thought, as the sun radiates warmth. The scarlet cloak, that Wemyss and his fellow goldsmiths affected to impress the populace with their superior station in life, hung on the wall where the man stood. The vulgarity of it pleased Brodie. Ruby red on a scarlet ground. These merchants must flaunt their wealth. He compared the man's dress with his own subtle silken attire.

'What can I be doing for yourself, Mr Brodie?'

'Take my money I expect, Mr Wemyss.'

Brodie enjoyed the retort and enjoyed it even more when Wemyss laughed with a noise very like a pig snorting. Brodie knew and disliked the man from Clark's tavern where the goldsmith got drunk quickly and often, and then roared and bellowed noisily about both himself, his business and his astuteness in worsting his customers.

'I'll take your money over the counter, Mr Brodie! Devil if I'll take it at cards!'

He honked to himself with his mouth in a piggish grin.

'They're the great leveller, Mr Wemyss.'

'The great reducer!'

'I want something for my sister Jean's birthday.'

'Oh, is it her birthday now?'

'Yes,' Brodie lied.

'What sort of a thing would you be wanting?' Privately Wemyss was thinking maliciously that he would never see it round Jean Brodie's neck, but he would keep his eyes open! Brodie was idly looking around the shop, but he was mentally absorbing it all, inscribing it as though he were drawing a picture. This way he found he could retain the small and essential details. He searched for something not displayed within the shop.

'She would like something pendant, on a gold chain.'

'Aye, Jean might like that!' Wemyss said, with what he hoped was heavy irony. He put the back of his meaty hand to his mouth and attempted to whisper in a conspiratorial manner, which in him was a strangled bellow. 'I have more in stock than ever at the moment. You come at a good time.'

To Brodie's dismay, Wemyss buffeted his way round to a position behind the counter, and tried to stoop to look underneath. Finding it impossible to bend, a thing which he already knew but never ceased attempting, he stooped on one knee on the floor, puffing loudly. It was a false alarm. Within seconds the man heaved himself upright again, holding on to the counter until he got his breath back.

'I have nothing of that sort up here. I'll have to go downstairs.' He said this with some distaste, obviously hoping that Brodie would change his mind.

'Thank you, Mr Wemyss.'

Wemyss grunted in a displeased fashion. 'Security, you see. I won't keep you long. There's that many thieves about these days that honest traders are put to extraordinary steps, and I do mean steps, to protect themselves from such-like individuals. It's a sign of the times. However, I hear, Mr Brodie, that you have persuaded the Council to pay for a more rapid method of despatch. If we had a proper Guard now, we might be able to make good use of it! Damned old fools.' He started to puff and wheeze his way down the 'steps' to his cellar below the shop. 'I can leave nothing in the shop!' The breathy complaint came from the cellar. Brodie was about to move, when an exclamation stopped him.

'Bugger! I mean damn, Mr Brodie! I have forgotten the candle. God-damn and take all this villainy and felony and treachery ...' he puffed out the words as he re-emerged from the opening '... and dishonesty and these steps and all the swindling ...' The ruby colouring of Wemyss' face looked alarming after this exertion. A sac of blood, thought Brodie. That's all we are. Wemyss took a candlestick from the counter and lit it from the soldering-lamp. He heaved and puffed his way back again, without any pretence of jollity. Brodie, who had been worrying about the time, eased the japanned box from his pocket and took off the lid. The shop key hung just above Wemyss' working recess. He could be seen from the windows, but the glass was too rippled and obscure to be able to espy anything but movement. He unhooked the massive key, and quickly took a pressing of the enormous wards. Brodie was perpetually amused by the impression that these people had that the size of a lock was directly proportional to its strength. The bigger locks were simply easier to open. Satisfied with the depth of the impression in the putty, he quickly wiped off stray traces. Clipping the box shut, he slipped it back into his pocket and rehung the key on its hook. He moved over and leaned idly on the counter. There was a delay of perhaps fifteen seconds during which he could hear Wemyss muttering and puffing below. Then the man started his slow progress back up the steps. From the corner of his eye, Brodie was alarmed to see that the key, being so heavy, was still swinging gently on the hook. He spoke to Wemyss quickly.

'What have you there?'

Wemyss stood and puffed speechlessly, slapping his well-covered ribs by way of response. He then laid out on the counter an array of gold and silver chains, some with pendants, some with set stones and some with simple gold or silver crosses. Brodie examined them, pretending to compare them for appearance but in reality judging which would be the cheapest to buy without arousing suspicion.

'I'll have that gold cross on the gold chain. This one. Very simple.'

God, thought Wemyss, it must be for his sister!

'That's seven pounds, Mr Brodie.'

Brodie paid, Wemyss put it in a small satin-lined box, and the business was done. The assistant did not return for another ten minutes. Wemyss was left contemplating the fact that there was little extravagance within families. Only mistresses really encouraged trade.

The black cock stumped about with the arrogance of an admiral. His golden eyes were hard, alert and unfriendly. He was a handsome bird. Nevertheless, Michael Henderson and Will Brodie stood in front of his wooden pen, shaking their heads. Around the walls of the out-building, stood other similar wooden-slatted pens and from them a continuous rustling and clacking could be heard. The black cock bristled his feathers and darted his head suspiciously from side to side as though expecting immediate attack from any quarter.

'He's a bonny bird,' Henderson was saying, 'but that's about all about him. A showman. Mair suited for a clapper-claw than a main!'

Brodie looked at the cock, obviously depressed.

'But he killed in training. Ye said so.'

'Oh aye. We wasted three scraggy dung-hill cockie-leeries on the beggar. If one o' them had had spurs and a decent meal, he wouldna' be here the day! He's not just what ye would describe as a wonder! Hoosht ye, beast ... !'

Henderson flapped at it. The cock immediately threw all dignity to the winds and shot to the back of the pen clucking.

'It's a bloody hen. Look at it. Fearty-gowk!'

'Is it getting the mixture?'

'Will, I could live on it masel' and get fat. And fightin' drunk. That creature gets Bell's beer, half a bottle, and bran mash mixed wi' wheat and oats, three times daily. And a spoon o' dried blood mixed in. The bird's magnificently fit for the table, but he's no' fit for the pit! Still, ye'll be havin' him after that!'

'He has to go in or else I'll only have the six.'

'Aye, I doubt he will. But we need new stock or we'll be going on like this. Give me the money, Will, and I'll get the fresh blood. There's a fault in these birds. I hear there's some new cross-breeds in England that havena' been seen up here yet. They say there's old Nick himsel' in their black little evil hearts. Javanese or some sic thing. We need new blood!'

Brodie pondered on Henderson's emphatic declaration. More money, and soon. Or else he would lose more. He was already in a perilous financial situation, but there was no going back on it. They must break Wemyss immediately. Smith could fence the pickings in less than a week, Chesterfield and back. If the shop held even half he thought, then they would both be nicely afloat. Besides with his re-election as Council Deacon six weeks ago, the work was beginning to flow his way again. Now it was Hill's turn to feel the pinch. Even if the devil had finished the Tolbooth and billed for it, exactly one week before losing office. There would be no more work for the energetic Mr Hill.

'Right, Michael.' Brodie had decided. 'This lot must go to the main as they are and tak' their chances. They've already cost me a small fortune, After that, whatever the result, find me new birds.'

'Grand, Will. If you pay me now I'll . . .'

'I'll pay you tomorrow, Michael, or certainly next week. Make it next week. I have a lot of things tae settle.'

'The earlier the better. We've no' had much o' a run.'

'Will I win the day?'

'Man, ye ken I never commit masel' on matters of gambling. It only loses friends.'

'But what about Buchanan's birds? Have ye seen them? Are they good?'

'I have and they're nothing special.'

'No worse than mine though!'

'That's so.'

'You're a canny man, Michael Henderson. I pay well, don't I?'

'You do, Will, you do.'

'Then do what you can. Give them a spot o' brandy. It'll either mak' them stand up or fall down!'

The 'main' at Henderson's was crowded as a cattle pen. His stable-men struggled and punched at the door, trying to control the crush and prevent the entrance of non-paying spectators. In the end, however, they were borne away by the weight of numbers. The ring was kept clear for Jamie by two hefty carriers with a fine vocabulary who thrashed out at anyone encroaching on the sacred circle. Fights had already broken out amongst the crowd and a mis-directed bottle crashed on to the pit. One of the carriers hurled it back in the approximate direction from which it had come. There was a vicious dull crash, and part of the crowd collapsed and struggled up again.

Brodie was white and nervous and was aware of it. The blood whistled in his ears and he seemed to hear the workings of his heart. Buchanan, the other cocker, was a sandy-haired, freckle-faced cloth merchant from Leith. He was chewing his lower lip and was equally pale. The main was for a majority win, seven cocks pitted against seven cocks. The whole of 'sporting' Edinburgh seemed to be there, together with Fife and the Lothians. Brodie felt a sense of panic at the density of the crowd. They were packed so close there was no room to sweat.

Brodie was taking no casual bets this time. This was between him and Buchanan for one hundred and fifty pounds sterling. For Buchanan it was the biggest wager he had ever laid. For Brodie it represented the only cash he had, including the men's wages, except three guineas he kept in his pocket. It was a desperate time. And yet it was desperately exciting too. Smith at this moment was in the basement of the grocer's shop. The forge would be furious-red. Brodie imagined him working with hammer and saw, the rasp and ring of iron. The key would be half-made and finished by the time the fight was over. Even this wild gamble was only a prologue. Buchanan shouted to him from the other bench.

'Henderson will make his fortune from this lot anyways!' Buchanan was nervous and envisaged losing. Brodie saw that. But the man, like himself, was enjoying it. He felt a warmth for him, and smiled and doffed his hat. They were charging two guineas now for admission and still people were pushing in. Henderson's men finally managed to swim back against the human tide and slam the solid outer doors to. They shut these with a stout iron bar. With the door closed, the screaming pack of spectators could be heard in full tongue. Money was being held aloft in fists that shook and gestured. Wigs were trampled underfoot, and bald men held their heads as though attacked by thunderous insanity. Bailie Dickson lost one shoe and had to hop throughout, or stand in unspeakable mire. Someone's faithful dog, which had found a gap in the wall, bounded through to fling itself joyfully on its master. Instead it was hit on the head with a heavy cane and expired on the floor. Men who had drunk too much pissed where they stood. Even thieves were robbed.

Jamie was flapping his arms up and down for the fourth time and screaming at the top of his voice,

'Shentlemen! Shentlemen! This is a full main of seven cocks each between Mr Brodie of Edinburgh and Mr Buchanan of Leith! Winner take all. There will be no draw in this contest! Shentlemen, if you will be silent please for God's sake we can all get started. Shentlemen! Shentlemen! Winner take all! If a bird or birds is disabled or maimed, then she will be put peak to peak ...' This Highland announcement produced roars of laughter from those who had heard it, which made Jamie blush furiously, but had the effect of quietening the barn.

'Shall be put peak to peak ...' he tried again, to even more laughter and cheers.

'Shall be put with their mouths together!' he concluded triumphantly. 'The bird which strikes will be declared to have won. If neither bird strikes then both birds will be withdrawn and the next two birds set to fight, reducing the number of contestants to five, so that there will always be a majority!' In the quietening barn, he began to reel off the rules. 'All the birds have been weighed before Mr Curries the referee who has satisfied hisself that the birds is evenly matched to within an ounce. There is, I repeat, shentlemen, seven fights—to the death!'

The crowd roared and cheered. Henderson joined Brodie on the bench where he sat.

'Well,' said Henderson, 'here we go, Will.'

Now that it had come to it, Brodie felt sick in the stomach and violently excited at the same time. His pale cheeks sported a hectic pink glow, so that he looked almost clownish. Buchanan, glancing at him, thought that they looked like the red patches on a pale apple.

'No shentleman who is a cocker shall in any circumstances enter the pit, nor clean the beak or eyes of his bird nor adjust his spurs, nor . . .'

'They might do it,' said Henderson, 'those birds of Buchanan's are a dreetie-looking lot o' gallants!'

The setters-on had taken the first two birds from their pens, and were holding them aloft where they could see each other. Then, while they screamed with malevolence, they were brought to Will Brodie to check the spurs. The first away was one of Brodie's best, a dark red. Buchanan's was a grey. To the accompaniment of a bestial shriek from the crowd, the two birds were released. They did not at first fly at each other, but strutted their ground glaring. Both birds simultaneously started crowing—in this breed a shrill scream. Their heads were poised like cobras. Brodie's bird appeared to be pawing the canvas, as a horse paws at the earth. Then it flew, projecting itself with its massive legs and pounding its clipped wings. The other bird was momentarily flurried, and backed off. Brodie's bird hit it in the breast with both spurs, and blood immediately appeared. The crowd roared. They loved the first claret. Buchanan's bird, however, did not even appear to notice and pecked viciously back. They were now locked into each other and neither would let go. They pecked and bored and tore into each other at close range. This bloody business went on for over three minutes when, as if by mutual consent, the birds released each other and backed off. The full extent of the damage was visible. Buchanan's bird had been wickedly cut in that first encounter and was dripping blood as it walked. There was no strut left in the creature, only an unfulfillable hate. As Brodie's red hit it again, it collapsed, unable to get up under the weight of the other bird. It appeared to try to get up twice, then lay, its beak open and tongue showing, the head arching slowly back. The red regarded this with curiosity and experimentally pecked at its throat. Finding this produced no response it leapt off its victim, fluffing its feathers as though in contempt. Brodie unclenched his fists and tried to appear calm and relaxed. He nodded to Buchanan.

'One to me I'm afraid, Mr Buchanan.'

'Aye, Mr Brodie. But happen you've put your best bird in first!'

'I have no best bird.'

'Well I have, Mr Brodie!'

'We'll see!'

The setters-on had captured Brodie's red, which they penned. It was bleeding itself from numerous scars, but paid no attention to these, continuing to stick its head through the wooden slats of the pen and scream defiance. The setters-on ignored it. They were too busy bringing out the next birds. Brodie lost three fights in a row.

'God, Will, it's that black hen o' yours next!'

Henderson, like Brodie, was leaning forward on the bench. But his was a relaxed and professional interest. Brodie was tense and his face burned like a man with fever. This was the stuff of life! To lose all or win all. This was a rare sensation that for a few moments made a man live on a plane above all other men. Perhaps this was what dying was like.

Perhaps Francis had experienced it, just the once. Will Brodie would experience it again and again. I am like a man drowning in boredom, he thought, who is again and again able to fight to the surface for a desperate breath of air. All around me there are drowned men who think they are alive. Give me air sweet air even if it means destruction.

The black cock was released against Buchanan's red. As in the first fight they did not immediately fly at each other, but strutted and stared. They cautiously approached each other towards the centre of the pit. The magistrates, Guards, burghers and thieves of Edinburgh roared at the uncomprehending beasts to fight. Then the unexpected happened. Far from attacking the red, Brodie's black, under some misguided notion, mounted the red bird. The crowd collapsed with hoots of ribaldry and laughter. The red bird was apparently so astounded that it was a second or two before it reacted. With a sudden flurry it shook the black bird off and flew at it. The black took to its heels and ran, jumping out of the ring despite the efforts of the setters-on to prevent it. The crowd still roared and hooted. Eventually it was recaptured, but immediately fled again. The match was awarded to Buchanan.

'I told ye, Michael. That bird's a disgrace. Cut its throat!'

'Aye well, Will, but ye canna deny it was a cock! Misguided maybe, but a cock all the same!'

Buchanan came over, trying to maintain a grin of decent proportions on his freckled face.

'It was a funny bird that last yin! We'll pretend he wasnae quite sober! Bad luck, Mr Brodie.'

'No, Mr Buchanan, ye had the better o' me. My birds were no good. Collect your money from Currie, Mr Buchanan, ye deserve it. But, Mr Buchanan,' Brodie's mind was racing like his blood, 'do me the honour of a return one day. Mr Henderson has orders to introduce some new blood to my birds ... I tell you, Mr Buchanan, I am going to buy some birds that will kipper yours with a trussed leg!'

'Aye? And not this new variety, the Roger!' Guffawing, Buchanan made his way back to his pens. 'I accept, Mr Brodie. Tell me when you're ready.'

Now Brodie had three guineas in the world. But that won't be for long, he thought.

Brodie had already changed into dark clothes. He was loading a ball into a pistol, by the light of a lantern in the basement of the grocer's shop. Smith was still putting a finishing touch to the key which he had clamped in a vice. He was filing the wards smooth to his satisfaction then, taking it from the vice, daubed it with grease from a pot. He put it on a thick piece of linen and took it over to Brodie.

'There it is. Done.'

Brodie looked at it expertly, holding it by the linen underneath to avoid the grease.

'It looks a good job. Let's see the putty.'

Smith handed over the tin and Brodie slipped the impression on to the key. The fit was perfect. He nodded approval.

'Are you armed?'

'Yes,' said Smith, 'one pistol, double ball.'

'Then let us take to the road!' Brodie brandished his pistol dramatically in the air.

'Here's to rich pickings and a dark night!'

'Aye,' said Smith shortly, thinking Brodie seemed over-excited.

'Are you not enjoying it, man!' Brodie was grinning. 'It will be all right. Easy. You have a long face, George! Put some of the devil into ye! Out on a blind-man's holiday.'

'I keep my smiling for when it's over,' said Smith. 'I laugh when we add it up, and I crack my jaws when it's fenced.'

Smith had worked with many accomplices before. Fear and nervousness he understood. Pale faces, few words and acrid sweat. But Brodie looked as though he had just strode in from the opera. As though to confirm this alarming impression,

Brodie suddenly started to hum a jaunty tune to himself, filling his pockets the meanwhile with the necessary tools. Smith had misgivings about the whole expedition, but told himself that the man had done well enough in getting the key, and on the basis of his record, was certainly no mug at this sort of thing.

'I'll go in first,' said Brodie, 'because I know my way about. There's precious little room and we don't want us fallin' ower the furnishings. I'll take the key, and we take a stocking each tae fill. Now you're clear where we're going? The cellar's the place. Keep to the virgin metal and ignore his pewter brass and bronze.'

'I'm no flat. I know my metals.' Smith sounded sharp.

'Then away!'

Brodie tucked the pistol into his cape pocket, pulled out his father's wig from his coat, and jammed this on his head. They went out by the stair to the street. Smith's dog heard them and barked as they passed the shop door.

'What of your wife. Does she know you're off?'

'Aye. But she keeps to herself. That way she knows nothing, and it's the truth.' Brodie was impressed.

'I'm a great believer masel' that a woman deceived is a woman relieved!'

They walked to the goldsmith's shops quite openly, keeping to the black recesses of the streets. The feeble yellow glow of the Town lighting wasted itself on soot encrusted walls. It held no perils for nocturnal prowlers. They passed many people, unrecognised and unrecognising in the moonless night. Outside Wemyss' shop, they stopped, and before Smith had time to ask what he was doing, Brodie had boldly unlocked the door, concealing his actions under his cape, and they were hurrying inside. Brodie re-locked the door behind them. It made little noise.

'That is what I call a good key,' he said.

'God, man,' Smith hissed, 'have you no idea of caution and prudence! That was mad.'

'It was good sense—never hang about, just walk in as though it belongs to you. Who could suspect that? Now, follow me.'

Smith felt out in the darkness and took hold of Brodie's shoulder.

'We have to go round the counter to get to the back.'

Brodie moved along the counter to the end of the recess, with Smith holding on. They clattered a bit as they felt their way through the gap and behind to the head of the cellar steps.

'Stop. I'll light-up here.'

Brodie lit the dark-lantern carefully. Smith noted that his hands were completely steady. By the narrow beam he left they descended the stone steps into the cellar, feeling their way down the wall. At the bottom, Brodie slid back the shutter so that the full light leapt out. This was only a candle but, after the intensity of effort of staring into the dark, the light made them blink. The cellar had roughly-dressed stone walls and a stone slab floor. It was windowless as they had guessed. Along the end wall there was a bank of plain, heavy-fronted drawers, with a bench-top over them. The drawers were unlabled in any way, but each was fitted with a small iron lock. Smith eased a small crow-bar out of his sleeve.

'This should do it.'

Brodie held the lantern close while Smith inserted the crow between lock and keep. He pulled down, then leaned his weight on the short bar. There was a sharp creaking then a crack. The keep had ripped out of the wood. They stood listening for a long time. Brodie moved to the foot of the cellar stairs and listened. When they were sure that they had not been heard, Smith set to, and each drawer was systematically broken in the same way. They completed this operation before opening them. At a nod from Brodie, Smith pulled the first one out as he held the lantern up. Smith had his back to Brodie, so that Brodie could not see, but he heard Smith swear softly to himself, great oaths, little oaths, a monotonous tone. It was the first sign that Smith had shown of excitement.

'What have you got?' Brodie asked. He could not see inside. Smith silently turned with the drawer and showed the contents. Brodie had been right.

The first drawer they pulled out was full of solid silver show-buckles. They counted at least twenty-five pairs. The next drawer was exactly the same. Three drawers contained cheap imitation stuff, and pewter brooches. They ignored these. The next drawer contained so many knee-buckles, that Smith nearly dropped it, as he pulled it off its slide. Brodie clapped him on the back and laughed. He pulled out the next drawer and whistled. Smith jumped and gestured to him with one hand while holding a finger to his lips. Brodie ignored it and said: 'No one can hear us down here! Just look at this ...'

Smith peered into the drawer. Lying on a bed of blue silk was a whole drawerful of gold rings, set with stones. Smith was mesmerised. He picked them up, one after the other, to examine them. There were opals, amethysts, cairngorms, diamonds, rubies and pearls, and any number of combinations. Twenty-six in all. Brodie nudged him and gleefully showed him the next drawer. On red silk lay twenty-four solid gold rings. They were weighty and sparkling-new, intended for signet rings. Other drawers contained silver spoons, earrings, seals and brooches. One drawer contained two pieces of plate and another a soup tureen.

This should keep the wolf from the door!' said Brodie.

'It's a fortune,' said Smith, 'we'll never carry it all!'

So they filled one stocking with silver buckles, but it sagged, distended, and ruptured under the weight of them. They tipped them out on the bench and decided to fill their pockets. The tongues of the buckles had caught in the stockings and they spent some minutes swearing and unhooking them. When they had transferred them all, their clothes hung about them heavily and clinked when they walked. They laughed and walked up and down, and ran on the spot clattering like cutlery. Smith was allowing himself to be carried away. Brodie swore that if he could not take the tureen then by God he would take the top, and put it on his head, pulling the wig over it. Smith laughed as Brodie solemnly paraded up and down, until he realised that Brodie meant it.

'No, you can't. You'll drop it! We'll be arrested.'

'I won't drop it. Look. I just have to walk like this. Like a whore or a bishop.'

'No, no, no!' Smith burst out. 'For Christ's sake stop being a fool!' Brodie stopped suddenly and looked at him sardonically.

'Now don't be getting excited, Mr Smith. It's light stuff anyway.' He set the top down, and began to tie up the rent in the stocking. They silently stuffed the two stockings full of the rings and other bits and pieces.

'If I can't have the tureen,' said Brodie, 'at least I can have the spoon!' So saying he pushed the soup spoon in after the rings. Smith realised yet again that Brodie was a dangerous man. Two dozen more spoons followed it, swept up from other drawers. The stockings were immensely distended by the weight of the goods, so that at chest height, they reached the floor. They tied them up and picked them up in their left hands.

'Are you ready?' asked Brodie. On Smith's nod, Brodie blew out the lantern. 'Give it a couple of minutes till you have your night eyes.'

They stood in the sudden blackness, aware of every sound again. People in the street. A hawking cough and a spit. Dogs barking. What goes for silence in cities. A sedan chair was carried past, with the clatter of shod feet on cobbles. They began to be able to see clearly. Brodie made for the steps and went up again, followed by Smith. It seemed glaringly bright in the shop, and their first reflex was to seek cover under the counter. It was only a street lamp across the street that they had not even noticed on their way in. Brodie undid the door and listened. He waved Smith on. Smith walked out. Brodie locked up, openly, without haste, just as any respectable citizen would do. They walked down the street together without talking, rather unsteadily, their clothes rather dishevelled. They might have been slightly drunk.

The following evening, Brodie and Smith sat in Smith's small parlour. A fire crackled and sparked up the chimney, providing the only light. Mary Smith sat to one side, while the two men, with their feet up on a wooden bench, cracked their boot-soles in front of the fire. On the bare boards of the floor stood several bottles of Bell's 'black cork', thick, black ale more intoxicating than wine. Mary wore a gold brooch, gold earrings which were lopsidedly fixed and four gold and gemstone rings that she had managed to push on to her work-curled fingers. She too held a tankard of beer and was evidently drunk, laughing to herself, and flashing the stones in the fire-light. They would only be hers for a day. Smith was reading from the *Edinburgh Evening Courant*. He had just read out a list of the articles stolen, which to their surprise was exact, nothing extra having been added.

'"As the public, as well as the private party, are greatly interested that this daring robbery be discovered, it is requested that all Goldsmiths, Merchants, and other Traders through Scotland, may be attentive, in case any goods answering to those above mentioned shall be offered to sale"—they won't find them throughout Scotland, I'll guarantee that. These parochial Scotch!'

'I think I have seen the same sort o' thing in English papers,' said Brodie, in good humour. Smith grinned.

'Aye, and very much to the advantage of us. Never take it as a complaint! It goes on, and this is where we get to it, "offered to sale, and to enquire how the persons who may offer them to sale came by them, and to get them examined before a Magistrate, and secured in prison, in case they cannot give a good account of themselves, and prove how they came by the said goods".'

Brodie laughed and slapped his knee.

'That's grand stuff! It has a magnificent pompous flow about it that shows what learned and literate men we have as magistrates. It takes nine years o' training to write a piece like that. Fine comedy!'

'Now we come to the best bit,' Smith continued. '"Letters containing information may be addressed to Mr William Dempster, deacon of the Incorporation of Goldsmiths in Edinburgh, or to Mr David Downie, Goldsmith there, treasurer of said Incorporation ..."'

'An old woman!'

'"... or to Mr William Scott, procurator-fiscal of the shire of Edinburgh; and in order that the person or persons guilty of the said robbery may be discovered, the Incorporation of Goldsmiths hereby offer a reward of ten guineas ..."'

The two men broke into more laughter, in which Mary Smith joined. Brodie poured more beer into his tappit-hen, his hands shaking with merriment.

'We must apply!' he shouted. 'A very fortune within our grasp. Ten guineas, by God! The earth will take another revolution today! Mr William Dempster, who would steal a crust from a bairn, provided he didn't have to waste shoe leather in the pursuit o' him, is offering ten whole guineas reward. He would sell his shite in the street for sixpence!'

'There's a bit more,' said Smith, wiping tears of laughter from his eyes. '"Ten guineas to any person who shall make such discovery, to be paid by Mr Downie, their treasurer, upon conviction of the offender or offenders." It's tempting, Will, really tempting.'

'I have worked out, with my magnificent business brain, that the reward must be all of one and a quarter percent. These Goldsmiths have gone daft with extravagance! Damn it, we'll write a letter. "Dear Mr Dempster, we have hid the jewellery up a cow's arse in a field just out of Hawthornden. We cannot remember which cow, but we trust that your investigations will be fruitful!" We'll do it. Have you paper, I'll send him the scrive.'

Smith suddenly realised that Brodie was serious.

'No, Will! That's a risk. Forget it.'

'There's no risk attached. I'll shove it through his door at dead of night.'

'You'll be seen. They're bound to be watching the offices.'

'The man deserves it. Ten guineas!'

'No, Will, let me get rid of the stuff!'

Brodie looked disappointed.

'I suppose you're right. Will you take it?'

'No, Mary will. She'll leave by stage for Chesterfield tomorrow. She won't be suspected. The whole lot will go in a hat-box, well padded.'

'It'll be heavy. They'll suspect.'

'She'll take it inside.'

'But will she get a good price from this man Tasker?'

'Mary?'

Mary Smith spoke up with sudden acute vehemence. There was no sign of stupidity in her face, or indeed her manner.

'I know the price of it. Tasker would never dare cross me. If that fencing benedict tries to bite me, his wife can know about certain things. He's a horning bastard like all men!'

Brodie was quite shocked at this unexpected drunken outburst, and Smith was clearly embarrassed. Brodie thought there was a whole concealed side to Mary Smith that he had been misled upon. He should have guessed.

'That's no language to use, woman, in front of Mr Brodie.'

'Is it not? We're gentry among thieves, are we? Then get a whey-faced, pink-arsed lady to do your work. Tasker will give her tuppence and the rest in kind. What do you think this is? A club for the fancy?'

'She's sometimes like this when she's been drinking,' Smith whispered.

'Don't you whisper about me, George Smith!' she exclaimed.

Smith pacified her. Brodie sat and thought. He was both attracted and repelled by this sudden manifestation of a real personality from behind the vacant façade. He felt a strange thrill at the contact. She was the real thing. For the first time he fully realised that George Smith was also the real thing. No gentleman adventurer in crime, but a professional criminal. He looked around the small parlour, with its minimal furniture and bare boards, and bottles of beer. It was really a thieves' kitchen. It reminded him of the opera. This was a new and exciting vista. He had hunted alone, and in a way this had begun to prove boring. In this new phase he would run with a mangy pack.

'George, I have been thinking about the future. In fact I have been making a list. I think enough time has gone by to have a look at Bridge Street. In fact I already have the impressions for keys.'

'You're a smart man, Will. You keep ahead of things.'

In fact Smith was worried in case his wife's outburst had put off this Edinburgh amateur.

'I have a key for Davidson McKain, the hardware shop, and one for Andrew Bruce—they're jewellers.'

'God that was clever.'

'No, it was easy, and they're stupid. But we should crack one in between, or it will be too obvious. I have an eye on Law, the tobacconist at the Exchange. For a diversion, you understand. The goods must be portable. But I have some grand plans for later.'

'What's that.'

'Have you heard of the University mace?'

'Aye.'

'Solid silver. Then there are some real challenges about this town which a man with some daring might easily do well to investigate. Have you ever been to the Excise?'

'No.'

'A child could walk in and fill his pockets. Then there is the mace belonging to the respectit Council itself! That thing is heavy. I sit and look at it at every meeting. It's there for whoever helps himself.'

'No! That's too risky, Will!'

'But think o' it. The Town Council theirselves—the tragedy o' it!' Brodie was smiling to himself as he contemplated it. 'Then there are the banks. We should try a bank—and the Chamberlain's office. They are awful careless with their money. And a stage coach. We have never tried that.'

'No! That's madness!'

'Is it? The Stirling Stage carries all the wages for the Carron workmen, once a week. They have no armed guard. The driver carries a pistol. Think, George. Keep thinking. Find an opportunity—then go for it. My father would have approved of it! It's good business thinking!' Brodie smiled wickedly to himself, and stared into the fire. Then to Smith's surprise he waved at the fire and addressed it.

'Hello, father! Keeping well?'

'What are you saying?' Smith was uneasy.

'It's Francis Brodie, my well respected father. A man of the Renaissance. He's in the fire.'

'Stop it, Will. Don't behave like that.'

'He is, you know, because I've put him there, and he's not coming out 'till I let him! I would be an awful disappointment to him the day!'

Mary Smith cackled and threw back her head. All the gems with which she had adorned herself sparkled.

* * *

Edinburgh Evening Courant, 1786.

SHOP BROKE INTO, AND ROBBED

In Parliament Square, Edinburgh.

WHEREAS betwixt the night of Monday the 9th, and Tuesday the 10th of October current, the shop of Mr James Wemyss, Goldsmith in Edinburgh, situated betwixt the Goldsmith's Hall and the Council Chambers of said City, was broke into and the following articles carried off, viz. 26 gold rings, some set with diamonds and the rest with stones; 24 plain gold rings; 5 seals set in gold, 1 gold broatch; 2 silver set broatches; 2 set crosses; 3 set ear-rings, one of them gold; 4 cut shank silver tea spoons, and one old plain silver do; 10 new silver table spoons; 1 silver tureen spoon, and the mouth of a dividing spoon; 2 silver punch spoons; 12 silver tea spoons, not quite finished but ready for burnishing; 1 silver seal with a ship on it, and one seal block; 12 silver stock buckles; 36 pairs silver shoes buckles; 3 single silver shoe ditto; 46 pairs of silver knee buckles, and four single knee ditto.

As the public, as well as the private party, are greatly interested that this daring robbery be discovered, it is requested that all Goldsmiths, Merchants, and other Traders through Scotland, may be attentive, in case any goods answering to those above mentioned shall be offered to sale, and to enquire how the persons who may offer them to sale came by them, and to get them examined before a Magistrate, and secured in prison, in case they cannot give a good account of themselves, and prove how they came by the said goods.

Letters containing information may be addressed to Mr William Dempster, deacon of the Incorporation of Goldsmiths in Edinburgh, or to Mr David Downe, Goldsmith there, treasurer of said Incorporation, or to Mr William Scott, procurator-fiscal of the shire of Edinburgh; and in order that the person or persons guilty of the said robbery may be discovered, the Incorporation of Goldsmiths hereby offer a reward of TEN GUINEAS to any person who shall make such discovery, to be paid by Mr Downie, their treasurer, upon conviction of the offender or offenders.

CHAPTER SIX

October and November 1786. Notable meetings

The Town Council was outraged, and when Edinburgh was angry, wig-chalk flew unspared. Bailie Gloag, a fiery little man, alternated with Old Bailie Shaw in condemnation of the recent outrages committed against the property of the merchants of Edinburgh.

Gloag, with wholly uncharacteristic extravagance had made the reckless proposal that the town guard should be increased by perhaps ten men. This, he explained (for he obviously felt explanation was necessary for everything that he said), was in order that the frequency of rotation of their patrols around the Town might be increased. Deacon Dewar, a hard-headed man representing the Masons, indicated with a hand his desire to speak. Lord Provost Grieve interrupted Gloag, who felt that he had just reached the nub of his explanation and sat down, looking pointedly about him and simultaneously shrugging. This had the effect of making him look like a settling hen. Grieve gestured with his quill.

'Mr Dewar.'

'An increase o' the Toon Rotten,' he said broadly, 'will merely mean a decrease correspondin' in the amount o' space left for shelterin' frae inclement weather an' blaw aneath the Luckenbooths!' He sat down again, amidst some laughter.

Old Bailie Dickson leaned backwards in his seat in front of Brodie.' Brodie, who had been contemplating the mace on the

'A pity you lost so much to Mr Buchanan from Leith, Mr Brodie.' Brodie, who had been contemplating the mace on the table as though it were barley-sugar and he a small boy, quickly feigned surprise.

'And were you there, Mr Dickson. I would never have thought it. I took it you were opposed to all sic things.'

Dickson did not reply. Instead he continued.

'How is business? Good? Trotter, I hear, is building up a business to be proud of. And him not a Bailie yet, nor even a Deacon.'

'I hear he's doing well,' Brodie replied equably.

'And you yourself? You're not feeling the loss of it.'

The man was impertinent. He chose to fight in whispers. Brodie could not easily respond.

'There's room in Edinburgh for Brodie and Trotter.'

'Aha. And Hill too? Francis would never have agreed to that!' With a look of triumph Dickson swung back to face the Chair. Dickson had won thirty guineas on Buchanan's birds, a fact that Brodie had been told. While he was still trying to master his rage, Dickson indicated that he wished to speak. Brodie found that he was cold and shaking. His last encounter with Dickson had left him with half-formulated apprehensions. There were some who might suspect and say nothing, but Dickson was none of that sort.

'Lord Provost, gentlemen. We have heard remedies suggested. I sympathise with those merchants who have suffered loss, but it is not, I regret, the continuing number of felonies themselves that prove alarming. It is the skill and knowledge of their committing that, I submit, should be our chief concern. They are, I fear, carried out by a determined and intelligent man. A common thief would have been dancing on Mr Brodie's trap months ago. M'Kain's shop and Wemyss' shop were opened with a false key. Mark it. Just how Law the tobacconist's was broken on the eighth of this month. In every case the outer port had been opened professionally, without force, and damage done only to the drawers or cases inside. We advertised as such, I remember, when Johnston and Smith were robbed. Mr Lord

Provost, I suggest that all these depredations are the work of one man or a man with accomplices. He is no common felon. He is someone who moves amongst us, and knows what we have! We are harbouring a felon in our midst. We must root him out!'

There was uproar as Dickson sat down, much of it indignant and resentful. Brodie felt the hairs on the back of his neck prickle. Dickson hinted too much, but did he know anything? Was it directed at him? He could not tell. Dickson did not look his way, but stoically faced front while the Council was hammered to order by Lord Provost Grieve—Grieve whom Brodie knew to have a finger in every commercial pie in the town, Grieve the merchant, Grieve the floater of companies and corporations, his name on every subscription head. Grieve the Lord Provost. For once he loved Bailie Shaw, who shot to his feet, his thin face pink with rage and his voice quivering.

'It is intolerable,' he was blathering, 'that such a construction —no, such an insinuation should be made among the elected representatives of the Town Council! Is Bailie Dickson implying that someone known and respected in this town could be responsible for this? I say no! We must keep a watch on all Englishmen —and Highlanders—and Lowlanders too!'

Grieve was holding his head in his hand and smiling. 'With Mr Gloag's ten extra men? They are going to be awfu' busy, Mr Shaw!'

'Does not the Bible say, Psalm eleven, "For lo, the wicked bend their bow, they make ready their arrow upon the string, that they may privily shoot at the upright in heart"?'

It was Dickson's turn to become angry now. Brodie felt panic at what the man might say as he struggled to his feet, but Grieve, wily Grieve, waved Dickson down.

'If this was a pulpit, Mr Shaw, I daresay there would be few here but you. It isna'. But as you have seen fit to quote at me, may I remind you that I am as well versed as yourself. Isaiah had a more optimistic view you may remember— "And I will restore thy judges as at the first, and thy counsellors as at the beginning, afterward thou shalt be called the city of righteousness, the faithful city." Isaiah Two, verse twenty-six. Take care, Bailie Shaw!'

Amid polite laughter, Shaw wisely sat down and said no more. Brodie had much to think about and, after a decent interval of attention to commonplace business, he left. To heed what might be a warning and stop, was probably more dangerous than to carry on. In any case Dickson might well have been acting on behalf of Trotter or Hill for motives of his own. He was aware that a guilty man sees fear in his own shadow, but the inference although squashed was too blunt to ignore. He had one more shop to crack, then he must give it a rest, wipe the floor with Trotter, get his business back in order. He decided to order up a new copy of Chippendale's designs, together with London and Paris catalogues. But first, to confound Dickson, there was Bruce's shop.

'The Coffin' was as crowded as was usual whenever Burns was in command. He was in a sour mood tonight and had been drinking steadily. His usual friends were there, but could not persuade him out of his depression. Willie Nicol was trying to rouse him.

'What point is there in this gloom, man? You are a contrary beast, as I have tell't you often enough. You fight your life awa' for expression, and when your subscriptions are assured and Mr Creech is at this moment printing, you want nothing o' it. You said yoursel' that you were likely to be inserted in the Almanacks, along wi' black Monday and Bothwell Brig! You wrote it. There are men who would give both arms if it werena' for the impossibility thereafter o' writing, for the patronage o' the Duchess of Gordon and Lord Cunningham, not to speak o' me and Masterton here, and Davie, and thon paint-smoored fellow Naysmith!'

'I am an ungrateful peasant. I apologise.'

'Ach the hell with your apologia! Humility doesna' suit you. It rings like a cracked bell.'

'What sort of wight am I? Full of whim and fancy, in the

company of the best of friends. This is an uncivil beast. I shake hands with you, drink and folly. Pass the Jemmy-John!'

Brodie, acknowledging Johnnie Dowie's greetings, joined the group in the 'Coffin'. He was immediately shocked by the sight of Andrew Bruce with Burns at the table. They were in conversation. Although in great confusion, Brodie stood his ground. To slip away would be suspicious. He had no knowledge that Andrew Bruce, Jeweller, knew Robert Burns, Poet. They appeared indeed to be friends. Burns was slapping Bruce on the back and saying, 'My good friend here, now that I am no longer under the protection of Henry Erskine, has honoured me and the Arts by providing a roof. That is all we poor muse-mongers ask!' He winked broadly and downed a draught from his demi-john. Looking up as he did so, he caught sight of Brodie, conspicuous in his light clothes. Willie Nicol, as a matter of courtesy, introduced them.

'This is Mr Brodie, Rab. Deacon of Wrights and a member of Canongate Kilwinning. You'll be meeting him at the Lodge.'

'You dress well, Mr Brodie,' said Burns with more than a hint of discourtesy.

'I am not above getting my hands dirty,' said Brodie defensively. This new circumstance almost disarmed him.

'Now, now, Rab!' said Willie, 'Mr Brodie is the best wright in Edinburgh. Beneath all that silk weskit and crockats is a man with craft in his arms. He'll cut you a chair yourself frae a log o' mahogany.' Burns smiled.

'That's more than a mere poet, Willie—I can only scrawl on that most unreceptive medium the heart!'

'In the fair sex you find it the most unreceptive medium? By what I've seen it is the most receptive.'

'By God, Willie, it's not, but decency forbids me from saying it!' There was laughter in which Burns joined. He still looked at Brodie.

'You are the man,' he declared, 'that knew Boswell.'

'I drank with him a few times.'

'They have showed me the record of it at the Lodge. And now he practises at another Bar. The man who towed the Ursa Major on his chain is another pedagogue, chained himself, to the awful weight of law. I am pleased to meet a man who spent an evening of social glee and heard him sing. He studied under Adam Smith, you know, and met Voltaire, Rousseau and Wilkes. What did he sing?'

'I can't remember now. It's over ten years ago. It was something patriotic, and something lewd, and something to the ladies. Things that young men sing.'

'And have you given up singing, Mr Brodie? You cut a bit of a dash. Which is a great change from the damned dull government of this Town!'

Brodie was nonplussed.

'I sing a bit to myself.'

'Man, why are you ashamed o' it? I wrote my first song before I was sixteen in celebration o' pure enjoyment, if that is the way to put it, o' a strapping, big-breasted, round-nippled, strong-thighed, hay-making lass that made hay with me. By God I could hardly stand straight in front o' my faither. "What's the matter lad?" he says. "Hae ye strained yoursel at the hay?" and he knew!' He looked at Brodie again, curiously. 'And what is it that a Deacon of the Wrights may decently sing to himsel' in Edinburgh?'

'The Beggar's Opera.'

'I wouldna call that very suitable matter.' Burns was amused now. 'I never met a Councillor yet who believed in the redistribution of wealth, except his way. It was Gay who said, "I must have women. There is nothing unbends the mind like them." I would give this hand or maybe, to be realistic, the end off this finger to have thought of that first. But do you know he also wrote that

> "Envy's a sharper spur than pay,
> No author spar'd a brother,
> Wits are gamecocks to one another".

And to that end, I'll have another drink, sirs! Good health to you, Mr Brodie.'

The conversation rolled on, Burns alternatively ebullient and depressed. Brodie slowly allowed himself to drift to the rear of the crowd, edging out to beckon for a bottle. He must think what to do. The key was made and the plan was laid for tonight. Smith was ready, and even now would be waiting at Clark's for him to turn up. They would play a game or two of cards, then quietly leave. He had no idea when Burns and Bruce would leave, but they looked settled for a long while. He sidled away from the group, when they were absorbed in a political discussion. Burns supported the American Revolution, maintaining fervently that it was no more than the new order after the Civil War. Brodie would have liked to have listened, but there was no time.

'Mr Burns spends a long time in here, Johnnie,' said Brodie to Dowie.

'He does that. He'll be here come the morning I doubt. He's to be Poet Laureate or some such thing for your Lodge.'

'He is?'

'Aye. He's Depute-Master of St James Lodge Tarbolton too. I heard them talking it ower. The Grand Master is to come down.'

'Is he staying with Henry Erskine?'

'Naw. He's changed, out o' civility. He's staying wi' Andrew Bruce, in Bridge Street. Are you off, Mr Brodie.'

'I am. Good night to you Johnnie. He's a powerful drinker.'

'And a powerful poet, Mr Brodie. Good nicht to you.'

Will entered John Clark's tavern, and stopped to wrestle with the spasms of the usual coughing fit. It was like inhaling the bowl of an old pipe.

He wiped his watering eyes, and could then see Smith and Ainslie at a table together in the sick light. They were talking. He was not altogether happy about Ainslie, for all his skill at cards. They must either enlist him or get rid of him. Of Brown there was no sign, and he found he was glad of it. He crossed over, avoiding arms and legs as best he could, and sat down beside Smith. Smith immediately sensed that something was the matter.

'Hello, Will? Are we on?' His face was alert and Brodie realised yet again that Smith was shrewd and had that extra sense of the professional—he could smell worry. Brodie had already considered the whole thing. Their last expedition to M'Kain's had been a débâcle. They had broken in successfully, Smith entering while he kept watch, but there had been nothing but seventeen steel watch chains and a red leather-bound pocket-book. Smith had given the latter to Henderson's daughter, which had delighted the child. There had then been a desperate second visit, with Smith fleeing when someone started out of bed overhead. They had had a bad row, Brodie accusing Smith of carelessness, and Smith accusing Brodie of running off, which, Brodie pointed out, was in the circumstances the only sensible thing to do. And, he had added, he had not noticed Smith hanging about either. Later, much pacified, they had gone by arm in arm as two drunks to find the shop watched by a Town Guard in full red uniform, who somehow thought he could blend in with a doorway.

They would have to proceed. If he called it off, Brodie sensed that Smith might throw it all in. But *he* would not go, and he reckoned on Smith's impatience to achieve this.

'Aye, we're on,' he said. 'Have you the necessaries?'

'I have.'

Ainslie was looking from one to the other, bright as a finch.

'I don't want to discuss this in front o' others,' he said. Ainslie was hurt.

'Tell him, George! It's no' fair, it isna'.'

'Tell me what?'

'Ainslie here wants to join us, Will. He thinks he could help. He might be right.'

John Clark's young Ganymede abruptly appeared, put down a pot of claret on the table, swabbing up spills with a cloth in his other hand. He then dematerialised into the gloom as silently as he had arrived.

'How?'

'Tell Mr Brodie,' Smith asked, but it sounded more like a command.

'Well, there's nothing and nowhere in Edinburgh about which I have not got what you might call a familiarity. I can go about, Mr Brodie, and speer where a gentleman of quality and appearance would be like a sprat in porrage. Naebody gledges at a wee skite like me!'

Brodie hated the man's obsequiousness but recognised the sense of it. It would allow them to extend the area in which they could work. Whereas Deacon Brodie was a familiar figure in the High Street, he would be like a two-headed man in Leith. What might Smith and he have achieved at M'Kain's had they had a look-out? It was only prudent, and would allow the two craftsmen to work. They needed a look-out. On another and very realistic level, Brodie recognised that Ainslie knew too much already, and it would be wise to take him in with them. But there was no reason why he should be informed of everything. With things becoming tricky, he could scout out new ground. The women were becoming discontented with him. All of them including his two sisters and that could lead to trouble! Time was the problem, and the fact that there was only one of him to go round! Rab Smith the foreman was openly criticizing his lack of attention to the wright work, saying that he was acting in the position of employer and being forced to take decisions that it was not his position to take. He had even hinted that he might go. He must have more time which meant he must have more help. His house must be kept in order, as this constituted the cornerstone of everything. He vowed to concentrate on the wright work for an extended time.

'All right. But you must do exactly as told, and the price is silence.'

Ainslie nodded eagerly.

'And a share in the proceeds I trust, Mr Brodie.'

'You will get your share.'

'An even cut?' persisted Ainslie.

It was a side of the man that Brodie had not noticed before. He might be all humility, but he intended to drive a bargain.

'It's an even risk, Mr Brodie, and if I introduce you to the work, then I think it is only fair. I'm sure the Magistrates would be very even in the distribution of their blessings if we ever got caught!'

Brodie's face took on a strange expression of intense alertness. This emphasised the cast in his left eye, so that he appeared slightly cross-eyed. He smiled and Ainslie felt ashamed by this reaction.

'Why should we ever be caught? My philosophy of life does not include such a possibility.'

'Well, it would be true,' Ainslie said, justifying himself. Brodie merely smiled at him again, making Ainslie feel that he was estranged from the workings of the man's mind. Smith interrupted this awkward exchange.

'I think it would be fair, Mr Brodie, if Ainslie sets up a crib for us. That's what we hope he'll do.'

Ainslie nodded.

'But not on our immediate affairs?' Brodie said, looking at Smith.

'Not on our immediate affairs.'

'Very well, Mr Ainslie, find us something interesting.'

'I will. No trouble.'

'Out of the centre. Something I would not cover myself.'

'I understand.'

The tavern was noisy with laughter and harsh voices. The ladies had disappeared with their trade, and tables were cleared for cards and dice. Men wandered between tables, joining a game, or watching. The fire was loaded with more logs. It was a bitter cold night, and the draughts that wheezed and sighed under the door made the candle-flames flatten out like dragon's breath. The rattling of dice had a cold sound like teeth chattering. Brodie suggested that they should play, and Smith agreed readily enough. Ainslie said that he had little money and could not yet afford it, although he hoped that would be remedied before too long. Brodie called out for any who would care to join in. Robertson of course came over, bringing with him Will Bell, a grocer and fellow Cape Club man.

'We'll join you, Will,' said Robertson. 'What are we playing?'

'Hazard.'

'That's fine with me,' said Bell, but looking at Smith. Brodie made the introductions.

'Mr Smith here is in the same line as yourself, Mr Bell, but in a very small way.'

'Aye? Is that so?'

Within a few minutes they were chatting relaxedly, and the game got under way. Clark produced the house dice, and everyone satisfied themselves of their impartiality with a few trial throws. Brodie had an identical pair in his pocket, but his were loaded. He would substitute them when the time seemed right.

They rapidly became absorbed in their play as Brodie intended they should. Brodie was in an agitated state of mind, and in gambling all other worries and concerns were completely forgotten. Smith, who was no expert gambler and took risks that ran against all logic, was soon losing money steadily. Brodie knew all the odds attaching to each number, and never tried to achieve a difficult 'main'. His skill with the dice was obvious. They played in almost total silence, except for the rattling of the dice, and the thump of Bell's fist on the table when he lost. Smith began to give Brodie meaningful looks across the table, even going so far as to pull a silver watch from his pocket and consult it as to the time. It was nearly midnight already, and they looked well settled in. In another half-hour, Smith had lost all the money he had about him, to Robertson, who like Brodie was ahead. He got to his feet.

'I'm cleaned out. Are you coming, Will. We were going to get that bit of business out of the way, or have you forgotten.'

Brodie looked up at him blandly.

'No, no, George. I'm well up. Never break a good run. The chatts are mysterious things, that need tae feel appreciated.'

Smith frowned.

'But it's late and we were going to leave. Don't forget the business.'

'It's not that important,' said Brodie quickly, 'it can wait.'

'But we agreed,' Smith persisted.

'Not now, George.' Brodie rudely turned his back. Smith, now angry, turned and went over to the fireplace, signalling the boy for a drink. While this brief conversation had been going on, and while everyone's attention had been upon Smith, it had been a matter of the greatest ease for Brodie, who had gathered up the dice in his right hand, to slip the loaded dice in his left into the dice-box and set it on the table. He withdrew his right hand, casually slipping it in his pocket.

'Were you going somewhere, Will?' asked Robertson.

'I'll give you no such luck, when you're still ahead. Ye know fine that I wouldna leave now!'

Robertson, a dour man normally, smiled bleakly.

'On we go then.'

They were however interrupted by Smith again, who stalked over from where he had been warming his legs by the fire.

'I'll ask you once again before you get started. Are you coming or not?'

'Not now, George. Give me time.'

Smith shook his head disparagingly and, watched by Clark, proceeded to hover between the table and the fireplace. Robertson looked at Brodie, and with a slight inclination of his head in Smith's direction, asked in a low voice,

'What's the matter with your English friend? He's not so happy.'

'Ach, it's a nonsense. He gets worked up.'

The game continued. Now that he had his 'despatchers', Brodie was 'nicking' as they called it, or winning on most of his calls. He began to take in money steadily from both Robertson and Bell. Clark, leaning against the chimney mantel, saw what was happening and knew too well why. It was being done skilfully however, and if he kept to it in that way, there was no reason why Brodie should be suspected. At at least four of the eight tables being played at the moment, he could see false dice in use. Smith came and stood beside him with his back to the fire, drinking and glaring with increasing anger at Brodie. Smith was on edge. He was thinking that this confirmed all his earlier worst fears. They had a rich crib to pick, it was all set, the key was in his pocket, and this gambling fool, this sham, this amateur would throw the lot away for thirty guineas. He found himself questioning what the man wanted. Was it the thrill of the thing, that he seemed to get, or the money. Smith wondered if he got any thrill out of it, and decided he only got fear. But to Brodie it all seemed to be the same—just a gamble. If he wanted proof, here it was. To this gentleman fancy there was no difference between cracking a crib and a game of wild dice. As though reading his thoughts, Clark remarked,

'You won't get him away from that now. Bide your time.'

'For how long?'

Clark shrugged. He puffed out a thin jet of smoke. Smith suddenly felt very angry again, but realised he must control it. They could not afford to attract attention. He could not give to his demands to Brodie the proper urgency they deserved, he could not remind him of the preparation and planning. He strolled over again, trying to appear casual, pot in hand.

'What about it now, Will? Are you coming?'

'Not yet. Look! What a bonny pile o' coins o' the realm that is.'

'But we have to go.'

Brodie looked up with a sudden flash of anger.

'I am not going now. What sort o' a sportsman would these gentlemen think I was if I didna give them the opportunity tae redress some wee parcel o' their losses? I can hardly leave with my pockets this full and no' give them the chance o' combat. Is that not so, gentlemen?'

Both Robertson and Bell had reached the stage in losing where it was unthinkable to retreat. They would risk their last guineas for the slender chance of winning back their losses. Brodie's offer seemed perfectly honourable to them. They nodded and agreed with a grateful solemnity which should have cheered Brodie's heart. This made Smith momentarily lose control and flare up.

'All right, I'll go alone!'

Brodie completely ignored this, realising that it was the sort of remark which might be remembered and should therefore be treated as of no consequence. He felt suddenly that he was a man beset. There was Dickson with his innuendoes, Young and Trotter, or Hill with their ambitions. He thought of Jean Watt and Ann Grant and all the women that were continually clamouring, however gently, however lovingly around him. He thought of Rab Smith, foreman, and of the Town Council; of customers and orders, timber, lint, veneer, shellac, gum arabic and glue. He was a man with too many mansions. He felt under pressure, and he was afraid. He was caught in the snares of his own duplicity. Life had acquired a momentum which he was no longer able to control. It was the last straw that Burns should be staying at Bruce's house. It was almost as though it had been ordained.

'On we go then,' said Robertson impatiently. Brodie realised he had fallen silent and that they were waiting. Brodie called his number, and skilfully rolled the dice. The number came up. It was automatic. He could cheat without thinking. But he could not go through with the robbery of Bruce. The rake-hell thrill had entirely gone out of it. His private life, that made such a mockery of his public image, no longer seemed to afford him any amusement. Burns had talked of freedom and equality. He admitted that his freedom often ran to licence, but this was no more or less than the true expression of the man. Brodie reflected that he might be drunk, but he was certainly depressed. His own activities seemed tonight to be a hollow jape. To Smith it was only a crime—had no other meaning. Smith had no conceits. Brodie thought, I am a juggler who has raised too many clubs in the air, and do not know how to bring them down without dropping them. I can merely keep them going. Mouths must be fed, backs must be clothed, jobs must be maintained, a style of living must be preserved. I have raised a structure that is too complex, but I dare not let any one part go, for that part may destroy it all by exposing me.

The dice came round to him again as caster and he played them, not 'nicking' but throwing a chance. The stakes went up. He threw once and missed without losing, he threw twice and the same thing happened. He threw a third time and threw his chance. Bell, who was banker, swore. Brodie raked in the winnings and the game went on and on.

Smith waited and watched, judging the passage of time by the candle. When it guttered down to a waxen pool, only to be replaced by the lad with another, he made up his mind. He looked at the watch in his pocket. It was nearly four!

'I'm off, Will. It's four in the morning. I can't wait any more. Are you coming?'

'Presently, presently.' Brodie sounded abstracted, as though he scarcely noticed Smith. But he had heard. Nearly four, he was thinking, but God the time flies, and drinking and gambling stop those thoughts from intruding that you would rather not have. He had lost a little and won a lot more and was still gaining. He hardly noticed Smith going out the door, because he did not want to notice. He wanted the man to slip away out of his conscience.

Outside, the coming day promised to be clear and cold. The stars were beginning to fade and there was a perceptible lightening of the darkness along the jumbled gables. A subtle change, just enough to cause a reflex in the optic nerve. Smith soundly cursed Brodie for wasting his time. He would have to hurry, for in an hour there would be stirrings in the town. Early workers would be opening their doors, blowing on their hands and watching the white gusts of their breath. Smith was concerned lest Ainslie should try to follow him, and quickly doubled and re-doubled two closes, stopping only when he was sure he was alone. The effort had made him puff, and the frosty air caught at the back of his throat, trying to make him cough. He pulled his coat around his neck and tucked his chin down. God it was cold! The streets and wynds were deserted at this hour, which made it more dangerous than ever, as he would be more conspicuous. Far off in the Grassmarket he could hear the sound of horses' hoofs and the calling of voices. The carriers would be up and about, some on their way. Sound travelled far on a frosty night. He must take care.

Bruce's shop was at the head of Bridge Street, and exposed as a result. Fortunately the doorway was set back, affording cover and shelter from the wind that thrashed round the corner. Smith approached the shop very slowly, setting his feet down deliberately and with care. At this moment he was glad to be without Brodie, who would probably have insisted in striding straight up to the door. Brodie's bold manner quite simply scared him. And as for his behaviour tonight! Slipping into the doorway, he pulled the crêpe mask out of his pocket and put it on. Then he carefully took out a bundle of false keys, wrapped in a wad of cloth to stop them clinking. They seemed to chime like bells as he tried them one by one in the lock, and he paused, heart beating. The fourth key did the job. He felt the wards move, and eased it open. Taking out the keys, he slipped inside. He immediately took a wooden wedge from his coat pocket which he slipped under the door on the inside. The door was firmly shut. Next he took out Brodie's dark-lantern, which he lit. He paused, listening, giving his eyes time to adjust. There were no sounds from above.

All the brothers Bruce's goods seemed to be below or behind glass. When he slipped back the lantern shutter, he had to slide it back again quickly, because the room flashed and shone with multiple images. The counter top was formed of three glass show-cases lined with velvet. Behind the window was a similar case. The walls were lined with glass-fronted cabinets. He reduced the lantern light to a slit as thin as a playing card, and investigated these. The cabinets were locked securely, and he was afraid that an attempt to force them might break the glass. He needed a cutter, but did not have one. The show-cases on the other hand proved to be easy. They were fastened by an ill-concealed 'secret' snib. Smith shone the lantern inside the counter cases. The thin pencil of light danced off gold and silver watches. The case behind the window contained rings, seals, some lockets and chains, brooches and more watches. This was good. He pulled two old black stockings from his pocket, and filled them cautiously, slipping them in as though placing eggs in a bag. He moved quickly but without any appearance of haste. In under ten minutes the show-cases were emptied, and he tied up the stockings and then tied the legs around his belt. Taking another quick look at the wall cabinets, he saw that the drawers inside were labelled in fading ink. He could read 'Brooches', 'Chains-gold', 'Buckles-Men's silver', 'Orders'. There was much more there, but not only did he not have the tools, there was no time. He blew out the lantern, having selected the correct key, and removed the wedge from the door. He listened and, when he was sure that it was still silent, he opened it carefully and stepped out. He was shocked by the gathering light. He could clearly see his hands. He locked the door behind him as best he could, his hands shaking a little now with nervousness. He was very exposed. It seemed to take minutes to shoot the lock back, but it only took seconds in fact, and then he was off, walking carefully along to the first Close then doubling through on himself. In the Close he stripped off the mask and hid it in his pocket. Within a few minutes he was walking in the Grassmarket. Here, to his relief, people were about, and seeing to their business. No one gave him more than a passing glance. Horses stamped to keep themselves warm. Shaggy ponies, carrying impossibly large panniers, dozed as they stood, impervious to all conditions. Highland carriers, armed like brigands, burst into spates and torrents of Gaelic, laughed, clapped each other on the back and passed a bottle. Border men cursed and muttered, trying to fix straps with numb fingers. It seemed to Smith that no one had told the Highlanders that it was cold, because they did not seem to notice. Some of them stood squarely in bare feet on the frost-white cobbles. It made him shiver. He went round the back of Henderson's stables, where some of Henderson's men were warming themselves at a fire. They nodded to him, knowing his face, and he nodded back. At the rear, adjoining the cock-pit barn was an outbuilding, unused for many years, but still littered with decaying straw. In one corner was a worm-eaten wooden manger, caked with flakes of oat-husk. He untied the two stockings and thrust them under the manger, stuffing straw in on top of them and spreading it about so as to hide the disturbance. Satisfied with the hiding-place, he walked out again, and made for home.

At Clark's, mid-day or dawn had no effect. The lad, red-eyed and weary, was dozing on a stool against the chimney-breast. Almost everyone had left except Brodie and his party. Clark had conceded the lateness of the hour, by straddling a chair so that he could lean his arms over the back and support his pipe. He had intended turning Brodie out long ago, but there was something about his performance tonight that fascinated him. He had seen Brodie in the madness of gambling fever often enough, but never quite like this. It was as though he was playing for his soul.

Bell and Robertson had lost all they carried and now stood watching with a small group of three others that included Ainslie. They only remained in the pious hope that Will Brodie would get what he deserved at the hands of his present companion.

Will was now playing with a corn-merchant named Weir, a habitual gambler, ardent as himself. Weir was a man who backed horses, played cards and kept cocks. Also, to Brodie's certain knowledge, he kept at least one other bedfellow beside his wife. The man was skilled, quick, rich and shrewd, but he had no standing in Edinburgh because of the vulgarity of his manners. He belonged to no Guild and no Lodge. However Weir knew the odds at a gaming table, but suffered from a gross impediment—he did not know how to cheat.

Weir was becoming increasingly furious with the wayward fall of the dice. He had worked it out, and it seemed to him impossible in the run of chance, that he should be so consistently unlucky and Brodie so consistently right.

Brodie was cheating without subtlety. To Clark it seemed he wanted to be caught. Even that he was putting on a display, in the hope of recognition. He had never seen anything like it. Brodie normally let his man win every third throw, then every other, then every third, so that he gained steadily but only over a time. He was treating Weir as he had treated Bell, with an expert contempt, ringing the changes like an illusionist running through his repertoire. There was neither subtlety nor cunning in it. It was not expert gaming, it was an intemperate and rash display. It was insulting in its audacity. Clark was alarmed at what would come of it. Robertson and Bell would make nothing of it, but Weir matched Brodie in skill.

'Brodie, you have bewitched these things,' Weir growled, as he threw again and lost. His face was becoming increasingly sullen. He was accustomed to winning some and losing some, but not to this steady rapacious decline.

'Skill,' said Brodie, slightly slurred, 'skill and application and love. They are like women. They need all these to bring out the best in them.'

'They're bedevilled,' Weir said rudely, dismissing all this soft talk. 'Or their damned funny dice!'

'What are you saying, Weir?' Brodie's voice was hard and humourless. 'I hear a loser talking.'

'Gentlemen,' Clark interrupted, 'allow me to get you both a drink to refresh yourselves. It sweetens the mind and the tongue.'

'I want no drink,' said Weir. 'I ken plenty of inn-keepers who mak' it their job tae befuddle the mind. I hope that's not your intention, Mr Clark!'

Clark stood up, dangerously silent.

'Sit down, Weir,' said Brodie, realising the danger at long last. 'We'll change the dice. That's a fair offer. You choose some other pair.'

'Aye but!' exclaimed Weir. 'I want tae see these yins.'

'Is that an accusation?' shouted Brodie.

'Aye but it is!' Weir declared. He grabbed out at the dice box and turned them out on to his hand. 'Light another candle. I want tae see these closer.'

He examined them by candlelight. They glowed along the edges with a thick translucency.

'By God! They're loaded!' he shouted. 'You're a thieving cheat Brodie!'

Roaring like an angry bear he lunged at Brodie, shoving him in the chest. Brodie flew over backwards, taking the bench, candle, bottles, glasses and table with him in a tremendous crash. Almost simultaneously, Clark seemed to spring from his chair like a frog, and hit Weir on the jaw. Weir staggered backwards and collapsed. Clark went over as though to examine him, and quietly took hold of the dice. Ainslie and Robertson were trying to haul up Brodie. Clark, unseen, threw the loaded dice in the fire.

'Get some water,' Clark shouted to the startled lad, who was watching it all wide-eyed, 'and get a cloth.' Clark pushed the others back and helped Brodie on to a chair, where the full damage could be seen. Going down in a heap with the pots and bottles, he had a gash under the right eye which bled copiously down his cheek, dripping off the end of his chin. On Brodie's face was an enigmatic smile.

Clark shouted at Bell and Robertson.

'Are you satisfied now? See what you've done to Mr Brodie. Pray God he doesna' prefer charges on all o' ye! See to that thing Weir over there!'

During this diversion, and while stooping over Brodie, he removed the good dice from Brodie's coat pocket. He then set about righting the table and bench, and replaced the dice with the unbroken pots. 'Right, Will?' he hissed. Brodie nodded and smiled. The lad ran in with a bowl and soft linen, and Clark set about washing Brodie's face. He gave the cloth to Brodie to hold on the wound, then went over to where Weir was getting to his feet aided by the others.

'Weir, ye can either come ower here and see for yourself, or I will throw you oot on the street wi' the greatest o' pleasure!' he bellowed at the semi-conscious man. 'Set him at the table. Robertson, you and Bell do me the honour o' examining they dice tae see what in the name o' the devil is supposed to be wrang wi' them.'

Weir was dumped on the bench where he held his head in his hands. Clark kept up the pressure.

'Bring a candle. Bring twa. I ask you, gentlemen, examine they dice! I won't have things like that said in ma' house. If ye have charges tae make, then make them! If ye havena, then out.' He gestured to the door with his thumb. 'I have nae truck wi' bad losers. Weir, you never enter here again!'

Bell and Robertson were examining them by candlelight, and shaking their heads.

'When you're satisfied, tak' your friend and go.'

'He's no friend of ours,' Robertson volunteered.

'Aye, that's as maybe. Will you lay a charge, Mr Brodie, for this insult and injury and defamation o' character? This scunner Weir shouldna' be allowed to play. A ban on him an' his like!' Poor Weir groaned and shook his head. Nobody gave him a cloth to wipe the blood that ran down from a split lip.

'I'm closing the place tae give Mr Brodie attention. Now get him out.'

Weir, still half-drunk and bemused, was supported out by Bell and Robertson. They were telling him he had made a mistake, he had best go home. They asked him where he lived and, receiving a muttered reply, set off like scolded schoolboys. Clark packed Ainslie and the others off after them. When he and the lad were alone with Brodie he sat down in front of him.

'That's the last time I do that for you, Will. Yon was lunatic. What devil got into ye? A bairn could have managed things better.' He alternately scolded Brodie, and pressed at the cut to try to staunch the bleeding. Brodie had begun to shiver with reaction. He hated and feared the thought of personal injury, and now it had happened. It terrified him. The massacre of two fighting cocks was like setting two men-of-war in the Forth. He was a merchantman, helpless in such things and skilled in others. It was a waste of him. The thought of his injury made him feel sick. He had never been hurt before.

'How bad is it, John?' He knew his voice was trembling. His stomach was heaving.

'It's not so bad,' said Clark cautiously.

'But will I be marked?' Brodie's voice was that of a small child. It shocked Clark, who realised for the first time that he was dealing with a crustacean with a thin shell. He felt involuntary contempt.

'I'm afraid you will. I'd be no friend to deny it.'

Brodie was sick, quite suddenly. Clark sprang back as he vomited.

'Ach man, watch yoursel! You'll be in an awfu' state.' His upper clothes were drenched with blood. The cut, being on his cheek bone under the eye, bled out of all proportion to its size. His cravat, waistcoat and coat were soaked. Clark told the lad to get another cloth and a bucket to clean up.

'I'll get you home, Will. This'll keep you from the tables for a stretch, and the way you were carrying on, there can be no harm in that. You'll be bandaged up, and one-eyed for a bit. I tell you, Will, in the kindest way, you have been taking risks that frighten me. What gets intae ye? You're a man o' skill and performance. What for do ye behave like that? A wean wouldna' be deceived!'

Brodie said nothing. He was thinking that he was tired of the whole thing. He felt flat and miserable. This was the anti-climax. The joy had gone out of it. When he carried pistols, he carried them for show, he never intended to use them. He had never done any human being an injury to his person. There was no skill or craft in this barbarity. There was no dash or cunning in it, nor any pride to be had. It was nothing but sordid to be knocked down by a chandler. He knew his own physical weakness, and wanted to hide away, nursing this new deformity. He wished that he could turn time back and undo it.

'What can I do?' he asked Clark, as though Clark might have some magic suggestion or some potion that he could rub on the gash to make it disappear. His voice was the same small voice of a hurt child.

'Go home,' Clark responded roughly, 'and get your sister tae patch you up. She's a handy woman, and will make a good job o' you. Make up a good story, and stay away from the tables. That's my advice. Wait for your sanity tae return!'

These blunt words had the desired effect. Brodie pulled himself to his feet with Clark's assistance, and cleaned himself as best he could. To his disgust he smelled terrible now as well. The lad went about his unpleasant task quite cheerfully. He was accustomed to it.

'Look at me!' Brodie exclaimed. 'I canna' go about the streets like this!'

'I'm afraid you'll have to, Will. There's no choice.'

'Get me a chair?'

'I'll dae that for ye.'

Brodie jolted home in a sedan with the curtains drawn. The two Highlanders who carried it laughed and joked with each other all the way. Brodie could not understand a word of it but suspected it was about him. In his misery he vowed to apply himself to the business, and throw over this whole monstrous existence that pressed on him like an invasion of his soul. But even as he made his vows, he knew it could not be done. He was in too far.

Jean Brodie's reaction to Will's five o'clock arrival was entirely predictable. Alarm was followed by anger. She scolded and raged at him but nonetheless got the maid to boil water on a new fire and produced linen strips for bandages. Brodie took off his ruined and reeking clothes and was washed and his wound bound up. He told Jean that he had been assaulted by a bad loser. This received scant sympathy.

'You can't have that sort of story put about,' she declared firmly, 'you'll bring us all and the firm into disgrace. I always knew it! Your father knew it! There's a wild gambling streak in you. You should be ashamed to have the Brodie name involved in a thing like that. You were hit in the face by an end of timber in the yard, that's what you will say!' Shocked by her own sudden mendacity she added, 'It happens, doesn't it?'

It was a good story, and simple. He was eventually put to

bed after many earnest promises to devote more time to the business. He would sit down with Rab Smith tomorrow and they would go through the orders together. He would confirm all those orders he had been given by word of mouth that he had never bothered to pursue. He would get out the tool box and clear himself a space. Jean felt that there was hope yet. Cousin Milton, a humourless lawyer who had formed his own poor opinion of the shape of the business, despite his tender years, had said they would be out of business in a twelvemonth. Jean would prove him wrong. She supposed this disgraceful business was a blessing in disguise, and prayed devoutly that night to God for being so good to her in showing her brother the right path and making sure he walked it. Ann Grant, who was already wakened by the crying of the smallest child, wondered where Will had got to. He had not called for days. Jean Watt was fast losing patience with a sleepy butcher whom she was trying to get out before dawn. He kept dropping his boots and complaining that he was tired and wanted to go back to bed. She knew he had no intention of sleep. She was taking a chance, but why had Will deserted her like this? The devil deserved it! She gave up and let the butcher stay. He was a grateful sort of a man.

George Smith turned up at Brodie's Close at eight in the morning. He had gone home but had not been to bed. He was not sure whether he was excited, or meant to have it out with Brodie, but would decide that when he saw him. Mary Smith had made no bones about it and had tried to dissuade him from going at all.

The Brodies' maid answered the door, telling him to keep his voice down as the master was still in bed and was not well. Smith, put out, left a message with the girl in equally frosty tones, saying that when the master felt well enough, he might bother himself sufficiently to call on Mr Smith where he would see that his business had prospered.

When Brodie finally arrived at Smith's house at about two in the afternoon, Smith did not at first recognise him, and when he did he tactlessly roared with laughter. Brodie flushed angrily.

'Good God, Will, what happened to you!' Much of the anger went out of him at the sight of the bandaged man carrying the hat he could not wear. The whole of the right side of Brodie's face was a mottled yellow and green, turning to black. The bandaging covered the whole of his right eye and cheek, so that Brodie had to turn his head this way and that to see.

'I was hit in the face by an end of wood.'

Smith roared again.

'Who was holding the end!'

Brodie turned on his heel, and would have left, but Smith called out.

'I'm sorry, Will. No offence!'

Then Brodie told the whole story, watched the whole time by Mary Smith, who stared at him with her vacant eyes. Smith then went on to tell of his success. Mary Smith interrupted, 'I don't see it's any business of his!'

Smith paused.

'Will, you weren't with me last night. It was part of our bargain. But in view of what happened I'm prepared to let you have some things of your choice. Not half, but some things. I did it all on my own.'

To Smith's surprise, Brodie readily agreed, and Smith went to the stables to recover the stockings. Brodie sat silently, regarded by Mary Smith with considerable hostility.

'You'll get my George into trouble, you will,' she said. Brodie did not deign to reply.

Smith returned quickly, carrying the stockings under his coat. He pulled them out triumphantly, holding them aloft.

'Look! Blunt sausage!'

He untied them and tipped the contents on to the bed. Mary Smith sprang over them like a harpy, but Brodie's reactions seemed disappointingly dulled. He kept rubbing at the bandage on his cheek.

'Watches, rings, seals, lockets and chains! They must be worth, I calculated, about three hundred and fifty!'

Mary Smith was handling them all, one by one, her eyes quite bright.

'And that's not all,' Smith continued, his heavy-browed face for once lively and excited, 'there are drawers of buckles and brooches. Gems for all I know. I didn't break them. Although I could have done if there had been the two of us!' he added reproachfully. 'However, we can go back and sweep it clean. I locked up with no trouble. They'll never know it was done.'

Brodie was looking at the haul.

'Aye, I agree, it must be worth three fifty. A good haul.'

'I reckon there's more than that in there. Wait until next time.'

'Not for me, George. No next time.'

'What!' Smith was angry and incredulous.

'I'm a marked man. Really. Look at me. How can I go about the place like this. There's too much attention attracted to me already. I would do well to lie low.'

'But just tonight.'

'Everyone in Edinburgh knows I'm bandaged.'

'The mask will cover it.'

'You know it won't.'

They spent almost an hour arguing. Smith insisted time and again that they should return and Brodie demurred. They even went out for a stroll in the biting air to look at the shop and see if it was being watched. There was no sign of anyone, and the lock looked undisturbed. Still Brodie swore he would not go, and Smith swore he would not take the risk alone a second time. They walked back to Smith's apartments in a blinding red sunset. Brodie selected only token items from the collection—a watch-key set with garnets, a gold seal and two gold rings. Smith even found himself offering Brodie more, saying that he had set it up and was entitled to it, while Mary Smith dragged at his arm and yelled at him that he was a damned flat and mad benedict to give money to this leary bloak. With their friendship just intact, mainly due to Mary Smith's antagonism, they parted. Brodie stopped at the door and clapped Smith on the back.

'You're a good fellow, Smith. I know you can't help your wife in there. She gets ower excitable at times. Ye do understand, I can do nothing until my damned eye is healed.'

'Aye, but we'll keep in touch, won't we?'

'We will.'

Smith looked after Brodie, shaking his head to himself. There had been little conviction in the reply. An amateur after all.

* * *

Edinburgh Evening Courant, 1786.

A SHOP BROKE.
Sheriff Clerk's Office, Edinburgh.
Dec. 28, 1786.

Between Sunday night and Monday morning last, a Hardware Shop here was broke into, and the following articles carried off:— A lady's gold watch, enamelled back, figure offering up a gift to Hymen—A large plain gold watch, caped and jewelled —A small secondhand gold watch; maker's name of these three J. J. Jackson, London—One small single cased watch, maker's name Innes—Two silver watches, name Armstrong—Several gold rings, breast pins, and lockits, plain and set round with pearl for hair devices—A few pairs set knee and shoe buckles —Two lancet cases full of lancets, maker's name Lavignie— All the rings, breastpins, lockits, and set buckles, are marked, in the underside with a sharp nail, the initials of the shop mark, and the selling price plain figures; so that if any attempt is made to erase any of these marks, it will easily be noticed.

Whoever will give such information, within three months

from this date, to William Scott, procurator-fiscal of this County, as shall lead to a discovery of the person or persons who committed the above theft, shall, upon conviction of the offender or offenders, receive a reward of TWENTY GUINEAS, and the informer's name, if required, concealed.

WILLIAM SCOTT, Proc. Fiscal.

N.B. If any of the above articles are offered to sale, it is requested they may be stopped, and the person offering them detained till notice is given as above, for which a handsome reward will be given, beside all charges paid.

CHAPTER SEVEN

Edinburgh, 1787. The new year

The new year had seemed reluctant to emerge from its frozen placenta of ice. The scavengers had given up their jobs, as the rubbish froze solid where it lay, discolouring the whitened streets. They had chipped the steps of public buildings clear, only to return the next morning to do the same again. People complained about shortages of everything, and unknown to them, in the Highlands, thousands died.

There had been little fuel, food was short and unvaried, travel was impossible. Several respected and elderly citizens were laid prematurely in the ground from falling over on the icy cobbles. The grave-diggers had been paid double wages and a gallon of whisky to chip their way to a respectable depth through the frozen ground.

The spring of the year had attempted to make a showing but was blighted by fierce frosts that turned petals into brown paper and stamens into bristle. Further north, trees exploded like cannon. The undertakers did a brisk job in the poorer houses of the 'lands', and the manhandling of coffins on ropes became a daily show, eagerly attended. However, this year, not one was dropped. The castle rock turned itself into a magical ice-berg which shone in the weak sun that had no more warmth than moonlight. In the Highlands, thousands more died, and bands roamed the country, digging for nettles and heather shoots under the snow. Edinburgh knew nothing of them. Work virtually ceased on the New Town. The workmen, with blue hands, became clumsy. Accidents were commonplace, but there was an ample supply of replacement labourers. The newspapers in the spring talked of an Anglo-Prussian alliance to stem the influence of France over Holland, but like the Government it all seemed too far away to be relevant. What was more important, that spring, was that the fishing boats from Newhaven, Mussleburgh and Fife could not put out for the weather.

Walking to and from taverns and clubs became a matter for mountaineers who could be seen scaling the High Street by means of pillars and doorways. It was said that Bailie Shaw (who never drank, as he often stated) slipped right down the West Bow, without touching the sides.

Whatever else had been short in the sour cold of the early year, the supply of alcohol had never faltered. Ladies were heard to say they had been forced to it, for they could not obtain their tea. Barrels had to be rolled by hand up the streets, causing consternation as they racketed about like curling stones. Brodie applied himself to business, for men were eager to work.

The year dissolved lazily, and last year's mess defrosted. By May the town had become filthy and sodden again, and the castle rock had returned to its glistening-wet black. The smells returned. By July the weather was alternately wet and scorching. It made more good trade for the undertakers and the earth was loamy and soft for them. The New Town was springing up with astonishing vigour, the stripped land beyond the old loch cut into swathes of yellow and brown mud. Brodie was getting a good deal of work.

He lay on his back with an arm around Ann Grant. She was pressed close to him, sleepy and warm. He had heard the Tron bell strike six and knew he ought really to be up, but he felt lazy and enjoyed the feel of her breasts on his chest. The bristle of her mound of Venus scratched softly against his thigh, but it did not excite him. They were both replete. Her breasts, Brodie thought, were far from perfect, had become full and pendulous. But she was a woman he could relax with and this was a quality he cherished. She took him in simply, like a hungry man who needed to be fed, without coquetry, shyness or play. She welcomed him and needed him. That damned whore Jean Watt must make a performance of it, as though to prove her youth. Her latest trick was to run round the room in a shift squealing and shouting, 'Catch me! Catch me!' He had no time for it. Then when he caught her she pretended to struggle and scratch. He had not asked for all that, and hit her for scratching. He needed no more marks. He wondered who had asked for the performance. He also felt that she found him boring. With Ann, on the other hand, it was like coming home. Jean, he noticed, had taken to putting rouge on her nipples.

The cut under his eye had completely healed now, but it had inevitably left a scar. He had, as he vowed, devoted himself to the business for seven solid and respectable months until even Jean, Cousin Milton and Rab Smith the foreman approved of him. He still played the tables at dice and cards. He could not help that, and he had tried. It was a compulsion as necessary to him as drawing breath. But he played mainly with Smith and Ainslie, and then for small stakes. He wished to attract no attention. The whole Town Council had expressed their commiseration at the injury to his eye, hoping it would not impair his excellent work. It had, he thought, if they only knew it. There had been no robberies by breaking and entering in the Town, since the raid on the brothers Bruce.

The enigmatic Mr Brown, who had seemed a promising recruit in those days now past, had left for Stirling in a hurry, saying the hounds were on his heels. True enough, two Messengers from London had arrived within days, asking for his whereabouts. Now they had returned, unsuccessful.

I am, he thought, the very model of respect again. I am hailed in every street and shop. I have joined them in hypocrisy, and I am welcomed into that brotherhood of corporation-packing, conceited rogues that feel fit to pass judgement on their fellow men. Burns had burned out Edinburgh like a consuming fire and left it, but Brodie remembered. Freedom, he had said, was like a mounting lark in a May morning. Men net larks in France for their tongues. Ann stirred, and woke. She did not move, but he could tell by her breathing.

'Are ye awake, Ann?'

'Yes,' she rubbed herself against him, 'and comfortable.'

'Am I the very model, the paragon o' respectability that I seem to myself?'

'You know what I think. A body is what they think they are. The rest o' the world can go hang.'

'Then I think that I am the biggest hypocrite in Edinburgh.'

'Oh Will, Will! Dinna' flatter yoursel'. Ye dinna' even signify.'

'Aye, but I dae. Because I am pretending tae be what I'm no' and they are revealing all the time what they are. I can't stay with it, Ann. This trade is the devil, it bores me. Now, makin' things, I enjoy. But I can't keep shop. And where does it lead a man to be able to say that he has made of his life, thirty dozen beech chairs and as many of elm, twenty mahogany tables or as many beds. My life is devoted to the support o' the human arse and elbows with the occasional hoch-magandy!'

'You were never averse tae that!'

'No, but I'll no' support another's!'

'It pays you well, and that suits me fine. It suits you too for all your moanin' for you've bought a fine new set of cocks, and have them in the yard.'

'Who told you that?'

'I should think half of the Town knows. They're waiting for the main.'

'I'm not ready for it. They'll need to wait some more.'

'Don't be cross, Will. Ye can't fool me, I know ye too well. Ye've given nothing up. It's lying low like a hare. All this act may fool a town, but it'll not be fooling me. Come on, ma' wee mannie, share your problems with Ann, afore ye go ...'

'I must get down to the yard. Leave off of me, lass ...'
'Protest ye may, but by the feel of you it's a' lies again!'
'I must go. I'm a respected citizen. I must be at my work!'
'Ye can't keep your true nature down, but!'

Ainslie had been having a lean time, and he was not well. A terrible thick cold had turned into a chest infection that inhibited his breathing so that he wheezed like a man sawing wood. He wore a ragged and dirty coat and looked no different from any other of the loungers, paupers, thieves and wharf-rats that attended the docking of a well-found ship at Leith. The Quay was busy with pack-horses and waggons. Rich men—owners, shippers and merchants—came and went in carriages. Lesser men arrived in sedans, with bearers too exhausted to speak. Even their deformed legs could not take the long carry from Edinburgh. Ainslie pulled the coat about him and rubbed his hands together to preserve some feeling. The bitter salty winds buffeted in from the Forth, frisking the puddles of seawater. A slithering horse clattered and fell, amidst sparks from its hooves. In the midst of this diversion Ainslie worked ever nearer the ship.

He had not heard anything from Bruce's shop, and he was almost certain that Brodie and Smith had robbed it. However, he had never been able to prove it. Smith simply denied it and Brodie treated it as a joke, nudging Smith and saying, 'Not me, Ainslie, not me!' He had lived off meagre pickings, dog's scraps for a minor thief. He had lifted a bundle of leaf tobacco, a barrel of brandy from a cart. He had 'eased' a watch from a sailor who stood unconscious against a wall. He had taken one good purse, and one alone, in that whole time. The wind was cracking his bones.

Sauntering to a waggon, he leaned on the tail-board and watched the *Meg* unloading tea. The air smelled of it. Orange pekoe, congou, souchong, hyson, bohea, imperial and caper. The merchants strolled and puffed pipes, dipped their hands into chests and inhaled, making wise faces and nodding or shaking their heads. To Ainslie, the names meant nothing. Tea was either black or green, and it sold for over seven shillings a pound. The good Lord had sent in a ship of it.

He watched the boxes swung ashore, in nets from spar tackle. The consignments were separated out on the quayside and Ainslie could read the names stencilled on the sides of the boxes and hessian bales. By far the biggest weight was for Carnegie, Grocer, Leith. John Carnegie, who kept a shop at the bottom end of St. Andrew Street, no more than a minute's walk from the quay, and who lived way up in the Town, safe from the German winds.

Ainslie had never dealt with tea before, but if a man could carry off seventy pounds or so of it, then it would be worth over twenty pounds sterling. 'Bitch', the fancy called it, after the delightful use the ladies put it to. It could easily be had from Carnegie's shop, and in quantity too. He knew Smith was tired of his prolonged idleness and, of course, Smith had a grocer's shop! If they could do it together there could be no better idea. He needed Smith, for he was weak and knew it. Even walking fast made him gasp. He sawed and rasped his way back up the long climb to Edinburgh. Both of his boot soles had gone, and he had stuffed them with hay. It hardly kept out the cold of the cobblestones.

Brodie could not be counted upon. Ainslie had watched the man recover from his eye injury and at the same time grow in respectability as a tree puts on leaf. He was industrious, he drank and gamed and gambled, but he kept his distance. You could always tell, Ainslie thought, by the mode of these dignitaries' address. They called him Deacon now, not Mr Brodie. It was a sign of his standing. He had lost it last year, but he had it back again. They would soon be calling him Bailie, or so the whisper said. Then after that it would only be a matter of time.

Smith was as enthusiastic about the project as Ainslie had

imagined he would be. He proposed that they should waste no time, but should go out that night, and he made Ainslie see the reason of his argument. The tea would have been hastily checked on arrival, and stored. In a day or two, or even on the next day, it would be split into smaller consignments and distributed. They must get at it in quantity. Furthermore, due to the lateness of the *Meg*'s arrival and the time taken in unloading and checking against her manifest, the tea had not arrived in Carnegie's storehouse until late and no special provisions would have been made for its security. Ainslie had cautiously examined the door from a distance on his way back, and seen that it carried both a padlock and a stock-lock. The stock-lock was big and looked old, even from where he stood. The padlock would present more of a problem, but both would be susceptible to a 'tickling' from a pick-lock. The two of them were pleased with the idea, and Smith showed Ainslie his collection of pick-locks, pointing out the ones for the job, and explaining the workings of the wards. Then they set off for Clark's to brace themselves with a bottle. The wind had dropped and the August air had lost its sharp edge. Nevertheless Ainslie started coughing.

'You'll have to get rid of that, Andy,' said Smith, giving him a thump on the back that only made matters worse. When he had recovered, Ainslie, his eyes watering, asked the question that had been bothering him.

'Are you going to tell Brodie?'

During the early months of the year, a greater familiarity had grown up between the two men, mainly from Brodie's abstraction, and the earlier hours he kept.

'I don't know,' replied Smith. 'He may not even want to know—you've seen how he's been. But I'll tell you one thing, we won't let it stop us!'

'He's become ower fancy for my poor taste. Just a wee patter flash dandy. No! I like the man, don't misunderstand me. But I like the kind o' cat that is consistent in where it loups.'

'It does us no harm to have a fancy friend.'

'Maybe for you, but it makes me poor!' said Ainslie with satyrical vehemence. 'About what you and he have been up to, I ken nothin', except there's been no part in it for me. And now I'm skint for sure.' He coughed and hawked violently, as though to give it dramatic emphasis. His illness was abundantly real to Smith. 'I'm reduced tae robbin' poor jack tars who have already been dispossessed o' the rest of their possessions by unscrupulous persons who leave me nothin' but a steel watch. Is that not terrible! I call that uncharitable. Tae prop a defenceless man against a wa' wi' nothin' on him but a watch. A less compassionate man might hae just tupped him intae the sea!' Ainslie laughed drily, and started coughing again.

'Where can I take you?' said Smith. 'With a hawk like that we're not safe in a graveyard.'

'I'm all right. I just need the sustenance, ye ken. That watch and a purse wi' some silver. It's no' much tae keep out the cauld, and put fat on me. Nor buy a decent coat nor boots wi' real leather below. I'm a battered ship. I'm getting short o' drinkin' money, and what sort of life is it for a man like me, havin' tae be seen cheatin' at cairds!'

Smith laughed. There was a clownish streak about the man that amused him.

'Ye can afford tae laugh,' Ainslie continued, stopping at a corner to wheeze for breath, 'but cheating at the cairds is a poor living, especially at Clark's. The place is that full o' jiggered dice and brief cards there's no' a natural game going. Now how's a man tae live like that!'

Smith held up a hand in protest, and they walked on again.

'All right, I've said we'll do it.'

'But what about Brodie? Do we need tae bring him in? Look at the times we've suggested things. The man's right off it—and he can afford tae be. It's a third less for you and me.'

'Now that's not sensible, Andrew. You don't use your head.

The more we carry the more we make. It's bulk that counts.'

Ainslie was silent for a minute as they walked up the High Street. The sun was low and golden. The pantiles looked on fire. The sky was clear and Venus twinkled in the fading blue.

'Yes, you're right.'

'And it still does us no harm to keep things up with him. Neither you nor I, Andy, will reach his station in life and he has very powerful friends. The ones we don't see, the ones that give him the jobs—the lawyers and publishers and literary creatures and even judges. Now no harm ever came of a criminal man being on port-bibbing terms with a judge! The Town, Andy, has a blind eye for its own. They won't see what they don't want to. But you and I are visible. Brodie provides the cloak.'

Ainslie knew it was all true, but elaborated on the fact that it was all right for a rich amateur to stop and start when he liked, but for poor pyking rogues like him, it was his work and life. It required regular application to make a proper living. Smith agreed and settled it.

'We'll mention it in front of him, but not, mark you, as though we invite him. Treat it as a bit of our own business. You'll see. Curiosity will get the better of him. If he wants in, let him ask. If not we'll go on anyway. There's nothing encourages a man like that so much as not being indispensable.'

Smith's approach proved to be correct. Brodie arrived at Clark's in good humour; he had the brisk and busy air of an honest toiler settling down for a deserved drink. His lazy swagger, which had a certain insolence, had been replaced by an element of bounce, that did not entirely suit him. He complained vigorously to Clark, and anyone else who greeted him, that he had a cold. Everyone in Edinburgh had a cold, and discussed theirs in return.

Within a few minutes of joining Smith and Ainslie, he sensed that something was going on between them. There was a certain coy air, and they made easy references to their 'business', their 'proposition' and their 'tea-party' which irritated him. Yet, against his will, it excited his curiosity. He drank deeply and wiped his mouth.

'What is it all then? I'm obviously supposed to ask. What kind o' skoddy mystery is this?' Ainslie was about to reply, but Smith put a hand on his arm to stop him, and spoke instead.

'A bit of enterprise, Will. We thought it might be best ye didn't know. Perhaps at the moment you might be averse to it. We have taken a passing interest in the tea-trade. Only figuratively, you understand, and in a small way of business taking.' He lowered his voice. 'And that's our business—taking.'

'Aye?'

'But we thought you would not be interested, as you have been concentrating on the more legitimate ways o' relieving rich people of their money. Please don't take it amiss, Will, but you have been a very busy man! We had these other schemes, remember, and you would have no part in them. So we thought, as we are feeling the pinch a bit, that it was time to be feathering our nests for winter. The nights are getting darker, and a man may freely move.'

'Or tae put it simply,' said Ainslie, 'my purse is as fat as a lamb's scrotum.'

Brodie looked at Ainslie, controlling the distaste he felt for his vulgarity.

'So you thought I would have no interest in such a thing? Well now. Have you considered these last seven months from my point of view? Have you considered the insufferable boredom of my respectability?'

'It has its rewards,' said Smith.

Brodie dashed his cane on the table with a whack.

'Damn it, Smith, it does not! Money is only a reward when you are without it. But when you have it, it is a fetter and chain, leg-iron and manacle, cat-bar and stocks to all self-respecting activity. You make me angry. Who set you up in business, eh? How do you propose to get rid of this tea?'

'Will, Will, keep your voice down, for God's sake! We had no intention of keeping you out of anything. We thought it was going counter to your present interests. I can't say we would welcome you in, because that would sound as though I had the right to invite you. If you want to take this on, then you're in charge, that's right, is it not, Andy?' Ainslie nodded eagerly. Brodie regarded them suspiciously.

'So you laid this on to test me. That's right, is it no' Smith? To see if Brodie's ready?'

'Ainslie found the tea.'

'Aye, but it's you that's baiting me, George, dangling carrots before my neb.' He paused. 'Where is it?'

'Carnegie the grocer, at Leith.'

'And have you examined the locks?'

'Ainslie has.'

'And what is there?' Brodie asked Smith without looking at Ainslie. Smith nudged Ainslie, who spoke up.

'The *Meg* unloaded the day at the quay. Carnegie has ten boxes, each o' a hunnert-weight.'

'It's not exactly that portable!' said Brodie drily. Smith leaned forward, and spoke urgently.

'No but, man, just to keep your hand in, just to keep in practice. It's down in Leith, it couldn't be easier. The nights are dark, and Leith is as dark as a cellar anyway. Come on, Will. Just to get us going again. You haven't foresworn it, have you? For if the business is dead, then with respect, we will have to start our own under new partnership arrangements. It is fine for you, but we *are* feeling the first nip of winter frost, and it reminds a man how cold he can be. I can't live off a grocer's shop, no more than Ainslie can live off a sailor's pockets. We are skilled men, with pride in our profession. Say the word, Will!'

'I must go for dinner. My sister will be waiting. I'll say

good-night to you gentlemen, until this evening. Shall we say about eleven?'

'Are we going, Will?' Smith persisted.

'I think I have been persuaded. You'll bring the tools then, George? And something for carrying it off. This is no job for stockings. We'll need to carry it ourselves, because we can't risk horses. Keep our hands in, did ye say? It'll mair like break our backs!'

'It's training.'

'What about my cold?'

'You'll work up a sweat, Will—it's good for the constitution.'

Brodie smiled with his mouth, but his eyes were concerned. He saluted them with his cane and left them, stopping on his way to exchange a few words with friends here and there. Smith watched him anxiously, for he had accurately read the face. Ainslie had too, and voiced the doubt.

'Do ye think he'll come?'

'I don't know, Andy, but I think so. He's a man you often do not understand, but have to take as he comes. He's bored with being respectable, and he's being driven from inside. Would you not be nervous of having such a thing inside you that you find difficult to control. It has a terrible attraction. You and me, Andy, we are common criminals. It's our way of earning a living.'

'Away with your nonsense!'

'Well, would you risk what he has to lose for a pack of tea?'

Ainslie was silent.

Dinner had become a fixture in the Brodie household. Will had given up his habit of remaining in Clark's or Dowie's and dining off claret and toasted cheese, or the occasional chop or herring. Now the maid served as waitress, and did her offices nervously, as though being asked to proffer the Host.

The main room had acquired more furniture now, and Jean was well pleased with it. She held her afternoon teas and entertained good society, and she had perhaps to some extent settled to the fact that she would not marry. These compensations softened her attitude, and the sight of her brother's success made it seem worthy to her. She still wept to herself at night that he had no men friends that he brought visiting, although she had often hinted that they would be welcome. However he continued to go out, rather than bring them in. It was common enough, and her consolation lay in knowing she was far from alone in her situation. She discussed it all with her sister Jacobina. They had decided they should be grateful to God that William had settled to the business, and thankful in the name of their father. But Jacobina was a married woman, and Jean could not help feeling that it tripped off the tongue more easily in her circumstance. Not only that, her husband Matthew Sheriff prospered considerably from William's industry, as he carried out the upholstery. Yet the year had been good to them. She knew that Will still gambled more than was proper, and that he frequented taverns too much, and of course there were his fighting cocks at Henderson's and in the timber yard. But that was the way of gentlemen and there was nothing she could do about that. As far as her modesty would permit, she had considered whether William consorted with women. She had no evidence to confirm it, but she supposed he must, particularly when he stayed out at nights and arrived in time for breakfast. She blushed furiously when she thought about it. Men's needs, she had always been told, were greater in these things, and he was at least discreet. She found it difficult however to meet his eyes for that day.

Brodie had finished his meal and was contemplating a glass of wine, twisting the stem backwards and forwards in his hand, noticing how the wine stayed still. A fire had been lit despite the fact that it was August, and he admired the glow through the glass. They had over the year arrived at an intimacy of discussion between them that sprang from Jean's approval of the new William Brodie. She had withheld her words before, and withheld her mind from him in silent reproach. The maid clattered about them, collecting plates and dishes. Jean found it all thoroughly domestic, and was happy.

'Do you think about life, Jean?'

The question startled her.

'What do you mean? I go to the kirk.'

'And you believe in the life everlasting! No, what I meant was, have you considered life as we lead it? The world is full of change. Why should I have so much work, and why should I prosper?'

'Will, don't be daft? You had father's business and you are good at your craft. Don't drink any more!' She put the glass stopper in the decanter, as though this would banish maudlin thoughts, or somehow stop them emanating from the bottle.

'Do you know that I find the whole thing entirely, absolutely boring? It is founded on principles of privilege and hypocrisy that God-fearing men call order and civilisation.'

'Will! You have been to Dowie's again. That place is a house o' rebels and insurrectionists. All this talk is unquieting. The servants should not be allowed to hear it. Father looked always to the example of the past, and to perfection of order and proportion. He was a man before his time. Look at the new town now. James Craig is following the same sense of order and the correct arrangement of things. Don't bite the hand that feeds you. You would do well on it!'

Brodie listened to her, smiling to himself.

'No, Jean, you have not taken my meaning. I get my work because I am a respected man—a Town Councillor, a mason, and a Deacon of the Wrights. The fact that I can use a chisel or fret-saw is neither here nor there. The work would still come my way. I am given these things to do, not for any merit o' my own, but for the station that I hold and the name I bear. If a collie dog could be a Deacon and a Councillor, and God knows he would make a good one, then they would give their orders tae him! Francis Brodie made me! As on the bottom of a paintin' or an engravin'. Francis Brodie fecit. Is there anything in it that truly represents me, or am I only a projection, like a mere thin shadow, of what they want me tae be?'

'You're in a mood o' choler.'

'It's the truth and plain enough to be served up ungarnished. I am other things, Jean. In my own right. No man deserves tae be kent all his life as bein' an Edinburgh Deacon!'

'I don't know what you're talkin' about, Will, but stop it, for it's wild. Father would have set you right. He was never ashamed, and he loved his work. What's wrong with it?'

'Father, that good and pious man that gave me everything, took from me everything I might expect to have! He hated me.'

'He loved us all. You were a disappointment to him for no' applying yourself to books, not involving yousel' in design but concentratin' on the making. And he was right. He taught you what you know of classical ornament and that is what folks want! There's no gratitude in you, Will! He forgave you and gave you the business. Is there anything more he could be expected to do? How dare ye say he hated you! He was full o' love, a fulsome, kind, goodly man. We owe him everything. You have no gratitude in your soul, Will, if you deny him that!'

The maid had retreated in alarm as the voices rose. Jean was beginning to sob and tears ran down her cheeks. Brodie on the other hand was very calm, and pale. He continued to regard his glass, never once looking in her direction.

'Has it ever occurred to ye,' he said with cold venom, 'that I have never ceased being grateful to the man? This very wine is the old man's blood. The whole town reminds me o' it as though I am another metal of no worth. "Aye, he was a good hard-working man, your father." Sweet Jesus! It seems tae me sometimes that every piece I make is seen by you, Jacobina and the rest o' Edinburgh as nothin' but an offering to his sacred memory! It might have been better for me if he had left me a pauper and spent his money on a whore!'

Jean started to emit a crooning moan, stuffing a handkerchief into her mouth as though to staunch the outpouring of her soul. Brodie got up and threw his glass of red wine on to the fire.

'That to father!'

The fire hissed, and a gout of sodden ash slopped on to the boards. Jean gave vent to muted screaming, by removing the handkerchief from her mouth. Brodie put the glass carefully on the table and walked to the door.

'Leave me my ane life, Jean!'

'You have plenty o' it!'

'But not inside masel', can you not understand that?'

'Father was a fine man. He loved you ...'

'Aye, damn it, and don't raise it, woman!'

'You're not going out?'

'I am.'

'But don't go out in anger. Please, Will.'

'Jean, Jean. It's not anger. Can ye not see that I hate masel'? That I cannot abide what I am. I am a living artifice.'

He picked up his cane from the stand by the door, and his hat from a hook. He looked white and wild, and this seemed to emphasise his slightness. Jean's simple motherly heart could not maintain forced anger. She saw him as a small child.

'You have a cold, Will. If you must go out, wrap yourself well.'

Brodie's reaction was almost violent. He shouted at her for the first time in their exchange of words.

'Jean! Do not look after me!'

It was almost a scream. He quickly left the room. When the maid, hearing no further shouting, decided to come in again and complete her tidying of the remains of the meal, Jean was staring at the fire, her face unhappy and puzzled. The mixture of red wine and ash had dried out so that it looked, as Will had said it was, like blood. Things had been going so well and they were progressing so splendidly in society. She could not comprehend why he should wish to upset all that. She had a steady programme now of teas, and even ladies of rank attended. They had their feet on a new social ladder, and he had tried to kick away the steps. She wondered if he was ill; she had heard that unmentionable diseases could affect the brain. She burst into tears, and the maid rushed over, putting an arm around her. How was she to find out? There was no way. It was a woman's burden to keep social life going.

Brodie, Smith and Ainslie were also deeply engaged in the difficulties of tea. The long walk to Leith had started Brodie sneezing. He had ignored his sister's warnings and wore his usual cloak which, although wrapped around him, was not proof against the sea winds. Ainslie perspired freely, and was running a temperature. Smith continually moaned at the two of them.

'All I need is two cripples for help. Why not invite half the Infirmary?'

'Hold your wheesht, Smith,' said Brodie angrily, 'it might be you. When it is, you can expect scant sympathy from me.'

Brodie was left outside to keep watch, as they could not risk his sneezing. Although he would not admit it to them, this seemed to suit him well. He considered that daring seemed to diminish with lack of practice, and this would do him good. Or maybe it was just the cold that made him feel so low. He was wedged in a black and uninviting corner at the junction of two walls, with the door of Carnegie's store-room just in view. His feet squelched in something unmentionable and he tried not to think about it. It was the sort of corner that would be used. To give the alarm he had a small whistle, which he was to blow twice, but for the time being he was concentrating on not sneezing, pressing hard beneath his nose with a knuckle, and sniffing.

Inside, things were going well enough. The locks had been no trouble to Smith, and they had prised open four chests of black tea. Smith had brought two pairs of canvas wallets, the type that carriers used over their donkeys, and these they were filling with tea. The job took an alarming time, for they had forgotten to bring anything to shovel it with and consequently were cramming it in by the handful. The tea seemed like mercury, slipping through their hands and pouring over their shoes, the panniers, floor or anywhere rather than go where intended. Ainslie was cursing steadily in a whisper. Smith suddenly stopped.

'I've an idea,' he said in Ainslie's ear, and took off one shoe. Ainslie sniggered and did the same. He had to hold a hand over the sole.

'It'll add tae the flavour!'

Ainslie suddenly sneezed violently, three times, and Smith leapt on him clapping his hand over his mouth.

'You damned fool!'

'It's the dust! The stuff's full o' it.'

'Wear a handkerchief!'

'Man, that's a joke. Where dae ye think I'd get one o' those!'

So Smith lent him his, and with the shoes they ladled out the contents, filling all four pouches. The floor was covered with their spillings and they moved about on an aromatic crunching floor. When they had replaced their shoes, they tried to lift the pouches. Smith got under his like a yoke and, standing upright, walked without too much difficulty to the door. Ainslie, adopting the same practice, stood upright and, with a strangled grunt, stopped dead.

'Wait,' he called, 'I canna move the bugger!'

'For God's sake!' Smith hissed. 'Try, you undernourished ... idiot.'

'I can't.'

'Well, what do you want me to do? Stand here all day with this on my back? Get under the weight!'

'I canna!'

'Christ!'

Brodie was surprised to see the warehouse door open, and Smith appear, loaded like a horse and beckoning in Brodie's direction. Brodie was reluctant to come out of his corner where, complete with crêpe mask and cocked pistol, he had finally made himself comfortable. He looked cautiously around, and crossed the street.

'What is it?'

'Come in.'

They stepped inside and shut the door.

'We have the tea but Ainslie can't carry it. You'll have to give him a hand.'

'I'm not dressed for it.'

'For the love of God, Will, we're not expecting society! Take a pouch with him, or he'll be stuck here till dawn. They're only a hundredweight and a half and I can carry mine!'

'It's ma' chest,' said Ainslie. 'I canna' lift things because o' it.'

'I have a cold,' said Brodie.

Smith put down his wallets and looked at the two of them.

'What is this? Is this a house party? Are we to stand here till the Guard gets us? Shall I go out in the street and get help?'

'There's no need for sarcasm, George. And stop your bawling at us, or you'll bring them anyways.' Brodie went over to Ainslie and together they managed to lift the other pouches. Once outside, Smith waved them to continue clear of the building, while he did what he could to secure the door, swaying like some grossly inflated creature under the weight of his load.

The remainder of their journey was a nightmare. While Smith trudged stoically on through the dark, Ainslie and Brodie, coughing and gasping, could find no way of distributing the load evenly between them, as both of them could not get it on their backs. Ainslie took one pouch on his back in front, and Brodie brought up the rear, holding the other pouch in his arms, which soon wearied him. They lurched along out of step, stopping frequently to change over. When they had finally cleared Leith, Ainslie collapsed at the roadside, his face and shirt running with sweat.

'It's no use, George,' said Brodie, 'we can't carry it.'

Ainslie could not even speak, but wheezed and whooped.

Smith had got beyond anger, and his own exertions had taken their toll.

'Then ditch it. I'll go on alone. I'll take this lot to your house.'

'No!' said Brodie. 'Not tonight. Jean is in a takin'. She'll be up and waitin'.'

'Suit yourself!' Smith spat on the ground and lurched off up the Bonnington Road. After a pause of several minutes Ainslie and Brodie recovered. In the faint light of false dawn they saw a ruinous shed in the adjoining field. By common consent they staggered over the wet grass and concealed the pouch inside an old cupboard of rotting wet wood. Neither man bothered to speak about it. They needed all their breath to complete the walk to Edinburgh. Brodie was deeply ashamed of the disaster and was convinced it was because they had tried such an unsuitable target. He was losing his position with Smith. The man was becoming conceited and was not treating him with proper respect. There would be no more of this trivial stuff. They would try for one of his favourite fruits, and he would show them what planning and daring could do. They would lift the University mace. By the time he had reached the High Street, he was determined upon it. It was a masterstroke that Smith would never conceive. Smith would have to give him his due for that. Above all, the whole Town would know of it. He had no time for this petty pilfering. He felt better, the more he thought about it. The tea had been an indiscretion and now he would cancel it out. He spent the rest of the night at Jean Watt's, to get his revenge on Francis.

* * *

Edinburgh Evening Courant, 1787

SHOP-BREAKING

That in the Night betwixt Thursday the 16th and Friday the 17th of August instant, the Shop of John Carnegie, Grocer, at the foot of St. Andrew's Street, Leith, was broke into, and about 350 pounds of fine black tea stolen and carried off.

Whoever will give such information to William Scott, procurator-fiscal of the County of Edinburgh, within three months from this date, as shall lead to a discovering in the premises, will receive from him a reward of TEN GUINEAS, on conviction of the offender or offenders and the informer's name (if required) concealed.

N.B. It is assumed the above theft has been committed by some of those who stroll the country under the pretence of hawking tea, and who may have had access to know Mr Carnegie's shop. The tea was turned out of the packages, and yesterday several parcels of tea were observed lying at different places on the Bonnington road, as if dropt from a parcel, which is a farther confirmation of the above suspicion, and that the tea stolen is carried to the country for sale by some hawker. If, therefore, any considerable quantity of tea is observed in the custody of any suspicious person or persons, it is intreated they may be secured, and notice given to said William Scott, who will pay all reasonable charges, besides a reasonable gratification for trouble.

* * *

The elegant Mr Brown had joined them one evening at Clark's, as though he had never been away. That things were not at their best with him was evident from the state of his clothing. For all his care and its quality, his coat was holed at the elbow, and a seam of his waistcoat split. His shoes were scuffed and worn. He had not shaved. He had sat at their table without waiting for an invitation and nodded to Brodie, Smith and Ainslie in turn. They were all too surprised to speak immediately, and Brown availed himself of it.

'Gentlemen, I am glad to see things have not changed for the worst in any way. You are all here.'

'What do you expect?' demanded Smith. Brown ignored this and continued.

'Stirling is a rocky place. Do you know it? But it is no nest for fine birds!'

'What happened to your English hounds?' asked Brodie, unsmiling.

'They must have snuffed up a stray fox. They're safely baying in England.'

Smith had enlisted him on the raid, Brown at first pretending to show little interest. He could not however conceal the hole in his coat, although he leaned on that elbow while talking.

'How can you be sure it's there?' he demanded. 'Perhaps it's locked away at night.'

'It's there,' said Ainslie, who was chewing away at his supper of mutton chops. 'They made me go a second time and inspect it. Mr Brodie went the first time. It's never moved from its case.'

'And not guarded?'

'Feech! There's an old man wha sleeps in his box like a corpus. We'll not be near him.'

Brown pondered. 'It seems to me that this is the sort of offence that would not be taken too lightly.'

Brodie smiled at Brown and, when he spoke, his voice was sarcastic. 'What's bad for civic dignity is well enough for us, Mr Brown. Surely ye're no' afraid of a wee bit hubble-show? Perhaps they'll think a scholar did it!'

'With pick-locks?' It was Brown's turn to be sarcastic.

'We have damned clever scholars in Edinburgh, Mr Brown.'

Brown was silent for a moment while the others watched him.

'I don't know why you need me,' he said. 'This sort of thing ends in all the fun of a tuck-up fair.'

Smith pushed a bottle over to him.

'Give yourself a shove in the mouth, John, you look as if you could use one. None of us here has any wish to be baptised by the twelve honest god-fathers.'

'Fifteen,' said Brodie.

'Aye, ye get fifteen here in Scotland,' repeated Ainslie with patriotic enthusiasm.

'Damn, I don't care to be reminded how many,' Brown growled, 'five or fifteen is all the same thing if you're dancing on air.'

'If you're nervous, Mr Brown,' said Brodie softly, 'then maybe you should miss this expedition?' Brown glared at him, furious. For a moment quite a different creature seemed to inhabit the elegant frame.

'I'm not afraid! Me? It's prudence. I won't be cropped for some foolishness, some bungled cull. All right, Brodie, I'm in. Now are you sure it's silver, and that Tasker can and will fence it? Is this thing planned?'

'Tasker can take it,' said Smith.

'And the silver?'

'As for the silver,' Brodie replied, 'I won't pretend tae gammon ye. I can only describe what I have seen with my eyes. What with the academic authorities have loaded it, or whether or no they have scooped the marrow out o' it like a bone I have no idea and canna' hold myself responsible for. But what it is supposed to be is solid and, like all such municipal trinkets, ye must take it on trust!'

The four men gathered outside the University at one o'clock in the morning. The bell of St Giles' rang out quite clear. Brodie had brought four crêpe masks, which he insisted they wear. Brown was surly and unco-operative, declaring in tones of derision that he had not come out at this hour to play the fool. When the others put theirs on, he accepted his with ill grace declaring the thing was a pantomime.

'I have a pair of pistols for you, George,' said Brodie to Smith, drawing a pair from one coat pocket and handing them over. 'They're ready loaded, double ball.' The butts with their silver mounts gleamed briefly before Smith tucked them away. 'Have you your own?' he asked. Brodie nodded, shifting one of his own pair to the pocket he had emptied. Brodie seemed elated and his movements were quick and nervous. Brown watched these movements with shock. His face paled and he tugged at Brodie's arm.

'You never told me you were going armed!'

'It's a pantomime, Mr Brown. We must have a bang here and there! A good discharge of powder. We shoot anyone who tries tae stop us ... Bang!' Brodie pointed the gun at a window pretending to fire. 'Have you never heard the song?

> "See the ball I hold
> Let the chymists toil like asses
> Our fire their fire surpasses
> And turns all our lead to gold!"'

'Quiet, Will!' hissed Smith.

'You're mad, Brodie,' Brown whispered, 'we'll all be cropped for you.'

Brodie turned to him, smiling, and took his mask away from his face. He bowed with a flourish.

'It would be a pleasure, Mr Brown.'

It was Smith who speedily intervened.

'This is no place for this sort of thing! We are here with common purpose. If we can't get on with it, we might as well heave our lines!' It had the necessary effect and, although neither showed any signs of cordiality to the other, they nodded and under Brodie's direction, made for the outer gate at the rear. This was a solid pine door, heavily studded and much scarred by batterings and student troubles of the last hundred years. Smith opened it with a pick-lock in less than a minute, while the others stood in cover; then they all slipped inside.

'I'll lead,' said Brodie, 'I know the way.'

However silently they contrived to move along the corridors, their heels clopped on the flooring, sometimes hard on stone and sometimes booming on timber. They moved in single file, hissing at each other to be silent. Brodie stopped and lit the lantern, when they were deep within a corridor, and they moved more silently, tip-toeing like pantomime villains. At the end of the corridor they came to the library door. It was solid mahogany and heavily panelled. The lock was almost new. Brodie held the lantern to allow a slit of light on the keyhole while Smith again tackled the lock. He struggled for some minutes with no success.

'Damn it, Brodie, I can't turn it! The wards are wrong!'

'Use another key!' They continued. Eventually one key seemed to make it give.

'Now what's wrong?' demanded Brown.

'Stow your patter. The bugger won't turn.'

'Let's leave it,' said Ainslie. 'We're makin' enough noise tae wake Greyfriars.'

'You're going nowhere. We didn't come here to be flummoxed by a chatty lock. Give me the dubs. You hop the twig and you get nothing!'

'What?' Ainslie gawped at Smith.

'If you want to go, go.' Ainslie shuffled and stayed. 'Give me more o' the glim, Will.' Brodie advanced with the light and Smith selected yet another key. Sweat was trickling down his face. With a snap the key broke off.

'God damn it, man!' Brown exclaimed. 'What sort of game is this?'

Smith turned on Brown with real anger.

'Take a carrot!' Ainslie looked ready to run. Brodie on the contrary remained serenely calm.

'Gentlemen, gentlemen. When rogues like us fall out, then there is trouble. Allow me. We have nothing tae fear. The old gowp is miles awa' and fast asleep in his cups.'

They suddenly all looked to Brodie. His nervousness had gone and had been replaced by a lordly ease. He alone appeared relaxed and unconcerned. It was a strange and uneasy calm in the situation. Brown summed it up.

'It seems to me, Brodie, that you don't care one way or the other if we get caught. And I know well why. A man of your connections in this town has nothing to fear. But we have! Let's call if off!'

'Are you not my friends? What is there tae fear? The mace is municipal nonsense solidified intae pure silver. Now naebody would tak' the mace, ergo, there is no guard on it. There are no scholars. There is one old greybeard, deaf in one ear. Should he hear us, I warrant he'll be deaf in both. Pull your pistols, have your lead ready. We'll break the door with a small crow. One noise and all over.'

The others looked at each other uneasily. His air of calm inspired confidence, but each was thinking at what stage calm became foolhardiness. Brodie had set his heart on the mace and it seemed to have become a crusade in which life, limb and value were of little consideration. Yet what he said was true. It was Smith who nodded. 'Come on then, Will. It's best done fast.'

Brodie took a short crowbar from his cloak and inserted it between the keep and the lock. He levered hard until there was the creaking and groaning of crushing wood.

'Now George!'

Smith gave the door a heavy thump with the whole weight of his body directly alongside the lock. There was a rending sound and the crackling of wood fibres as the keep tore out of the frame. The door swung lazily open. They stood in utter silence, each man hearing his heart. They listened for three minutes, four, five. There was no sound. A leathery, saddle-soap smell came from the library. Brodie led the way in.

The mace occupied the pride of position on a table in the centre of the room. It was enclosed in a glass showcase.

'No worry,' said Smith, 'I'll star the glaze quite silently.'

Putting the tails of his coat over a side panel, he gave it a confident clout with his pistol butt. There was the slightest tinkle like the rattling of silver coins, and the case was open. It was magnificent in a grotesque and vulgar manner and they all felt the weight, exclaiming at it. Brodie was delighted.

'Did I not tell you! Did I not tell you!' he kept exclaiming. 'We'll have it melted down. The whole of University pride can be melted down in a pot on a fire. That is man. That's the worth of his pride. Not the heat of a fire can it stand. This mace has worn its silver off on more hands that have ruled the kingdom and hung its thiefs than anything you are like tae see. Yet all it's worth is its weight. And that is the symbol o' man's pretension!'

But the others were not listening but guessing the weight. Brodie's eyes were sparkling. He began to hum to himself noisily and would have broken into song if they had not hissed at him to be quiet.

'I'm a happy man!' he said in explanation. 'We should all be happy men. This is a rare thing!'

'What is it you're really after, Will?' said Smith who was next to him, and out of the hearing of the other two. 'Is it the money, or do you want to steal the pride out of the town? Do you want to rob men's hearts and steal the Assembly Hall?'

Brodie looked at him with a smile.

'If pride's a chunk o' siller it deserves tae be melted down. Men are proud, and they melt down just the same.'

Ainslie interrupted them.

'How dae we get it out? It's monstrous large. Muckle great poker!' It stopped them for some seconds. Brown could not resist being derisive. 'Don't worry, Mr Brodie will think of something.'

'And I can, Mr Brown. I'll put it down one leg of my breeches and the head under my cloak. You see, Mr Brown, a cloak is a very practical garment.' Together they managed to get the shaft of the mace down Brodie's breeches, where it stuck fast in the buttons at the top of his stockings. He enveloped the heavy silver head in the cloak, which would not fit under his armpit, but which he wore in front with his right arm around as though shielding it from the cold.

'Now for God's sake,' Brodie said, 'walk slow. I'm in ma prime!'

They left the building as they had come, Smith holding the lantern in front and Brodie hobbling behind him. At the outer door they agreed to split into pairs to be less conspicuous. Smith and Brodie clutched each other in a parody of drunkenness and staggered off to Henderson's to conceal the mace in the stables. Brown and Ainslie agreed to go their separate ways.

'That was well done, George,' Brodie said, highly delighted. 'There will be such a gweeshing and tutting the morrow that Edinburgh has never seen! God, ma leg will be raw!'

'We'll clear it to Tasker tomorrow.'

'Aye. But it'll seem a shame to lose it. I have a fancy, George, for just a wee bit siller out o' it to put a plate on ma father's coffin.'

'He's buried!'

'Och, ye can dig him up again! Just tae give him back a wee bit something for all I'm told I owe him. Would that not be nice now?'

'No. That would be mad!'

They staggered along in silence. Caddies passed them, on late-night errands. Sedans swayed past, some of their occupants singing, and one of them being very sick.

'I daresay you're right, George. It was only a notion. I have them, you see, and I can't help it. Do ye understand? I want tae make something of myself.'

'You are rich and respected.'

'Not that, man! I hate it!'

Brodie spoke with such vituperation that Smith was silent all the way to the Grassmarket. They hid the mace in the manger and said good-night outside. Smith would arrange for the mace to be trunked up and sent by carrier to Tasker. Brodie decided he would like to see Ann Grant. He could hardly contain his delight, and yet he would never tell her. She would be immensely upset. Now, he thought as he walked, there is Inglis and Horner for silk, the Excise office—the Council mace! That would be a summit for a man to set his eyes upon. He could sit in the chamber with the rest of them and bemoan the theft. He could make a pretty speech on the immorality of the times. He could rail like Galloway and beat his breast like Shaw. There was the Lottery office and the Chamberlain's office. Edinburgh was like a dead sheep and the hoodie crows would sit on it and peck their fill. He swung into a kind of shuffling saunter and whistled to himself from *The Beggar's Opera*. It was a moment of rare exultation and he felt the very devil of a man.

Ann was happy. Will had seemed so cheerful, waking her with a kiss on each eye, calling her his heary, his hinny, his grand fleshed queen. He was himself again. The solemn Deacon of the last year had only an appetite for gruel. Now he wanted a meal of her, vigorous and delighted. She lay with him snoring in her arms as the sunlight filtered through the curtains. She could hear the children with the servant-girl in the other room, romping and squealing. For these moments, life was good. His black cape and trousers were flung over the back of a chair and other clothing was scattered around the room. Ann could not understand this continual change of dress any more than she could understand his changes of mood and fortune, but she knew very well that the way to keep him happy was never to ask. He was a good father to their children, and they lacked nothing except the dry-bone blessing of the Church. There's plenty of bastards in Edinburgh, she thought, and most of them not so well provided for. She wondered what would happen when they grew older. Would they have to be told? Why not? They had a lot to be proud of as a Deacon's kin. Even the neighbours were impressed. Flora Maclellan had a rich baker, and she was jealous.

She gently eased herself from him. Will Brodie snorted, but

remained asleep. Getting up, quite naked, she started to set his clothes out in some order, folding them and putting them on a chair. She picked up the cape and was struck by the weight of it. Patting the inner pockets she found the pistols and quickly put it down again. Why should he carry pistols? They frightened her, and she retreated back to bed. Her movements made him turn over on his back. He opened his eyes, and shut them immediately.

'Tak' away the light . . . tak' it away . . .'

'It's day, Will, and time you were up. It's late—near nine.'

He said nothing but lay savouring the warmth. It was as though he had come out of a long and virtuous sleep in which he had done nothing but labour. That is the way a cocoon turns into a butterfly, he thought, and there is no merit in it, it simply happens. But when it is free of its encrusting shell, life begins again. Francis my father lies in his cocoon of shrouds, and all he is is a bladder of corruption. He is the embodiment of the worthy citizens of Edinburgh, as he always wanted to be! Light is an unpleasant thing for it brings out the pretensions in man. In the dark he is his true self, no better, no worse. Satan is the prince of darkness, they say. All wrong. Darkness is truth. Darkness is the time for the execution of dreams. Prisoners are executed in broad daylight, so that the citizens may have the protection of donning their full pretensions and have no sympathy for what they see.

He did not like this run of thought, and turned to Ann, putting his arms around her and pulling her to him. She did not respond. He half opened his eyes.

'Come on, lass. You're never wearied yet. What's the matter?'

'Why do you carry pistols, Will?'

He opened his eyes and stared at her.

'Tae protect maself at night. There isn't a gentleman in Edinburgh that does not carry arms.'

'That's not so.'

'I'm a well breached sort of a man, Ann. It's just wisdom.

Ye ken I keep late hours and there's many a rascal might fancy ma purse.'

Ann seemed satisfied and allowed herself to be drawn to him. At that moment the door was flung open and the children ran squealing into the room pursued by the maid-servant, who exclaimed apologetically that she could not keep them out.

'We knew ye were here, faither! We never get a chance tae see ye!' Cecil, aged eleven, hurled herself on him on the bed. The two had immediately rolled apart. Jeanie stood regarding them with large glowing eyes at the foot of the bed. The maid-servant, now that the damage was done, went next door and returned with the baby Jamie, just gone two, who wriggled and struggled to get to his unsteady feet.

'They're grand bairns Will, and they love you and miss you when you're away.'

'Don't reproach me, Ann, there's nothing I can do.'

'Did you bring us something?' demanded Cecil.

'She'll grow up to be no sort o' lady at all!' said Brodie. 'Young lady, ye dinna go through life demandin' things off gentlemen, or ye may get more than ye want!'

'Will!'

Cecil giggled knowingly. She persisted.

'Have ye got something for us? Ye brung us something last time.'

'I have. Bring me ma coat. Not the cloak! Aye that's it.'

From the pocket of his coat he brought out a handkerchief which he unwrapped on the bed.

'I have been carrying these around for ye, ye hussy. And your sister there who has mair manners than tae throw herself awa' for trinkets!' From the handkerchief he produced a locket on a fine gold chain, which Cecil grabbed with excited shrieks. Round-eyed Jeanie had to be coaxed to shyly accept a brooch. The maid was beckoned over, and Jamie, still wriggling and kicking, had a garnet mounted on a pin attached to the nearest part of his clothing. Tears welled up in Ann's eyes.

'Ach, Will, the bairns have no need o' jewels ...'

'Take them for the future, Ann. They won't go poor. There's nae wizardry can foretell events in these times. What if something should happen tae me? Nothing wards off want like jewellery.'

'You're soft, Will. What can happen to you? You'll spoil the weans.'

Brodie unwrapped a thick chain and pendant from a fold in the handkerchief. It sparkled with a ruby encircled with pearls.

'This one is for you. Now you're all provided for.'

Ann was taken aback. She shied away from the pendant as though she dare not touch it.

'It's worth a fortune. I can't wear that! I'd be robbed! Me, in my clothes, wi' that round ma neck! ... No. You mustn't do it, Will. Take it back!'

'I can't take it back. That, I assure ye, is impossible.'

'I don't know what to say.'

'Then don't. Put it by, and think of it. There's mair security there than in the Castle.'

Reluctantly Ann was persuaded to take the gift. She was troubled by the size of it and she was troubled about his continual reference to security. There was fear in her heart that he intended to leave her and that this was a parting price. She smiled however, between tears, and thanked him and kissed him. The baby cried too, but Cecil was enormously delighted and danced around, looking at herself in a glass. Jeanie stared at the cornelian in her brooch as though it contained the secrets of the universe and stared at the man with her mother. She wondered what the brooch was for, because she had never seen one before.

* * *

Edinburgh Evening Courant, 1787.

By the Right Hon: The
LORD PROVOST, MAGISTRATES, AND COUNCIL,
of the City of Edinburgh

WHEREAS, on the night between Monday and Tuesday the 29th and 30th current, some wicked persons did feloniously break open the doors of the Library of the University of this City, and steal the UNIVERSITY MACE, a reward of TEN GUINEAS, to be paid by the City Chamberlain, is hereby offered for the discovery of all or any of the persons above mentioned, or of any person in whose possession the said Mace shall be found.

Edinburgh, Oct. 31. 1787.

* * *

Brodie was in the counting-house at the end of the Close when Rab Smith tapped at the door to say good-night. Around him was the usual litter of books and leather-bound ledgers that he detested. Because Jean was angry with him, he had decided to pretend to keep up appearances.

'Good night, Mr Brodie. I'll be going now.'

It was a statement that brooked no argument. Brodie noticed that as he paid less attention to the work, Rab Smith's words became bolder, even insolent. He had other things to do, however, than wrangle with his foreman. The man was after his own concern, and would no doubt get it before many years. Brodie realised, not for the first time, that his own future was not in this. Yet what was it in? He looked up at Smith. The man had his coat on. He was well dressed and prosperous-looking. Rab Smith would make his way in the world, and like Francis Brodie would work hard and honestly to prop up the arse-ends of Edinburgh.

'Good night Rab. Thank you. Have you locked up?'

'Aye.'

Of course he had. Rab had always locked up, put away the tools, supervised the men and done everything fitting to a worthy man. He, William Brodie, would shed his skin and the real Will Brodie would be shucked loose. Perhaps Rab, like Francis, would end with the guineas on his eyes, and for a brief moment Edinburgh would pause and remark that he was a good man and a loss to them all, then they would elect another Brother, a new Deacon, a new Council, arrange another member of Parliament and life would go on undisturbed.

He shut his books the moment Smith had left the Close and went down beyond the timber racks to see his game-cocks. Henderson had six and he looked after four because it gave him an excuse to get away from Jean. They rattled and shook at the wooden bars of their pens, recognising his steps. Under cover in a small timber building, he kept their feed corn. Filling a bucket with corn he walked past the pens, throwing in handfuls, talking to the birds and praising them. The birds looked at him suspiciously, their black eyes glittering. They screamed and pecked if he put a hand in the pens. There was no way of winning the love of a fighting cock. They were pure hatred, encased in feather and down.

'You're bonny bastards,' he said to them, 'eat up, eat up.'

When he had emptied the corn pail he went further down the Close to his tool-shop and, taking a key from his pocket, unlocked the door, closing and locking it behind him. He lit two lanterns on a bench. The interior was filled with pieces of metalwork, and wall-racks held saws, chisels, spring metal, lock parts, augurs, pincers and key blanks. The bench was fitted with two metal-working vices. Brodie opened the drawer under the bench and took out a half-formed pick-lock. He clamped it into the vice, whistling to himself, and began to work on it alternately with a file and a hammer, bending and shaping, occasionally taking it out and peering at it against the light. Although he had made hundreds of keys from impressions, this was the first time he had attempted to make a pick-lock. Each Sunday, when Edinburgh exhibited its piety, he and Smith had gone to the shop, with Ainslie and Brown discreetly behind. While the devout listened to a good long sermon, Brodie and Smith idly strolled about the shop front and examined the padlock. It was a design that neither of them knew, and Smith said he thought it came from England. Brodie saw what he could of it and, while he tried to find the position of the wards with a slip of waxed stick, he could hear the preacher in St Giles', in full exhortation. It was a moment to savour. Smith said that he could make a pick-lock for it, but Brodie determined immediately to make one himself.

He worked late into the night, unconcerned about the noise. At the foot of the Close there were few people to overhear, and it was not at all uncommon for Brodie's men to be working late. All Edinburgh knew what an industrious man the Deacon was. By midnight he was satisfied. The work had been difficult as he had been working as much as possible with cold steel, so as not to ring the anvil. He was determined to try it very soon and show Smith where he stood. If the man proved more expert, then he might easily lose control. And there was the matter of pride. The old dog would show them!

It was Brown who first raised the question of Tapp's shop, although it had been on Brodie's list for a long time. He said that he had passed it daily and that, instead of risking their necks in the University, it looked a sweet little nut to crack. Brown had struck up an acquaintance with Tapp, a rough-and-ready man who was flattered by the attentions of a man he took to be an English gentleman. He had twice been invited to dinner with Tapp and his wife, and during the course of his wanderings about their premises had discovered that Tapp's house key fitted the lock on the shop. Brodie and Smith were both put out by this sudden piece of free enterprise by the deep Mr Brown.

'I didn't know you knew one lock from another,' said Smith,

'are you sure?' They were sitting over a 'gill bell' ale in Dowie's, which was crammed with respectable gentry.

'I'm sure,' said Brown and to their horror pulled a large key from his pocket which he set down on the table in plain view. 'That's the key of the shop.'

'Christ, man, you'll have us hung! Put it under the table.'

'There's no worry,' said Brown, 'Tapp's over there drinking, the shop's empty. He won't leave these thirty minutes.'

They all turned and took surreptitious looks. Tapp was indeed sitting at a table deep in conversation and his cups.

'The man drinks like a fish, and his liver will be a specimen for the Infirmary,' Brown continued. 'Have a look at it, George, and see if you can make a match.'

The key was passed nervously under the table. To their alarm Brown got to his feet and gave Tapp a hearty wave.

'I'll go over to talk to him. I'll be back in ten minutes.'

Brown's boldness had left them stupefied, but nevertheless Smith examined the key and passed it on under the table to Brodie.

'What do you think o' it, Will?'

'What about you?'

'There's nothing in it. It's easy.'

'God, that man has strange ways. I don't trust it,' said Smith.

'He's a cool one,' said Ainslie, with admiration in his voice.

'That's stupid.' Smith was incisive. 'Give him a nod. We want that back.'

Ainslie went over to Brown and they saw him take him by the sleeve and exchange a few words, Brown occasionally looking their way. Finally Brown and Tapp shook hands, and Tapp waved a hand in their direction. They both waved back, rather stupidly and very discomfited. Brown and Ainslie rejoined them.

'Well,' asked Brown, 'what do you make of it?'

'It's an easy job. Nothing in it. God, Brown, will you take the damned thing back?' Smith was white and upset.

'Easily done,' said Brown. He doffed his hat, said farewell

and, with a further wave to Tapp, left the tavern.

'That man will be the hanging of us,' Smith said.

'He's a canny man.' Ainslie looked after him, shaking his head and smiling in a way that neither Smith nor Brodie liked. Brodie got to his feet decisively.

'Come on, George, make the key.'

'But I'm making the other one!' He lowered his voice. 'For the silk. Inglis and Horner ...'

'Can you make a key by tonight?'

'What?' Smith was astonished.

'I think we should oblige Mr Brown—as he has been so obliging tae us. It is, after all, the festive season and in a week it'll be Christmas. Let Mr Brown renew his cordial sentiments with Mr Tapp, who is a man who likes his beverage—and we three will do the shop!' Brodie smiled at them with his down-turned grin. Ainslie and Smith looked at each other, undecided.

'Christmas, George. A wee present for ye! Strike while the iron is hot. Mr Brown has a good idea. It would be a pity tae disappoint the gentleman.' Smith was silent, pondering, which he did by wrestling with his jaw as though to tear it away. He finally made up his mind. 'I can make it, but it's not much time ... there'll be a little shank, we'll need to turn it with pliers.'

'Never mind, George, let's hasten on with it. Don't sit there.' Brodie twiddled his cane and stood over them until they got to their feet. His face was aglow and his eyes sparkled.

'But which one is it to be?' asked the puzzled Smith.

'The house, of course. The man has nothing but rubbish in his shop. If Mr Brown wants it done, we'll do it. There should be a guinea or two, or else how does he buy his claret?'

All three left Dowie's: Brodie to consult with Brown, and Ainslie to make the key. Brodie savoured the idea. It was sweetly just. Mr Brown was not the only one who could spring surprises, and by God he would pull this one off. The perfection lay in the fact that Brown would take no part in the robbery. He would engage Tapp in a seasonal drink in his shop, and they would clean out the house.

The evening was the kind that thieves pray for. The sky darkened at four, and was black at the half-hour. A heavy pall of low cloud and smoke hung over the city like a tarpaulin, blocking out the quarter moon. Later, a sea mist rose, determined to fill the void. The weather was sharp and cold, and snow was in the offing. Mr Tapp, true to his name, was delighted when Mr Brown stopped by with a seasonal bottle of brandy. He closed the door and bolted it, turned up the lamps, and they made themselves comfortable by the fire in the corner. They talked of the state of the Union, the conduct of Warren Hastings, the future of British India and Pitt's Act of '84 and all the other things that gentlemen break their brains on when they enjoy a bottle. In the house next door, Brodie and Smith were picking their way carefully through the furniture. By the light of the lantern they saw Tapp's desk, and began to pull out the drawers. They were immediately successful. The first drawer, which was not even locked, contained a purse with eighteen gold guineas and a pound note. Another contained some gold rings, a few with stones. On top of the desk they even found Tapp's own watch. Brodie smiled, his eyes gleaming behind his mask as he showed Smith the name on the case.

Swinging round the lantern so that they could see the whole room in narrow segments, they saw an escritoire against the far wall. It was locked, so Brodie broke it easily with a jemmy. It was a fine piece of furniture and he felt genuinely sorry when the top fractured along the lock edge. Inside, it was full of papers and letters, some in drawers and some loosely scattered about.

'There will be nothing there,' said Smith, 'it's a woman's escritoire.'

'Aye, it'll be Mrs Tapp's,' Brodie riffled quickly through

the drawers. There were quills, ink, a blotter and a bible, nothing of any value. Brodie was about to close the lid when he noticed the secret drawer at the bottom of one nest of drawers, fashioned like a piece of the framework and only an inch high. He pressed it in and it gave slightly.

'Wait, George.' He pulled out all the drawers above and was unable to find a catch.

'Leave it,' whispered Smith, 'it'll be woman's trifles.'

'Damnation, George, it might be a stack o' gold. It's worth a bit noise for a look. I'll jemmy it too.'

He slipped the short iron crow into the narrow crack above the drawer and wrenched. The wood was strong and merely creaked and groaned.

'You pull, George. Put some weight behind it!'

Smith braced himself against the front of the desk and heaved. There was a resounding crack and Smith nearly crashed over backwards. The whole drawer front had torn away. With hearts beating, they listened. Smith made a wry face at Brodie. Brodie shrugged and held his arms up in the air, as an actor does when taking a bow. In mime he indicated the whole room by turning. There was nobody there. They advanced to the drawer and Brodie held the lantern low so that they could see inside. Smith pointed excitedly and drew out a piece of folded blue silk. He unwrapped it quickly. Inside was a miniature portrait of a young man, set in a gold frame studded with four pearls. Brodie started to laugh.

'I know him! That's Sir Soldier!'

'That's who?'

There was a screech from behind them that made them both jump so much that the lantern nearly went out. Mrs Tapp, taking her courage in both hands, had looked into the room.

'Who's there? What's going on wi' my desk? Thieves!' She had started to shout.

'Run,' yelled Smith, but that was not Brodie's intention.

'Mrs Tapp,' he said amiably, 'I trust ye have no intention

o' making a noise that might bring your husband. Ye ken well what I have here and no doubt we can all be discreet about it . . .'

'How do ye ken ma' name?' she demanded. 'Who are ye? The devil tae your cheek!'

'I had heard ye were a spirited woman, Mrs Tapp. But ye won't scream. We are, you understand, but poor gentlemen passing through, and it's not our job tae moralise. It is by the merest chance that we have discovered this portrait of a young gentleman of your acquaintance that you would rather keep hid.'

'Thon's ma son! Give it tae me, you rogue!'

'No, no, Mrs Tapp. Young men can be untimely loose wi' their tongues, and I have heard that this young blood was mightily impressed by ye! Ye take ma meaning clearly? Impressed. And with your husband in bed and watching. Now I'm no judge and damn me if I should spoil a lusty woman's fun, but, Mrs Tapp, you must not spoil ours.'

There was a silence. They could hear her breathing quickly, her dress rustling with every small movement.

'Who are you, and how do you ken sae much? You're no an ordinary thief and I ken your voice from somewhere!'

'I doubt it, Mrs Tapp, and if ye did, it would mak' precious little difference tae the situation. We can't stop here all night, pleasant as it is chatting tae such a well formed and forward woman.'

'How dare ye!'

'You may keep the picture, but I think we'll have the wee bit gold around it, as your husband is a prudent man and keeps little about the house. But we'll have your silence in return for our consideration for not spoiling your fun with your young buck. Really, Mrs Tapp, I have heard that you are a woman who cannot be denied!'

'You damned devil!'

Brodie lifted his hat and bowed to her with a flourish.

'Your servant, madam, and good night to ye!' He motioned Smith to the door, and allowed the other man out in front of him. He bowed to her again from the doorway.

'I know who you are!' Mrs Tapp said furiously, but nevertheless she kept her voice down.

'I very much doubt it, madam. And if ye did, ye couldna' say and nobody would believe ye. One screech, madam, and you lose that portrait.' He tossed the miniature on to a chair then ducked out of the door. Mrs Tapp heard his footsteps following Smith's out of the house. She was furious but frightened. Try as she might, she could not place the voice or clothes, but was sure they were familiar to her.

Mrs Tapp was a resourceful woman. She had to be with her clamorous appetites. She snatched up the miniature, and hid it in the bottom of an old trunk of clothes. It took her no time at all to realise that she must be in bed and appear to be asleep when her husband returned. She had heard and seen nothing, naturally. It would be a miracle she had not been molested!

She was sure that, somehow, she knew that voice.

CHAPTER EIGHT

Edinburgh, 1788. The fatal year

The new year was a time of intense excitement to Brodie. Since the sale of the mace to Tasker in Chesterfield and the robbery at Tapp's, his game-cocks had also been doing well. After his prolonged period of abstinence, the devil had got into him. Brown was highly critical, saying over and over again to the others that Brodie seemed to set more store on the style of the raid on Tapp's than any actual profit. Brown was disgusted with the trifling haul, as he described it. Ainslie was by nature pleased with anything, but Brown's insistence had transmitted itself to him too. There was a feeling of division between the two pairs of men. Smith had little patience with Brown. He reminded him continually that Tasker was his, Smith's dolly-shop, and that both he and Brodie were the craftsmen of the enterprise.

To Brodie, Smith confided that he did not trust Brown.

'He's a fawney-rigger, as we say, a ring-dropper. There are two sorts in our family, Will. In one sort there is trust and in the other there is treachery. These flash coves are not our sort. He's a cat-in-the-pan. When all's well he's with you, but they have long noses. At the first whiff of trouble, watch him. See how he arrowed off to Stirling.'

Despite Smith's words, he also had his reservations about Brodie's behaviour. He felt he now understood that the man had to have some bravado in the performance, and he admired the way in which Brodie had handled Mrs Tapp without any apparent alarm or fear. At the same time he was conscious that it could have been disastrous. Mrs Tapp might tell her husband even now, and might easily remember the voice. Smith still felt that they should have fled, however undignified it might have seemed.

'There's no dignity about dancing on the end of a rope,' he had said to Will, trying to make his feelings clear.

'If we dance here, Georgie, you need have nae fear o' the rope. I've had my hand in the design o' it. Did you not know that? It can be fixed.' Smith stared at him incredulously. 'Oh aye. Get the length right for the drop, and with a harness there need be no trouble. I have thought all that out.'

'It is a subject I would rather not discuss or think about, Will! You're an inhuman cool sort of man at some times.'

'No, Georgie, but I am awful prudent. I am also the best wright in Edinburgh so it is my job tae understand these things. As my chosen profession may link me with the child o' my brain, it is prudent tae have a way o' mastering it invented at the same time!'

Smith was quite white as he thought about it.

'You talk as though you want to try it, Will. For the love of Christ, be silent. It turns my bowels to soup. No one survives a cropping!'

'Oh, but they do, and they have, Georgie. Here, in this town. And if certain precautions are taken, there is no reason why it should not be contrived. The last time it happened, it was by accident. Did I not tell you all about it?'

'No, and I don't want to hear!'

'It's a matter o' scientific study and curiosity.'

'It's a matter that makes me sick.'

Brodie's general elation led him to return to gambling. A contributory factor to this was the heavy pressure that Jean Brodie, Jacobina and Matthew Sheriff, were putting on him to return to his cabinet work. Jean had started a campaign of afternoon teas that Will was supposed to attend, but which merely drove him from the house. She had also stopped the maid from preparing a formal dinner, in the hope that hunger would wear him down. It was such a pathetic manoeuvre that Brodie actually felt sorry for her despite his dislike for her righteous nagging. She simply had no comprehension how to deal with human beings. He ate instead at Clark's.

Brodie had been pressing them eagerly to raid Inglis and Horner, silk merchants at the Cross, as they had recently received a new consignment. In friendly conversation at the shop, he had discovered that they had taken delivery of a considerable quantity of lutestring, armozeen, florentine and rasdimore silk, in addition to both cambric and white satin. George Smith had passed quietly by one night and had duly tried the picklock he had made. It worked perfectly and he had simply relocked the door. They had all agreed to Brodie's insistence that time was important, as the stock was being sold every day, and were to go there that night.

As usual they waited in Clark's, playing cards to while away the time. Ainslie, Smith and Brown were already present, but Brodie was late. Brown, who allowed no opportunity to slip by, was becoming impatient.

'Look, George, you have the key. How much longer do we have to sit here and wait for our friend? You know as well as I do that he may be off anywhere. Let us do it. We'll give him his cut.'

'No,' said Smith. 'It was his idea, and we'll wait. There's time yet.'

'You were always a great man for supporting the Deacon,' said Brown. 'I wish I shared your trust in him. I don't understand him and I make no bones about it. When I can't fathom a man I'm suspicious. What need has he for this way of life? I don't trust a man who pykes for pleasure. What has he got to lose in this place? The likes of him have it sewn up tight as a sailor's shroud. Have you ever considered it—in his position if he was caught blundering down the High Street with the regalia of Scotland in broad daylight, they would ask him to put it back and make a stronger box into the bargain! It's us who should worry. That means you and me and Ainslie, for they'd top us for lifting a purse. You and me especially, for you have form, George, I'm prepared to wager on it.'

'Damn your patter!'

'I'm not interested—it's your affair. But I have no intention to hop the twig before my time for the vanity of the Deacon.'

'Brown, I wonder if you use your brain-cannister. If the man has the power he has, then he has everything to lose, and have you considered that he is our protection?'

'Aye, it might be, if we were all innocent as babes. But, George, none of us is, are we?'

Brown smiled knowingly at Smith, who felt sudden anger and only kept his temper with difficulty. It would serve no purpose to fall out with the man at this stage when he knew too much, but he decided to have it out with Brodie. They must get rid of the man as soon as possible. There was an insinuation in everything he said, and he always seemed to take an oblique view of everything. There was nothing straight in him. Smith wondered what private enterprises Mr Brown had running on his own. He should be watched and checked up upon.

Brodie's entrance immediately alarmed Smith. He saw him come in, and make straight for them, not pausing to chat to left or right. He ignored greetings called out to him, and sat down immediately at the table. His naturally sallow face was paler than usual, and he had been hurrying, not sauntering, for the sweat stood out on his forehead and ran down his side-whiskers. His scar seemed to stand out like a purple comma below his right eye. He immediately waved for a drink, not waiting for Clark. After this flurry he sat in silence and stared at the table. They all looked at him in some bewilderment. When the lad had brought him a drink of ale, which he gulped at eagerly, it was Smith, naturally, who asked what the matter was. Brodie seemed embarrassed. From a sallow yellow he gradually reddened.

'Gentlemen, I am ashamed tae say that I have probably cooper'd Inglis and Horner for us all.'

'What?' All three almost shouted simultaneously. Heads turned throughout the tavern. A red-nosed lawyer, very drunk, stuck his head round an adjoining partition and demanded to know what was the matter and would they all mind not shouting as it was disturbing the peace, by God. A smiling girl pulled him back and they saw no more of him. Brodie leaned forward and spoke in a very subdued manner.

'It may be all right. You see, I thought I would try my hand at making a pick-lock. I have never tried it, ye must understand, and for a man o' my craft it offers a considerable challenge ...'

'God, no!' moaned Brown. 'Don't tell us, we've guessed.'

Smith was holding his head in his hand and massaging his broad forehead. He could think of nothing to say. Finally he asked how bad it was. Brodie, almost eagerly, like a child who sees the promise of forgiveness, explained the situation. He had only tried the key to see if he was capable of making one, and by God he was, for the lock had opened. Like Smith he had intended to re-lock the padlock and come straight on to join them, but it would not lock. He had struggled with it for five minutes in mounting panic. The Guard had gone by, and various caddies and chairs, and each time he had been forced to flee and return. In the end he had wedged a small piece of wood in the lock to keep it shut, and left it as it was. 'There's no way,' he continued eagerly, 'that anyone can tell it has been done. We must go back tonight and clean the shop, and Smith can lock it with his key.'

'Count me out,' Brown said nastily, 'I want no part in a mess like this.'

'There's three or four hundred pounds' value in silk alone.

The place is crammed with it! It must be done. You can't leave it.'

'For a Deacon I take you for a damned fool, Brodie,' Brown said angrily. 'What do you expect in this life? Smith had a key, it was perfectly set up, it was a good job. You coopered it and, in my opinion, you were going to do it yourself!'

'I'll listen to that from no man!' Brodie leapt to his feet, but Smith with comparative ease dragged him down again. Smith controlled his own anger, but his fingers rapped on the table as he made his point.

'Will, you've buggered it. Because you had to try a key. What sort of flat's foolery is that. The thing's all to smash, and it's you that's done it. What do you want us to do? Smile at you, congratulate you? Congratulations, you have just made your first pick-lock. It's a very expensive affair, this professional pride of yours that costs us three hundred pounds. How do you propose to put that right?'

'Aye,' Ainslie chipped in, 'maybe such as you can afford tae throw it tae the winds. But poor folk such as me find things different. I'll remind ye that we did well enough out o' the tea. Now did I go in and star the job?'

Brodie sat silent. His embarrassment was turning to anger under their combined attacks. He came back at them.

'What sort of seven-sided fools are ye? It's all right, I tell you. The bit o' stick will hold it. Go and see. There's no harm done. I'll remind you, sirs, that this was my idea, and when talking of the money you say you have lost, you are talking of money you would never have had but for Will Brodie. Devil take ye! Saw your timber elsewhere, if that's the way ye take it! I never came here tae pitch the fork, but to explain what had gone wrong. I don't apologise. I was wrong, and that's that. Now the matter must be corrected.'

'I'll correct it,' Smith interrupted. 'Like I corrected our friends Bruce. Remember, you never showed? Well, don't expect your share of this if we do it for you!'

'I am coming with you. I won't be cheated that way!'

'No, you aren't, Will Brodie. Not after spending half the night strolling up and down the street, locking and unlocking the padlock. We don't need you. If we go, we're going alone, and fast. You'll have been seen, man!'

'No!'

'Well, we can't take the risk,' Smith insisted. Brown got to his feet.

'Count me out. I want no part in this nonsense. If Brodie likes playing against a stacked deck, then I don't. I like to do the stacking. I'm off to perch, and that's the end of it, and I won't stir from there till morning and I shall make damned sure my landlord knows it!'

Brown strolled out of the tavern without a backward glance. No one spoke until he had gone. Smith then leaned over.

'Now, Will, you must see the sense in it. Tell us when the Guard passes by, and at what interval, and we'll go and see the trouble. But understand this. We don't want you tonight.'

'Tae hell wi' ye, George Smith! I'm not to be spoken to like a child. I came here in good faith, and not tae be scolded by the likes o' Brown. Yon bastard I do not like. And I do not like this conversation. I'm awa' home and maybe when I have friends wi' civil tongues we may talk about it again. Good night sirs.' Brodie stormed out angrily, growling a farewell to Clark.

Smith thought hard about the situation. If there was no watch on the shop, then they should do it quickly. It was a risk, but calculated. Brodie, he considered, had two knacks, one for dealing with awkward situations on a personal level, as with Mrs Tapp, and the other for wrecking things at the last moment, for some trifling reason. It was as though his mind were divided and in eternal conflict. One part of it was astute and perceptive, able to set up a job and plan it and then look forward to it with an uncommon glee. The other part, almost against his wishes and certainly, it seemed, outside his control, tried to wreck it. What earthly reason was there for Brodie to have made his own key and tried the door? Firstly the man had the skill to make keys, he had no need to prove it. Secondly he had the courage to carry the job through—he had shown that already. It was so unnecessary. Smith wondered if that second part of the divided man actually wanted to be caught in order to prevent the crime. He could understand that Brodie might be struck with guilt, for after all he could afford it. Then why commit the crimes? Smith sighed. It was all too much for him. Ainslie looked at him, his bright little eyes glittering.

'Well, George? Are we on?'

'We'll go and have a look anyway. And as we're passing by, we may as well take our tools.'

'Will we split it?'

Smith thought, not for the first time, that Andrew Ainslie thought foremost about money in any situation.

'Yes. We'll give everyone a fair share.'

'After we've done it! Come on!'

'Listen Andy, Brodie and Brown will get no more than they deserve, and as we take the risk we take the major part. But everyone gets his cut, understand? It makes sure of people's silence.'

'Aye, I suppose that's true,' Ainslie replied innocently, 'but surely you're not saying that John Brown would turn stag on us?'

'I mean nothing but what I say. Now wipe your eye and we'll go.'

'What?'

'Drink up, man.'

* * *

Edinburgh Evening Courant, 1788

SHOP-BREAKING AND THEFT

Sheriff Clerk's Office, Edinburgh, Jan. 9, 1788

That this last night the shop of Mess. INGLIS, HORNER, & CO.,

Silk Mercers at the Cross of Edinburgh, was broke into, and the following articles stolen and carried off therefrom, viz.

A considerable quantity of black lutestrings, black armozeens, black florentines, and rasdimore silks, some of them whole, others cut pieces. Most of the armozeens and lutestrings have yellow lists or selvedges, with some red threads on the outer edge; others of the lutestrings, and all the florentines have white selvedges. All of the silks were rolled on pins or blocks, upon the end of most of which is the following mark I.L.S. with the number of the piece and quantity of the yards in figures. Several pieces of cambric, some whole, some cut—also a piece of plain white sattin. It is more than probable that the said goods may be cut in a manner such to cause them, when exposed to sale, to have the appearance of remnants.

The value of the above goods is equal to from £400 to £500 Sterling, so far as yet discovered.

Whoever will give to William Scott, procurator-fiscal of this County, within three months of this date, such information as will be the means of leading to a discovery of the person or persons who committed the aforesaid shop-breaking and theft, or will cause apprehend or imprison the said person or persons, shall, upon conviction of the offender or offenders, receive a reward of ONE HUNDRED POUNDS Sterling, and the informer's name, if required, concealed.

N.B. If articles, similar to those above described, are offered to sale or discovered in the custody of any person of suspicious appearance, it is intreated that the goods may be stopped, and the person or persons in whose custody they are found secured, till notice is sent as above; for which a handsome reward will be given, besides all charges paid.

CHAPTER NINE

Last fling

As in the previous year, January was a bitterly cold month when harsh winds from the Arctic seemed determined to scour out the city. Business as a consequence suffered and men took to spending more time in their haunts of entertainment. Fires blazed in every chimney that could afford one, and a pall of greasy black smoke hung about the roof-tops, dirtying the washing. The shaded streets of Edinburgh with their heavy overhanging gables and damp vapours and gutters were rimy from morning to night. Everything seemed to have frozen, from the Magistracy to the Town Guard to the water pails that the carriers still brought from the icicled town conduits and left on steps. Dogs were frisky and ran about barking to keep warm. No fishwives visited, as it was too cold to carry wet creels.

It was the time that Will Brodie loved, for people stayed inside and only reluctantly took to the streets. Even the law seemed to have frozen in its administration, for lawyers seldom strayed from their bottles except to crack their boot-soles by the fire. It was no time to be in the Tolbooth.

Brodie had recovered from his rage and chagrin over the affair of Inglis and Horner, reminding the others how right he had been. He still remarked bitterly from time to time that he thought he should have had a greater share of the goods. Brown, who had taken no part in the affair, was naturally well pleased with his cut, which he soon squandered on his current girl, Mary Johnston, in exchange for favours granted.

The size of the reward that had been offered, together with the promptness of its publication, had surprised everyone except

Brodie who had sat through an extraordinary meeting of the Council while they debated the matter. The merchants and magistrates of Edinburgh were becoming desperate. Inglis had needed some persuading, but the Council were well satisfied and quickly dispersed, puffing their hands and wiping their noses in the frosty air. After all, they had not had to offer the reward out of public funds.

The remainder of the silk lay concealed in Ainslie's cellar to be taken by the Newcastle carrier, the first consignment having been despatched in trunks by the Berwick carrier. The trunks were labelled 'Tasker. "Bird in Hand" at Chesterfield', and they were expecting a good price. It was a time for good humour and friendship. Brodie was anxious to make amends for his blunder with the key and, as they sat in Clark's, he talked eagerly of their pursuing his most ambitious plan to date—the breaking of the Excise Office, which should contain upwards of five hundred pounds. It was pleasant to conspire in Clark's with a hot glass of punch steaming on the table. They gambled for pennies with a pair of dice, and talked and thought. The place was packed and noisy and there was no chance of their being overheard. Brodie had explained the layout of the interior and given them a very thorough briefing on the difficulties, and despite the residual animosities and reservations that the others still held, they were impressed. Smith complimented him.

'You've been through it thoroughly, Will, I'll give you that. Can you get an impression of the key?'

'Aye, there's no bother there. But only the outer door. The key to the inner door is kept by a clerk about his waist, so that he may close it at any time of the day to prevent public admittance when they have money lying about. We will have to force that door. It will need a strong crow.'

'Have you nothing that will do the job?'

'I doubt it,' said Brodie, 'I have a strong chisel, but it is tempered steel and will snap. We need cold iron. Someone must see to it.'

'But what aboot the Guard?' Ainslie asked.

'Ach, nothing! But there are two watchmen employed by the Excise that have nothing better to do than spy on the building. However, I have been watching them of nights. Ye see, gentlemen, Brodie is a thorough man for all ye say about me sometimes. Now these two bonny fellows take it in turns and there is a time that there is one off and the other yin not back again. Perhaps that could be observed upon so that we can be sure it is a regular event, for it would be awfu' embarrassing if it proved otherwise!'

Ainslie volunteered that it was his sort of work, and Smith said that, as he would be making the key, perhaps Mr Brown would like to take it in turn with Ainslie so that one face should not become too familiar. Brown agreed with some ill-nature. He did not look forward to such a cold prospect. Brodie was delighted with the way they had taken to the job. What was more, they were willing to accept his instructions. He had planned it all himself, in detail, and he was to run it. He continued:

'Now I can get an impression of the key tomorrow. I have only to go in and ask to see some man whom I went with a week ago and does business there—a man from Stirling who is certainly there right now. The important thing about the Excise is the cashier's desk, for they are a bunch of dainty rogues as ye might guess and distribute the money in two places for security. Now I will draw you the desk quickly and, George, I will show you how it's locked, for it's hidden, with false escutcheons.'

They continued in their deliberations until each had a clear picture of what they should do, and Ainslie, Smith and Brodie settled down to another glass of punch. Brown, who had been consulting his watch from time to time, announced that he had an engagement and, despite their protestations, would not stay. Smith remarked amid laughter that he supposed that Brown 'was following up the silk', and left amidst their ribaldry.

'He's a man with no humour,' Brodie observed. 'Who is this Mary Johnston anyway? He has a great capacity for keeping things to himself.'

'Maybe that's not so bad, Will,' said Smith.

'Maybe, but I like to know more about what a man gets up to.'

Ainslie laughed obscenely.

'Hochmagandy! Hochmagandy! It's all the same for beggar or dandy!'

Brodie was embarrassed by Ainslie's crudeness. Smith wanted to know what it meant.

'Ach he's only a crude devil. Let's get on with our game.'

Before Smith could ask any more, their solitude at the table was roughly interrupted by a large man, over-clad in thick black trousers and coat, with a leathery-looking face. He was obviously half drunk and thrust his hands on to the table, leaning forward for support.

'Good evening to ye, gentlemen. I see ye have the ivories out, which means that ye are sportsmen, and I see that ye have a chair just emptied. Now I am a sportsman masel' who is short this moment o' company. I would take it an honour tae join ye!' Without asking their permission, he sat down heavily, knocking the table and slopping their punch. 'Ach, gentlemen, the chairs in this place are ower sma' for the likes o' me. I'll order some mair!' He clapped his hands and waved. The others stared at him. 'Don't be unfriendly tae a visitor now! My name is John Hamilton, master chimney-sweep, frae Portsburgh. I have heard that you gentlemen are ever keen.' Clark's lad brought a steaming bowl of punch, and Hamilton started to ladle out the liquid into their glasses. He spilled so much that Smith impatiently took the ladle from him and did it himself. Ainslie looked at Brodie.

'Shall we have a wee game?'

'Why not.'

Smith was the only one who seemed reluctant, but he joined in nevertheless.

Brodie produced his own dice from his pocket, taking the others off the table. Hamilton did not notice. Brodie winked at Ainslie, and suggested they played hazard, which Hamilton readily agreed to, throwing his purse on the table with an extravagant gesture. Then things happened with alarming speed. Hamilton appeared to have little idea of what he was doing. He mumbled to the dice and muttered and cursed when his 'main' chance failed. Between throws he helped himself steadily to the punchbowl. Brodie and Ainslie were gaining steadily and Smith had lost a trifling amount. Hamilton continued to dip in his purse for guineas.

'Ye have the luck o' the devil!' he roared. 'There's nothing I can dae! Damn, just one more game!' He slapped down a guinea note. 'In Portsburgh, I have a good business, ye ken. Men work for me. It's not like here mind. God damn! Ye've taken ma' money again! What are you? Ma' luck is as good as the next man's! Ye'll not frighten Hamilton off a board!' He slapped down another guinea note, and picked up the dice, as caster. He rattled and shook them, crooned to them and swore at them, and finally threw them, throwing a chance. The stakes went up. Cursing continually now, he threw again and lost it. Brodie collected the winnings.

'Now it's my bank!' Hamilton shouted. Heads were beginning to turn, and the cautious Smith did not like the look of the man. The fire-light shone directly on his face and Smith thought he looked dangerously cunning. Nor was Smith sure he was as drunk as he pretended.

Brodie was too cautious to 'nick' first time but, following his routine, threw a chance. He added to his stake. He threw once and missed, but not losing. Watched grimly by Hamilton he threw a second time and got it. Hamilton appeared resigned.

'It's yours, it's all yours . . . tak' it awa'!' He slumped back in his chair. Brodie reached out to rake in the money. At that moment, while his attention was distracted, Hamilton moved like a striking snake. He whipped the dice off the table and, clutching them in a huge fist, bellowed, 'Bring some light! I want tae look at these! It's my belief they're loaded!'

Smith would have flown at the man but Brodie grabbed his arm. 'That is a slanderous suggestion, sir! Merely because ye are losing. How dare ye! Do ye know who I am?'

'Aye, Mr Brodie, I know very well who ye are, Mr Brodie. A pigeon-fancier Mr Brodie, who would take a man like me. Bring us a light, I'll prove it!'

'By Christ, you've come here from Weir!'

'Is that so, Mr Brodie? And who is this Weir? Another poor dove ye've plucked with your innocent friends!' He saw Clark quietly edging off the mantelpiece, and pointed a finger at him. 'Now, Mr Clark, I think you had best keep out o' this, for I am saying this in public. Let us examine the dice.' He held them over a candle so that the ivory became semi-transparent like hard wax. 'By Jesus, the things are loaded! See, gentlemen, see. I invite ye all. And this by a Deacon of your fair town, who practises the fair art o' theft with the assistance o' these little friends. Come no nearer, Clark, or by God I'll split your skull! Be sure, my friends, that I will lay this before the magistrates in the morning!'

Brodie got up from the table and advanced on Hamilton. Although he was deathly white, his voice was steady enough.

'Take care, Hamilton, or whatever you call yourself. These dice were supplied by the house. You had the use o' them too. So are you such an innocent bird?'

'Is that so, Mr Brodie? In that case I can only regret that ye did not instruct me in their use before we started, so that we might all have been even! And is it the habit of Mr Clark tae keep the house dice loaded?' Clark exploded with rage.

'Get out o' here, Hamilton, or sure as I stand here I'll fetch a horse pistol and blow you out in the gutter where trash like you belong!'

'By your leave, Mr Clark, I'll go, but I note ye never answered the question!' Quite composed, and obviously sober, the big man went to the door, the dice clasped firmly in a huge fist. He stopped and addressed Brodie.

'Good night to ye, Deacon. This evening of innocent amusement has afforded me great pleasure. You will hear from the magistrates tomorrow. It is truly sad to see men of standing demean themselves to these tactics!' Before Brodie could reply, he went. There was a moment's silence before the tavern broke into an uproar of talk, Brodie protesting his innocence at the top of his voice and condemning the man's outrageous behaviour as being that of a rogue and the worst sort of loser.

'Gentlemen,' he proclaimed as a sort of final announcement on the subject, 'don't let this spoil your pleasure. Let the magistrates decide. God knows, I am innocent. When did Brodie need a sweep's soot!'

Later Clark took him aside to remonstrate, telling him yet again that he had had it coming and that it would bring the tavern into evil repute. 'Don't worry, John,' Brodie replied, 'I can put a word or two in the right place. You'll hear no more of it.'

'So you say and I hope you're right. I want no more of it. Understand?' Brodie nodded. He was in fact worried. He would have to act fast.

The following morning, he made it his business to seek out Councillors Galloway and Smith. Galloway, for all his cant, understood well the need to keep the name of Edinburgh clean, and Smith was a friend he could rely on. He caught Galloway in the street at gill-bell, although naturally it was not to be supposed that Galloway was visiting a tavern. Brodie explained his situation.

'I'm sure I don't have to emphasize tae ye, what an embarrassing position this . . . sweep has put me in,' he was saying, 'and I cannot conceive of his vindictiveness not only to myself but to the Council.'

'Is that so?' Galloway was scandalised. 'And did he say so in as many words?'

'He made implications about men of standing in this town.'

'He never!'

'Aye, before the whole clientele.'

'The man's a rogue. And is it true the dice were loaded?'

Brodie smiled slightly. Galloway was his man.

'Aye, it may have been. Or else the man may have thought they were. What I am trying to say, is that the man may have deceived himself. It makes no difference for we all had the use o' the same dice. But his imputations are too much for a family like my own to bear. Consider the name of Brodie pulled through the muck and stour by the whim o' a sweep. And I have no proof, as the Lord is my guide, that the man did not substitute the things himself.'

'Is that so? Well, Mr Brodie, it's a sorry affair right enough, and not one that I would want to see a Deacon and Councillor of the Town in. But ye have brought it on your ain heid. Gamblin' is a ferocious evil, man. Did ye know no better? Come now?'

'Aye Mr Galloway, you were always a wise one. I should ha' known better. You could not have called it gambling, until the sweep came along. We were merely chatting, enjoying a warming cup and playing with pennies. Ask anyone who was there. The sweep suggested the thing.'

'Aye well, but ye should know better than tae be drawn in. The Book says, "The righteousness of the upright shall deliver them; but transgressors shall be taken in their own naughtiness." Proverbs, eleven, six.'

'How true.'

'Aye. Well I'll speak tae the magistrates for ye. I dinna think that the word o' a sweep wi' his abominations about the men of standing in our town should be allowed. Rest assured, Mr Brodie, I'll put it tae rights. But it is a lesson and a judgement. Heed the Lord!'

'He shall be my guide, Mr Galloway.'

'Aye, well there's none better. Now I must away. I have my business. Good day to ye, Mr Brodie.'

'Good day.' Galloway hurried away for his gill.

Donald Smith was a good deal more forthright.

'I told you your gambling habits would bring you into trouble, Will. It's no' the most savoury of company ye sometimes keep.'

'Now, Donald, Clark's tavern that evening was filled equally with whores and lawyers, including some Writers whose names I will not mention.'

'You know what I mean, Will. All men have private lives, but they normally keep them private. Whatfor do ye have to get mixed up with a sweep.'

'He intruded upon us. Not by invitation, in fact the very contrary. Have you never found yourself in that position?'

'Indeed I have. It is good sense to just get up and go. Aye, I'll not read you lectures, for we all make mistakes. Do ye think the things were loaded?'

'I don't know. He lifted them before we could see. I have no doubt that the ones he puts before the magistrates will be. The man was drunk and a bad loser. Everyone will tell you that. It's the disgrace to the name, Donald, and folk saying there's no smoke without fire. Not just me. But think o' my sister.'

'That's true. I'll enquire after this Hamilton for you. He sounds a known sort of man. I'll have a word with the magistrates, just you leave it to me.'

'I hope some day I can offer the same sort o' service to you.'

'Damn it, Will, I hope you never have to! I'm not without blemishes as you know, but I keep them under my own bedclothes so to speak!' He laughed and smacked Will on the back. Brodie smiled back. They sauntered up to the Cross, chatting. Their route took them up the Canongate and, as they passed the Excise Office in Chessel's Court, Brodie thought that all would be well.

Edinburgh Evening Courant, 1788

SHOP-BREAKING AND THEFT

Whitehall, Jan 25, 1788.

Whereas, upon the night of the 8th or morning of the 9th of January instant, the shop of Mess. INGLIS, HORNER & CO., Silk Mercers in Edinburgh, was broke into, and articles taken therefrom amounting to upwards of £300 value; and as the persons guilty of this robbery have not yet been discovered, notwithstanding every exertion that has been made, and the offer of £100 of reward for that purpose, his Majesty's most gracious pardon is hereby offered to an accomplice, if there was more than one concerned, who shall, within six months from this date, give such information to William Scott, procurator-fiscal for the shire of Edinburgh, as shall be the means of apprehending and securing all or any of the persons guilty of or accessory to the said crime.

SYDNEY.

Besides his Majesty's most gracious pardon, the sum of ONE HUNDRED and FIFTY POUNDS Sterling in place of £100 formerly advertised, is now offered to any person or persons who will, within six months from this date, give to the above William Scott such information as shall be the means of leading to a discovery of the person or persons who committed the aforesaid Shop-breaking and Theft, or will cause apprehend and imprison the said person or persons in any sure prison, to be paid upon conviction of the offender or offenders; and the informer's name if required concealed.

* * *

Brown and Ainslie sat behind a hedge, shivering with cold. Their breeches were wet and their shoes soaked and white with their tramp through the snow. Brown was convinced he was contracting frost-bite, and one foot had lost all feeling. He sat down in the snow and massaged it.

'This was a bloody clever idea of Smith's,' he complained, 'and when you sit down you freeze your arse. Five minutes and

I'm going home!' Although they had stopped at the village of Duddingston and drunk a bottle of porter apiece, its effects had long since worn off. Blowing snow buffeted them in the face and rushed over the hedge. They were the wrong side for shelter, but the right side for concealment.

They had brought Smith's black dog Rodney with them, to lend them an air of respectability. Men with dogs were less suspicious, especially if they walked them boldly on the moor. They would appear to be either rabbiting, or taking the dog for a stroll. Men alone would be suspicious.

The dog Rodney, oblivious to the cold, still leapt and bounded about in the snow, snapping at mouthfuls and yipping with excitement. It refused to be caught and kept in cover.

'Listen to the bloody row of that mongrel thing!' Brown's teeth were chattering. He pulled the hedge with one hand, to make a parting in it through which he could see its antics. A slab of snow slid off the top and disintegrated over his head and shoulders. Letting the hedge go sharply, he was caught by a further fall, and sat back cursing and wiping his neck and face with his handkerchief.

'Bugger this! Two miles' walk and now how long do we have to wait?'

Ainslie tried to whistle to the dog through his teeth, with a thin noise like a rabbit screaming. The dog heard, for it stopped and cocked an ear. Then it ran off again, lolloping round in circles, sniffing the yellow patches of urine left by rabbits, hares and voles. 'He must go in for his dinner,' Ainslie insisted.

The two men were above Duddingston Loch looking towards Prestonfield. The scene in other circumstances, or even two hours earlier, would have been strikingly beautiful. A fresh fall of snow lay on old snow so that each step made a noise like cutting cabbage. The Loch was frozen over, except for the very centre where a throng of ducks and seagulls had broken and stirred the ice. A coot ran about clownishly, doing the splits when it fell. But below them a farmer was hammering away at a pair of harrows, preparing for the spring levelling. His ploughs, in true fashion, had merely been turned into the hedge. Ainslie and Brown wanted a coulter as a crowbar. It would be ideal for the job, and if they left it behind it would never be traced. Brodie was worried about his own tools. They were distinctive, and they were tempered steel. The small crow he possessed would be no match for the Excise door.

The farmer was in no hurry. His breath rose in steaming clouds. He had paused to look at the dog several times, but had then got on with his job, hammering the tines straight. He had no sheep to be worried, but he was obviously curious about it. The dog finally came galloping back, with a face that seemed to expect a reward. Ainslie grabbed it by the neck, and held it, panting, behind the hedge. Its breath smelled from hunger.

'What about the reward then?' said Brown. 'A hundred and fifty pounds and a free pardon. By God, it's enormous.' He looked cautiously at Ainslie to see what the other's reaction would be.

'Aye,' Ainslie replied, 'it's no bad when ye consider that they offered ten guineas for the mace!'

'Tell me truthfully. Are you not tempted?'

'Me?' Ainslie affected to be scandalised. 'Turn stag? I would never peach a man, not for money nor nothing!'

'I know that, but have you not been tempted. Damn it, Ainslie, it's almost twice as much as your share!'

'And yours. What's in your mind?'

'There's nothing in my mind.' Ainslie was studying him carefully and Brown was equally careful to keep a blank face. 'What's money? But consider a pardon. Me a free man. I was bound for Botany till I flipped the coop. If they ever catch me I'll be lucky to avoid a cropping. Consider yourself in that position. They must know it's wanted men.'

'How?'

'The way it's put. First the reward, then the increase and the pardon. A softer man than me might go for a thing like that.'

'A man who went for a thing like that would get his throat cut. And here we would see tae it.' Brown was uneasy at this reply. As though to emphasize it, Ainslie spat into the snow, leaving a neat round hole. 'So you wouldna' be thinking o' it, Mr Brown?'

'What do ye take me for?'

'A pretty fancy operator. I have no convictions on me and likewise have no intentions o' collectin' one! As long as that's quite clear ...'

Their conversation suddenly stopped, as Brown nudged Ainslie. The farmer had picked up his tools, cleaned his boots off on the harrow, and was making his preparations to leave. In a minute he was tramping homewards on the lea of a drystone wall. All they could see of him was the puffs of his breath.

'Come on,' said Ainslie, and pushed his way through the hedge, snarling at the dog to sit. Brown followed, and the dog immediately rushed after. Ainslie kicked it soundly as it passed, and it let out a high-pitched squeak but was otherwise undeterred. They scrambled down the slope to the ploughs, which were partly overgrown with dead brambles and nettles. 'We'll need a stane,' Ainslie said, picking up a handy-sized one from the field. He set to knocking out the wedges that held the coulter on one of the ploughs. The noise echoed and bounced with a terrible din, emphasized by the bone-yard quiet imposed by the snow.

'Christ, Ainslie, what the hell are you about!'

'A lot o' noise but quickly. If I dunt it less, we'll be tappin' awa' here all day. Just mind your business and watch!' Ainslie dealt it another dozen ferocious blows. There was a sudden clatter of metal. 'Got it!' he shouted. 'Then move!' Brown hissed. 'That farmer's on his way back!' They could see puffs of breath speedily returning up the lea of the wall. The two of them quickly clambered up the slope, covering themselves further with mud and snow, and dived through the hedge. The black dog amused itself by dancing round in the field where the ploughs lay.

'Oh God,' Brown groaned, 'get that whoreson mongrel beast out of there, can't you.'

Ainslie whistled. He stood up and waved. He waved and whistled. The dog was digging for moles.

'Let's get out of here,' Ainslie urged, 'the farmer's nearly on us!' Ducking low, they ran as fast as they could and were soon out of sight round the curve of the hill. The dog stayed where it was, scooping out earth, until it heard the bellowing of the farmer, then trotted rapidly after its masters, disdaining to run for a mere human. It overtook them at the foot of Salisbury Crags, where at that very moment Ainslie was holding back a boulder while Brown tucked the coulter and two wedges under it. Bounding up joyfully it stuck its freezing nose in Ainslie's face, almost causing him to drop the stone. Cursing, he gave the animal such a kick on the rump that it followed them all the way back to Edinburgh with its head hung low.

'I tell you, Ainslie,' Brown said, 'if that were my dog, I'd shoot it. We want nothing more to do with that bastard beast!'

'So the farmer saw a stray dog, so what! There's hundreds o' black dogs in Edinburgh.'

They trudged homewards, clutching their coats about them. Their feet and hands had lost all feeling. Mr Brown however was rapt in thought. A pardon and a reward was too much to ignore without consideration. By taking the King's pardon on the theft of the silk, he could wipe the slate clean in two kingdoms. Or could he? The advertisement referred to an accomplice coming forward. Might he not end up as the condemned? Brodie had connections. What about Scotch law, he thought, could it clean off his English conviction? Same King. He must check on it with someone. The thought persisted that here was a great chance merely waiting to be seized.

While Ainslie and Brown had been taking their rural stroll

in the cold, Smith was busy filing, the sweat running down his face. The cellar in which he was working had no ventilation and the heat of the small forge in the corner could only build up. The air was foul and inadequate, as the fire had consumed much of the oxygen. The small chimney originally intended for the laundry copper, was inadequate for the blazing coals. Brodie had obtained the impression for the key in a manner which characterised his coolness and skill at that part of the job. He had called time and again at the office, asking for business clients, and in particular searching for, he said, a Mr Corbett of Stirling. Upon these frequent visits, at each of which he was warmly greeted, he was able to observe the comings and goings of the staff, together with the detailed layout of the offices and the drawers in which they could expect to find the money. There was no strong-box.

The impression he had taken of the key was not one of his best, as he was almost interrupted, by the door opening to admit a customer, but Smith found it good enough for a skilled man. It presented a little challenge, and he whistled to himself with the honest joy of a craftsman earning his pay. Mary brought him beer and bread where he worked, together with a slab of cheese. They sat and talked in the thick air, spending fortunes five times over in the treasure-halls of their imaginations. They had decided it was the big job they could retire on. Mary was full of plans, and her lethargy had lifted so that she appeared almost animated. The husk of drudgery had fallen from her shoulders, neck and face, and she emerged almost new like a caterpillar changing its skin.

The return of the exhausted and complaining Ainslie and Brown brought them back to reality. The dog Rodney bounded at his master in a fit of passion, staining him with mud and saliva. Smith cuffed it without malice and threw it the cheese rind in the corner, where it ate it in one gulp and sat dribbling, its head bobbing from one to the other as they spoke. Ainslie and Brown stood by the forge where they quickly began to steam from head to foot, a sight that set Mary Smith laughing. With the red glow behind them they appeared to be emerging from the vapours of hell. Smith threw the dog the crust of bread which it swallowed whole, and then sat shifting from paw to paw, its tail sweeping the stone flags. It was a dog that loved its master.

Smith asked, 'Did you get it?'

'We did.' Brown sounded aggrieved.

'We've christened it!' Ainslie announced proudly. 'I call it Great Samuel.'

'What?'

Ainslie looked at him in astonishment.

'The ignorance o' you English is truly astonishin'! Great Samuel, for great strength. It's in the Bible,' he added wisely, 'every man should read that.'

Smith roared with laughter, shaking his head. No one else knew what he was laughing about.

Brodie, feeling that he had already made a substantial contribution to the campaign by taking the impression of the key, had decided it was a good time, before their expedition, to see how his cocks were shaping up under the care of Michael Henderson. They were alone in the feeding barn, and Henderson had with him two dung-hill cocks of a lamentably disposable appearance. They had been given to him by a farmer for no longer fulfilling their functions. Brodie was dismayed.

'Could you not have got something just a wee bit better? What a bundle o' sticks. If ye ate them you'd pass them whole!' Henderson held up a hand.

'Will, they're rubbish. Of course they are. But what do ye want? Your birds maimed? We have the main afore us. No, this will just give them a wee bit taste o' blood. Now watch the following. One, how fast they fly at the bird, two, their persistence and above all lack o' mercy. We need no gallant knights. It's murderers we're after. These scrae and scranky auld wrecks are difficult to kill, mark me. Man, ye can't kill a bone!'

So the two skeletal birds had been sacrificed to two of Brodie's best birds, Henderson making observations on the movements of the birds throughout. He understood their timing precisely and seemed to know when they would retreat, and when they would charge. The scrawny victims, as he had said, put up little fight, but took a long time to die. The floor was covered with feathers and both birds were almost naked at the end of it. Brodie, looking at their torn and blue flesh pimpled like human skin, suddenly felt disgusted. He did not like the training. Two birds in their prime was one thing, with the mass hysteria of the crowd, and with a fortune to win or lose. This cold execution was another. Henderson sensed it from his face. 'This is not your pot of ale, Will? Aye, it's no' much fun but it has to be done: I canna raise fighting-cocks on mother's milk and affection. Good soldiers must be trained to kill and do it fast and fearlessly. I've never seen ye taken like this. Is anything the matter?'

Brodie was indeed suffering from an uncomfortable depression, which he put down to the waiting before the action. But there was something more to it than that, he felt. He had come to recognise his own moods. His present one was of unease. It had prompted him to give Ann and the children the jewellery. It might be the raw weather and he might be catching a cold. Whatever it was, he was depressed. He felt, moreover, that in raiding the Excise, he was not only achieving an apogee in his career but by the same token ending it. Even the Royal Bank would be no more difficult or rewarding. His confederates, far from being a jolly set of rogues, able to lift him from his depression, carped and criticised him. They scorned flair, and ridiculed his enjoyment and fun. George Smith was a nice enough man, but they were a dreary bunch and not what he had intended. He could not help feeling that he had allowed himself to be trapped by reality while trying to escape through the window to romance. Ah, Macheath! Ben Budge! Matt o' the

Mint, Polly Peachum! Instead of whom he thought, I have Solid Smith, Arse-bare Ainslie and ... what about Mr John Brown? He determined to make a show of it and shock them all this time.

Henderson was looking at him in a peculiar way and he realised he had not replied.

'I'm sorry, Michael. Business worries. You will look after the cocks, won't you?' Henderson stared at him with genuine stupefaction. 'Good God, Will, ye know I will! That's a pickle insulting.'

'I don't intend it, Michael. I trust you like no other man, ye know it well. And, bye the bye, I would appreciate the borrowing of a brace of horse pistols.' Henderson was silent and thoughtful. He picked up a pail of corn and began to feed the penned birds.

'I suppose you know what you're about.'

'Aye.'

'Well, you're guy doleful for it. Tell me nothing, Will, what the ears don't hear cannot be extracted frae the tongue. But take care, man. Ye may have them of course.'

'You're a good man, Michael. You'll see no more o' this mood, mark me. My fortunes will shortly change. Ach, it's just worry.'

'Watch John Brown.'

'Why do ye say that?'

'I don't trust the man. He steers his own course. He's clever, and he'll make use of you.'

'Don't worry on it, Michael. I have Mr Brown's measure.'

Nevertheless, Will Brodie could not rid himself of his unease. The reward was enormous on the silks, and that, with a King's pardon, was very dangerous indeed. He cursed the intrusion that had starred the glaze of his dreams. He would carry out such a depredation on the Excise office as would enable him to sell the business, the Brodie name, and everything he possessed. He would take to the sea, as he had dreamed as a boy, renounce

Edinburgh and its stew of corruption, and blow over the blue sea to a new freedom in an innocent world. He would dismember everything his father had created over so many years in so many short hours, with Jean and Jacobina clinging to his knees and sobbing. But where should he go? He had the world to choose from? He walked home from Henderson's, his mind buzzing with ideas. No man should be fettered by indulgent love and nailed to the cross of gratitude. He cursed Francis and the fanatical burden he had piously imposed. That was the great hypocrisy. It had all been for the benefit of Francis Brodie's soul. Will Brodie hoped he roasted in hell.

The final planning took place on the afternoon of March 4, the day before the raid. The four men met in Smith's house, where they liberally indulged in bottles of 'Black Cork'. The plan was gone through three times until they were all familiar with it. On the following night the guard was an old and wizened man, long accustomed to sleep quietly at his post, and he should give them no trouble. Brodie proposed that should the man appear, they should take rope along to tie him, and pretend to be smugglers in search of their confiscated property, a story that was doubly appealing to Brodie as he remembered the popularity of Wilson. Brodie had also brought a coil of stronger rope so that, if surprised at their work, they could bolt the doors and escape out of the back windows to the garden below. It was agreed that Ainslie should remain on watch, preceding them to the building and giving the all-clear when the last clerk had left. They would be masked, and Brodie undertook to provide a whistle for Ainslie, one blast to be given if it was the watchman, who would then be tied up, and three blasts if it meant trouble, or more than one man. The other three were impressed. It seemed to them that Brodie had thoroughly mastered the situation, and his contingency plans for escape showed a new prudence he had not previously displayed. Brodie's inventive thinking did not stop there. If everything went to plan he intended, he said, to leave a spur, torn from its buckle as though by accident, to give the impression that the robbery had been carried out by horsemen, and confuse the magistrates. The others thought this a clever idea. It should lead them to conclude that the theft was committed by a different gang from those who had robbed Inglis and Horner. In Brodie's mind, however, the robbery was going to be done by highwaymen. It would be part of his dramatic role and he intended to enjoy himself. He also arranged to bring a strong chisel, pick-locks, false keys and the dark-lantern. Brodie, Smith and Brown would carry a brace of pistols apiece, but Ainslie who would remain outside would go unarmed, so that he should appear innocent of any intentions if stopped by the Town Guard and searched. They toasted their success in great humour. Of all the plans they had laid, this seemed the most complete. They had provided for every eventuality and particularly for their own escape. Brodie's manner was determined and commanding and no one saw any reason to challenge him. As to the haul, they could expect to find anything from five hundred to a thousand pounds. It was Brown who introduced the only discordant note, arguing bitterly that he had not yet had the opportunity to enter a premises and do the inside work. Brodie, in great good humour, declared that he would guard the door then, and protect them from the wrath of Edinburgh. He explained where the drawers were, and where to search for money. The four agreed to meet again at seven the next day, Smith with the false key for the outer door, and Ainslie and Brown with the coulter for the inner door which would have to be broken. As they parted, Smith observed that it had almost been like a business meeting, and they toasted its successful conclusion.

CHAPTER TEN

Alarms and excursions

Dinner the next day was proving to be an ordeal, which was how Jean Brodie had planned it. William had already delivered the pick-locks, whistle, keys and chisel to George Smith and then immediately had returned home at three for the party. Until the day before he had forgotten it had been arranged. Jacobina and her husband Matthew Sheriff had come, to which he had no objection, but so also had his aunt Helen and his cousin Milton, a young lawyer for whom he had never had much affection. In Will's opinion he was too righteous to be real. Aunt Helen was small, old and determined to speak her mind, trusting implicitly in her seniority to protect her from rebuffs.

Jean insisted that it was a family occasion and the best china and linen had been laid out. The girl had even been sent out for the best wine. Will was to be punished for the recent lapse in his business attention and the return to his former ways. He thought, I sit at the head of the table and it is my house, but I am still the sacrifice. Then he thought of dead Francis with the guineas on his eyes, of Mrs Tapp, and the Excise office, and smiled. Why should he bother? It would be infinitely easier to bend the head of a penitent to receive these feather-weight blows.

It started well enough, with the usual pleasantries and an inspection of the house by Helen and Milton, guided by Jean. Will wondered privately if they were making an inventory to see if he had sold anything off. When they came back, he asked jokingly if they had found it all there, to be met by a frigid stare from his aunt. Milton on the other hand had the grace to laugh. At least he had some human tissue. Helen immediately brought the subject round to business. Matthew Sheriff however remained staunch in that camaraderie of men harassed by the same women. He insisted on Will's behalf that business was well enough, and that he should know for he would be the first to feel it. When times were hard, chairs were hard too. There was no money for upholstery. Aunt Helen was not to be turned by humorous speculation, nor by a man who had no Brodie blood.

'I have heard, Will, that ye spend too much time wi' gaming. Indeed I have heard that at this very moment there is a cloud over the name o' Brodie because o' it. Is there any truth in it? That sort of thing is no good for a respectit family. Edinburgh is a fierce town wi' reputations. They go like that!' she snapped her withered fingers with surprising strength. 'Now, Francis was a man careful o' his reputation, and when he passed awa' there was many folk wha commented on his piety and honest hard work. A good life and a clean death. That's what Edinburgh likes.'

'No doubt, aunt, but should there be nothing else?'

'Aye,' she came back, sharp as a whip-crack. 'Work!'

'To make a virtue out o' work is to make a vice out o' pleasure, is that not so?'

'It's the first sensible words you've spoke. But I want to know about this sweep.'

'If all pleasures are vices, then clear the table, Jean, for we'll have no gluttonising in this house while I'm master o' it!' Brodie issued it as a command and regarded their startled eyes around the table. Only Matthew was smiling.

'Awa' wi' it! Sinners begone!' There was a thunderstruck silence until he broke into roars of laughter. 'Want o' a sense o' humour should also be listed amongst the great sins o' mankind, for it leads pious folks tae mak' fools o' themselves.'

Jean began to storm at him, followed in turn by Jacobina, complaining about his rudeness. Aunt Helen affected to swoon, which she did not succeed in doing convincingly, for her chair was jammed too tight to the table, and she dare not fall forward on the china and glass. It was noticeable that even young Milton's eyes had the suspicion of a sparkle. Matthew hid his face behind a handkerchief, suddenly suffering a bone in the throat, although he had not lifted a knife.

Aunt Helen, when comforted, never really returned to the hunt with the same vigour, as it took much strong wine to revive her, and soon the subject was forgotten. In the midst of the chatter, Brodie went over the plans again and again. They were proof against any disaster. It filled him with a fanatical pleasure to consider the evening ahead while submitting to the strictures of his aunt. She is Francis's sister, he thought, and to her as to him—may she roast in hell. He smiled at her and nodded, not hearing a word, as one might smile and nod to an idiot. Live but a week or two more, sweet aunt, and you will see William fly the pen, spread canvas wings and away. Francis with golden guineas on his eyes. I hope they have two for you.

The meal finished as the maid lit more candles. It was no longer dusk, but darkness outside. Matthew, Milton and Will stood by the fire, and the women gossiped at the table. Jean, determined to display her status in manifest contradiction of all she had earlier said, was insisting that they should now partake of tea. Aunt Helen was slightly shocked, believing as her generation did that excessive partaking of tea led to excessive desire for alcohol. The two women persuaded her it was fashionable and she was soon converted. The men made themselves easy with another bottle. In this way, time passed too quickly. After tea, Cousin Milton was summoned by Helen to take her home, and went in search of a sedan. The young man was not at all pleased, having found, under the liberating influence of the claret, that Brodie and Sheriff were good company.

'We must meet again, Will,' he called on leaving. 'It's not right that cousins should live so close and not meet.'

'I'm not sure that's proper,' Aunt Helen remarked with a return of spirit.

'Nonsense, aunt,' Milton rejoined to her amazement, and the two passed bickering, into the darkness of the stair. Matthew laughed and sat down in a comfortable chair.

'Although I say it masel', Will, we make damned good furniture! My, this is a comfortable piece o' work. Damn me but this fire makes a man thirsty.' Brodie passed a new bottle, and they discussed the ways of the world that well up from the bottom of a glass. It was a violent shock to Brodie, when Sheriff looked at his watch and announced that he must go because it was almost eight. Brodie should have been at Smith's house at seven. He was an hour late. With as much haste as was decent, he packed off Sheriff who had reached the back-slapping stage, and if not braced for the short journey down the close, looked quite capable of falling asleep in the chair. When Sheriff and his wife had gone, he had no trouble with Jean. She announced in dudgeon that he had insulted his aunt and behaved without courtesy. It gave him the opportunity to retire. Leaving Jean in the main room, he entered his bedroom and shut and locked the door. With frantic haste, he undressed, almost tearing off his silk waistcoat and cravat. He put on instead his old black suit and greatcoat, pocketed two pairs of pistols and his dark-lantern and finally removed from the top of his clothes press a black cocked hat, a black wig and three crêpe masks from a box. The masks he thrust into his trouser pockets. The whole change took him only three minutes and he found he was trembling with concentration. He made himself stop and rake his mind for anything he might have forgotten. Nothing. He hurried out, making little noise and passed the main chamber where Jean would still be sulking. Outside, he hurried down the stairs and walked as fast as he could to Smith's house. He knew they would be angry and would not understand. He determined not to apologise, as it would only make them worse.

Smith, Brown and Ainslie had almost gone beyond the stage of worry into that of panic. It was only Smith's stoicism that held them together. In this frame of mind they were completely stunned when Brodie threw open the door. He wore his cocked hat on his head, and the crêpe mask over his face. His great-coat swirled about him, and he dashed into the room, kicking the door closed behind him. In each hand he brandished a cocked pistol, which he pointed at the three in turn, singing loudly at the top of his voice:—

> 'Let us take the road;
> Hark I hear the sound of coaches!
> The hour of attack approaches;
> To your arms, brave boys, and load.
>
> See the ball I hold!
> Let the chymists toil like asses,
> Our fire their fire surpasses,
> And turns all our lead to gold.'

They were too stupefied to speak or interrupt, but stared at him open-mouthed. When he had finished singing, he uncocked the pistols, which were evidently charged, thrust them back into his pocket, and sat down on a bench with a smile. 'I was unavoidably detained, gentlemen, but here I am prepared. George, I have your pistols, and here's a wig for ye, for your face is getting too familiar by my way o' thinking, and your hair is too distinctive.'

'We've been waiting here an hour!' Brown shouted furiously. 'Christ have you no concept of time? What is this, a fancy dress ball?'

Smith cut through the looming row.

'There's no time for fighting. We all know what we're about and we're all here. Let's get on with it. We're late already.'

'Aye,' said Brodie, 'Ainslie must go ahead. He'd best be off now. Have ye your whistle, man?'

'I have,'

'And the code.'

'One for the watchman. Three for danger or mair than one.'

'Good luck.'

'Aye and tae all o' us.'

Ainslie left. The others, still with some acrimony towards Brodie, laid out their equipment. It now consisted of Smith's false key, looking very professional and new, a pair of toupee curling tongs which he had squared off at the end to make a lever, a small crow-bar and the chisel, the heavy coulter and two wedges, a pick-lock, two coils of rope, one thick and knotted for escape, and finally the torn spur as a decoy. Brodie displayed the dark-lantern and Smith and Brown had wax tapers to light from it. Smith and Brown, who were to force the doors, loaded themselves with the implements, Brown complaining of the weight.

'What are you carrying, Brodie?'

'I'm no' going inside. I have a brace o' pistols, and I'll take the ropes.'

'Do we need all this scrap? It's ridiculous.'

'We'll need it. You haven't seen the doors,' replied Smith.

'Mr Brown is not experienced in our arts, George,' said Brodie. 'The tongs and chisel will take care of the outer cashier's door, but we need the coulter and wedges for the inner. The crow and chisel will account for the desks and drawers and the pick-lock is a little precaution. That is when George's key has dealt with the main door. They don't make it so ye can just walk in and fill your pockets, Mr Brown.'

'Damn you, Brodie, I know my business. What do you take me for? Some flat?' Smith intervened again.

'For the love of God, let's go. If we carry on like this, we'll get napped for sure.' Following Smith's sensible advice, the three men left the house. The night was raw. Fresh snow had fallen and frozen on old snow, so that it crunched underfoot. The streets were almost deserted.

'We'll go our own ways,' Brodie said, 'and here, I have the masks.' Taking one each and adding them to the collection in their pockets, they split up to rendezvous immediately at Chessel's Court.

Ainslie was crouched down behind the railings so that he was sheltered from the freezing wind by the low wall on which they stood. He was invisible in the darkness, watching. When first Smith and then Brodie arrived, he appeared out of the gloom and waved them into cover. Sharp light and sharp shade lay in bars on the court, the product of the moon and snow. Ainslie's teeth were chattering and he was holding his nose so as not to sneeze.

'The porter's gone. He locked the door five minutes ago, and straight home. God Almighty I'm cauld. Can I no' go elsewhere?' His voice was nasal and plaintiff.

'Stay here.' Brodie was peremptory. 'Where's Brown?'

'Not arrived.'

Brodie motioned to Smith and together they crunched their way to the head of the Close, keeping to the black rims of buildings. Brown made them both jump, by appearing at the head just as they arrived there.

'Christ!' Smith exclaimed, soon recovering. 'We came to look for you.'

'I was seeing the porter home,' replied Brown coolly. 'Seeing him leave I thought I'd make sure of it.'

They all crunched back down the Close, hissing at each other to be quiet like stage conspirators. They need not have worried, the place was deserted. Smith took the key from his pocket, and Ainslie slid shivering into the most comfortable position he could find between the snow, the granite wall and the iron railings.

Brodie's heart was pumping in his ears, and he looked about him continually, flourishing his greatcoat. Brown told him to keep still. All three were bright with nerves.

The outer door opened with an oily click, and in three seconds they were all inside. The watching Ainslie permitted himself a sigh of relief that set him coughing into his patched coat.

Inside, Brodie and Brown set the main door back on the latch, while Smith tackled the spring catch of the inner door with his improvised crow made from the toupee tongs. After a brief struggle that too gave way. At a nod from Smith, Brown advanced to the cashier's door. Brodie doffed his cocked hat to the two of them and took up a picturesque lounging posture behind the front door, arms akimbo and with a loaded pistol in each hand. His eyes gleamed with delight. It was all going exactly as planned. Through his mind ran phrases and challenges he would use on an intruder. He practised gestures, and striking poses, stepping out from behind the door, both pistols levelled. All the time he hummed to himself in a low musical way. He was enjoying himself.

Brown had taken out the small crow, which he called 'Little Samuel', and with Smith forcing the coulter and Brown levering on the crow, they were attacking the most intractable of the doors, the inner door to the cashier's room. It was of thick pine with massive hinges. They set to work knowing it would take some time. Meanwhile the Deacon had given up play-acting and was feeling drowsy and leg-weary. He wished he had not had that extra bottle with Matthew Sheriff, as he could not prevent himself yawning. Behind the door in a recess he found a chair, used in the normal course of things by the porter on the door. Pulling it up, he sat comfortably in the shadows. It was pleasantly warm compared with the night outside. Within minutes he was gently nodding off to sleep, clutching his pistols. Smith and Brown had meanwhile made good progress and, with the splintering efficiency of the coulter and wedges, had forced the cashier's door. Inside they lit the dark-lantern and from it the tapers they carried for better vision. The toupee tongs and 'Little Samuel' made short if crude work of the desks. They started to ransack the room, at first with trembling excitement, then later with anger and desperation.

'There's no bloody money!' Brown was almost frothing at the mouth. 'That's your friend the Deacon! There's no bloody money!'

Drawers were strewn everywhere, and the raw edges of splintered wood shone white in the light of tapers.

'He saw it come in. It's here somewhere. Stow your lumber and keep looking!' They started to research the desks, hunting for secret drawers. An exclamation from Brown brought Smith over.

'Here's something anyway!' He pulled out a purse and they counted it. 'Sixteen pounds! God Almighty, is that what we've risked a cropping for!'

'Shut up, man. There may be more in here.' They set about the desk.

Mr James Bonnar was a conscientous men, a fact he kept telling himself, and others too if they would listen. To fortify this opinion of himself he decided, notwithstanding the bleak weather, that he would return to his office to collect the papers he needed in the morning. It may have been conscientious but it was also prudent for then he could work at home the next day by the comfort of his own fire. He was not surprised to find the outer door of the Excise on the latch. The clerks often worked late, but then they were only clerks. Pushing open the door and beating the snow from his boots, he was startled by the door suddenly hurtling back in his face, to be immediately thrust open while a figure in black hurtled out into the night knocking him against the wall. Mr Bonar was outraged. These young clerks had been told about their behaviour.

'You!' he shouted. 'How dare you! Have you no manners, man? In this building you walk. It's as weel I can't see you, I'd have you dismissed!' His yells were lost to the Close for the figure was already gone. Cursing, Bonar kicked aside the chair that he had upset on opening the door, and made for his room upstairs.

Ainslie, still chittering with cold behind the railings, was petrified by the sudden turn of events. He had no idea what was going on, and could not even see who was involved. He had seen a man hurrying into the Excise, and before he could blow his whistle, he had immediately seen a man burst out of the same door and run up the Close. He had no idea what to do. Bonar had no sooner run up the stairs than he collected his papers, still in a fury over the insolence of the clerks, and ran down again. Ainslie was even further stupefied to see a third man—Mr Bonar on his way home—suddenly emerge and hurry out of the Close. In a terrible dilemma of anxiety, he hesitated and cursed and finally gave three blasts on the whistle, stuffed it in his pocket and took to his heels. Assuming that Brodie, Brown and Smith must be making their way out of the back of the building, as none of the night runners had stopped for him, he slipped round by St John's Street, clambered his way through the gardens of the Canongate, getting himself even more filthy, wet and wretched in the process, and turned up like a faithful dog at the rear of the Excise Office expecting to find them. There was no one there, and no window was open. He examined the ground for footprints, but there were none. He decided to get out of it and wait for the gang at Smith's.

Brown and Smith had heard the commotion with terror. They had been about to leave the cashier's room, which they had thoroughly ransacked, when they heard footsteps pounding down the stairs. Mr Bonar was angry and in a hurry. They quickly shut the door again. Brown whispered to Smith, 'Treachery! Get your pistols out, and cock them.' This they both did, hearing the ominous clicks in the dark, as they drew the hammers back. The front door closed with a crash that made them both jump, and nearly made Smith discharge a shot. They listened. To their amazement there was no hue and cry and sound of searching. There was a dead and total silence.

'What in hell was that?' Smith asked in a trembling voice. Brown did not bother to reply. His mind was running ahead.

'Where was Brodie? Where was Ainslie? They've all gone. I told you that Deacon was a flat, a bloody flat. I'll swing for the bastard yet!'

'Shut up.' Smith had recovered his calm. 'We don't know what happened. First let's get out.'

'Where's our thousand pounds, just tell me that? Sixteen miserable pounds. This is the Excise office!' But Smith had gently opened the door and peered out.

'Brodie's gone!'

'I knew it!'

They crept into the hall and gently opened the front door. The two slipped out and up the yard to where Ainslie had been.

'Him too!'

'Scotchmen! I told you! They were in it together!' Smith made no reply to Brown's continuing outbursts but suggested they should get back to his house as fast as possible. In the Excise office they left the coulter which was too awkward to conceal, and the spur that Brodie had provided. Smith undertook to hide the rest of the tools out at Salisbury Crags, as soon as possible. The expedition had been a disaster.

While the other three were all on their way to Smith's house, Brodie, who was very shaken by his experience, was making other plans. What if he had been recognised? He had only woken up when the door pushed his chair over. Had the man seen him? He had no way of knowing. His main concern was to provide an alibi. His mind was centred entirely upon himself and he gave the others no consideration. He was a known man, they were nothing. He must have an alibi! He considered where he should go. He did not want to bring Ann Grant into this, nor did he want to alarm her. That witch Jean Watt was made for this business, and could be silenced with gold. He hurried home to change.

Jean Watt was alarmed by Brodie's appearance. He was dressed in his day-time finery, but he was obviously worried and ill at ease. Nor had she expected a visit from him, and she did not like being taken unawares. It could lead to unfortunate coincidences.

'Will, I never expected ye! This is a surprise.'

'Why? Who's here?'

'Naw naw, hinny, there's naebody here but me and the boys and Peggy. Go see your sons, they're asleep like wee cherubims!' This overstatement did not prevent him from going into the next room where the two boys were tucked up asleep. Neither was particularly clean, and Frank snottered as he slept.

'Jean lass, sit down. Close that door so we can talk. This is important.'

'What's the matter, Will? Ye are in a fine stramash!'

'I want ye to get this clear in your heid. I have been here since eight and mak' sure Peggy knows it too. Do ye understand me?'

Jean Watt laughed.

'What have ye been up tae, Deacon? And you such a respectable man.'

Brodie suddenly lashed out and hit her on the ear.

'Listen, woman, this is no a matter for laughter!' Jean stared at him like a puzzled child. She made no fuss about the blow. They were commonplace to her, but Will Brodie had never struck her. 'You'd think we was married,' she said, rubbing her ear. 'What is it, Will? Can ye tell me?'

'No, and it's better I shouldn't.'

'Ye've killed a man!'

'No.'

'Ach well, it's not that important then.'

'You'll say I was here.'

'Who to?'

'Some may ask.'

'The sheriff-officer?'

'Aye.'

'What have ye done, Will?' Her eyes showed less concern than admiration.

'It's no concern for you. What about the boys?'

'How do ye mean?'

'How will you care for them without me?'

'How so? Why should I be without ye? Will, what's it come tae?'

'God, Jean, I canna tell ye without putting ye in peril. Come tae bed, woman, I'm tired and need ye all at the same time. I have money for ye, such as I could raise. Look after the boys. If ye tak' another man make sure he's a guid one.'

'Will, Will!'

'But if they should come asking, lass, you will tell them, won't you?' He was strangely anxious and pathetic. The peacock, plucked, was a ridiculous bird. Jean Watt thought he looked like a very small boy, hiding from the bigger ones. She cared little for mothering men, and little enough for children.

'I lost my nerve tonight—made a coward of myself.'

Jean's heart sank. She had no stomach for lame confessions. Yet she tried.

'So? There's nae harm in that. All men do it but few admit it.'

Brodie was still thinking, not really paying her any attention. She did not like that either. It made her feel frightened. She considered the day when men would no longer pay her any attention, and what she would do then. If Brodie was really in trouble, was there anything in it for her? She must be realistic, as Peggy was always saying. 'What use is one man,' Peggy continually nagged, 'he'll only die or leave you!' Brodie took her by the arm and looked her earnestly in the face. The affect of his sincerity was to draw his mouth down and emphasize the cast in his eye. She almost wanted to laugh. He gripped her hard. 'Say I had a sore throat—we went tae bed early. Make sure your Peggy has it perfect. If it comes tae it, it may be evidence. In court, lass, do ye understand? They'll hang me an' they get me, Jean. You're the only one I've told!'

'Well, it's not the thing you'd go bawlin' frae the Cross!' Brodie tried to smile, but failed. Jean shook him by one ear, as though he were a child. 'They canna hang a Deacon. It's never been done!'

Brodie considered what she said, and at last relaxed.

'Aye, that's so. There's no call for excitement. Bring a good bottle, Jean!' There was a flash of swagger about him again. The pathetic look had gone from his face. 'There's nothing wrang wi' me that a good dram and a warm mowe willna' cure!' He gazed in almost childish awe at her full breasts as she took off her bodice. It was an expression she did not want to see return.

'Dinna stare at me, Will!' her voice was sharp.

'Damn it, lass, get yon damned kirtle off, so I can really see ye!' Before she could protest her embarrassment further, he pushed her backwards on to the bed and stripped her with flattering lust. That she understood.

The three other men had waited for Brodie with increasing disgust and vituperation. Brown bluntly accused him of running away. Ainslie's confused account of events would in no way turn him. 'There's no saying whether the man's more green than yellow. For my money he has a fine streak of both!' Eventually they simply exhausted their invective, and turned their minds to more practical things. Brown declared that he was going to the New Town, to make an appearance there. No one would accuse him of being near the Canongate. Ainslie was keen to accompany him, offering to be his guide to the hostelries. Smith's reaction was however more complex. He was hurt by Brodie's performance, and venting his anger gave him little relief. He guessed, accurately, that neither of the other two was guided by any motive but self-interest. He could not relieve himself of the feelings of friendship that had grown between them. He had no time for drinking and drowning of woes, he said, he was going home. He tried unsuccessfully to find some excuse for the turn of events and to forgive his friend. No matter how he looked at it, however, Brodie had deserted his post and fled. At this moment he was hiding. There could be no going on with the Deacon.

Ainslie was an able guide. Brown and he soon ended up in Fraser's tavern, brisk and cold from the walk. Brown was still vindictive, referring continually to Brodie's station, his airs, fine clothes and swagger. Ainslie cared nothing about that side of things, but bemoaned his loss of earnings. He complained over and over again that he had blown his whistle and that he had played his part and that it was not his fault if no one had heard. In this way they passed most of the evening, neither listening to the other, until Brown finally tired of Ainslie's whining voice.

'The man's a green fool—a trained monkey behind the door could have held a man at bay. A boy could have done it. The Deacon throws a fine hatchet, but he can't point a gun. Deacon, my arse! The gallant highwayman, cloak, pistols and swagger. The strutting blade! He's just a toffed-up bladder of fart. This moment, he's eating his supper on an easing-chair, mark me! Sixteen miserable pounds!'

* * *

Excise Office Broke Into and Robbed.

On the night betwixt the 5th and 6th of March, it is reported that some persons did feloniously enter the Excise Office by means of false keys and other implements, including the coulter of a plough, the which has been discovered on the premises. The loss from the Office is not known for sure at this time but seems slight, the criminals having failed to gain access to secret drawers containing, it is reliably reported, more than eight hundred pounds Sterling. In breaking the front door a false key was used as is evident by the lack of any damage and its being open. The inner doors and the cashiers' desks however have suffered the most severe abuse under the hands of these criminals so that much expense will be required to repair the Offices and make them safe.

Mr James Bonar of the Excise Office discovered the criminals in the very act of theft. Indeed if he had not fortunately returned to his office, disturbing them, they might yet have found the great sum of money no matter how well it had been hid. Mr Bonar has made a full report of his information regarding this terrible crime to the Sheriff-Clerk's Office and an Advertisement relating to it is expected daily. This crime seems to be one more in the never ending attacks on the property and reputation of our city to which we have recently been laid open. The Magistracy has undertaken to discuss the matter and see what further precautions may be taken to deter such persons as will consider such a crime as robbing His Gracious Majesty's Excise.

* * *

At Smith's house the next day, Brodie received a sour welcome. Brown, who sat opposite the door, immediately picked up four pound notes from the centre of the table, and flung them at him. He had conceived the idea the night before. Brodie noted it for the contrived gesture it was.

'There's your share, Deacon, and may you prosper and grow fat on it! Live well!' He made it sound like a threat. Ainslie spoke up, a rare thing for him.

'While we're at it, Mr Brodie, I'll remind ye forbye that ye owe me a debt o' honour from last November, I believe it was. Ye will remember it was in the sum o' five pounds as ye were temporarily embarrassed and it escaped your memory the following day to repay me ...'

Flushing with rage, Brodie turned from one to the other, to be met with the same stony stares. He gathered up the notes and tossed them at Ainslie, felt in his pocket and flung over a guinea, which Ainslie caught.

'Keep the change. Christ, stand me on the trap!' he pointed at his own chest, jabbing away excitedly. 'It was not my fault, I tell you. What about you, Ainslie, and your whistle? That was a fine concerto. And the cracksmen! Fine lads with the tools.

What was I supposed to do? No warning, then the door is flung on ma heid! Had I loosed off a shot, we'd none of us been here the day. We'd be manacled tae the bar in the 'Booth, that's for sure. So what's sae damnably clever aboot that?'

Brodie's outburst was listened to in silence. Brown broke it, speaking slowly, in between lighting a clay pipe with a taper. 'They say ... in the journals ... that there was ... more than eight hundred ... in secret drawers.' He looked up at Brodie, pausing dramatically while the taper still burned in his hand. He blew it out. 'It seems to me that your information has cost us dear.'

'You wanted to break it, Brown. Had I been there the pickings might have been richer. I'm no' accounting for your incompetence!'

Brown got up boldly and snapped his fingers in Brodie's face.

'That's what I give for your fancy ways, and that for your green ideas, and that for your miraculous and divine holy inspiration!'

Brodie went white with rage. His eyes shone with an unnatural gleam, so that Smith thought he would attack Brown. Smith leapt to his feet and got between them.

'That's enough, John. Bugger the Excise, we'll send the silk to Taskers. We have cash in hand. Forget it, just for now. At least we got the fare for that!'

Nobody laughed at his thin joke.

'It's a fine day,' said Brown, 'when we break the Excise office of Edinburgh to get the fare for a coach! We can't afford to keep you, Brodie. You're becoming an indulgence.'

'Are you a peaching cove, Brown?' Brodie returned with an attempt at his old flash style, but it was thin on his lips. 'Are you the sort tae shoot the cat with fear?'

Brown smashed a pewter mug on the table with such violence that he ripped the handle from the body. Claret sprayed everywhere. For the first time he dropped all pretence of an urbane manner, and stood snarling, the wine dripping from his hair.

'By Christ, Brodie, don't tempt me! There's more reward for you, you flat and fancy fool, than there's been in two takings. Don't you ever forget that, my fancy friend!' Brodie was flustered and had lost control of the situation. His fear of violence left him powerless, and Brown, with true animal instinct, smelled the fear. Brodie stammered slightly, his normally lazy speech forcing his tongue through his teeth like a strangled man.

'There's mair jobs to do. You would be fools to stop now. Is that not so, George? There's the Bank, there's the Council Chamber—that's the mace again, the Chamberlain's office, the Stirling Stage for the wages of the Carron men, that's a new sort o' job ...'

It died on the air. Shrugging, Brodie returned to the door. 'You think on it, you'll see.' As he went out, Brown spat at the door. The drool ran down the panels, released its hold unwillingly and slipped on to the floor. Smith looked at him with disgust. 'Do that in your own house, Brown, not in mine.'

'Join your friend then,' said Brown obscurely. Getting his hat from a hook, he kicked the tankard into the fireplace and walked out. It took him only five minutes' rehearsal before he walked into the Sheriff-Clerk's office. It had been on his mind for weeks.

Smith and Ainslie had meanwhile decided to make the best of the situation. Ainslie paid the fare for his wife to go to Taskers by the Newcastle stage. They did not trust him without her watchful eye. Ainslie paid for it with Brodie's money, which he had changed from the takings for a five pound note.

CHAPTER ELEVEN

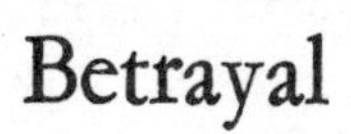

Betrayal

The Sheriff-Clerk's office was not intended to be inviting, and Middleton looked as though he had been chosen to blend with the furniture. He was a craggy, bleak-faced man given to speaking his thoughts aloud without further consideration. His face was parchment-yellow and his hands seemed to Brown like two eagle's claws. His face was that of a predator. He looked as though he digested men whole.

His reaction to Brown was one of detached distaste, and his politeness smacked of judicial manners. Brown feared Magistrates that called him Mister. However, Middleton was not immune to a certain eagerness, as he contemplated the advancement of his own career. He was careful to conceal it. In front of him on the ancient oak desk lay a large ledger in which he wrote with a quill, during their brief meeting. The scratching irritated Brown as it was meant to. So did the Town Guards who stood on either side of him as an indication that he was already a prisoner, their axes over their shoulders. He felt trapped, and Middleton knew it. He had used the technique for years.

'You have certain discoveries to show me concerning the recent robberies in the town. Now let me see, what do you mean by that? One robbery or more. Maybe these recent robberies are connected?'

'I'll say no more until I have promise of a free pardon.'

'Aye, that will be so. But maybe we'll hang you, Mr Brown, for being part of it yourself ...'

'You can't! I have come here of my own free will to lay information in return ...'

'In return for what!' Middleton shouted. 'Don't bargain with me. You are a criminal, Mr Brown, and you and I know it. Now I am not, in fact I administer the law. It is on my side. It takes my word for things. Now where's your bargain?'

'I heard that you had a jury, even up here. I heard it was them that had to be convinced. I heard that you even had judges.' Brown was pale but calm. He would not be bullied, he was too experienced for that. 'I heard you have a Procurator before whom I shall have to appear. I have proof, and I can name names. In exchange I expect pardon.' Middleton regarded Brown for a minute in silence. The man was well dressed, intelligent and articulate. He looked experienced in the law.

'What proof have you got?'

'False keys, used for entering the Excise office.' Brown played his trump card. It was effective.

'Have you, by God! Where are they?'

'Now I must not say. You'll prejudice your own evidence. Take me to the Procurator, and I will lead you to where they're hid, before witnesses. A clever lawyer might otherwise say you had put them there, and that would spoil your case.' Brown managed a faint smile. Middleton had stopped scratching and laid down his quill.

'You fancy yourself as quite the lawyer, don't you, Mr Brown? Don't be clever with me. Try to tie me in knots and you'll be trying to untie one about your neck. Who are these others?'

'I'll be glad to say when my conditions have been agreed. It is after all a matter of some importance to me, and it would seem that I shall have plenty of time.' He indicated the Town Guards. Middleton suddenly swung himself from his stool.

'Right, Mr Brown, we'll see the Procurator, and by God if you're not telling the truth, I'll be glad to attend your hanging!'

Brown still managed to smile at him with impressive calm.

'I think you can trust me.'

'Trust!' Middleton yelled. 'I trust nobody. I don't trust myself. Why should I trust you? You're a thief and a rogue and don't you forget it. You call the Procurator "sir" and try none of your airs with him.'

It was nearly midnight when a bizarre party staggered through the scattered snow and rocks by the light of lanterns at the foot of Salisbury Crags. Brown was preceded by two of the Town Guards, aged veterans who made slow progress and slipped about a great deal. They were unbalanced by being obliged to carry their axes over one shoulder and hold a lantern in the other hand. Sheets of ice lay black and unseen over the rock and they took several tumbles, followed by yells and Gaelic cursing. Each time the whole party stopped until order was restored, then moved on in the feeble light. Behind the Guard came Brown, shivering in the bitter frost, for no one had given him a coat. His hands had been manacled, and he like the Guards was having difficulty keeping his town shoes firmly planted. Behind Brown were two more Guards, then Middleton and the Procurator, accompanied at the rear by two clerks, who being spry young men were impatient at the speed of progress. Brown occasionally gave directions to the Guards, who never appeared to hear him, so that he had to turn round and repeat everything to Middleton, who then called them out again when they were obeyed. He was the only one who could see properly as the other men all appeared to be near-sighted and town-eyed. Brown suddenly stopped.

'There's the stone.'

'Guards, pull that stone up. Come on, hurry. Well, put your damned axes under it, it's the first practical use they've had!' Middleton's ranting upset the Guard and two of them set lanterns on the boulder they were lifting so that they immediately fell off on to the ground and went out. After more bickering and shouting while the lanterns were re-lit, the stone was turned aside.

'Keys, sir,' shouted a clerk, producing a clattering tangle of metal that he straightened out on a bright steel ring.

'False keys,' said Middleton after a brief glance.

'Well, Mr Middleton,' said the Procurator who had remained silent on the walk, 'shall we go back to civilisation now, or have you a longing for these midnight strolls?' He turned to Brown. 'It seems you were right, Mr Brown, and now we will try them on the door, then we will get down to a few facts. We have the whole night after all, as Mr Middleton is fond of observing. It makes interesting listening forbye. Middleton, you will of course make the necessary arrangements to apprehend our friend's companions, Ainslie and Smith.'

Middleton nodded.

'Tomorrow at first light.'

Mr Brown was keeping Brodie for later. He was after all a rich man, and if Ainslie and Smith kept silence, his benefits would be a reward, free pardon and a lifelong hold over the Deacon. It seemed a good plan. If Ainslie and Smith talked, it was only a financial alteration. Even if Brodie talked himself out of it, he was finished. Brown viewed it all with considerable satisfaction.

Saturday was a brilliantly clear day, with the early yellow sun like a brass trumpet for spring. Brodie rose without any premonition. He had weathered the storm, and today he was going to Henderson's to inspect the progress of his fighting-cocks. They had to be ready for his next 'main', and Henderson had arranged a training fight for each bird. He felt that today he could watch the massacre of the unfortunate dung-hill birds, without revulsion. The excitement of the main was on him. He had only one more week, and he intended to make this one pay. He whistled to himself as he sauntered down the West Bow in the sunlight. Edinburgh was busy and cheerful this morning. Carriers and caddies were full of good humour, and expressed it in joking and shouting. Even the chair-carriers had stopped grumbling, which for them was near to high ecstasy. Will felt in great good spirits as he passed through the Inn passage to the pit at the back. As he opened the door, Henderson was stooping over a pen, talking to one of the cocks, and feeding it corn. He straightened up, looking worried and grim.

'Well, thank Christ you're here, Will. I thought ye might hae been part o' it! You want tae watch your friends!'

Brodie stared at him. Henderson saw that he genuinely did not understand.

'Ye havena' heard, have ye! Christ man, where have ye been ... no, I know well where ye've been, but not which one. Will, prepare yoursel'. Smith and Ainslie have been arrested.'

Brodie was thunderstruck. His tongue wobbled about in the cavity of his mouth as if searching for sounds. He made guttural clucking noises like a mute. His face was ashen and he looked about to collapse.

'Sit down, man, afore ye fall down.' Henderson was firm and fatherly, but nevertheless appeared wary. 'The whole Town kens about it, man. Your friend Brown has peached on them. They robbed the Excise. I hope you had no part in that.' It was a question although not put as such.

'What do they say about me?' Brodie managed to ask.

'Nothing. But should they, Will? I have heard it remarked that they were Brodie's constant companions, as the worthy folk say. There's comment. Aye, the muck sticks, and Brown has turned out tae be a rare skite. If you've any part in it, get out.' He made a broad sweep with his hand, palm down. 'Right out. They'll hang them, for sure. Now, Will, listen tae me, look at me, and tell me for your ain sake—did you have any part in it?'

Brodie looked at him, pale and shaky. It was a horrible dream. His father wanted to know if he had stolen a penny. He denied it and denied it because that was what Francis wanted to hear. He did not want the truth. People know the truth, they don't need it put into words for then they are committed. They want to hear what they want to believe. Of course he had stolen the penny, why did Francis keep asking and asking? He looked away from Henderson's grim face.

'Of course not. Do ye think I'm that stupid?'

'Consider it well. They'll get ye if they can.'

'Tae hell, Michael, tae hell! I've told you. We'll have no training the day. I'm shaken. I'm astounded, surely ye understand. Let me be. You go on. Brown! Smith and Ainslie! Good Christ...' Words failed him again and he walked out of the barn, his mind racing. Henderson looked after him, dismayed with what he had seen. There was, as Brodie had rightly guessed, little doubt in his mind.

Almost before he had barged blindly across the Grassmarket, he knew what he had to do. He had not been named yet, if Henderson was right, in which case Smith and Ainslie were keeping quiet, and so was Brown for some reason of his own. He had to know how the land lay and the only way would be to talk to the two prisoners. He was a Deacon and he would use it. He started off for the Tolbooth.

Bailie Dickson would have been hard pressed to be honest with himself over his real motives for hanging about in the Lawnmarket, outside Brodie's house. But as he was rarely honest with himself it did not trouble him. He simply found himself there rather than at the Cross and considered it rather a surprise. And as he was there he might as well enquire after Brodie considering the fate of his friends.

He was delighted therefore to see Brodie coming down the Lawnmarket towards him. He appeared jaunty enough, but he was abstracted and Dickson noticed he jumped when addressed.

'Good day to ye, Mr Brodie. You're in a hurry I see.'

'I am, Mr Dickson. Business is pressing.'

'Aye, always, always. Those scaff-raff got up tae some fine business, I hear. That's the English for ye. No morals. No good comes o' gamin' and gamblin' for it only leads to other vices. And the English love their vices. Man, but I'm glad ye had no nearer acquaintance or ye could have found yourself involved.' Dickson inclined his head and looked at Brodie maliciously. Brodie ignored the insult.

'I've only just heard of it.'

'Is that so? It'll come as a great shock, no doubt. It does a body's name no good at all tae get mixed up in such things however indirectly. You should have seen them for what they were, Mr Brodie. We all kent well they were thieves.'

'Did ye, Mr Dickson? Ye never had the manners tae tell me.'

'Tush tush, Mr Brodie, this is no time for hard words between friends. Mind, after that trouble with the sweep Hamilton, ye could have been mair careful. Still it's done . . . aye, ye'd best attend to your business. It grieves me, ye understand, to see ye in such a position.'

'What sort of position would that be, Mr Dickson?' Brodie was quietly furious.

'Brought so low by others. The family name. Francis was aye awfu' careful with his name. But then he always understood. Good day to ye, Mr Brodie.' Brodie did not reply. He waited until the fat figure had waddled out of sight past St Giles. The man haunted his life like a ghoul, reminding him always of Francis. Francis had not died, he had transferred himself as a memory into other people, where he lodged, spying.

Will Brodie strolled casually towards the Tolbooth and entered at the street door, where relatives were permitted to visit. The front chamber was as black and filthy as the cells. Two Guards who had been lounging on benches leapt to their feet, pikes presented. The senior man, a sergeant, recognised him.

'Good afternoon, Mr Brodie.' The two men looked uneasy. Brodie strolled casually about the room as though inspecting it.

'I hear ye have the two rogues prisoner who broke the Excise.'

'That's so.'

'I congratulate you, sergeant, and your men. The town may sleep easier for your work. I hope they're secure.' The sergeant permitted himself a smile.

'Aye, they're secure. But it wasna' us that took them. They were informed upon.'

'I heard you took them this morning.'

'We arrested them true enough, but there was nothing in that.'

'I congratulate you anyway.' He strolled over to the door leading to the cells.

'Can I see these rogues? I'd like fine tae look at the devils.'

The sergeant shook his head.

'I'm sorry, Mr Brodie. We have orders no one is to be admitted.'

'But I'm a Councillor, surely I have a right. The town's affairs are mine, sergeant. Can I not just glance at your notorious villains? Come now, there's no harm in it.'

'I'm sorry, Mr Brodie, we have orders.' The man was uncommonly adamant. Brodie was worried and it showed as annoyance.

'So ye said, man, and I heard ye, but I'd still like a glance, a minute, a look. I don't want tae have to remind ye of my position ...'

The sergeant was unmoved. 'Look, Mr Brodie, I can't let ye! Town Councillor or Lord Provost, I canna let onybody through that door, and I'm tae shoot onybody that tries.'

'Would ye shoot me? Don't be ridiculous ...'

'Aye,' said the sergeant calmly. 'I wid have tae. I might stick ye in the legs wi' ma pike first, seeing as ye're a man o' position and entitled tae favourable consideration.' Brodie lost his temper. 'Damn your cheek, man. I'll see your captain and I'll see your prisoners. The militia in this town think too much o' themselves!'

'But we're tae be congratulated, Mr Brodie,' the sergeant said slyly. Brodie cursed them roundly and stormed out, slamming the heavy door. The sergeant sat down again. The soldier, looking quite frightened, spoke for the first time.

'Will we get in trouble?'

'No. That's a civilian, and that's the way they carry on. If the captain says no, it's no, he's got no rank. Yon's a friend o' them in there too. Is that no' interestin'?' He smiled to himself knowingly. Brodie was hurrying home. He had guessed by the sergeant's attitude that his game was almost up.

Smith and Ainslie were taken that afternoon to the Fiscal's office. They stood before his desk, manacled by the hands. On the Fiscal's desk lay the bunch of false keys, the coulter and the torn spur. Two Guards stood by the door. Clerks sat in adjoining benches scribbling down everything that was said.

The Fiscal picked up the coulter.

'Regarding this object, which I am told is the coulter of a plough, the theft of such an object was reported by one John Kinnear. I am concerned to establish its identity. Present John Kinnear.'

The Guards opened the door and a farmer, poorly dressed, entered. He was nervous and turned his bonnet perpetually in his hands. 'Stand forward,' hissed a clerk and he shuffled towards the desk.

'John Kinnear, you are a farmer of Duddingston and you reported the theft of a coulter and two wedges by two men from a plough.' There was silence. 'I am asking you.'

'Aye, I did, sir.' The farmer looked nervously at the manacled men.

'I understand that you saw two men making off at about the time it was stolen. Can you see either or both of these two men here?'

The farmer looked around him hopefully, even studying the clerks.

'No, sir. They were hauf way up the hill. It was impossible. Ye see ma farm is . . .'

'Aye, no doubt. Would you be good enough then to look at the coulter and tell me if you recognise it.' The man picked it up and turned it over and over.

'It's the same. But I can't say it's mine, sir, coulters is all much the same. I never had occasion to study it.'

'There is no way, no distinguishing mark by which you would know it?'

The farmer shook his head. The Fiscal sighed.

'Very well, Kinnear, but think hard.' The farmer scratched his head, but stood looking blank. Suddenly enlightenment came to him. 'There is something, sir, but no' here. There's a big black dog tied up oot there in the other room. And sure as I stand here, that beast was the yin they had, loupin' all ower ma field.'

The Fiscal smiled bleakly.

'Release the dog then!'

Dog Rodney pounded into the Fiscal's office, delighted to be loose, and hurled himself at Smith, licking his face and barking. He could not understand why Smith cursed and kicked at him. The Fiscal sat back with a broad smile.

CHAPTER TWELVE

Flight and netting

There was an atmosphere of desolation in the room. The big west window engulfed a setting sun as it had done the day that Francis died. Jean's grief was hardly less. It was Milton, white, shaken, but practical that did all the talking and made the arrangements. Will had confessed to them that he had been guilty of taking part in the burglary at the Excise office. He said nothing of anything else. He declared he had been led astray, that it was a momentary lapse, that he had no intention to steal, but had come along on the spur of the moment. He had been drinking, he hardly knew what he was doing. Milton came straight to the point.

'There is no reason at all to believe that you will remain protected. You must get out, leave the country. I'll talk in confidence to your friends.'

'I have none.'

'Your friends at the Lodge. You are accused of no crime, there is no reason why they should not help you. I can arrange a ship from Blackwall. I know the owners and you can be taken aboard in secret. But where will you go?'

'I always wanted to travel when I was a young man, I dreamed of running away to sea,' Brodie managed a smile. 'It's strange how things catch up with you in later life.' The whole room was suffused with a fiery glow. Brodie thought it looked quite beautiful and at the same time realised that a great calm had come over him now that his guilt was out. He was relaxed now, where before he had acted like a confused man. He now recognised this for what it was—a new direction in his life. He could strike the shackles from him and be free. It seemed to him that he had been working towards this for a very long time. He would leave Edinburgh forever, and leave behind him his whole dead past and all those people who were hosts to the memory of Francis. The town was peopled by them. He wondered why he had not seen it so clearly years ago.

'I'll go to Holland. It's close and there is a Lodge in Amsterdam will keep me in touch. Then I'll take ship to America. To Philadelphia, or Charleston. We have a Lodge in Charleston. They'll keep me in touch with you.'

'Then I'll arrange your passage to Holland. You must leave immediately. By that I mean tomorrow. Even that could be too late. We'll get you on a coach at Dalkeith. You will carry a letter to Alex Walker, a friend and solicitor at the Adelphi in London, who will take care of you from there. We must work this out in detail.' Will looked at Jean who sat huddled in a chair, a wet handkerchief clutched to her brow.

'Must we bother Jean? She should lie down.'

'That's the first scrap of human decency you've shown this day, Will,' said Milton with surprising authority. 'I'll take her out.' While Milton led her away, Will walked up and down the room, viewing it all over again. He had an irresistible desire to snigger as he looked at his own furniture and his father's proudly placed in the room. So much work, he thought, running his hand over the table, chairs, a cabinet, and all for what? He looked at himself in a glass that his father had made. The sun gave his face the red glow of a devil and at the same time made a halo of his hair. He laughed aloud. How simple it all was, if once you made up your mind. If he could get Milton alone, he could tell him about Jean and Ann and see that they were well provided for. Everyone should be provided for by someone else, which was only fair as he had provided for so many. He would give his cocks to Henderson, and he should provide for them. His workshop could go to Jean and Jacobina together with his other properties. That would provide for them. He, William Brodie, would provide for himself. But first he would need cash. The thought stopped him suddenly in his tracks. Where could he lay his hands on cash before tomorrow? Milton would provide it. He had to, there was no one else. He felt light-headed with relief and, when Milton returned, he spilled out his affairs with Ann Grant and Jean Watt, half giggling like an idiot. Milton wondered if he was entirely sane. He was shocked at the revelation of so much turpitude, and disgusted by the creature he saw.

'I do not propose to judge you, for there is a divine judge who is more able than me, but I cannot conceal from you my disgust,' said Milton, appearing even younger than usual. 'My one concern in this matter is to keep the name of our family out of it for the sake of all the family, excluding you. I make that plain, Will, because I want you to know I am not doing this for you, but for everyone else. I am removing the rotten apple from the barrel, which I don't do for its own sake.'

'Milton, Milton. I can quite understand your shock. I am an older man than you and have mair vices. I have strayed intae vulgar ways, as you see it. But, believe me, there is nothing in my behaviour that ye will not find in the commonalty o' the worthies o' Edinburgh! Even the Lord Provost. Particularly the Lord Provost! I could tell ye things about Grieve that would mak' my transgression seem no more than a summer cloud.'

Milton held up a hand as though in benediction.

'I'll hear no more. If you continue, you will make me sick!'

'Look out the window, Milton. It's what's out there should make you sick.'

'I won't argue with you. We have no time.'

'Aye, and we have no money either. I thought of it just now. I will have to depend on ye for cash.' Milton seemed to grit his teeth before replying.

'Yes, that's so. But you won't live in your accustomed style, not out of my pocket, anyway. I have your thirty guineas, for that's all I can manage.'

'Thirty guineas! For me to go to America?' Milton nodded. 'It's not enough for London.'

'It'll have to do.'

Brodie looked quite downcast.

'I never thought to be treated this way by my ain family,' he complained.

'They say every man has redeeming features,' said Milton censoriously, 'maybe yours are late to develop.'

Brodie looked up at him with a sudden sly grin.

'Aye, maybe. But I was never mean wi' my money. And look at the state of my clothes! Could you not have done better than that?'

'It's prudence,' said Milton sharply. 'What do you want? To strut the streets of Ostend like a peacock? An old black coat is the same everywhere. You are not being sent as an ambassador!'

Brodie looked at Milton in some surprise at his heated outburst. 'You know, Milton, you have a head on your shoulders. Maybe a moth in the pocket, but nevertheless a good head.' Milton was about to interrupt hotly but Will went on. 'I have just emerged from a great blackness into light. Do you understand, I am a free man, for the first time. You never knew Francis, or you would understand. I have had pressures on me that tore me. I am my own victim. Can you understand?' Solid, capable Milton shook his head.

'No, Will, I can't, and it would be dishonest of me to say otherwise.'

'It would have cost you very little!' Brodie said with emotion.

George Smith was told that same day that Brodie had now quit the city and that all his haunts had been searched. He demanded to see the Fiscal, wishing, he said, to make a clean breast of it all, and ask the King's pardon. The Fiscal was delighted to listen, but needed no more witnesses. He would rather have more criminals.

Sheriff Clerk's Office, Edinburgh, March 12, 1788

TWO HUNDRED POUNDS
OF REWARD.

WHEREAS WILLIAM BRODIE, a considerable House-Carpenter and Burgess of the City of Edinburgh, has been charged with being concerned in breaking into the General Excise Office for Scotland, and stealing from the Cashier's office there a sum of money—and as the said William Brodie has either made his escape from Edinburgh, or is still concealed about that place—a REWARD of ONE HUNDRED AND FIFTY POUNDS STERLING is hereby offered to any person who will produce him alive at the Sheriff Clerk's Office, Edinburgh, or will secure him, so as he may be brought there within a month from this date; and FIFTY POUNDS STERLING MORE payable upon his conviction, by William Scott, procurator-fiscal for the shire of Edinburgh.

WILLIAM SCOTT.

DESCRIPTION

WILLIAM BRODIE is about five feet four inches—is about forty-eight years of age, but looks rather younger than he is—broad at the shoulders and very small over the loins—has dark brown full eyes, with large black eye-brows—under the right eye there is the scar of a cut, which is still a little sore at the point of the eye next the nose, and a cast with his eye that gives him somewhat the look of a Jew—a sallow complexion—a particular motion with his mouth and lips when he speaks, which he does full and slow, his mouth being commonly open at the time, and his tongue doubling up, as it were, shows itself towards the roof of his mouth—black hair, twisted, turned up, and tied behind, coming far down upon each cheek, and the whiskers very sandy at the end; high topped in the front, and frizzed at the side—high smooth forehead—has a particular air in his walk, takes long steps, strikes the ground first with his heel, bending both feet inwards before he moves them again—usually wears a stick under hand, and moves in a proud swaggering sort of style —his legs small above the ankle, large ankle bones and a large foot, high brawns, small at the knees, which bend when he walks, as if through weakness—Was dressed in a black coat, vest, breeches, and stockings, a striped duffle great coat, and silver shoe-buckles.

* * *

The Geddeses were tormented by curiosity over Mr John Dixon. Why had he arrived at midnight and what was the nature of his ill-health? They had heard him moving about freely enough and even talking with John Dent, the master, in their own Scots tongue.

The sloop *Endeavour* presented a dramatic picture. She was stuck fast in the mud off Tilbury and had lain there ten days, waiting for the neap tide. Day after day the yellow sun dispersed the wreaths of fog and rose over her as she sat sail-less, and at night it sank far over the flat Essex coast, making a hard black silhouette of her masts and spars. To the Geddeses' annoyance, Mr Dixon kept to his cabin and slept at night beside a fire in Dent's stateroom. They conjectured who and what he was. Mrs Geddes, a silly and romantic woman of fifty, was sure alternately that he suffered from leprosy, that he was a spy, that he was a Crown agent, and finally that he was the ageing Young Pretender returning to his native land. They were after all bound for Leith.

Brodie alias John Dixon was for his part thoroughly bored by his enforced confinement. All there was to see from the stateroom was Thames mud or Thames water, both of which looked remarkably similar in colour and consistency. He played draughts with Dent in the evenings when this was possible, and he wrote letters to Ann Grant, Matthew Sheriff and Michael Henderson, filled with depression and remorse. When he was not active, depression seemed to settle about his head like a swarm of bees that could not be beaten off, and he had violent nightmares from which he woke sweating. In the triumph of his escape, this delay had brought him dreams of death. This was no bird-like escape on to a blue sea with a fair wind. It was like a prison hulk in the marshes.

From the stateroom windows he was able to watch the big ships, as they slipped down the channels, sails full set in this windless reach. They passed to London, or outwards to every point of the Globe. Seamen clambered about their decks or up the rigging in constant motion. Whistles blew and orders were bellowed that rang across the water. They were vibrant with life, but his ship lay dead. Sailing barges rushed close by, their masters shouting ribald comments. They knew their way through the narrow channels. There was nothing unusual to them in seeing a grounded vessel. Brodie watched all this activity for hours, dreaming of far-away lands. Clippers swished by, bound for India or Australia on the tea and woollen trades. Merchantmen for the Americas, fat-bellied, low in the water and rich. Frigates and men of war tacked briskly about, smart, sparse, and bristling like terriers. He had enjoyed it at first, but the contrast of their stubborn immobility dragged him into a depression. In this state he began his letters.

The ebullient rudeness of his departure left him with an aftermath of anxiety and remorse. They would certainly be searching for him by now. Would Milton, who was tight-fisted as a clam, really look after his bastards? There was too much righteousness in the man. He wished now that he had been more moderate and appeasing. He missed Henderson, that rock of calm, and he missed Matthew Sheriff, a steady, kind fellow. What would Rab Smith be up to? The devil would be in his glory! The worries ate at him worst in the Thames mists that crept up when the cold in-coming tides subtly covered the warmer mud. He saw that he had behaved with the arrogance of an unknowing child, but he had been unable to prevent it. Milton had arranged things well, but by God he was insufferable!

It amused him that the Geddeses were due for a surprise

journey, for he had delivered sealed orders from the owners to Dent, who was to make for Ostend, on his way to Leith. They would have a taste of foreign travel. Pulling over another sheet of paper, he wrote to Ann Grant. As he told her how much he missed her and how he hoped the children were well provided for, he sank into deeper melancholy. What could a letter really provide? He had asked Henderson to do what he could. Pulling out that letter he read it through. He had ended it with an appeal that, on re-reading it, brought tears to his own eyes.

'I am very uneasy on account of Mrs Grant and my three children by her; they will miss me more than any other in Scotland. May God in His infinite goodness stir up some friendly aid for their support, for it is not in my power at present to give them the smallest assistance. Yet I think they will not absolutely starve in a Christian land, where their father once had friends, and who was always liberal to the distressed. My eldest daughter, Cecil, should be put apprentice to the milliner or mantua-making business; but I wish she could learn a little writing and arithmetic first. I wish to God some of my friends would take some charge of Cecil; she is a fine sensible girl, considering the little opportunity she has had for improvement.' Tears of pathos ran down his cheeks as he re-folded the letter. He prayed to God with sincerity. To Jean Watt and the two boys he gave a passing mention. He had never believed they were his. But Cecil, sweet Cecil ... she was a beautiful child, and he loved his girls.

Mrs Geddes had insisted on a boat being provided and she and her husband had taken to going ashore to relieve the tedium of waiting. Throughout the long wait, Williamson the King's Messenger had scoured Edinburgh and assured himself Brodie had left the city. He picked up his trail in Newcastle where Brodie had taken the 'Flying Mercury' to York and London. From the coachman he learned that Brodie had left the coach at the foot of Old Street, Moorfields, instead of continuing to the coach stop at the Bull and Mouth, and there he lost him.

With the dogged persistence that characterised the big man, who was built like John Bull, he combed London's gaming-dens and found no trace. He moved on to the channel ports of Margate, Deal and Dover, rightly assuming that his man would flee the country. Finding nothing there, even he was obliged to give up. He returned from Margate by the Rochester road, less than half a mile from the river. Jolting along in the stage in the evening sun, he considered how like a Dutch painting these flat reaches of the Thames appeared, with the dying sun picking out the mastheads and spars of the ships. It was a rare moment of relaxation, and he was very tired. He looked out with pleasure at the barges, frigates, barquentines and sloops lying out from Tilbury. He was glad to be on his way home, even if he had been unsuccessful. The man would turn up one day.

Mrs Geddes proposed it and her husband John had to execute her desires. He was a pliable, happy man, rich with the tobacco trade, caring little for others and liking nothing better than a full belly and another bottle.

'Why don't we invite that Mr Dixon ashore, my dear? It would be good for his health,' she added unconvincingly.

'Ach, woman, you want to see the man, so why not say so!'

'But it would be good for his health,' she persisted, unabashed, 'it can do him no good cooped up in that cabin day and night. Have you heard him coughing? The mists are damp and drear. We have to meet him sometime. Maybe we can get him out of himself?'

The Geddeses presented themselves at Brodie's cabin. They could hear him coughing into a handkerchief. Brodie let them in, feeling that it might ease his boredom and depression. They must see him sometime.

'Why, Mr Dixon,' exclaimed Mrs Geddes tactlessly, 'you're not an old man at all!' she blushed. 'We thought you were old and ill!'

'For the former, no, for the latter, yes. I have been confined for a weakness of the chest and now have a throat like a tube of fire. I can eat no solids, and must be careful o' the weather.' This was now, to his annoyance, entirely true. The throat was giving him the devil.

'We have a boat to go ashore,' said Geddes, 'and we wondered if you would join us? There is a good inn at Northfleet, called the Queen's Head.'

'I'm sure it's a haunt of smugglers,' gushed Mrs Geddes, 'it is so exciting. But it is really quite safe. Say you'll come with us!'

Brodie needed little persuading, and even before they left the Thames, the Geddeses and Mr Dixon were on convivial terms.

The neap tide floated the *Endeavour* and the ship came to life, sails snapping at the wind and timbers creaking. She battered out of the Thames into thick Channel weather with heavy winds. Before long the three passengers were suffering the discomforts of sea-sickness, Mrs Geddes lying on her bunk groaning and saying prayers by turns, while John Geddes sat miserably with a bottle of rum, declaring over and over that it tasted the same going down as coming up. Neither showed undue concern when Dent informed them that they were now off the coast of Holland, having been driven there by strong winds. In fact he had been unable to make for Ostend and was anchored off Flushing. Brodie was to go ashore. Mrs Geddes, now that they were at anchor in calm water, recovered her spirits and took it all as a treat. 'My dear,' she told her husband, 'we are to visit Holland, and all this on the way to Leith. What an adventure! Captain Dent says he will put in there for supplies, at a place called Flushing, and the Dutch make such fine lace! We may go ashore, he says, and make some purchases.'

John Geddes was also surprised. 'It's a strange course you've struck, Captain. Still, there's nothing like Dutch gin!' and he winked broadly. They were however very surprised at Mr

Dixon. Mrs Geddes came bursting into their cabin later that day, full of the news.

'Mr Dixon is leaving the ship, John! He is taking a skiff for Ostend. I heard him talking about it to Dent.'

'That's damned queer.' Geddes was not a stupid man. 'It seems to me that Mr Dent was blown off course by his helmsman.'

'What do you mean?'

'Who ever heard of going to Leith by Flushing? It's over wrong for an error of navigation. There's something peculiar in this.'

'Well, anyway, I'm sure it's none of our business. After all we're being charged no more for the journey, for I specifically asked the captain! I've never been in a foreign country before.'

'Aye. But it's still damned queer.'

'I told you he was an agent,' she gushed. 'How much can I spend on lace? This is all very exciting!'

The next day Brodie said good-bye to them over a bottle of brandy, which Mrs Geddes affected to find a powerful liquor, while drinking a third of the bottle. 'You have business in Holland, Mr Dixon?' she asked.

'I have. But not tae talk about.'

'I told you, dear!' She was triumphant. 'Mr Dixon is on government affairs!' Brodie roared with laughter in an unrestrained way, and Geddes was embarrassed.

'There is something I would like ye to do for me,' Brodie said, producing a packet of letters wrapped in oilskin. 'These are for delivery in Edinburgh. I would be eternally grateful to ye both if ye would see they are properly delivered.' He was suddenly serious, almost pleading. 'You will mak' sure o't won't you?'

'Certainly, Mr Dixon.' Mrs Geddes seized them. 'They'll be safe with us.'

Eventually the small party broke up on a surfeit of farewells.

Mrs Geddes watched Brodie's departure down the rope ladder to the skiff, hanging on to the side for support and giggling. John Geddes waved like royalty, looking flushed and content. Dent gave orders over the side, and a farewell salute. Within twenty minutes the skiff was a white speck in the distance, heading for Ostend. Dent called to the Geddeses, 'If ye want ashore, there's a boat going in an hour.' He had no idea who Dixon was, and being a sea-captain had no anxiety to ask.

* * *

Scots Magazine, May 1788.

In the night between the 4th and 5th of May, George Smith, prisoner in the Tolbooth of Edinburgh, accused of shopbreaking and theft, had the ingenuity to make his way from his own apartment to that of Andrew Ainslie, a supposed accomplice in the same crimes, though Ainslie's room was situated two storeys above that occupied by Smith. This it would appear, was achieved by his converting the iron handle of the jack or bucket of the necessary into a pick-lock, and one of the iron hoops around the bucket into a saw. By a dextrous use of these instruments Smith took off one door from the hinges, and opened the other which led to Ainslie's apartment. They then both set to work, and cut a hole through the ceiling of Ainslie's room, as well as through the roof of the prison itself. Luckily, however, the falling of the slates and lime into the street, between three and four o'clock in the morning, attracted the attention of the sentinel upon duty, who immediately gave the alarm, and the inner-keeper had them soon after properly secured. In order to let themselves down from the top of the prison they had prepared 16 fathoms of rope, which they had artfully manufactured out of the sheets of their beds.

* * *

It was Margaret Geddes who succumbed to temptation. She was holding the bundle of letters as though it were Pandora's box.

'I can't keep myself from them,' she cried in exaggerated despair. As they had returned to Leith three weeks earlier, they had so far managed very well.

'No!' John Geddes was striding up and down their main room. 'They must be handed over intact. They will be evidence.'

'The man must have been Brodie,' his wife insisted, flapping at an open newspaper on the table before her, 'the description fits exactly. We could have been murdered on the ship!' Her eyes gleamed with excitement.

'Don't talk such damned nonsense, woman. The man killed no one. The thing is, how do we explain not delivering them? We've had all this before. Of course it was Brodie.'

'You know fine why we didn't deliver them, nor hand them over! It was your gin!'

'And your lace and nankeen.'

'It was your nankeen.'

'Aw, away tae hell!'

'John! No profanities, please!'

'I am too respected to be mixed up in this sort of thing. It will mean the court for us if they catch him, and all this brought up in evidence.'

'He'll be clean away by now.'

'Anyway, I repeat what I said at the beginning, we have only a suspicion. How do we know it was Brodie?'

'Open the letters!' said Margaret Geddes triumphantly. John Geddes stopped striding about.

'Well, at least we'll know for sure,' he said doubtfully. Mrs Geddes needed no more prompting. She picked one from the pack and broke open the seal. She read in silence, her face red with excitement.

'What does it say, what does it say?'

'It was him!' She sounded delighted. 'Listen! It's dated Thursday, 10th April, 1788.

'On the ship.

Dear Michael,

I embrace this opportunity of writing to you, and I make no doubt but it will give you, Mrs Henderson, and a few others satisfaction to hear that I am well.

Were I to write you all that has happened to me, and the hairbreadth escapes that I made from a well-scented pack of blood-hounds, it would make a small volume.

I left Edinburgh Sunday, the 9th, and arrived in London Wednesday, the 12th, where I remained snug and safe in the house of an old female friend until Sunday, 23rd March (whose care for me I shall never forget, and only wish I may ever have it in my power to reward her sufficiently), within 500 yards of Bow Street. I did not keep the house all this time, but so altered, excepting the scar under my eye, I think you could not have rapt to me. I saw Mr Williamson twice; but although countrymen commonly shake hands when they meet from home, yet I did not choose to make so free with him, notwithstanding he brought a letter to me; he is a clever man, and I give him credit for his conduct.

My female gave me a great uneasiness by introducing a flash man to me, but she assured me he was a true man, and he proved himself so, notwithstanding the great reward, and was useful to me. I saw my picture six hours before exhibited to public view, and my intelligence of what was doing at Bow Street Office was as good as ever I had in Edinburgh. I left London on Sunday, 23rd March, and from that day to this present moment, that I am now writing, I have lived on board a ship, which life agrees vastly well with me. It is impossible for me at present to give you my address, but I beg you will write me, or dictate a letter to Thom, and let it be a very long one, giving me an account of what is likely to become of poor Ainslie, Smith, and his wife; I hope that neither you nor any of your connections, has been innocently involved by those unfortunate men, or by that designing villain Brown; I make no doubt but that he is now in high favour with Mr Cockburn, for I can see some strokes of his pencil in my portrait.'

'Is there anything in it about us?' There was a pause while she finished.

'No.'

'We'd best read the rest.'

'Then what shall we do?' Geddes thought for a while.

'We'll ask your brother. He knows a man who knows the Dean of Faculty. He can get advice. Now read the others quickly.'

Secure in the belief of his safety, Brodie had settled down to a quiet and pleasant life in Amsterdam enjoying the watery beauty of the city, and strolling the canals. It was an idyllic interlude. The weather was warm and balmy, the city rang with innumerable carillons of bells and street organs played in every square, drums thumping and monkeys with red hats dancing on top, strapped to them with a thong round the loins. It was made for idle strolling. He had even made friends with a fellow Scot who had been a successful forger, up to a lucrative point, at the expense of the Bank of Scotland, and like himself had decided on a change of air. They employed quiet hours in the gentle pursuit of the fine craft of draftsmanship, Brodie observing it might be a useful trade in the Americas.

He had taken rooms in an alehouse, whence he had been passed from Ostend by one Bacon, another Scot, on production of a letter from Alex Walker. This building, like every 'herenhuis', overlooked a canal. Brodie had thrown open the window, listening to the comfortable noises outside. Clogs clopped on the cobbles, and horses clattered with a heavier metallic sound, jingling their harness as they strained on barge-ropes. The water shushed peacefully under the bows of the vessels as they made their slow progress, causing wavelets to dance with small plopping noises against the banks. The house itself was tall and gaunt, squeezed into a row of houses that all looked too narrow, as though they had been compressed from each end and extruded upwards. Brodie had every reason to be relaxed, for he embarked the next day for Charleston.

He lay back on his bed, pale, but with the appearance of a man who has found peace. The light was beginning to fade, and the screaming of swallows brought him to the window. He liked to watch them in their hundreds, dipping and dappling into the canal, then streaming over rooftops in the wink of an eye. They seemed to him to have a rare freedom, unlike any other bird. They shot over men's heads within a foot of their caps, utterly confident in their speed. He was mesmerised by them. Tytler and his balloon might provide an escape, but the liberty of these birds was sublime. Time and again they danced on the water as though they would swim, playing with the other element. They seemed to be filled with joy.

The sound of voices down below caught his attention. They were speaking in English, and one of them was asking if John Dixon was in. A horrifying panic seized him so that he almost fainted at the window. His landlord was answering yes, he was upstairs, was he a friend of the Captain? There was more talking and steps sounded inside the house. Brodie looked round, desperate. There was only one steep stair, and the man would be on him in seconds. He wrenched the door of a small cupboard beside the chimney, and clambered in, pulling the door to behind him. Almost immediately there was a thumping on the door. This was followed by a pause and renewed thumping. The door was opened. Brodie, almost compelled to hold his breath, heard a man moving about the room, obviously searching it. He heard the bed being moved and the furniture searched. The large wardrobe was rifled and the doors slammed. There was a brief pause. Brodie's door was suddenly pulled open, and he was looking, speechless, into the face of a big man, holding a pistol. The man stepped back with a grin and a flourish, keeping the pistol steady.

'How do you do, Captain John Dixon alias William Brodie? —would you be so good as to come along with me.'

Brodie stiffly climbed out of the cupboard and the two men looked at each other.

'Don't you remember me, I'm John Daly, who met you at

Ostend. Sir John Potter, the consul there, employed me to find you. You'll make me a rich man.'

Brodie seemed to have sagged within his clothes, and looked even smaller than he was. He said nothing in reply. The game was up, and in a curious way he accepted it, as though it had always been what he expected. All his dreams, he thought, came to nothing in the end. He wondered briefly if the swallows had dreams of being earthbound.

* * *

From the Tolbooth

Edinburgh, August 17, 1788.

Dear Sir,

The nails of my toes and fingers are not quite so long as Nebuchadnezzar's are said to have been, although quite long enough for a Mandarine, and much longer than I find convenient. I have tried several experiments to remove this evil without effect, which no doubt you'll think says little for your Ward's ingenuity; and I have the mortification to perceive the evil daily increasing.

Dear Sir, as I intend seeing company abroad in a few days, I beg as soon as convenient you'll take this matter under consideration, and only, if necessary, consult my Guardian and Tutor sine qua non; and I doubt not but you'll devise some safe and easy method of operation that may give me a temporary relief. Perhaps the Faculty may prescribe a more radical cure.

Dear Sir, if not disagreeable to you, I'll be happy to see you. You'll be sure to find me at home, and all hours are equally convenient.

Believe me to be, with great esteem,
Your most affectionate Ward, and very humble servant,
WILL. BRODIE.

To Don. Smith Esq.
Edinburgh.

* * *

From the previous night into the early hours of the next day,

August 27, Edinburgh could not settle to a peaceful rest. Crowds gathered, dispersed into taverns and re-gathered again around the Tolbooth, shouting and singing. Tired, work-worn men could not sleep in their beds for the singing of roving drunkards who wandered the streets and visited each other's houses. There was a sense of unease. Disturbances continued until dawn. Men fighting and swearing, windows thrown open and abuse and filth thrown out. It was a blowsy ring-eyed city in the morning, and people yawned and were short-tempered at the table.

Outside the Tolbooth, several hundred people had gathered by dawn, occupying the vantage points from which they might view the prisoners leaving. They were mostly working men, who would disperse to their labours afterwards. In the Justiciary Court, every seat had been bought by five, but no one thought it was full. Extraordinary scenes of choler and violence occurred at the door, between old and respected citizens. Old men, whose coffins were bought, ran ram-like at the crowd in an attempt to get in. The door-keepers, men of immense corruptibility and hoarse voices, cursed, shoved and hit out at the crowd as they pleased. They had the right to refuse admission, and everyone must pay their price. They had started charging two shillings at four, a heavy sum, based on the size of the crowd. By half-past four it was three shillings, and by seven they had crammed the crowds up double and were charging a crown for admission. Even the agents of the Court had to pay, puce with rage and pushing, as they surged their way slowly to the doors. Those who would not pay were excluded, for all their station, as were those who were unpopular. An undignified clamour of yelling and promises of retribution amused the crowd within, who cheered on either the party outside, or the keepers at the door. Ladies lost their bonnets, and gentlemen their wigs. Some declared it the best show they could remember, short of an actual hanging. Inside the Court, soldiers stood at their positions by the jury and the judges' bench, with fixed bayonets in their muskets, chatting to those in the crowd around them who called pleasantries or begged them to move over so they might see.

Inside the Tolbooth, Brodie was dressing himself with particular care in the scant light of his apartment. His fellow Councillor and friend Donald Smith had seen him respectably equipped and attired, for as he remarked, 'At a trial it is even more important to be seen about with a certain style. It doesna' do tae let the City down.' On the bench beside him were a folded coat and hat. His nails had been cut and his hair dressed and powdered. For the occasion he wore a fancy waistcoat, black satin breeches and white silk stockings. He could hear the crowd in the Lawnmarket through the small barred aperture that gave him light, but could see nothing but the building opposite. People leaned out of the windows, waiting.

Two warders watched his preparations in silence. When he was satisfied with the adjustment of his shirt and waistcoat, he turned to them.

'Gentlemen, it's gone half-past eight. We must not be late for their Lordships. Will you help me on my way?' He stooped, picked up the coat and held it out for one of the men to take. Surprised, the warder automatically took it, shook it out and held it for him to put on, giving it a professional tug here and there to straighten the seams. Brodie turned to him in surprise. He was gratified at the courtesy. 'Man, ye were a tailor sometime? No? Or a valet? It would have been thoughtful o' the Town tae have provided me with a valet!'

'Sorry, Mr Brodie, I was in the Army.' Brodie appeared quite crestfallen.

'Aye,' he responded, after a slight pause, 'they were always flashy dressers.' He gave a smile that was no more than a thin front and put on his cocked hat. For all his efforts, he was obviously nervous. He adjusted the cocked hat with an adroit tap and announced that he was now ready to receive or, as was more likely the case, to be received by Lord Braxfield himself at his audience.

Smith in complete contrast, was a sorry sight. He had been in his cell for six months now since arrest, supported only by what his wife could raise on their possessions, and what his own needle and thread could achieve. His trousers were worn through at the knees and the seam of one arm of his jacket had split at the shoulder, where constant mending had sundered the weave. His stockings were old and yellowed and his shoes were mostly uppers, filthy with food and urine. They had recently been polished with straw and chaff stuck to them. He smelled foully of the ordure of his cell and his unwashed body. His breath stank from his wretched diet, and the warders steered about to the lee of him.

Brodie had ordered sedans for them so that they could pass through the inquisitive crowd without their close attentions. He wanted no mementoes torn from his clothes. Nor did he wish to become a victim of the sport that the crowds might have with the Guards, for which they armed themselves with rotten fruit, night-soil and bags of flour, despite the penalties. The sedans waited outside the main street door, escorted on each side, and front and rear by soldiers. Their white straps crossed them back and front with the saltire. A yelling, breaking into a roar, alerted the crowd that Smith and Brodie had emerged from the door. Even as he climbed into the sedan, dazed by the light, the pushing of the Guards, the din and the hundreds of faces, Brodie could not help speculating if they were for or against him. It was neither—they were simply enjoying themselves.

Brodie's friends among the Canongate Kilwinning Lodge and the Council had obtained for him as good a trio of Counsel as he could possibly expect. He not only had the able Henry Erskine, Dean of Faculty, but Alexander Wight and Charles Hay, noted Advocates. Every one of them belonged to the Lodge. Brodie's other friends, particularly Michael Henderson, had been refused admission to Jean and Milton, and as his name was to feature in letters produced by the prosecution, he had not been allowed to see Brodie. Milton had arranged matters respectably, as lawyers do. The family did not visit the Tolbooth, for Milton said that was out of the question. In this Jean and Jacobina willingly complied, moaning and wailing like two harpies about the fate of the family. No one, and not for tact, mentioned the fate of Will.

Smith was in no such happy condition. As with his clothing, so with his lawyer. He had to make do with the cheapest, and found his case taken up eagerly by a thrusting young man called John Clerk, who seemed to Smith to be eager to handle the case. Clerk was at that time little known except for his tenacity and fire, attributes which Smith unwisely thought would help him. John Clerk had taken the case because he was sure that it would help his own career, and make an impression on Braxfield, the Lord Justice-Clerk. Smith was not even sure why he should be there, as he had confessed the breaking of the Excise, stating that he would give them no trouble and plead Guilty. To his surprise, his agent Mr Morrison, acting under Clerk's instructions, had persuaded him that such a course would leave him singled out, as Brodie might well escape the verdict. He had better link his lot with Brodie's and plead Not Guilty. He had reluctantly agreed, assuming the experts knew best, but how he was to get away with it, he had no idea as he had made three declarations when he had learned that Brodie had fled, all of which confessed his guilt. Nor did these limit themselves to the Excise Office for, in a moment of fear, Smith had given information on the robberies of Tapp and Inglis and Horner, as well as leading the law officers to Brodie's counting room and offices, where pick-locks, the wig and wedges, lantern and false keys had all been found. But the Magistrates thought two informers enough. Smith would stand trial.

The five judges hovered in their robing room, waiting the ring of the bell, at nine. They were as formidable an array as Scotland had ever produced. Lord Braxfield the Lord Justice-Clerk spoke his own fiery version of justice. Unlike many of his colleagues, he deplored the drinking, gambling and whoring that were to him the scourge of the city. He had a tongue as trenchant as a meat-cleaver, and his points were generally blunt, short and final. He was a man of immense ego, and equal courage, but treated the Law like a court-martial, delivering his opinions in the broadest Lanark so that even his colleagues were unable to understand. Above all, Braxfield believed that there was no crime that was not terrible by definition and that could not be solved by hanging. No single man in Scotland could inspire more fear. He freely bullied Counsel, and his fellow judges, but had no objection to forceful argument provided he won. In court he was inclined to tasteless jokes aimed at the defendant, and indecencies in general, with which he liked to shock the public. Young R.L. Stevenson had already singled him out as Weir of Hermiston, and watched his performances with care.

Lords Hailes, Eskgrove, Stonefield and Swinton were among the chief ornaments of the Scottish bar. Hailes was the scholar and gentle inquirer, a mole in the law books. Eskgrove was a repository of knowledge, but had become so rarefied as to no longer have a sense of the ridiculous. He had however a strong sense for procedure and would not be pushed by Braxfield. Stonefield was the cart-horse who had pulled long and hard, and although not brilliant was respected for the accuracy and moderation of his judgements. Swinton would provide the modifying force to Braxfield. He would plod solidly and carefully where Braxfield had already crashed through with the weight of his sparse emphatic words.

Ilay Campbell, the King's Advocate, was a man tormented by his inability to work up any emotion. Try as he might, his delivery was invariably tedious and his delivery of a warning of imminent disaster would have taken three pages of model prose. The crowd yawned and made exaggerated gestures of weariness whenever he spoke, and this only increased his tediousness.

At nine, the judges entered with due slowness and ceremony, bumbling, not hurrying, and the crowd which had been babbling noisily immediately stopped talking. The soldiers of the 7th Regiment of Foot straightened to attention. When the judges sat down, they looked like sheep peering over a dyke. A hum of activity took place amongst Counsel. Braxfield waited until Ilay Campbell nodded, then he spoke.

'William Brodie and George Smith, pannels at the bar, you are to attend tae the indictment which will now be read. Proceed, Mr Norris. We may as weel be off.'

Norris, the Depute-Clerk to the Court, rose and intoned the indictment in a reedy voice, while Braxfield made a point of staring at the ceiling.

'William Brodie, sometime Wright and Cabinetmaker in Edinburgh, and George Smith, sometime Grocer there, both prisoners in the Tolbooth of Edinburgh, you are indicted and accused at the instance of Ilay Campbell, Esquire, His Majesty's Advocate for His Majesty's interest; that albeit by the laws of this and every well-governed realm, theft, more especially when attended with house-breaking, and when committed by breaking into a house used or kept as an Excise Office, or other public office, under cloud of night, and from thence abstracting and stealing money, is a crime of an heinous nature, and severely punishable; yet true it is and of verity, that you the said William Brodie and George Smith, are both, and each, or one or other of you, guilty actors or art and part, of the said crime, aggravated as aforesaid: in so far as, upon the night of the 5th day of March, last, in this year present of our Lord 1788, or upon one or other of the days and nights of that month, or of February immediately preceding, or of April immediately following, you, the said William Brodie and George Smith, did, by means of false keys, or other instruments, wickedly and feloniously break into the house in which the General Excise Office for Scotland was then kept, in Chessel's buildings, on the south side of the High-street or Canongate of Edinburgh, within the royalty and liberties of the city of Edinburgh, and county of Edinburgh, and did thence feloniously abstract and steal money, to the amount of Sixteen pounds Sterling, or thereby, consisting partly of Bank-notes, and partly of silver and half-pence ...'

Brodie's attention wandered, and he searched the crowd for familiar faces. He was distracted by the number of them, so closely packed that they looked like skulls on ledges. If his eye caught one of theirs, the person either looked away, or grinned at him broadly. The heavy oak panelling of the chamber and the gallery was well made, he considered, and of substantial work. He realised he did not know who had done the work, or when, so long ago. Would it be like that with Will Brodie? More to the point, he thought sardonically, would it be like that with Francis? The man had aspirations to greatness, but human memory is fickle. People will remember me, Francis, he said in silent address, long after you are forgotten. The good men do dies with them. The evil they do lives after them. The massive coffered ceiling with its plaster pendants seemed about to slip on to his head. He turned his attention to Smith, with whom he had had only the briefest meeting outside the Court. Smith, as though conscious of his gaze, turned round to look at him. To Brodie's horror, Smith's cheeks were wet with tears. Brodie was struck with remorse. For him the game was almost played out, but for Smith there had been six months of miserable confinement on wretched food, yet Smith had kept silence until Brodie had fled. He owed the man a great debt, which he hoped to repay. That they would find them guilty there could be no doubt, on the strength of Smith's confessions and Brodie's careful letter alone. He had written it on the boat and hidden it in his trunk against just such an eventuality, confessing only to the Excise office crime. A matter of sixteen pounds could hardly buffet a Deacon but would poor Smith get away so lightly? He looked up and caught Braxfield's eye, quite unexpectedly. The result was like a physical shock, but he refused to look away. Braxfield stared him full in the face, the powerful eyes holding no leniency or sympathy. In Braxfield's view, hanging was equally good for all men. Surely he would be transported, he thought, at the very worst. The blue sea, open country and ferocious sun. Were there Indians in Australia? There was some savage race. Braxfield continued to stare, and Brodie thought it prudent to submit to his gaze.

'And you, the said George Smith, having been afterwards apprehended, and brought before Archibald Cockburn Esquire, Sheriff-depute of the county of Edinburgh, did, in his presence, emit three several declarations; the first of date the 8th day of March, the second of date the 10th day of March, and the third of date the 19th day of March, all in this present year of our Lord 1788: and having afterwards been brought before John Stewart, Esquire, Sheriff-substitute of the said county, you did, in his presence, emit a fourth declaration, of date the 17th day of July, likewise in this present year of 1788: the first of which declarations was signed by the said Archibald Cockburn, and the fourth by you, the said George Smith, and the said John Stewart. And further, you, the said William Brodie, having, in the month of March last, when the said George Smith was committed to prison, left Edinburgh, and fled from this country; and having afterwards been brought back, and taken into custody, did, upon the 17th day of July, in this present year 1788, in presence of the said Archibald Cockburn, Esquire, emit a declaration, which was signed by you, the said William Brodie, and the said Archibald Cockburn; the whole of which declarations, together with a letter written by you, the said William Brodie, and signed John Dixon, dated at Flushing, Tuesday, 8th April, 1788 and addressed to Mr Michael Henderson, Grassmarket, stabler, Edinburgh; an unsigned scroll, or copy of a letter ...'

The voice went on and on. It was all true. They would try his alibi against it, but he placed little faith in Jean Watt. She was what she was, and not designed to convince Braxfield. No, they would be found guilty. Brodie realised, quite calmly, that this was the second release from hypocrisy. He would purge his soul and purge the soul of Edinburgh. He looked again at the faceless crowd. You are Francis, he thought, and my trial is yours. My conviction will be the destruction of your lying cant. If a Deacon can be condemned, then look to yourselves, for you are next. He wanted Francis to be there, exhumed and propped in his coffin. The smell could be no worse.

'... a gold watch, with a chain, seal, and key; a chest, or trunk, containing various articles; a five-pound bank-note; a pair of curling irons or toupee tongs; a spur ...'

Brodie smiled.

'... a dark lanthorn; a pair of pistols; several false keys and pick-locks; and two spring-saws; are all used in evidence against you the said William Brodie and George Smith; and for that purpose, will be lodged in the hands of the clerk of the High Court of Justiciary, before which you are to be tried, in order that you may have an opportunity of seeing the same; at least, time and place foresaid, the said house in which the General Excise Office for Scotland was then kept as aforesaid, was feloniously broke and entered into, and a sum of money feloniously and theftuously taken and stolen therefrom as aforesaid; and you the said William Brodie, and George Smith, above complained upon, are both, and each, or one or other of you, guilty thereof, actor or actors, or art and part. All which, or part thereof, being found proven by the verdict of an assize, before the Lord Justice-General, Lord Justice-Clerk, and Lords Commissioners of Justiciary. You, the said William Brodie, and George Smith, ought to be punished with the pains of law, to deter others from committing the like crimes in all time coming.

Ilay Campbell.'

He sat down to rounds of applause and jeers. Braxfield immediately intervened.

'I want it made clear to all, that if there is ony disturbance within this court, then the soldiers have fixed bayonets and orders tae use them for the purpose of clearing the court!' There was silence. Brodie, in a slight sense of euphoria, wondered how lawyers could manage to say the same things so often in so many different ways and end up where they began. He had a feeling it was all really irrelevant. The jury were sworn in. He felt they might as well go out and decide on it.

The first day of the trial was of exceptional length, lasting from nine in the morning until six in the morning the next day, and in that time the whole evidence was heard both for the Prosecution and Defence. The Sheriff-officers gave evidence of the discovery of the concealed keys, tongs, pistols and lantern, revealed in the declarations of the luckless Smith. Andrew Ainslie, looking sick and white, gave evidence without once taking his eyes off the floor, and continually had to be asked to speak up. He avoided Brodie's eye. Brodie for his part had assumed an air of indifference and ease, crossing and uncrossing his legs, examining the ceiling and generally behaving like a man at a lengthy sermon. At times he brooded, arms folded, to all appearances asleep. Smith on the contrary was wearing himself out with anxiety. He had difficulty understanding the accents of witnesses and strained forward all the time, as if he might find some chink in the evidence. The Dean of Faculty, for Brodie, challenged the admissibility of Ainslie's evidence, hoping to show that it was the incentive of a pardon that had made him turn King's Evidence. After some argument that roused the Court, Ainslie was allowed to speak. During his whole testimony which was essentially accurate, as Brodie judiciously judged it, Brodie remained unmoving. Nor did he stir when Brown was called and the Court erupted with noise. He was jeered at, insulted and even spat at, by some ladies who were cleared from the Court. Brodie permitted himself a quiet smile. He was lost in contemplation of an oceanic paradise, like Leith Links on a summer day, but hotter. There would be palm trees and bright red flowers, and even men with their faces in the centre of their chest like Magellan had said. There might be mermaids, and beautiful girls with voluptuous brown bodies. He wished he could take Cecil. He cared for nothing in the world as much as Cecil.

Braxfield had ordered the soldiers to advance with fixed bayonets, and order was restored. To Brodie the murmur and shushing was the surf on the shore. The Dean of Faculty argued at length and with skill for Brodie, holding that the known infamy of Brown in connection with other offences rendered him 'infamia facti', which Braxfield with immense skill rebutted. John Brown gave evidence in detail and at length, from the cut of Brodie's dress to the details of the forcing of the cashier's desks. Mr Brown proved again that he had an excellent brain and a retentive memory. With the production and circulation of poor George Smith's belated confessions, from which he had hoped to receive a pardon, together with Brodie's letters, the Prosecution were happy to conclude their case. Smith in his anxiety had been as accurate as Brown.

At about midnight, the evidence for the Defence commenced, Smith offering no witnesses, but resting on his simple denial of the charge. Brodie on the other hand would attempt to prove an alibi. Matthew Sheriff, the only relation who would intercede on his behalf, testified that they had dined together until eight. Brodie's alibi depended upon the testimony of Jean Watt and her maid.

'Call in Jean Watt, residenter in Libberton's Wynd!'

Jean entered the court dressed in her finest clothes, which due to their gaudy tastelessness, gave rise to hooting and whistling. Brodie coloured where he sat, and looked about him angrily. Braxfield again had recourse to his threat, and the soldiers tramped about looking menacing. Ilay Campbell moved over to her. He could see she was shaking violently, and had daubed herself with rouge to hide the greyness of her skin. Her eyes were still red from recent crying, and she shot glances at Brodie, who for the first time showed interest by looking at her, attempting a smile.

'I wish to know,' said Ilay Campbell, addressing the jury, 'from this woman whether or not she is married.' There was a murmur round the Court and Braxfield scowled. Campbell turned to Jean Watt. 'Are you married?'

'No. I'm not.' It was a whisper.

'The witness will speak up, please.'

'No, I'm not.' There was renewed talking and much wagging of heads. Braxfield could contain himself no longer.

'This is intolerable! If this noise doesna' cease, I shall clear the Court at bayonet point and hear the case by jury. Spectators are here on tolerance. I hope I make masel' plain! Continue!'

Campbell asked Jean Watt to give her evidence, which she did in a trembling voice, occasionally stammering over words.

'Sir, I am well acquainted with the . . . prisoner . . . Will Brodie. I mind that on Wednesday the 5th day of March last, Mr Brodie cam' tae my house just at the time the eight o'clock bell was ringing, and he remained in it . . . there all night, and was not out from the time he came in until a little before nine o'clock next morning. We went tae bed early, around ten o'clock, Mr Brodie havin' a sore throat that night—he complained of being much indisposed.'

Ilay Campbell cross-examined her. 'How do you recollect that it was Wednesday night more than, say, any other night of the week?'

'On the following Monday I heard that Mr Brodie was suspected of being concerned in the breaking intae the Excise office, I heard his house had been searched for him and that he had gone away on the Sunday. This made me remember particularly, and also, because it was the last night he slept in my house. Would I not remember that? He slept with me that night,' she said, pride in her voice. 'I have a family of children to him! I saw him again on the Saturday night afterwards, but not till then; and,' she concluded triumphantly, 'he was in my house in the forenoon of the Tuesday preceding!' She looked around as though inviting more questions. She was taken aback when asked to stand down. Brodie thought her a spirited whore, but poor stuff to save his neck.

Peggy Giles corroborated her mistress's evidence, adding with relish that he was used to sleep in her mistress's house. She said it for effect, but the public were now so subdued by Braxfield that there was no response. Others followed, including his foreman, Rab Smith, who had really nothing to add. The evidence for the Defence was concluded in one hour, for Brodie alone, and very thin it looked. Between the hours of one and five-thirty, Counsel made their addresses to the jury, a circumstance that sent many of them to sleep, to be awoken by a fierce clash between John Clerk and Braxfield. Braxfield had become increasingly infuriated by Clerk's address. He had just declared to all and sundry, 'Gentlemen of the Jury, I ask you, on your oaths, can his Majesty make a tainted scoundrel an honest man?' There were roars and applause.

Braxfield reacted immediately.

'Macers, clear the Court if there is any more unruly din.'

Ilay Campbell tried to intervene.

'Sir,' he addressed Clerk, 'permit me to say, after this interruption, that the prerogative of mercy is the brightest jewel in His Majesty's Crown.'

Clerk responded vehemently.

'I hope His Majesty's Crown will never be contaminated by any villains around it!' There was pandemonium. Some roared with laughter, some jeered and pointed. Braxfield shouted to Campbell over the din. 'Do you want his words noted down?' Campbell, ever judicious, replied, 'Oh no, my Lord, not exactly yet. My young friend will soon cool in his effervescence for his client.' Braxfield waved a hand at Clerk. 'Go on, young man.'

'Gentlemen of the Jury, I was just saying to you, when this outbreak on the bench occurred, that you were the judges of the law and the facts in the case.' Now there was a silence in the Court like a frosty night. Braxfield spoke with his full dignity and bullying manner. 'We cannot tolerate this, sir. It is an indignity to this High Court—a very gross indignity deserving of the severest reprobation.'

'My Lords,' continued Clerk unbowed, 'I know that your Lordships have determined this question; but the jury have not. They are judges both of fact and of the law, and are not bound by your Lordships' determination, unless it agrees with their own opinion. Unless I am allowed to speak to the jury in this manner, I am determined not to speak a word more. I am willing to sit down if your Lordships command me!' Mr Clerk then sat down. Braxfield would not have it. 'Go on, sir,' he said menacingly, 'go on to the end of your tether.' Clerk got to his feet again and resumed his address to the jury. 'Yes, gentlemen, I stand up here as an independent Scottish advocate, and I tell you, a jury of my countrymen, that you are the judges of the law as well as of the facts.' Braxfield exploded into rage.

'Beware of what you say, sir!'

John Clerk resumed his seat as before, hands folded, and stared at Braxfield. After a pause, Braxfield, well aware of the legal niceties, was compelled to enquire,

'Are you done, sir, with your speech?'

'No, my Lord, I am not.'

'Then go on, sir, at your peril.' Lord Hailes, uneasy at what the reports might record, urged Clerk on.

'You had better go on, Mr Clerk. Do go on.'

Clerk was not to be so easily mollified. No one to his knowledge had ever had Braxfield on the run, and he would not let the moment slip from his grasp.

'This has been too often repeated,' he stated in offended tones. 'I have met with no politeness from the Court. You have interrupted me, you have snubbed me rather too often, my Lord, in the line of my defence. I maintain that the jury are the judges of the law as well as of the facts; and I am positively resolved that I will proceed no further unless I am allowed to speak in my own way.' Braxfield lost his temper, and turned to the Dean of Faculty.

'Then we must now call upon the Dean of Faculty to proceed with his address for the prisoner Brodie, which the Court will hear with the greatest attention.' The Dean, at this, shook his head. It was out of order. Braxfield chose to take it that he declined to speak. 'Very well. The Court will proceed now and discharge its duty.' The effect of this made the whole courtroom jump. John Clerk leapt to his feet shaking his fist at Braxfield.

'Hang my client if you daur, my Lord, without hearing me in his defence!' The confusion was absolute. The public gaped and it was the turn of the lawyers to jabber and talk. With as much dignity as he could muster, Braxfield rose from the bench and stormed out to the robing-room followed by the rest of the bench. If he could have hung Clerk alongside Smith and Brodie, Braxfield would have found a way. On their return, when they had calmed themselves with good sense and strong spirits, John Clerk was allowed to resume without interruption. He had made a name for himself, but, Brodie feared, had lost a client.

At four-thirty in the morning Braxfield rose to make the final address to the Jury. He was tired, and they too were yawning. He commenced his speech as a warning and admonition and delivered it as though it were already the sentence.

'Gentlemen of the Jury, the crime which is charged against the prisoners at the bar is of a kind the most hurtful to society. The situation of the pannels, and particularly one of them, is also exceedingly distressful. Mr Brodie's father, whom I knew, was a very respectable man, and that the son of such a man—himself, too, educated to a respectable profession and who had long lived with reputation in it—should be arraigned at this bar for a crime so detestable, is what must affect us all, gentlemen, with sensations of horror. This unhappy situation seems to have arisen from a habitude of indulging vices which are too prevalent and fashionable, but it affords a striking example of the ruin which follows in their train ...'

Brodie wondered what he was talking about, the hypocritical bag of wind. The jury struck reassuringly moral attitudes, and listened with the faces of monks, nodding wisely from time to time.

At six o'clock Braxfield finished. The jury were enclosed and the Court recessed until one in the afternoon.

The jury had handed in their verdict in an envelope sealed with black wax. The Court was, if anything, more crowded than the day before, as word of the trial spread. Smith and Brodie now stood in the dock, resting on its single wooden rail, Smith with his handkerchief to his eyes, Brodie with his hat in one hand. The Clerk of the Court had read the verdict in hushed silence. They had all 'in one voice' found William Brodie and George Smith guilty of the charges against them in the indictment. Smith seemed to have shrunk within his clothes, and presented a cowed and pathetic spectacle. The Deacon on the other hand appeared calm, almost resigned, and stood with a leisured easy sort of air. After all, he thought, I have nowhere else to go.

Lord Hailes responded to Braxfield's request to pronounce the verdict upon the pannels at the bar.

'My Lords, after the verdict of the jury, nothing remains for us but the melancholy task of pronouncing the sentence of the law.'

'Come on, George,' Brodie was heard to murmur, 'pull yourself together! We must make a brave show.'

'It is not left in our option what punishment to inflict, for the law has declared the crime of which these unhappy men have been convicted, capital. It is my opinion, my Lords, that the prisoners at the bar be carried back to the Tolbooth of Edinburgh, and that they be there detained, and that they be executed on Wednesday, the first day of October next.'

Smith suddenly slumped forward on the rails, sobbing and shaking his head in disbelief. Brodie stood quite still—it almost seemed as though a slight smile played around his mouth. Lord Eskgrove concurred, but with signs of genuine sorrow.

'My Lords,' he said, 'nothing is left for me but to agree with the opinion of my honourable brother. I sincerely commiserate the fate of these unhappy men; one of them I pity much. Now that I see him at the bar, I recollect having known him in his better days and I remember his father, who was a most worthy man. Their situation is a miserable one, and I hope that it will have the effect to deter others from being betrayed into the same vices which have led these poor men to this ignominious condition.' Lords Stonefield and Swinton remembered Brodie's father as well. Brodie gave no indication of his thoughts and Smith continued a muffled sobbing. But Brodie's mind was soaring beyond the coffered ceiling of the Court. Fear was conquered by an unholy glee. He had attached to the Brodie name a stigma that was heraldic. The family would have to carry Will for ever and ever amen. When men talked of Brodie, they would mean the son and not the father. Francis was a shade in the shade. Invisible. A reflection of his son, called Will's father. Francis was a shade within a shade, invisible. No more. As a large shadow eats a small one, or a great light consumes a lesser. Francis was no more.

And yet the fear was there and made him swallow. He looked at the sweeping horseshoe of advocates before him, scanning them slowly. Although they wore their death's-head faces, they caught his eye with interest. They were enjoying it.

Lord Braxfield had begun his address and, as though to snuff out such a vice, laboured it censoriously. Brodie listened with interest, for here was the authentic voice of Edinburgh hypocrisy, crying with all its outraged justice against a sinner. He noted that the whole proceedings were being written down, and prayed that this should be recorded for men to read.

'William Brodie and George Smith, it belongs to my office to pronounce the sentence of the law against you. You have had a long and fair trial, conducted on the part of the public prosecutor with the utmost candour and humanity, and you have been assisted with able counsel, who have exerted the greatest ability and fidelity in your defence.

'I wish I could be of any use to you in your melancholy situation. To one of you it is altogether needless for me to offer any advice. You, William Brodie, from your education and habits of life, cannot but know everything suited to your present situation which I could suggest to you. It is much to be lamented that those vices, which are called gentlemanly vices, are so favourably looked upon in the present age. They have been the source of your ruin; and, whatever may be thought of them, they are such as assuredly lead to ruin.'

Ah, the cards, and the cocks and the dice and the women and the claret, the ale, and the porter. Brodie smiled. Where would he be without them? At this moment, in the tavern with all the advocates and judges of Edinburgh. Braxfield growled on.

'I hope you will improve the short time which you have now to live by reflecting on your past conduct ...'

Ah, the cards, and the cocks and the dice and the women and the claret ...

'... and endeavouring to procure, by a sincere repentance, forgiveness for your many crimes. God always listens to those who seek Him with sincerity.'

Brodie begged devoutly that God would smite down Braxfield and promised to pray so every day. He would be sought with sincerity. Braxfield then read the formal death sentence.

'... the said William Brodie and George Smith to be carried from the bar back to the Tolbooth of Edinburgh, therein to be detained till Wednesday, the first day of October next, and upon that day to be taken forth of the said Tolbooth to the place fixed upon by the magistrates of Edinburgh as a common place of execution, and then and there, betwixt the hours of two and four o'clock afternoon, to be hanged by the necks, by the hands of the Common Executioner, upon a Gibbet, until they be dead; and ordain all their movable goods and gear to be escheat and inbrought to His Majesty's use: which is pronounced for doom.'

A long pause followed this pronouncement, broken by Brodie, who flung wide his arms to the advocates

'Gentlemen, I embrace you! Your lily hands have removed this fearsome sore from the city's fair skin. I die in my great mistake, and I do repent it. What I took for a raddled whore is a maiden!'

Inevitably uproar followed. Brodie attempted to say more, shouting that everyone had spoken save him, and he was the one to hang. Smith fell with a crash to the floor, momentarily diverting everyone's attention.

'Guards!' roared Braxfield. 'Prick any bonny fellow who moves! Order! Order! Sergeant, bring up your men, get the prisoner to his feet!' He banged away with his gavel as though he would nail the bench to the floor. Brodie was restrained from further speech by his advocates, but could not be prevented from waving to friends and acquaintances in Court. There was some delay while Smith recovered consciousness. He already had the skin of a dead man. They returned the way they had come, in sedans, through noisy and excited crowds. Smith was too ill even to know what was happening, but Brodie lifted his hat and bowed as he went, particularly to his enemies.

CHAPTER THIRTEEN

Execution

The condemned cell of the Tolbooth was dominated by 'the cage', a plate-iron cell no longer used, and the 'gaud', an iron bar, that spanned the room and was set in the wall at each end. It was supported and braced from the floor at intervals and at each of these divisions there was a chain and fetters. Four prisoners had previously shared it, Brodie and Smith having had the company of two men under sentence of death for robbing the Dundee Bank. These men had now at Smith's request been removed, as they had been given a six weeks' stay of execution.

Each man had a mattress that lay on the stone slabs in his allotted place, but Brodie, by the financial persuasion of some of his former associates of the Guilds, had been permitted a longer chain so that he could sit at a writing desk where he had ink, quill and paper. The room was dark, very cold, now that it was late August, and was otherwise unfurnished. They were allowed no candles or lights. On the floor beside Brodie's mattress a draught-board had been scratched out by him in the stone with a link of chain, and bits of cloth served as counters. Outside the Tolbooth, the noisy clack of carpenters' hammers echoed round the streets. They were putting the rails round the gibbet.

'George!' called Brodie to the heap of clothes huddled on the opposite mattress. 'Play me a game.' The heap of clothes moved, its chains clinking.

'I've no stomach for it.'

'It would take our minds off that damned noise. It reminds me altogether of ship-building, which is a damned waste for the short journey we're going.'

'How can you joke? You should pray, Will. Join me in a psalm, say a prayer. Can you not repent?'

'Repent of what? Have you not sung enough psalms and said enough prayers for the salvation of us all? Your Reverend Cleeve comes every day. I never saw you as meat for the Minister.'

'Have you no thought for your eternal soul? We're going to hang, do you understand? Do you want to hang unshriven?'

'At times like these, George, it is as well tae attend tae temporal matters. You sing psalms, and I'll write letters. No doubt they both have the same object, we'll see what gets us out o' here! Unless you and Cleeve have the power o' Joshua, we are here and here we are, and that's an end on't.'

'But you never got any reply.' Brodie was silent for a moment.

'Aye maybe, but wheels o' that size tak' time tae turn. If the Duke o' Buccleuch can be persuaded that we should be released, then rest assured, we will.'

'And the Town Council?'

'Them too.'

'Then you'd better start singing. You've heard nothing from them.'

'I shall die like a man. Think on it, I'm to be hung on the gallows that I suggested tae the Council with my own improvements. Is that not a fitting joke?'

The sound of a key in the lock made them all turn. The heavy studded door was pushed open, revealing Milton with a stranger. The gaoler called to Brodie.

'Your cousin, Mr Brodie, with a foreign gentleman dee-something. Ye ken, your cousin that aye leaves his purse at hame!' Milton flushed hotly.

'You can't speak to me like that, I'm a lawyer!'

'Can I not? Well, in here you're Brodie's cousin, and in my opinion every lawyer in Scotland should be in here the now. Next time bring the guinea, or I'll take great pleasure in slammin' the port in your face. Lawyer!' He spat scornfully and left, to stare in at them through the Judas.

'You'll have to pay, Milton,' said Brodie grinning, 'they all pay tae see me. It cost a crown in the Court I'm told.'

'Will, we've no time for nonsense. I have brought a gentleman with me that I advise you to receive. Dr Peter Degravers.'

The stranger stepped forward and shook hands with Brodie. They were of much the same height, but Degravers was fatter and sleeker. He spoke with a French accent.

'What is all that noise?'

'It's the gibbet. My dancing master.'

'Will, for the love of God be serious.'

'I was never more so. There's nothing like imminent death for concentrating the mind.'

'This is the gentleman I told you about.'

'Damn me, Milton, ye bring a man to prove my ain trap won't work? What next? I'll get no more work out o' it!'

'Will, you must be serious.'

'Milton, you are a good lad if inclined to be a little sparing with the money.' Brodie held up his hands to still Milton's protests. 'It's true, and becoming in a lawyer. But this is nonsense. Now do I look like Lazarus and does he look like Christ?'

'Be quiet!' Degravers had turned to Milton in irritation. 'This man will not listen to me. Good. Then let him save his soul, not his life. That is logic?'

'Please listen to him,' Milton insisted, 'just once.' Brodie nodded.

'How can I speak in here?' Degravers asked. 'The other one will hear.'

'Keep your voice down,' said Brodie pragmatically. 'The banging at hell's gates out there will drown it.' Degravers leaned forward on the top of the desk so that he practically whispered in Brodie's ear.

'It can be done. I have done it many times.'

'What can? I never heard ye was a miracle man.'

'No no. I have talked with your cousin and he has talked with your friends of influence. They got together to see if there was any way that you could be physically removed from your embarrassing situation, but it is impossible. So they have come to me.' He gestured expressively and awaited a response.

'Cheat death, by God? I have cheated mankind, and womankind too if it comes to that, but I doubt I'll cheat auld Nick!'

'Be discreet. I will slip a silver tube down your trachea on the morning before the ... when you take a little promenade.'

'Before I'm hengit!'

'Precisely. A harness will be sewn into your coat so that the weight of the body is supported, and the wind-pipe, the trachea, is not then constricted. The tube also prevents compression. When you are taken down, we will gallop you over the cobbles in a cart to restore the circulatory system, as that may be constricted, then when you arrive I shall bleed you from your veins and arteries. Then all will be well.'

'I don't believe it.'

'It's true, Will,' insisted Milton, 'he has a dozen testimonials to prove it.'

'It's a fool's game. There's nae dignity in it.'

'There is no dignity, my friend, in being suspended from a rope, kicking like a hooked fish while your neck stretches and your tongue swells ...'

'Quiet,' said Milton as Brodie swallowed uneasily.

'Cheat death.' Brodie contemplated the idea. 'Ye can cheat him but not beat him. But I can cheat the Law, and the sentence, and all Edinburgh and live out my natural days. I could want no other victory out o' life.' He looked up at Milton, suddenly doubtful and trusting. 'Will this work, do ye think?'

'I have to get someone to bribe the hangman. We must have a short rope, and the noose must go over the harness. That can be arranged.'

'Milton, I never thought you'd do it.'

'It's not just me, Will. There's Deacons Jamieson and Donaldson who are sorry to see you fall so low, and your lawyer Alex Paterson. Do you agree?'

'Have I any other chance?'

Milton walked between Brodie and the other prisoners while Degravers took out an indelible pencil with which he made various marks on Brodie's body.

'We'll save you yet, my friend,' said Degravers, putting away his pencil. 'Until tomorrow!'

'Aye that's tae be the grand day, a carnival o' animals.'

When the two men had left, George Smith demanded to know what it was all about. Brodie explained that Degravers was a doctor, who would bleed him before the execution, in the hope of saving him. Smith shook his head pityingly.

'You were ever an inventive man, Will. But the practical solution is prayer.'

'Ach, I only do it to please my cousin!' Brodie replied.

'The ministers will all be here this evening.' Brodie turned away with an impatient movement.

'There's no escape wi' them, George. They only help you on your way.'

Later, in the afternoon Ann Grant brought Cecil. Brodie was badly affected. The gaoler had flung open the door with a grin, calling to Brodie.

'Here's another of your pullets, Mr Brodie, with a bairn.'

Ann Grant rounded on him. She was dressed in black and, although pale and drawn, was composed and in control of herself.

'Mind your tongue, gaoler. Your job's not through!'

'Aye, and what might ye be? Number one, or number ten? Keep your airs!'

Ann put an arm round Cecil's shoulder, and turned on him, blazing, 'Call yourself a man? It takes the meanest sort o' gett tae taunt a chained man. I may be what I am, but hold your tongue or by God I'll see tae it through his friends that ye lose your job! Who do ye think ye are tae Mr Brodie? If I puff in your face, you're deid!' The warder was shaken and, muttering to himself, withdrew. 'I'll be outside, watching, mind!' he added as an afterthought.

Cecil, only ten, was terrified by her surroundings and the harsh words with the gaoler. She had been told, but could not believe, as no child could believe, that people would hang her father. She slipped from Ann's restraining arm and ran to him shouting, 'Father, father!' burying herself in his arms, incoherent with grief. Tears poured from her face and she sobbed uncontrollably.

'Hush, lass, hush,' Brodie murmured over and over again, holding her to him and stroking her hair, 'your father's fine, he's fine.' He could think of nothing to say. What consolation was there to offer in all the world? Her sobbing was so terrible that Brodie could stand it no more. Tears streamed down his face too. If there was any one thing for which he wanted to live, he realised, it was not to strut the streets of Edinburgh in defiance of all mortal laws. It was not to gloat with animal satisfaction at his victory over those sacks of corruption, that wallowed in mire but believed they smelled of lavender. It was this child. She was the one thing that loved him beyond reason, asking nothing in return but his love.

Ann put her arms around them both, torn with her own grief which was as much for Cecil as Will. Ann was a realist, and for her life must go on. She had lost other men, not in this way, but it was not the end of life. She wondered if it was because she was a woman. She was stricken, but knew that she would eventually recover, because she must. In Cecil there was no such knowledge, and Ann knew it. She rocked them both until Will wiped his eyes dry. He looked up at her.

'I've been no man, lass. You will look after her, and my other pretties?'

'You're more of a man for caring. You know I will.'

'God, lass, if I could undo this thing, I would do it. Would they hack off ma' arms and legs and leave the trunk it wid be better!'

'God bless ye, Will.'

'How are ye provided for?'

'I'm well enough. Your friends have helped.'

'Milton?'

'No. He wants no part wi' me. But Jamieson and Donaldson are good men.'

'I did little enough for them ever, that they should be so kind.'

'It's not anything ye did, ma bairn. They see the goodness in ye. Don't ye understand? No, I can see ye don't. Will ye are a wee boy. There's part o' you never grew. Life has been a wrestle wi' you.'

Brodie was calm again.

'Ann, will ye be there?'

There was a long pause. Her eyes were far away, as though she was testing the scene in her mind to decide if she could face the terrible sight.

'If you want me.'

'I want ye, Ann, if ye can bear it. No one of my family will come. It will be lonely. I canna believe in any God ... I have tried. George there has succeeded, but fool masel' I can't. Not on that.'

The gaoler unlocked the door and opened it.

'Time's up in there. Ye've had the regulation time an' more!'

'It was only a second!' Ann protested.

'It was the time!'

'It's best done quickly, Ann. No long partings. I'll put on a manly show.'

'Oh God, Will!' They kissed and embraced. Ann, very businesslike, took Cecil's arms from her father's neck. Brodie kissed her face and eyes again and again, then released her. Ann tried to detach the girl but she struggled and screamed. More gaolers appeared at the door, hearing the commotion.

'No Cecil, my dove, my cushat. Go. Go now, go with your mother. Father will be all right!' He was distracted with grief. Finally Ann Grant had to pick up the girl, restraining her with all her strength. The child screamed and screamed. At the door, she tried to kick and scream at the gaolers, 'You're going to kill ma father! Murderers! Murderers!'

Brodie called after them.

'I love you both, I love you both!'

Cecil's heart-breaking screams could be heard right down the stairs of the Tolbooth and out into the street. The screaming still did not stop, but went on outside until it disappeared into the distance. Even the gaolers were shaken. They were so subdued they withdrew, locking the door quietly. There was a long silence while George Smith heard Brodie sobbing in the semi-dark.

'Will?' he said tentatively, much moved by what he had seen and heard.

'What?'

'Take consolation in the Lord. You must. Take consolation in the Lord who will provide.'

'I can't!' It was a cry of agony. 'Nor can I pretend it to masel'. Who am I tae start dealing in hypocrisy now?'

Michael Henderson was his last visitor that day, before the ministers of the Church arrived. Brodie was composed again, and was playing draughts by himself, his left hand against his right, as Smith was too absorbed in prayer to play. They clasped each other warmly. 'Michael, I have come to the conclusion that the laws o' chance are entirely overrated. I have played my right hand with my left thirty-five times since I have been here, and my left hand has won twenty-eight times. Now that's no' possible! With that luck at the table, I would collect another o' these!' He indicated his scar. Henderson clapped him on the back.

'I'm proud of ye, Will. You're in grand shape.'

'I wish they would get it over.'

'It's the waiting?'

'Aye, it's a long suspension. They have promised us a good dinner the night. I tell you something, Michael, there's little chance it will come up again!'

'Will, don't joke. You're hurting yourself. Talk of other things.'

'It desna hurt me, Michael. It's how I feel. There is a quality o' light-headedness when the hours are slippin' awa'. It's like being fou as a sow, but with a clear, clear head. A moment's smallest pleasure is an eternity.'

'How's George?'

'Hear him.'

'Is that all he does? He was never like it before. George, how are ye, man?' Smith paused in his prayers and looked up at Henderson. Henderson was shocked at the change in his face. The eyes were hollow-set and feverish, and his skin was dirty grey with the pores picked out like pigskin. He had the wild look of a man not sane. 'It's not you I need, Michael Henderson, it's the minister. Mary will not see me. I am deserted. In the Lord I place my trust. Time is running out, I must pray. Pray for my soul.'

'Aye,' said Henderson kindly, patting the kneeling Smith on the back, 'I'll pray for ye, Georgie lad, as best I can.'

Henderson sat down with Brodie on the mattress, and Brodie asked him about the Town, and what was going on. He wanted to know all the details.

'What do they say about me?'

'Different things. The general opinion among the merchants is that you're well rid of. Man, you hurt their pride! As for other folk—Will, you'll be sadly missed.'

'But what about my petition to the Council? Why would they not listen?'

'Pride and viciousness, Will. They are exposed for what they are. Aye, there's a change coming. I have heard talk. There's mair doxies without patrons in Edinburgh now than in her history! And Burns has wrote a verse about the trial, or so they're saying.'

'About me?'

'No, Will, but about the whole cruel injustice o' it. It seems he was not impressed by Mr Brown. He read the defence that Clerk put up, and they say he put a pen to paper.'

'Tell me, you devil Henderson. What did he say?'

'Aye, well I might tell you, or maybe no ...' Henderson smiled. Brodie for a moment was almost himself again.

'By God, Henderson, it's come tae this, taking advantage of a poor wretch in gaol!' But Brodie too was smiling. Henderson thought for a moment. 'It goes like this,

"A prince can mak' a belted knight
A marquis, duke and a' that;
But an honest man's aboon his might,
Guid faith he mauna fa' that!"'

'Is it true?'

'They say it is. Is that not the same thing? But Burns remembers you.'

'Is that so? Michael, you've cheered me up. Him, but who else? That's a damnable noise outside! Gaoler, can they not stop that clamping!'

'What is it?'

'They're altering the gibbet, knock knock knock. Like some poor devil beating at St Peter's gate, which is what it is. I'll get no sleep the night. Come on, Michael, tell me how the cocks are doing? I freely bequeath them to ye, afore the Law thieves them from me. Keep them out o' sight, or those rabid hounds o' magistrates will have them—they've had aw thing else. By God it irks me sore, Michael. They take near two thousand pounds o' my property tae repay a debt o' four. By God, it's a good business the Law. It shows a fine profit. And all they need to do is murder me wi' all the due process! Don't let them get ma birds!'

'Come on, Will, it was mair than that.'

'Not that I ever confessed. Not that they're hangin' me on! Or are they hangin' me on something I haven't heard? Keep them fit, Michael, and feed them well, for when they go, I'm gone. They're Brodie's birds.'

Henderson stayed for half an hour and left telling Brodie he would be there in the morning. They parted awkwardly, shaking hands in the end, and bidding each other a formal good-night. Brodie lay down on his mattress feeling depressed by the void of his going. The monotonous drone of Smith saying psalms aloud was getting on his nerves. As it got dark and his spirits were at their lowest, the preachers would move in, sliding quietly out of the dark like familiar spirits. 'Confess your sins my son, confess. The Lord forgiveth, confess ...'

The Judas shot back with a smack, and the door was opened but instead of the clergy came Dickson. Brodie was amazed at first, but Dickson soon made his business plain. He stopped short of the desk and called to Brodie,

'Well, sir, it has come to this. Your father, had he not been dead, would have died of shame.'

'Go away, Dickson! Gaoler, take this canting humbug away. He smells in ma nostrils!'

'Come now, Brodie, I came tae ease your hours.'

'A hoodie crow shows the same concern for its dinner. It waits for it tae die. It's concerned all right. In case its dinner runs awa!'

'Ye may abuse me, Brodie, but I couldn't see ye hang without I should offer my condolences. There was a time when we was friends.'

'I canna mind it.'

'It has been remarked, Mr Brodie, that it is too often a fatal consequence to be involved with wicked women. It is ruinous—to the character and constitution. In all charity I must assume it is the reason for this fall. Ye were always a good wright ...'

Brodie interrupted him by starting to sing in a loud voice that drowned him out:—

'’Tis woman that seduces all mankind;
By her we were first taught the wheedling arts;
Her very eyes can cheat: when most she's kind,
She tricks us of our money with our hearts.
For her, like wolves, by night we roam for prey,
And practise ev'ry fraud to bribe her charms;
For suits of love, like law, are won by pay.
And Beauty must be fee'd into our arms.'

Dickson turned on his heel, furious at the insult, and hammered on the door with a little white fist. Brodie called to him. 'They won't let you out, Dickson, for you're a rogue! You'll see!' The few seconds it took for the gaoler to open the door seemed to Dickson like hours. He clattered down the stone stairs with Brodie's laughter in his ears.

Will Brodie went to bed at eleven and slept till four, declining to join Smith in his distraught pacing, observing that there was little to get up for when he would soon be lying down again. This tactless remark provoked Smith to further prayers and tears. Brodie's sleep had been haunted by the face of Francis, on which two guineas floated like bright moons. In his dreams Francis had come to the execution, dressed all in black, then when he turned, he wore an executioner's mask with only the eyes glittering like newly chipped coal. Will had stepped boldly on to the trap and Francis with a roar of triumph had pulled the lever, tearing off the mask to appear as Dickson. But Will had hung on to the rope above his head and to the cheers of a thousand people had let himself down. A nightmare pursuit had followed in which every step gave way, parting in the centre as though hinged, showing a great void into a pit of skeletons which gleamed like white fungus in damp earth mould. These pits were graves, unlined. At the last step to freedom, it sprang open like a trap and dropped him on to a shapeless mass of corruption below, that received him with a nauseating softness. The thing however was alive, and embraced him tightly, while earth rained on his head from above as the Councillors of Edinburgh, with spades in their hands and satanic leers, filled in the hole with all the speed they could muster, sweat pouring down their bodies in streamlets, so that it soaked him in his terrible embrace. The thing spoke with the voice of Francis. 'Welcome, William, ye'll not get out of this one, not ever!' The weight of the earth on him was crushing him so that he began to suffocate and his chest hurt with creaking pain. At that he awoke, wet with sweat, to find himself pressed face down on the hard stone of the floor. His ribs were bruised with the contact, and he climbed back on to the mattress.

At nine o'clock, a hairdresser was admitted under close supervision to powder and dress his hair, as Brodie still had manacles on his hands. He insisted to Smith that he should have the same done at his expense but Smith was too distracted, remarking that it mattered little what he looked like for he was nothing but meat. Brodie would have nothing of that.

'Come on, George, keep your spirits up, man! It is not often the luck of a man to know in advance the exact time and place of his going so that he can make the proper preparations. As we have the luck forced upon us, we may as well be decently dressed and groomed!'

Shortly after the hairdresser, he was visited by the Reverend Hardie. Brodie was polite but abrupt.

'Will Brodie, you must make your peace with the Lord. I am here as his voice and as your comforter and guide. The Lord is infinite in his mercy.'

'You have your business to do, Mr Hardie. I would never put a man from his job, but I beg you, be as quick as possible about it. There is little time.' Brodie showed some irritation about the visit. He was keyed up and active, and above all was waiting for his friends. Hardie was naturally upset, but persistent.

'There cannot be too much time devoted to saving your eternal soul.'

'No doubt. If the same Lord is listening to Georgie Smith there, I'll be saved a hundred times over.' Hardie then said some prayers with Brodie who recited them with him, kneeling. The manacles were taken off for this purpose. Hardie then left, much dissatisfied with his efforts. He wished Brodie a swift and easy passage to a forgiving Maker. Brodie wished Hardie the same.

At eleven, the visit he had been waiting for was announced by the duty gaoler, who stepped back with some deference to admit Deacons Jamieson and Donaldson. He clapped them on the back, shook hands and engaged them in animated conversation. Poor Smith looked on, alone. His last visit would be from the Reverend Mr Cleeve, and until then he decided to read the Psalms aloud, which he did whenever he was overcome with sick fear. Jamieson carried a new dark blue coat. 'Gaoler!' he called. 'I have brought Mr Brodie his clothes. May I help him dress?' The gaoler, who was more interested in the immense crowd that was beginning to gather in the Lawnmarket around the Luckenboths, hardly bothered to look before nodding. Jamieson slipped the coat on to Brodie.

'It's the special coat,' he whispered, making a pretence of patting and dusting the back and shoulders. 'The wires are sewn in on the inside. Feel them, they're in the piping ...' Brodie carefully felt the seams and sleeves.

'By God, that's clever. Did Milton have that done?'

'It was Degravers' idea. Now listen carefully because there is only one chance. As you come down the turnpike stair, take your time. On the west stair, we will meet you again, and give you a drink of cinnamon water. It will make you cough and splutter—see to it! At the same time Degravers will have the tube in a handkerchief, and pass it to you. Bend over, and he will wipe your face. That way he believes he can introduce the tube without anyone knowing. Is that clear?'

'Aye. But how can I speak? Folk will expect me tae speak. If I stand there bubbling like a wet pipe, someone's going to be mighty suspicious.'

'Degravers says it affects the voice box in no way. Don't feel your coat, there is a hook on the back of it around which the rope will be passed. The hangman has been seen to, and the rope will be short. He will arrange it right.' Brodie was moved to tears for the second time. He stared at the two Deacons, shaking his head. Finally he said, 'But why should ye do this for me? Gentlemen, there is no way I can repay ye.'

'There are some of us, Will, that believe the judgement ought never to have been made. If every man was hung for his indiscretions, there would be no Council in Edinburgh.' Brodie continued to shake his head mutely, then stepped forwards and shook them both firmly by the hands. Donaldson was practical.

'So that we can attend you, Will, ye must write to the Lord Provost. Now. Making it your last request. We will deliver it to him. Without us there, it may all go wrong.'

'You're right. I have paper and quill. What shall I say?'

'Are your family coming?'

'No.'

'Then we must. And further, you must be cut down straight away so that Degravers can get to you. You will be jolted in a cart.'

Brodie managed a grin.

'Man, I hope you're careful. I should hate tae break a bone!' He sat at the ancient oak desk, carved deep with dates, curses and initials, and wrote to the Lord Provost, the scratching of his quill drowned by Smith's steady intoning. Donaldson indicated Smith. 'How long has that been going on?'

'Smith would make a man welcome the noose!'

Brodie's letter was short and to the point.

'Edinburgh Tolbooth,
Oct. 1, 1788, Eleven o'clock.

My Lord,

As none of my relations can stand being present at my dissolution, I humbly request that your Lordship will permit Mr Paterson,' he paused ...

'What about Degravers. He must be there. And where am I being taken?'

'To your own workshop. Give him another name. Call him anything.'

Oates.' He continued writing.

'Mr Paterson, Mr Oates, with Deacons Jamieson and Donaldson, to attend, it will be some consolation in my last hour; and that your Lordship will please give orders that my body after be delivered to Mr ...'

'Say Paterson,' Said Donaldson. 'It sounds more reasonable.'

'To Mr Alexr. Paterson and by no means to remain in gaol; that he and my friends may have it decently dressed and interred. This is the last request of

Your most obedient
but most unfortunate,
WILL. BRODIE.'

The Deacons shortly left with this request and delivered it to the Lord Provost. He was so moved at the trivial nature of it that he immediately agreed.

'Aye that's so. We can't have a Deacon of the town hanging up there in public view. It's not proper. Cut him down when it's over. Bury him decently.'

At one o'clock the prisoners were brought their last meal of beef-steak and port. Smith was putting a brave face on things, but could do no more than drink the port, which he gulped greedily, only to be sick some minutes later. Brodie on the contrary ate with a good appetite, continuing to make tasteless comments.

'You would think, George, that they would have mair sense than to serve us with so much red meat and red wine on a day like this. I take their word it's beef-steak. They took care to serve it bloody!'

'I don't know how you can eat it, Will!'

'It'll not come up again. It won't get the chance. Try to eat, man. Death is less fearsome on a full belly.' Smith tried again, only to set himself retching. He had also begun to shiver. As the hour set for execution approached, a remarkable calm had come over Brodie. He had thought long and hard over Degraver's plan, and put little faith in it. If it worked, then so much the better. He would devote his life to Cecil. But death seemed irrelevant to him, as life had seemed irrelevant. He felt that he had always known that he should die this way. From that death would come release and absolution from all that the Brodie name had brought. He had been successful in its destruction and the final renunciation was his public guilt. Dying was merely a piece of theatre that gave everything else a finality. The curtain had already fallen on his life, his execution was merely the actor pushing aside the cloth to receive his bows. Francis had been slain in the play. He, the actor, had relieved himself of all his words.

The great bell of St Giles began to toll at two o'clock. Every thirty seconds the melancholy boom reverberated through the crowds in the narrow streets. All Edinburgh seemed to have turned out for the hanging. The Town Guard marched up in their best order, pursued by a volley of ribald remarks, and took up their positions surrounding the single-storey structure at the western end of the Tolbooth. The massive beam stuck out a good ten feet from the gable wall above the execution platform. To the underside of it were fixed two stout iron hooks, already draped with new hemp nooses that shone clean and yellow in the light. Windows, balconies, roofs and every vantage point were jammed to a dangerous degree. Men clung to window ledges and stood on boxes and barrels. Napier's

Laboratory that adjoined the gibbet was so over-swarmed by spectators that Napier was screaming and shouting and trying to pull some down. Windows were broken and barriers smashed to gain a view. In the Council Chamber, the Councillors were dressing up for the occasion. They put on their full robes of office, strutting and preening themselves, helped by servitors, and donned new white gloves. In their gloved hands they carried white staves to appear the more striking. They chattered and gossiped as though it were all a social occasion, which indeed it would be after the hanging, when they planned to sit down to a feast, or deid-chack, to celebrate the occasion. The menu was discussed with more interest than the hanging. They concurred with the views of Bailie Torry some four years earlier, who had observed of a prisoner engaged in long-winded prayer on the scaffold, 'I wish he would be done, that knuckle of veal will be roasted to a cinder.' It had been reported to them that Smith had got religion.

The magistrates were followed by the clergy in black gowns and bands. With so much dressing-up, it looked like a punch-and-judy show.

Word was brought by a sergeant to the Tolbooth.

'The magistrates beg to inform you, gentlemen, that they are ready.'

Soldiers were now stationed on either side of the prisoners with loaded muskets. At a nudge from the soldiers, the two men stepped forward. Smith began to incant:

'O Lord, rebuke me not in thy wrath: neither chasten me in thy hot displeasure. For thine arrows stick fast in me, and thy hand presseth me sore. There is no soundness in my flesh because of thine anger; neither is there any rest in my bones because of my sin. For mine iniquities are gone over my head; as an heavy burden they are too heavy for me ...' Brodie simply walked to the door, stepping aside to let Smith through first. As they proceeded to the second floor, from whence they would step out on to the platform, they were met on the turnpike stair by Donaldson, Jamieson and 'Oates'. With them stood a captain of guard. 'Say your farewells, gentlemen. I daur not keep the spectators waiting.'

'Farewell, Will,' said Donaldson. 'If there was anything I could have done, rest assured I would have done it.'

'I wrote to the Duke of Buccleuch,' replied Brodie, 'and if he will not intervene, then I must accept my fate.' He was calm and casual in his conversation. Smith was trembling and was held by the arm by one soldier.

'Have a sip of cinnamon water,' said Donaldson, 'it will fortify you.' He was about to hand it to Brodie when the captain intervened.

'How do I know that's not poisoned?' Donaldson drank some, coughing and slapping his chest afterwards.

'By God, it's cordial. It warms the belly.' The captain nodded and Donaldson handed the glass to Brodie who drained it down, then bent double coughing convulsively. Donaldson slapped him heartily on the back, while Oates gave him a large handkerchief with which he appeared to wipe Brodie's mouth in the semi-darkness of the stair. Brodie could be heard gagging and choking, and then he stood up.

'All right?' asked Donaldson.

'Aye, I'm all right,' replied Brodie in a slightly croaky voice. 'By God that was liquid fire. But I can still speak, ye see,' and he winked at Donaldson, quoting,

'Of all the friends in time of grief,
When threatening Death looks grimmer,
Not one so sure can bring relief
As this best friend, a brimmer.'

The party moved down the turnpike stair, clinging on to the greasy rope that formed the only handrail. They stopped in front of the door to the platform. It was solemnly opened, Smith giving a low groan, and the two prisoners were escorted out, blinking, into the daylight. An immense roar went up from the crowd. The prisoners were amazed by the number of people.

There was no conceivable place on which fingers or a foot might find a grip that was not occupied. Smith stood still, supported by a soldier, his head bowed. Brodie, on the contrary, walked forward to the edge of the trap, looking very small and dapper. There he bowed neatly to the crowd, in three directions, to roars of approval. The Magistrates pursed their lips and looked uneasily at the size of the Guard. Brodie then turned and bowed to the Magistrates to hooting and whistling from all sides. Don Smith, close by, enquired anxiously of Brodie, 'How are you, Will. Bear up.'

'I am glad to see ye here. My nails, as ye can see, are quite neat, as is my hair.'

'Will, I can't say I'm sorry to see you in this situation.'

'It is fortune de la guerre.'

The three clergymen then came forward and bid them kneel, which Smith and the clergy did. Smith and the three ministers then employed themselves in fevered devotion. Brodie himself, as though struck for the first time by the horrible reality of the black oak beam and its golden hanks of knotted rope, took a silk handkerchief from his pocket, and spreading it on the platform that he might not spoil his trousers, said his own prayer, a little apart from the others. It was the only indication he gave of being discomposed.

'O Lord, I acknowledge thee as the great ruler of the world; although I lament much that I know so little of thee. This much, however, I know, that Thou art a merciful God, and that, as I am a great sinner, Thou wilt have mercy upon me, through the merits of Thy Son Jesus Christ. O Lord receive my soul! Into Thy hands I resign it. Amen.'

The great bell tolled, and Brodie got to his feet, waiting for Smith to finish his devotions. The tube in his throat made him want to retch each time he swallowed, and it ached, giving him a pain in the right lung. The spread end of the tube that prevented it slipping further was pressed against the back of his palate and uvula. He was frightened and in no way sure that it would work. What if it only prolonged his agonies and left him to die there of agonised strangulation. He closed his eyes and prayed to God silently and in earnest. Smith rose unsteadily to his feet. Uncontrollable tears had again started to trickle down the man's face.

'Well, Will,' said Smith, belching with fear, 'this is it. No regrets!'

'You're a good brave fellow, George. No regrets.'

The hangman stepped forward to bind their arms. Brodie refused.

'No, no, man, I must have the use of my hands. I'll not struggle. You have my word on it.'

'They must be bound.'

'Then not too tight. The arms but not the hands.'

He was panic-stricken. The hangman ought to know. If he could not use his hands, he could not grasp the sleeve end of the harness. Did the man know? Had he been bribed? He looked into the man's face as he bound his arms, but his face was expressionless. Brodie's hands remained free. The hangman then bound Smith, and returned to push a white night-cap on each man's head.

'Up you go, gentlemen.'

The two prisoners walked up the flight of wooden steps that led from the platform to the trap immediately below the beam. Neither man could take his eyes from the yellow hanks of rope.

'Go up, George,' said Brodie, 'you're first in hand.'

Brodie was disposed to examine the apparatus, and made a show of sounding the woodwork of the trap with his heel, examining the trap and lever as though he were inspecting his own works and particularly inspecting the halter under which he stood, which he could reach with a hand. The crowd was becoming silent. Smith stood in an attitude of dejection, a man without any further resources of spirit or hope. Bailie Galloway, a man who knew the length of every bit of string, at that moment noticed the rope was too short.

'Lengthen that rope man,' he called. 'Officers, see to it.'

'I'll have tae tak' them down tae do it!' complained the hangman.

'We want no mistakes made,' said Dickson. 'Take them down and do it.'

In this terrible pause, Brodie descended from the trap on to the main platform while the hangman appeared with a pair of steps, climbed up amid cheers, and lengthened the halters. Brodie was becoming worried again. The sea of faces swam in front of him like tens of thousands of white skulls. Francis had once described the Church of the Capucini in Rome to him, reading from one of his books, where skulls by the thousand were stood on ledges and shelves. Donald Smith came over to talk to him.

'This is terrible, Will. Truly terrible.'

'It's no more terrible than dangling up there.' He was then joined by Jamieson and Donaldson. 'Is everything all right?' he demanded anxiously.

'It's all right, Will,' Donaldson replied, 'but this delay is terrible!'

Jamieson was red with embarrassment. As he was naturally sandy-coloured he glowed.

'Will, what can you think of me? I did the mason work for that engine of human evil.'

'Oh, it's none of your fault, man. The hangman's the bungler. Practice makes perfect, and he wants experience, which is a strange thing when we have the wisdom of Lord Braxfield. Were I not so closely involved, so to speak, I would be curious tae observe its functioning. As things are, my view will be rather skywards than in the machinery!'

'Ready, Mr Brodie?' called the hangman with a strike of the bell. Smith who had remained on the platform shaking, apparently immobilised with fear, now advanced for the rope. Brodie stepped smartly up the flight of stairs, almost appearing eager. The tube had begun to hurt him now and he was having difficulty breathing when he talked. It was Donaldson's turn to intervene, and with good reason.

'Damn it man, the rope's too long now. Know your business!'

In his eagerness to comply with the previous instructions, the hangman had now so extended the rope that Brodie would have touched the floor. The Magistrates were tutting and shifting like nesting doves, waving their white batons and flapping their ropes. The spectacle was beginning to lose its dignity. The crowd was also becoming increasingly restive with each blunder and the Guard feared violence. Brodie descended the steps again, shaking his head, and resumed his conversation as though he had been temporarily called away. Smith did not move, but stared, haltered, at the edge of the trap.

'That hangman's a bungler. He ought to be punished by the agonies he gives others. Still, what does it signify, provided the job in the end is right. Are you sure he knows his job? Damn it, it's the first exercise I've had in a month, and I think another trip down the steps will kill me!'

The hangman had now re-adjusted the rope for the third time. The huge crowd of nearly forty thousand was silent except for a rustle of movement that sounded like the riffling of wind through forest leaves. Brodie ascended the steps with the same springy gait. The hangman put the noose over his head.

'Have you got it right?' asked Brodie.

'I have. Just like you wanted.'

Brodie nodded and went to Smith and shook his hand. Smith was lost in a coma of despair and appeared scarcely to notice. Brodie adjusted the rope about his neck with the help of the executioner, who was most careful as to its final arrangement.

'When I drop my handkerchief, friend, you may let me jig.' He turned to Smith. 'God bless you, George!' Brodie folded his arms and stood on the trap in a braced attitude that seemed to express courageous resolution. The crowd applauded. Smith started to pray aloud but made no reply to Brodie. Brodie after some seconds, during which he seemed to scan the multitude with some satisfaction, dropped his fine silk handkerchief. The lever was pulled and the two men dropped so that the rope thrummed.

As soon as the Magistrates withdrew, Donaldson and Jamieson cut down the body, watched by the attentive crowd. Smith remained suspended, his neck cranked at right angles, turning round and back, back and round, according to the wayward draughts of the wind. It took them under three minutes to get the body from the gibbet by means of folding steps, then it was immediately lain in the back of a light cart, which set off through the crowd at a furious pace, scattering yelling people before it. Jamieson drove it, yelling, 'Make way! Make way! By God, I'll run ye over!' while Donaldson attended to the body. The cart clattered and jolted over the cobbles with such bone-shaking violence that Donaldson had trouble in loosening the noose which had sunk deep into the neck. Brodie's face was black and blotched, and his tongue stuck out, choking him like some monstrous slug.

The cart soon reached Brodie's Close where a small group of his workmen immediately picked up the body and ran with it, panting, to a workshop at the rear of the Close. Behind closed doors a bench had been laid out with a clean linen sheet and pillow. Degravers stood waiting with his scalpel, bleeding bowls and instruments. As soon as Brodie's clothes could be removed, he made incisions at the visible marks he had made and watched the flow of the deep crimson arterial blood. Forcing open the jaws, he got his fingers into Brodie's mouth, and began to extract the tube. No one from Brodie's family was admitted to see the hideously contorted body. The white linen was soon red with blood.

Player: But honest friend, I hope you don't intend that Macheath shall be really executed.

Beggar: Most certainly, Sir: to make the piece perfect, I was for doing strict poetical justice. Macheath is to be hanged; and for the other personages of the drama the audience must suppose they were either hanged or transported.

Player: Why then, friend, this is a downright deep tragedy. The catastrophe is manifestly wrong; for an Opera must end happily.

The Beggar's Opera.

* * *

Michael Henderson had won handsomely on Brodie's cocks. The canvas pit was stained and feather-strewn and the blood-hungry mob were leaving to drink away their gains or losses.

Of the seven birds he had lost two. Brodie, as he had said, was dying by degrees. He leant on the side of the pit, pulling at a long-stemmed clay, while his men cleared the barn of rubbish and drunken men. Buchanan, who had lost and had been busy paying off his debts from a leather purse with a draw-string, crossed over to him.

'Well, Henderson, Brodie had the last laugh on me. He cost me fifty-five guineas, which is not bad work for a dead man!'

'Aye, well they do say that there is a power tae reach beyond the grave.' Henderson looked very solemn but his eyes twinkled.

'Never, man! That's talk of the devil!' Buchanan blurted. However, the man was clearly curious about something, and not sure how to put it. He scuffled his brogues in the straw.

'Tell me, Michael, you were a friend of his. There is a rumour round the Town that he was seen in Paris, and that he was revived after the hanging. It has happened before, ye ken. And they say his coffin was awful light ...'

'I would not put much credence on all that, Mr Buchanan. There's aye one o' these rumours starts up.'

'Then you know he *is* dead?'

Henderson took his pipe from his mouth and ejected a thin cascade of blue-white smoke.

'The Magistrates are satisfied. Now who would argue wi' them?'

Buchanan nodded and moved away, still doubtful. Henderson watched his receding back. A secret smile lit up his long face. He would let them know nothing.

Glossary

Baptised by the twelve honest god-fathers	Tried by jury.
Benedict (n.)	Married man.
Bite (v.)	Cheat.
Blindman's holiday	An excursion by night.
Blunt	Money, valuables.
Briefs (n. pl.)	Shaved cards, taper for cheating.
Broadsman (n.)	Card sharp.
Cat bar (n.)	Iron bar holding the leaf of a double door without the lock.
Cat-in-the-pan (n.)	Turncoat.
Chatts (n. pl.)	Dice.
Chatty (adj.)	Lousy.
'Cheese your patter!'	'Shut your mouth!'.
Close (n. Scots)	Alley wide enough for foot traffic only.
Cocker (n.)	Cock owner.
Cooper'd (adj.)	Spoiled.
Crib. Crack a crib	A 'job'. Commit a robbery.
Crockats (n. pl. Scots)	Ruffles.
Cropped (adj.)	Hanged.
Cuittle (v. Scots)	Wheedle or coax.
Cull (n. and v.)	Dupe or fool. Also verb.
Deacon (n. Scots)	Master of a Guild. In 18th c. Scotland carrying privileges in the cities, a number of Deacons automatically becoming Town Councillors, in rotation. The title was held for life.
Despatchers (n. pl.)	Loaded dice.
Dreetie (adj. Scots)	Shit-stained.
Dubs (n. pl.)	Bunch of keys.

Ease (v.)	Rob.
Eeries and orries (Scots)	Ins and outs. Details.
Family man (n.)	Thief or burglar.
Flat (n.)	Dupe or fool.
Flying stationer (n.)	Pedlar or traveller.
Fou (adj. Scots)	Drunk.
Full feather (in.)	Wealthy.
Gammon (v.)	To deceive.
Gill bell	The stroke of eleven o'clock on St Giles' bell, the signal for general refection.
Gledge (v. Scots)	Glance at.
Grog blossoms (n. pl.)	The nasal erruptions of over-drinking.
Gull (v.)	Cheat.
Hengit, hauf-hengit (adj. Scots)	Hanged, half-hanged. Maggie Dickson revived after her hanging and lived to be an Edinburgh character for many years, her head permanently wrenched to one side.
Hochmagandy (n. Scots)	Lewd and ribald – (fornication).
Hop the twig	Clear off, or be hanged.
Hubble-show (n. Scots)	Riot, hubbub.
Ivories (n. pl.)	Dice.
Jemmy-John (n. Scots)	Demijohn. Tankard.
Jiggered (adj.)	'Rigged' or loaded.
Kipper (v. Scots)	Split in half.
Kite (n.)	One who preys on 'pigeons'. Sharper or cheat.
Knowing (adj.)	Cunning or clever.
Land (n. Scots)	Tenement dwelling or floor.
Leary bloak	Knowing fellow. Original spelling of bloke.
Main (n.)	A cock-fight of some importance involving several combats.
Mootie (adj. Scots)	Small, weedie.
Mowe (v. Scots)	Copulate.
Nick, main chance, etc.	Terms used in the gambling game of 'Hazard'.

On the pickaroon	Out on a speculative jaunt. Looking for prospective opportunities for theft. 'Casing'.
Patter flash (adj.)	'Flash' talking.
Peach (v.)	Betray, inform.
Pigeon (n.)	Victim or dupe.
Pitch the fork	Tell a piteous tale.
Scrae and scranky (Scots)	Shrivelled and lank.
Scaff-raff (Scots)	Riff-raff.
Scrive (n. and v.)	Write, writing or letter.
Scunner (n. and v. Scots)	Abomination. To disgust.
Setter-on (n.)	Ring man at cock fight who releases the birds.
Seven sided (man)	'Flash' term involving a heavy joke, meaning blind. (A blind man has a left side, right, inside, outside, foreside, backside and a blind side.)
Shoot the cat	Vomit.
Shove in the mouth	A tot of spirits.
Skite (n. Scots)	A nothing. A person of no significance.
Skoddy (adj. Scots)	Dishonest.
Smoored (adj. Scots)	Smothered.
Stow your lumber!	Shut up!
Tappit hen (n. Scots)	Lidded ale-pot of distinctive shape.
Too far north	English allusion to the Scots. Too canny or sly.
Toon Rotten (n. pl. Scots)	Town Rats. Nickname for the Town Guard of Edinburgh.
Traveller (n.)	Hawker or pedlar.
Tuck-up fair (n.)	A hanging.
Turn stag on	Betray or inform on.
'Ursa Major' (the)	Samuel Johnson.
Wean (n. Scots)	Child or infant.
Well breached (adj.)	Wealthy. Flesh well covered.
Weskit (n. Scots)	Waistcoat.
Widda (n. Scots)	Widow.
Wight (n. Scots)	A simple man.

Wouf (v. Scots)	Gobble.
Wright (n.)	Carpenter, joiner and cabinet-maker.
Wynd (n. Scots)	Passageway wider than a 'Close' and large enough to admit a horse and cart. Wynds and Closes formed the great bulk of old Edinburgh, running at right angles to, and connecting the main streets of the Cowgate and High Street/Canongate.